Anne of Hollywood

Also by Carol Wolper

Mr. Famous

Secret Celebrity

The Cigarette Girl

Anne of

Hollywood

CAROL WOLPER

Gallery Books

New York   London   Toronto   Sydney   New Delhi

G

Gallery Books
A Division of Simon & Schuster, Inc.
1230 Avenue of the Americas
New York, NY 10020

Copyright © 2012 by Carol Wolper

All rights reserved, including the right to reproduce this book or portions thereof in any form whatsoever. For information address Gallery Books Subsidiary Rights Department, 1230 Avenue of the Americas, New York, NY 10020

First Gallery Books hardcover edition January 2012

GALLERY BOOKS and colophon are registered trademarks of Simon & Schuster, Inc.

For information about special discounts for bulk purchases, please contact Simon & Schuster Special Sales at 1-866-506-1949 or business@simonandschuster.com.

The Simon & Schuster Speakers Bureau can bring authors to your live event. For more information or to book an event contact the Simon & Schuster Speakers Bureau at 1-866-248-3049 or visit our website at www.simonspeakers.com.

Designed by Davina Mock-Maniscalco

Manufactured in the United States of America

10 9 8 7 6 5 4 3 2 1

Library of Congress Cataloging-in-Publication Data

Wolper, Carol.
    Anne of Hollywood / Carol Wolper.—1st Gallery Books hardcover ed.
        p.   cm.
    1. Young women—Fiction. 2. Motion picture producers and directors—California—Los Angeles—Fiction. 3. Hollywood (Los Angeles, Calif.)—Fiction. I. Title.
    PS3573.O5678A56 2012
    813'.54—dc22   2011030577

ISBN 978-1-4516-5721-0
ISBN 978-1-4516-5723-4 (ebook)

For "Sid," again and always.

Anne of Hollywood

Anne

"The good news is you're fucking the king; the bad news is you're fucking the king." It's something my sister once said to me and at the time I laughed because I had just started seeing my "king" and I couldn't worry about whatever bad things might be waiting down the road. Not when everything about my guy made me smile. If you don't let yourself be swept up with optimism every once in a while, what's the point, right? I know, I know, romantic optimism can be dangerous. Some would call it foolish, my father among them. If I listened to everything he said I would run my personal life solely from the left-side neocortex of my brain. He believes rational, linear thinking is what gets one the crown. I guess he expects me to have the mind of Machiavelli and the wiles of a sixteenth-century courtesan. Well, I'm a California girl and this is the twenty-first century. I can't ignore the forces and influences (outside my family) that informed my spirit, including an appetite for the big thrill. Los Angeles is a place that encourages the belief that if you are skillful and lucky enough you can catch a big wave and ride it all the way in to shore. I say that even though I have water phobia and wouldn't even consider getting on a surfboard. My version of extreme sports is falling in love with someone out of my league. That said, I am my father's daughter. Acting recklessly is not my style. The problem is that even with a well-developed left-side neocortex, love still brings confusion and confusion almost always brings mistakes.

But before I go any further I should tell you about "the king," which is my term of endearment for him. His name is Henry Tudor but he doesn't need a last name. When you're as powerful as he is you achieve the rare status of owning your first name to the exclusion of all others similarly named. In Los Angeles, Steven always means Spielberg, Jack always means Nicholson and Phil (still) always means Jackson. When people in Hollywood drop the name Henry, they do it with such reverence he might as well have an *HRH* in front of it. It should be noted that reverence comes begrudgingly in this town and those who give it usually harbor fantasies of taking it away the second the adored one shows signs of slipping from the mountaintop. With no such signs apparent when it comes to Henry, he continues to rule with no one coming close to his accomplishments.

He's forty with the résumé of someone twenty years older. At thirty he created an Internet company that changed the Web. Anytime anyone seeks out information on the Net, chances are they're using Henry's search engine. He sold the company by the time he was thirty-five, making the kind of money that allows you to buy a sports team, radio stations, a cable network, all of which he did, including one kick-ass FM station in Austin. In the last five years, he's become a majority shareholder in a Hollywood studio, invested in medical research that could change the world and been touted as a likely candidate for political office. And now for the really annoying part: he looks like Paul Newman in *Hud*. That's not supposed to happen. If you're that rich and that smart you're supposed to have a receding hairline and pasty-looking skin. Or be tall and gawky. Or at least, just to keep people from going into a depression because you seem to have cornered the market on everything that matters, to have the decency to eat crap food and develop a paunch, for Christ's sake. The scary thing is, even if he did—and someday he will—lose the battle of flesh and gravity, this king has enough charm (not to mention power) to keep people kissing his ring and other parts of his anatomy forever. Who wouldn't find a man like that intriguing? So, I jumped in.

And what a wild ride it's been. No one would have guessed it would have lasted so long. People expect girls like me to fuck the king once and be gone. I'm not "A" list and I'm certainly not Henry's usual type. I'm attractive and alluring enough to get my share of attention, though not from royals, rock stars or any man who has ever owned a yacht, which is to say I'm not one of those girls who rates as a typical trophy. I do have my talents, though, and a summer in France taught me some valuable tricks in the bedroom. Unfortunately those qualities do nothing to elevate my status on this playing field and when the king consorts with someone not considered worthy it inspires hostility. I wasn't prepared for the enemies. Had I been as gorgeous as a supermodel, as rich as an heiress, or an actress with an Oscar to my credit, people would still not be happy that I had Henry's attention, but they'd understand. What they resented was the king coupling with a "nobody." In their eyes I wasn't special enough ("flawed but willing" has always been my credo) so therefore I didn't belong there and they hated me for defying their negative expectations. Worse, if a less-than-special girl could get a king it made them question why they couldn't. Their frustration turned into rage, directed my way. Doesn't matter how eco-friendly, quasi-spiritual or liberal humanitarian they might claim to be: when it comes to a king's power and politics, the game can get rough. In that sense not a lot has changed since the sixteenth century except shorter skirts and iPhones.

I was so naïve and I shouldn't have been. I should have known better. I should have understood that in any town where the stakes are high, where there are only a few top slots and numerous contenders, betrayal and banishment come with the territory. I have no one to blame but myself and maybe all the bad advice I got from everyone except from my brother George.

He's the one I miss the most in my banishment. For two weeks I've been living at Henry's ranch near the Santa Ynez Mountains, up the coast from Santa Barbara; it's a beautiful isolated spot with not a neighbor in sight. There are no locks on the doors but the emotional prison I'm in keeps me from walking away.

My life is hanging in the balance. I'm not sure what comes next. With so much time on my own I go over and over the events that brought me here to see if I could have done something differently or better. Yes and yes is the answer to that question. Some days I'm full of anxiety, other days full of anger and other times full of forgiveness. Just the other day I realized that in spite of everything I still really like some of my enemies. Then I panicked, worried that this is exactly the kind of generosity one feels right before the end. When all is lost doesn't forgiveness enter the picture right before the proverbial sword comes down? And then I perked up when I realized that I'd taken a Xanax and had finished half a bottle of that yummy lemonade marijuana drink that my brother brought me the last time he was allowed to visit. My forgiveness had been chemically induced. No worries. Not about that, anyway.

The phone rings. Caller ID tells me it's the call I've been waiting for. My hands are shaking as I pick up the phone.

"Hello," I say, amazed that I sound normal, almost relaxed. I don't sound like a woman whose future is at stake.

"Anne . . ."

I love his voice. It's gruff, raspy, a touch bestial. It doesn't match up with his Paul Newman in *Hud* face.

"Yes, Henry?"

It's not really a question. It's a drumroll to a decision that feels more like a verdict. The real question is, Have my enemies won or have I pulled off a Hollywood ending?

Part One

THE PARAMOUR

Chapter 1

Anne

FOUR YEARS EARLIER

"Silly me. To think that getting involved with a king would be challenging instead of what it really is . . . dangerous."

My sister laughs at my confession. It's her way of saying better you than me. We're at the Starbucks in Beverly Glen, a convenient meeting place, halfway between my apartment in Beverly Hills and her new boyfriend's house in Sherman Oaks. "The Glen," as the residents in the vicinity refer to it, is a small shopping enclave at the top of ritzy Mulholland Drive and is the only shopping for miles around. This commercial development is meant to provide the basics for those rich enough to live at the top of the canyon: a wine shop, a deli, a dry cleaner's, drugstore, a couple of restaurants and a charming oddity . . . a bookstore that looks like someone's home library and specializes in first editions. Though I don't think many people are picking up their morning coffee and stopping next door to peruse the stacks of leather-bound classics. Not this crowd. The *Hollywood Reporter* and Page Six are more likely their idea of reading and they're getting that off the Internet.

It's one of those overcast mornings with enough chill in the air to make a hot chocolate sound appealing. Yet that chill could be gone in fifteen minutes, the sun could break through and then the only thing on the Starbucks menu we'll be craving will be iced cappuccinos. We choose the middle ground and order lattes. She opts for a "tall"; I choose a "grande." I need the extra caffeine because I didn't get home until 3 A.M., but at that moment my sister isn't interested in the details.

"Is Henry's soon-to-be-ex wife causing problems?" Mary asks as she eyes a blueberry muffin at the next table. She doesn't seem too worried about any problem I might have.

"I don't know. I don't think so. Why? Is she dangerous?"

"She's bitter, she's got plenty of money and is the most likely to hire Jake Winslow."

"Jake who?"

"The new private detective in town. From Tucson. All the rich wives in town hire him to see if their husbands are cheating and the husbands hire him to see if their girlfriends are cheating. That's what Henry said anyway but he might have been joking."

My sister enjoys her role as the authority on all things concerning Henry and his world. I often pay attention because she did date him long before I was invited into the royal bed. Although that may sound like a worst-case scenario for siblings, at most it makes our relationship a little sensitive. Actually, I think my sister was secretly relieved when they broke up. The relationship required too much of her and my father was too invested in it succeeding. Pressure and Mary are not a good mix. She doesn't like having to work too hard for anything and hasn't had to for most of her life . . . and that includes temporarily snagging the most desirable guy in town.

Mary was chosen and wooed by "the king" without ever going out of her way to attract his attention. She didn't have to. The night she met the royal one at a party up in Coldwater Canyon, she was at the height of her power. Mary is one of those girls who succeed at being tantalizingly beautiful *for one season*. Not that she's not pretty now, but the summer they met she looked like she'd stepped out of a Raphaelite painting. Her curves and luminescent skin made her appear to be the ultimate fertility child-goddess. Girls were always asking her how she got such great skin, hoping the answer wasn't some imported Swiss moisturizer that cost more than two hundred dollars a jar. Mary loved to say her secret was her strict diet of avocados and peaches, which was kind of true except when she was stuffing herself with french fries and margaritas.

Beauty and youth weren't the only things she had going for her; timing was also on her side. After separating from his wife, Henry had gone through a number of exotic beauties and was in the mood for a blonde . . . and not just any blonde. The night of the party he was on a search for a blonde with an angelic face and the kind of tits that would, as Raymond Chandler once said, "make a bishop kick a hole in a stained glass window." Actually Chandler didn't mention tits but if he'd ever met Mary he might have. What guy wouldn't want to hook up with her winning combination? But the big shocker for any guy who does is the realization that Mary doesn't like sex. She loves kissing and is happy to make out for hours, but sex is too messy for her taste. Too invasive. Too sweaty. The irony is that she's addicted to the attention that comes from being described as sexy, which often made me wonder if one can truly be sexy if one doesn't like sex. And the follow-up question: How long can a sexy nonsexual girl hold the king's attention?

To Mary's credit, she wasn't in awe of the great one. She liked the perks that came with being the king's girlfriend and she adored seeing her picture in magazines but when it was over, she took a few days to recover from the rejection and then bounced back to her simpler life with gusto. I have to admit I was greatly relieved. This was my *sister* and she'd become a celebrity overnight, which meant that overnight I'd become the lesser sibling. Any accomplishments or attributes I possessed were no longer viewed in the context of a woman in her twenties trying to make her way in the world. Nothing mattered except my proximity to my sister and her proximity to the king. It was as if suddenly overnight I'd lost my last name and was now only known as "Anne, Mary's sister." Being on the verge of my own overnight fame lately I wonder if someday I'll miss that anonymity.

My sister has finished her latte but her attention is still on the blueberry muffin.

"Want me to get you one?" I ask.

She turns back to me, leans closer, conspiratorially. "I'm off wheat. I'm looking at the guy eating the muffin. Check him out."

The guy is a middle-aged man with a haircut that would be more appropriate on Maddox Jolie-Pitt. He's wearing a boxy, wrinkled, navy blue blazer over a white T-shirt. I watch him compulsively check messages on his phone while finishing off the last bit of that muffin. He looks vaguely familiar.

"An actor?" I whisper.

"Maybe like a thousand years ago. Now he's some big deal in the eco-green scene . . . and a major gossip."

I take another look at him. "Oh, right. Now I get it." I'd seen him being interviewed on TV. He looks older in person, and not as healthy. Maybe he's just having a bad day. On second thought . . . a really bad day. The interview he did on TV was all about living green. No toxins. No chemicals. No sugar. Yet there he is devouring a fat-filled blueberry treat and a syrupy frap (granted no extra whipped cream on it) in public. It's like seeing someone known for driving a Prius step out into the parking lot and get into a gas-guzzling Escalade. Not that he seems particularly worried about being exposed as a hypocrite. Judging by the way he's frantically working the keys on his BlackBerry, he has other things on his mind. He picks up his cup and sucks in the last bit of the sweet coffee drink like a sugar addict. Maybe he's indulging instead of exploding. Leaving green to keep from going mean.

"Hey Cliff."

He looks up when Mary calls his name.

"What?" He does his best to act like he doesn't recognize her. Befuddlement doesn't become him. His mouth gets slack-jawed and his eyes squinty. Not a good look. I feel sorry for him and have a momentary urge to wipe away a stray crumb that's lodged into a spot on his chin.

"Cliff, it's me, Mary."

"Mary," he repeats as if trying to place her.

"Mary Boleyn. We met through Henry."

"Mary Boleyn," he says slowly, as if meeting her had been so insignificant he can barely recall the event. And yet he's careful to be polite. "How are you?"

My sister may not be the sharpest girl around but she knows exactly what's going on here. Cliff is distancing himself from one of the king's ex-girlfriends in case she's not only an ex but has inspired the king's wrath. Cliff, like everyone else in the kingdom, does not want to be perceived as a friend of any enemy of the king.

"This is my sister, Anne," Mary says.

"Nicetomeetyou." He can't spit that out fast enough so he can move on.

Mary can barely hold back a grin as she adds, "Anne is now dating Henry."

I kick her under the table. No one is supposed to know *yet*. And didn't she just say he was a "major gossip"? Is this Mary being clueless or careless? It's always a toss-up with her.

"Is that right?" Cliff tugs at a clump of his punkish hair. Mary has definitely caught him off guard but he's already made his move, shown himself to be less than warm, and now his only option is to retreat to neutral ground.

"And no rivalry there?" He's trying to be cute.

"Mary's in love with a great guy," I reply as if the two things have anything to do with each other.

He smiles. "Modern love."

I have no idea what he means by that. Nothing about my situation or Mary's feels particularly modern.

Spotting someone outside the window, Cliff quickly picks his car keys up off the table. "Well good luck," he says and then, facing Mary with considerably more enthusiasm than he had two minutes before, adds, "Good to see you again. You look great." He's no dummy. He knows that, as a last resort, flattery is always an effective closer. With that, he dashes out of there . . . dying to get away from us or dying to get to someone else? Hard to tell.

Mary laughs. "If it wasn't for the green thing that guy would be so OTR."

That's short for Off The Radar. I hate my sister's habit of reducing everything to letters. It's so high school. Maybe that's why it works. "Hollywood is high school with money." That's how my dad and everyone of his generation describes not just Hollywood but all of Southern California. I think it's more like high school on steroids. The stakes, the wars, the consequences are all bigger. Everything is bigger except people's sex drive. It's amazing how that shrivels up when everyone is so worried about how much power they have or don't have. The king, of course, has no shrinkage problems. He wouldn't be a king if he didn't have a libido big enough to satisfy a bevy of women. Is he seeing anyone other than me? I don't think so but he is the king. Lesson number one: You can never rule it out.

"So what's making your life so dangerous?" Mary asks, finally ready to get back to the topic I raised.

I reach for my bag, which is hanging off the back of the chair. "Promise me you won't mention this to anyone."

"Yeah, yeah, yeah, of course I won't."

I pull out a white envelope and spill its contents on the table . . . a tarot card, the Queen of Cups stapled back-to-back to the King of Cups. The third card is the dark-haired (like me) Queen of Pentacles, torn in half, beheaded. "No return address, no name. Postmark is Los Angeles."

Mary picks up the card. "Obviously someone other than me knows who you're fucking."

"Did you ever get anything like this when you were seeing Henry?"

"Not like that but there are always a few wackos around. Once when I was crossing the street someone driving by yelled out 'fucking ho' but I took it as a compliment. I figured if a complete stranger hates me that much I must be doing something right. Did you show this to Henry?"

"No," I say a little too defensively. "Everything is so great with us. It's all new and exciting and I don't want anything ruining that."

"You sure? Henry likes a little drama. He's a sucker for the damsel in distress, wounded bird thing."

"Maybe at first, but I bet he'd get tired of it. After a while he'd start thinking, Why can't she fix her own fucking wing?"

Mary laughs, tosses her beautiful mane of blond hair, giving the impression that she's one of those fun California girls on a perpetual spring break. "You're right, might as well hold on to the honeymoon as long as you can."

Who wouldn't want to keep a royal honeymoon going? Putting aside the lust part, which is considerable, there are plenty of perks and I'm not talking about the silver-colored Lanvin shoes that cost a thousand dollars. It's great to be given something I could never afford but the bigger gift is the Big Yin Yang. The yin is the feeling that simply by being chosen by the king I've broken through the pack of the billions of people on the planet. Suddenly I feel as if I matter. I have access. I'm just one degree away from the best of the best. My ego inflated overnight, which is precisely when the yang part kicked in. Instead of going all super-diva bitchy, this voice popped into my head that said when much has been given, much is required, and suddenly a generosity of spirit infused me. These days I want to help everyone. I've become a terrible driver, constantly letting other motorists cut in, stopping for pedestrians the second they step off the curb. I've also developed an urge to tip, and not just the usual suspects. I tried to tip the guy behind the counter at Rite Aid when I was picking up a prescription. He looked at me like I was crazy and declined my offer. Most people take the tip, which is getting kind of expensive. The yin without the yang could turn me into a less beautiful version of Naomi Campbell and the yang without the yin could turn me into a Sin City version of Mother Teresa. But merged together they create the best buzz. Lately I've actually started to wonder if there's such a thing as being too buzzed but I'm not so concerned that I'm on the Internet looking for an antidote.

"Shall I toss this out?" Mary asks, scooping up the tarot cards.

As creepy as it is, it's possible the sender is just some girl with too much envy and too little judgment. I decide to give "jealous girl" the benefit of the doubt because that's the generous thing to do. However, if she (and I can't imagine the sender is a he) turns out to be some psycho, sperm-trapping grifter who interferes with my relationship with the king, well then, in that case competition and revenge win out over generosity. But for the moment . . .

"Yeah, toss it," I say.

Mary crumples the cards into a ball and stuffs it inside her empty cup.

I clean off our table and Cliff's table, too. Yeah, Mr. Ecology didn't bother picking up his own trash. I give him the benefit of the doubt as well, chalking up his bad manners to too much sugar. As my sister and I walk out, a group of guys, in line to place their order, check her out. Mary knows that at that moment she is the sole object of their attention and she walks past them like a star. Men in this town love blondes. Good for her.

Outside the sky is still overcast, though brighter than it was a half hour ago. The harsh glare has me reaching for my sunglasses. Mary already has hers in place.

"Give the big guy my love," she says, and then kisses me on the cheek. At that moment I wonder if she would ever hook up with Henry behind my back. I quickly dismiss the thought, glad to find a distraction in the sight of Cliff, one row of cars over, engaged in an animated discussion with a woman who is doing most of the talking.

"Who's that with Cliff?" I ask.

Mary glances over. "Oh, *her.* That's Theresa Cromwell. She's one of those women who lead with their brains. Makes a point of telling you how smart she is. Like I care."

"You know everyone, don't you?" I say, teasingly.

Mary opens the door to her convertible and gets in. "Comes with the 'girlfriend' job title."

Before I can ask if she considered being with Henry a job, she turns on the ignition. Gnarls Barkley's "Who's Gonna Save My Soul?" is playing on the CD. She lowers the volume. "I can't believe we didn't talk details. How do you like fucking Henry?"

I don't want to explain that, technically, I haven't actually fucked him yet. Mary wouldn't approve of my strategy and I'm not about to divulge the erotic techniques I use to keep Henry enthralled. It's not a conversation to have in the parking lot of the Beverly Glen Shopping Center.

So I just smile. "What do you think?"

She laughs. "I think next time I want details."

After she leaves, as I'm about to get into my car, I realize Cliff and Theresa Cromwell are staring at *me*. When they realize I've caught them, Cliff looks down at his BlackBerry and starts fidgeting again but Theresa doesn't move a muscle. Suddenly a chill comes over me and though there's no reason to think this, as I look at Theresa looking at me this thought pops into my head: She's wishing I were dead.

It's a feeling and a thought I've never experienced before (not even the beheaded tarot card elicited this fear) and it's so disturbing that I quickly turn away, get into my car and lock the doors even though nothing bad is ever going to happen at eleven o'clock in the morning up in the Beverly Glen parking lot. I slam the car into gear and accelerate, not slowing down for speed bumps. As I drive away I look in the rearview mirror but Theresa and Cliff are both gone.

When I get to the bottom of Coldwater Canyon, the sun has broken through and everything looks golden. Mexican gardeners are out tending to expensive lawns. Privileged children are playing at the jungle gym in the park. Rich tourists are stepping out of their bungalows at the Beverly Hills Hotel to stake out lounge chairs by the pool. Everything is as it's supposed to be. The ominous feeling I had just ten minutes ago has lessened but not before I've bitten two fingernails down to raggedy ends.

As I head east, I replay the first moments Henry and I really connected. It's something I do from time to time either because I'm indulging in a wonderful memory or as a way to fight any encroaching doubts. I love recalling that sunny afternoon in Malibu almost a year after he and my sister had split. It had rained earlier that morning, which almost never happens in June. People seemed a bit unnerved by that freak weather condition but by noon when the sun was out, all was back to normal. A fashion magazine was throwing a party to honor the actress on its latest cover and since I still had some trickle-down cachet as "Anne, Mary's sister," I somehow made it on the exclusive list. From the second I walked into the beachside rented mansion I felt like a misfit. The place was packed with girls who were young enough to be a size zero and still look healthy. Those who were on the other side of thirty got attention the old-fashioned way—they paid for it, strutting around in their best Prada or Dolce & Gabbana. There wasn't an Ugg boot in sight. This was not Pamela Anderson's Malibu. Nor was it mine but at least I wasn't in my usual Tory Burch flip-flops. And that was part of the problem. While I was coming in from the outside, drink in my hand, the heel of my shoe got caught on a slight ridge along the floor of the sliding glass doorway. Doing my best to regain my balance I managed to break my fall without breaking an ankle but the drink went flying.

"Didn't anyone ever tell you tequila and stilettos don't mix?"

I looked up to see Henry, standing there lending a hand. He pulled me up and didn't seem to mind that I was speechless. I guess he gets a lot of that. Truth is I was stunned to see him and rendered mute because at that moment I recalled what my sister had told me about the royal cock and it almost made me swoon.

"So take off your shoes, darling, and have a seat."

And so I did.

By the time I get to the commercial stretch of Sunset Boulevard, I'm no longer biting my nails and have managed to suppress an urge to call Henry and ask him what the deal is with Theresa Cromwell and her evil eye. I take a left at the intersection, hoping I can pop into a salon on Sunset and get a manicure. If you saw me a half hour later sitting there getting my nails prettified with a coat of Chanel's pale pink polish, a tall glass of purified water with a slice of cucumber floating in it by my side, soothing sounds of Brazilian jazz on the nail spa's speakers, my head leaning back on the chair, my eyes closed, you might think of me as the epitome of calm and content. Wrong. More like shell-shocked and paralyzed as I realize that even though I can't explain why, I know that Theresa Cromwell will be crossing my path again soon. Even more frightening is the certainty that this is the beginning of the end of my honeymoon.

Chapter 2

Theresa

Theresa was reassured by the sound of the doorbell's constant ringing. Thank God, her guests were arriving *on time*. She wanted a full house when Henry finally made his entrance. It was important to her that he walk into a house full of attractive, smart, lively people, all loosened up by her special mojito cocktail. Fuck the "just water for me" crowd. Didn't they get that drinking at a party is the price of admission? She didn't invite them there to soberly take notes on others' debauchery, though she herself never failed to take a sober assessment of who was there to play and who just came to watch. Those standing on the sidelines sipping Pellegrino would not be invited back again . . . unless, of course, they were rich, famous or powerful.

Checking her makeup in the bathroom mirror, she could hear voices and laughter coming from outside but was in no hurry to go downstairs. She knew the caterers had everything under control and her assistant could play hostess for another ten minutes. If she couldn't she didn't deserve the job and would be replaced by someone who could. There was a surplus of capable girls in L.A. Girls who could be counted on to size up and make whatever adjustments were necessary. Girls who always had a painkiller to offer, a pack of cigarettes (even though they didn't smoke) and every emergency number you could ever need programmed into their phone. These girls understood the nuances of the social scene, having developed a keen sense of who liked to talk about their kids, who liked to talk about their work, and more importantly, who would enjoy a good blow job joke and who wouldn't.

The sound of a car idling out front caused Theresa to anxiously look out the opened window. Nope. Not a limo. Not a Town Car. Not one of the three cars Henry owned (a Mercedes, a new BMW and an old Range Rover), all of which Theresa was aware of, down to their license plate numbers. It was only another Toyota Highlander SUV, the hybrid, in black, of course. What she wouldn't give for someone to drive up in a canary-yellow Ferrari for a change, something glaringly politically incorrect, just to break up the monotony.

Turning her attention back to her image in the mirror, Theresa carefully, almost brutally assessed her face. She was no beauty but in the right light she had a certain appeal. The nose job had been worth seven thousand dollars, back when seven thousand was considered a lot of money to spend on "correcting a deviated septum." Theresa took pride in having resisted the urge to go too cute. Her nose was still Roman, still big by L.A. standards, but the slight refining had taken the horsiness out of her face and left her with what she liked to consider "an aristocratic profile." Not bad for the daughter of a factory worker. Her eyes were too small but through the miracle of very black mascara they appeared alive and almost seductive. Her lips, though average in appearance, were her best feature because, as Theresa liked to say, "Very few secrets have passed through these." In a town where gossip was currency, where most women happily shared their secrets over dinner at the Tower Bar, Theresa was no cheap date.

The sycamore trees outside rustled slightly, causing her to shiver. A summer breeze back in Boston was always welcome but breezes in Los Angeles could be unsettling. Plus the last thing she needed was a dip in the temperature, having decided to forgo portable heaters for the backyard. "Not to worry," she told herself, everything would work out fine. Her astrologer had predicted a successful outcome, something to do with Jupiter's favorable alignment, which only happens once every twelve years. Apparently this was Theresa's year to thrive and she wasn't about to waste any opportunities. At forty-four (she admitted to forty-one) she had to seize the moment. It was time to tap into her "Sicilian" strength, time to tap into her savings account (these parties weren't cheap) and time to fully commit to what her father used to call her "watch this" routine. She could still see herself at fourteen, hands on her hips, determined not to let Cynthia Cavallo have the uncontested rights to hunky Johnny Quinn. Well watch this, L.A.

Opening a drawer full of cosmetics, Theresa pulled out a small jar. Almost as if performing a ritual, she carefully unscrewed the top and set it down on the counter. She then lifted up the skirt of her simple, almost demure black dress. She'd opted for just a hint of cleavage because she was wearing three-inch stilettos and the rule was you can't double-slut an outfit unless you're under thirty. With one hand she slid her lace thong aside and with the other she elegantly dipped a finger into the jar and scooped up a bit of lightweight lotion and applied it to her clit. When she was finished, she took a deep breath, exhaling out all her tension, knowing that within the hour this "female Viagra" would kick in and she'd be awash in a hormonal surge—the good kind, not the perimenopausal kind.

She intended to work her party with palatable sexuality. It was all part of Theresa's master plan for her and Henry. She wasn't delusional enough to think she could ever be his "queen" but that didn't mean she couldn't win in her own way. Sure, rumor had it that he was totally besotted by his latest paramour, Anne Boleyn, but Theresa wasn't worried. She had a plan. Step one, befriend the besotted one and to that end she'd invited her to the party. Anne got her own invitation, separate from Henry's, and had immediately RSVP'd yes. Would she come alone, with a supportive friend, with her king? Theresa knew each choice spoke volumes about Anne's confidence and cleverness . . . or lack thereof.

As the first hit of Theresa's self-induced surge washed over her, she couldn't help but smile. No one would bet on her to pull this off but she didn't care. She was smarter than all of them, just like thirty years ago she was smarter than Cynthia Cavallo.

Chapter 3

Cliff

Cliff hated mojitos but he had options. He could take an occasional sip and then, when no one was looking, leave the glass behind a sofa or chair. Or he could wait till the ice cubes melted, add more cubes until the cocktail was diluted down, neutered and tasteless, and then make a show of finishing it off. Or he could do what he did, which was to covertly pour out two-thirds of the drink into one of the exotic plants surrounding the outdoor patio. It did occur to him that this wasn't exactly eco-friendly and considering his position in the green movement not something he'd want to be caught on video doing, but he was feeling a little hostile, so fuck it. His marriage was falling apart, his career was going nowhere and, just yesterday, a chunk of the hillside in his backyard slid down into his small pool and it wasn't even the rainy season. His finances couldn't take another hit and neither could his patience. If there were only one thing wrong in his life, that'd be a problem and he could deal with problems. Two things wrong at the same time was a crisis and he'd weathered a few of those. But three things wrong at the same time was a cosmic reversal and no one could be expected to handle those very well. If he had a taste for alcohol he'd be slurping down those mojitos fast but booze wasn't his weakness. Sugar was. Sugar and Soma, that little painkiller that kept him steady, like tonight, when his wife had refused to come to the party because she said she loathed—dragging out the word so it seemed to be a block long: *looooooathed*—the way Cliff acted around Theresa.

"And how do I act around her?" he asked.

"Needy."

What she really meant was weak. Cliff understood that his wife expected him to be strong, yet sensitive. She also expected him to be successful, devoted, loyal and not lose his hair. She felt entitled to all this because over fifteen years ago, before they were married, she'd met and flirted with Billy Baldwin, which she had, over time, spun into a scenario in which she'd turned down a movie star to marry him. No truth to it but Cliff was too weak to point that out. He did feel a pull toward loyalty when it came to her role as mother to their son. She was exemplary in the parenting area but so was he. Did that mean he was entitled to a woman who was successful, devoted, loyal and free of cellulite?

She apologized later, when he was getting dressed for the party. "Look, it's not you, it's her. It's that woman. She toys with you. Makes me want to slap her."

"That would be something to see," he joked.

He kissed the top of her head. "I'll be in and out of there in an hour."

"Drive safe." She smiled at him.

As he backed out of the driveway, he stopped for a second to look at his house. Everything appeared calm, peaceful. The shrubs were neatly trimmed. Tiny white lights twinkled in the surrounding trees. Through the living room window he could see his wife on the phone, probably with one of her many girlfriends. She seemed relaxed in a way she never was around him anymore. There was no sign of the turmoil of his eroding backyard or his eroding marriage. In fact, from a distance his wife looked almost happy. He pulled a Soma out of his pocket, took a small bite and took his foot off the brake.

"Can I get you another, Cliff?" The bartender was ready to refill his glass.

"Uh . . . no, I'm good for now."

"What's the matter, don't you like mojitos?" The question came from someone nearby, a voice he didn't recognize. He turned to see Anne Boleyn, smiling. "I hear they make good plant food," she said as she sauntered by, a glass of Pellegrino in her hand.

He could tell himself he followed her inside because he was concerned he'd been caught poisoning Theresa's prized exotic orchid and wanted to do damage control. Or he could pretend he wanted to make up for the bad impression he'd made on their first meeting up at the Glen. The truth was he wanted to find out if she had arrived with Henry, which would be a significant statement and would have gossips blogging for days. He liked having the latest information. Being "in the know" was his secret addiction. There was no way he was going to pass up the opportunity to have a conversation with the new girl in Henry's life. If she was anything like her sister, Mary, she'd be blurting out personal details with the slightest encouragement, any one of which he could dine out on for the next few months. I wonder, he thought, if like her sister, she prefers being on top.

Chapter 4

Anne

What I wouldn't give for a glass of rosé champagne. The bartender is pushing the mojitos but I take a pass since it isn't on my alcohol compatibility list. I can drink rosé all night and never have a problem but a few sips of rum, tequila or vodka and judgment goes out the window and this is not a time in my life when mistakes can be made without dire consequences.

It's only early in the season but I know the summer is going to be full of drama and not only because Nostradamus predicted world doom in 2012. Though some Angelenos—those always looking for cosmic signs—take that prediction as law, even among the more down-to-earth there's a sense that conflicting energies are being stirred and their convergence will not be pretty. Uneasiness is everywhere. Everyone seems to be waiting for something to happen and worried that when it does they'll be on the losing side. There's a sense that we're about to see the changing of the guard but no one seems to be sure who will be guarding whom. People are on edge and everything is a potential debate. People coming out of the movies argue over the latest action-adventure. Is it visually brilliant or mindless spectacle? Comic books have gone seriously dark. There's no fun in the villains anymore. Sports fans are dealing with another fallen hero who was eliminated from competition for using strength-enhancing drugs while in politics another married congressman is exposed for his romp with an aging coke whore who likes to pepper her conversation with spiritual quotes from Eckhart Tolle's latest best seller. Pop culture is looking for its next princess now that Paris Hilton can hardly find a paparazzo to take her picture anymore and people are finally getting tired of those big fake glossy retouched magazine covers that are so Photoshopped you could probably make my grandmother look like a supermodel. Frustration and change are in the air and everyone is jittery. Long-standing relationships are crumbling and unlikely people are hooking up. Everyone's wondering what or who will be the next new thing, the next new wave, the next new high. Even Hollywood royalty is out there looking over their shoulders, when their eyes are not focused on the next curve in the road ahead. Henry is restless, too, and I know this is not the best time to step into his life but when a king knocks on your door, you answer it, or at least, I do. I was brought up to open that door, even though my father never thought I'd get the chance and my mother worried about what I'd do if I did.

With no pink (or even white) wine to be found, I stick to water even though I'm nervous knowing Henry will be showing up sooner or later. When we spoke earlier he wasn't specific about his arrival time and I wasn't about to interrogate him. And if you're thinking that sounds too submissive let me clarify . . . I don't want to interrogate anybody. If I have to work that hard to get information I've already lost the game. It's also not a very smart approach. I may be dating Henry but I'm not his official, designated girlfriend. I don't have any right to demand his itinerary. He's a free man, officially single. For years he's been legally separated from his wife, Catherine, as they work out the remaining fine points of what feels like the longest divorce in the history of the world. The delay has nothing to do with the custody of their teenage daughter. This is a battle over power, money, revenge (Catherine's) and control. Of course Henry's had a number of women in his life since his marriage fell apart, including his dalliance with my sister, but there has been no serious contender for the wife slot. For all I know, Henry may like it that way. As it is he's free to do as he pleases, showing up with whoever he's in the mood for . . . and there is no shortage of options. He could even show up with Catherine. There's a part of Henry that likes to shock and she would certainly put her anger on hold to step back into the spotlight, even if just for a night. It's a scenario that scares me but I know better than to quiz him on his plans for the evening, even though being forewarned is always better than the big ambush. But at this point I can't have it both ways. I can't have the comfort that comes from a conventional relationship where each party knows what the other is up to *and* an extraordinary adventure. If conventional is what I want I have no business getting involved with Henry. The problem for me is that I've always craved adventure and wished for an exciting life but I was born into a family that, at best, was only close enough to extraordinary to gossip about it. If I want an extraordinary life I'm going to have to work for it, which means never getting thrown by whatever gets thrown my way.

I wander inside and find a seat on a sofa next to a small table on which is displayed a framed sketch of a female torso. It's by Leo de Vince, a contemporary artist I recognize. Henry has a large oil painting by de Vince hanging in the hallway that leads to his bedroom. A young woman in a purple hat. I make note of the fact that Theresa is a fan of the same artist. I'm making plenty of mental notes as I look around the party, including how quickly Cliff settles himself down next to me.

"I'm on antibiotics, not supposed to be drinking at all," he says, though I suspect he's lying.

"Yeah, me too."

"You're on antibiotics?"

"No," I reply. "I'm not supposed to be drinking."

"AA?" He has a soulful expression when he asks this question, as if to say don't worry, I don't judge anybody.

"No, I just don't need the extra calories."

He looks at my body as if guessing my weight.

"One hundred and twelve pounds," I say, "and I'm kidding about the calories."

Relieved, he laughs. "I was going to say, you don't look like one of those Adderall girls." He smiles, letting me know that though he might be more than twenty years older, he knows what's happening out there in girl world. He knows the drug girls take to fit into their size-25 jeans. (I'm a size 27.) As he launches into a story about L.A. women and their weight issues, a story that's neither insightful nor funny, I nod encouragingly because there's something about him that is endearing, even though I know he can't be trusted. He's the type my father always warned me about, the type that can be found in any royal court, in the power halls of Washington, D.C., at Upper East Side New York cocktail parties, at Hollywood premieres or any upscale Los Angeles soiree he can talk his way into. He's one of those guys who carefully monitor the shifts in power and align their positions accordingly. I'm guessing his politics are conveniently vague, except for his position on the environment and even that is soft, more cause than crusade. His appearance, matching his demeanor, is studiously innocuous, except for the occasional idiosyncrasy (his hair) designed to suggest a touch of playful insouciance. I imagine his closet is filled with Banana Republic chino pants, Polo shirts and, for dressier occasions like this one, nondescript gray or black suits probably bought at Macy's, definitely not Neiman Marcus. His best quality is his deep brown eyes, which warm up an otherwise bland face. Add it all up and Cliff appears to be accessible and welcoming, a friend to all except in tough times, when, if my father's judgment is correct, he's a friend to none. His true allegiance is to whoever wears the crown. No crown? Then all you'll get is a polite, folksy "hey, how you doing?" In an earlier era he'd be the guy wearing a sorrowful expression as you were led past him on your way to being beheaded. However, once you turned a corner he'd be chatting up your replacement as if you never existed.

"I don't see your date around."

It takes me a second before I realize he's finally finished his Adderall monologue and has moved on to what he really cares about.

"My date? You mean the king?"

It takes him a moment before he gets it. "Yes, the king. King Henry. That's a good name for him." He forces a laugh and I realize the joke's on me. Cliff might incorporate that nickname into his repertoire. My term of endearment could go viral.

"I stopped by alone," I say, admitting to nothing more.

"Oh I thought . . ." He stops, confused. "You live in the neighborhood?"

"No. I live in Beverly Hills. Not 90210: 90212. One-two, not one-oh, the cheap part of Beverly Hills."

"Not that cheap," he says.

"It's a one-bedroom apartment."

I can see him trying to piece my story together and wondering if Henry might already have dumped me and if so what am I doing there. He can't help himself. He has to probe further.

"How do you know Theresa?"

"I don't. Strange, right? A woman I've never met calling me up to invite me to a party and I say yes."

"I'm sure you've got your reasons."

"Yes I do," I smile. "Yes I do."

At that moment, as if our conversation had been her cue to enter, Theresa appears at the bottom of the stairs. *Vivacious* is the word that comes to mind and that's an understatement. She looks as if she'd just gotten a shot of human growth hormone. To describe her as hyper-robust is no exaggeration and it makes her appear both attractive and slightly bizarre. The second Cliff sees her, he stands up, as if summoned by a bell. "You're lovely," he says, shaking my hand. Again he uses flattery as a way to make a smooth exit but at least he sounds sincere, and being a nervous wreck I have to admit it makes me feel better.

Chapter 5

Theresa

Henry showed up an hour and a half late . . . and not alone. That got people talking. In fact, it woke them up. Prior to his entrance the party was on the verge of never having enough escape velocity to rocket into a real celebration. Not even the mojitos were enough to overcome the lethargy of waiting for the main attraction . . . and waiting. Theresa was on the verge of second-guessing her strategy. She hated when that happened and it rarely ever did. A month before, when she'd been promoted to a vice president in Henry's corporation, she'd made the decision not to issue a formal press release and to keep the news under wraps until she could announce it with greater fanfare. This was to be her moment but it was a moment that required Henry's presence.

When he eventually raised his glass to toast the newest member of his executive team, Theresa was finally able to conclude that those many nights going to Suffolk Law School had finally paid off. She made the thank-you speech she'd been rehearsing in her mind since she arrived in Los Angeles. She was a tad sentimental, remembering how she worked her way through college in Boston and got her first significant job at an L.A. firm. She skimmed over why she left that career to pursue other (nameless) opportunities, which brought her to Henry's world and running *Daily,* his new magazine website, which was in a position to surpass the *Los Angeles Times'* readership in the next six months. She paused as her guests cheered (most vocal among them Cliff), then summed up by saying, with the requisite tears in her eyes, that "things sometimes come full circle," bringing her to this new role as an advisor to Henry on issues of law and business . . . "but not his art collection or his personal life. I know my limitations," she joked. People laughed. Most of the guests were on a second cocktail and now that the party was fully in gear, they were happy to respond warmly to anything anyone with a raised glass had to say.

Theresa glowed, bathed in good fortune and confident that news of her promotion and her VIP party would travel fast and with greater impact than some small second-page headline in any newspaper or blog. Her master plan was working, though the truth was that until Henry walked in the room, Theresa wasn't sure he'd show up. The bonus was the girl he brought with him as part of his entourage. Her name was Larissa, she was one of Henry's "friends" and her presence was unexpected entertainment for Theresa and potential trouble for Anne.

In the three years Theresa had worked for Henry she'd become a sharp observer of the background girls who floated in and out of his life and Larissa had always more or less been in the picture. Tall, blond and pretty in a generic way with no discernible talent, she was a typical "short-runner"—Theresa's name for those girls who at twenty think their beauty and youth will get them the big prize but by thirty are beginning to panic when they realize that all their good looks bought them was a short run on a crowded field. Larissa was thirty-one and she was holding on for life, hovering around

Henry, hoping for at least a semipermanent spot by his side. It wasn't looking good for Larissa, which isn't to say she didn't occasionally spend the night with him, but in his pecking order she was strictly an entourage girl. Only keen royal observers understood the nuances of all the categories and subcategories surrounding Henry. And Theresa, being one of the keenest of all, made it her business to know the difference between a short-runner, an entourage girl (often one and the same), a fluke, a fling, an inamorata (a fling with potential), a paramour (a relationship with potential) and a contender. She also made it her business to chart the rise and fall of each and at times even facilitate a showdown.

The second Henry walked into the party with Larissa, Theresa scanned the room for Anne, wondering how she would handle Henry's incorrigible habits. She spotted the Boleyn girl across the room, in conversation with another guest, nodding politely as if listening attentively. A picture of cool. She's faking it, Theresa thought, and she's pretty fucking good at it except for the fact that every ten seconds or so Anne's eyes darted back to Henry and his little traveling circle. Theresa had witnessed this kind of thing before and it was always a toss-up as to whether the new girl would eventually storm out, pout, cry (a rare few) or suppress the anger and insecurity and decide to be cavalier, sweet or, in a few cases, flirt with the competition.

While Anne contemplated the best move in this situation, Theresa made hers, as soon as she could do so. Politely putting off those wanting a convivial word or two with their hostess, she headed over to Anne, who was now no longer engaged in any conversation and had her back turned to Henry's side of the room. She was busy doing what everyone does when they're nervous and solo—checking messages on her cell.

As Theresa approached she was struck by Anne's seductive appeal, which had not been apparent in that first sighting up at the Glen. Certainly Anne's long dark hair was a big part of it but more appealing was the fact that she was nothing like those ubiquitous L.A. girls whose appeal is based on blond hair extensions, fake tits and little else. Though no model, Anne had a lovely face, nice skin, refined features, a beautiful, delicate neck and, judging by the way she filled out her simple Dolce & Gabbana pencil skirt and silk tank top, a slim but strong, athletic body. However, it was only when Theresa got really close that she became aware of the feature that probably captivated Henry—Anne's eyes, dark, almost black, full of spirit and mystery. There was something about those eyes that both beckoned you near and dared you to come closer.

Theresa gently touched Anne's arm and offered her warmest smile. "So glad you could make it."

"Delighted to be here," Anne replied. She was gracious with a hint of sarcasm, which Theresa knew was not directed at her.

"I don't usually invite strangers to parties at my house even when it's a party for a hundred people but—"

"You were curious," Anne interjected.

Theresa ignored the interruption. "I also don't usually allow crashers." She glanced across the room. "But Henry is an exception. He can bring whomever he wants."

"An exception and your boss."

"Well, yes there's that, too." Theresa softened her voice. "I'm on your side, Anne. It's a test, you know, that's all; nothing to worry about."

"A test, a message . . ." Anne shrugged, as if she'd survived harder challenges and this one wasn't enough to work up a sweat over.

Theresa wasn't buying the act but it's exactly what Theresa would say if in the same predicament. She gripped Anne's arm conspiratorially. "Darling, why don't we walk over there together?"

Chapter 6

Cliff

Cliff once heard Henry say, "I'm not a bad guy. I've been accused of being misogynistic and even cruel but never to my face and never by someone who had the whole story." Though Cliff didn't know for sure if Henry was a bad guy or not (and he'd never say a word against him in public), he did know that he didn't have the whole story and never would. He had pieces and the opportunity to acquire another gave him an adrenaline buzz that made him feel alive. A rare feeling these days and one he wasn't about to waste.

Cliff worked his way through the crowd over to where Henry, Larissa, Theresa and Anne were standing, chatting politely just like any foursome at any other cocktail party, except one of the four happened to be the man everyone in Los Angeles wanted to get close to. The man who practically changed the molecular structure of a room just by making an entrance. Cliff maneuvered himself within earshot by attaching himself to a small group of guests discussing their summer vacations. It was the perfect cover since he wasn't required to say anything, just look like he cared who stayed at which Four Seasons in Hawaii or who traveled halfway around the world to South Africa only to arrive at their hotel and run into their L.A. neighbors. It was all babble to Cliff because he couldn't afford those kinds of vacations and didn't care who could, not at that moment anyway, not when he was eavesdropping on three women and a "king."

Though he couldn't hear every word it wasn't hard to size up the situation. Theresa was pretending to be neutral, Larissa was pretending to be happy and Henry and Anne weren't pretending at all. Very few words were spoken by either of the two but the way they looked at each other was proof of their involvement. The way Anne said Henry's name, very formally, only made their connection more obvious. Using proper protocol with someone whose cock you were sucking twenty-four hours earlier probably added to the thrill, Cliff thought. Centuries ago a king's mistress probably could get a lot of erotic mileage out of a simple curtsy to "Your Highness." And just watching Anne do her twenty-first-century version of it got Cliff a little charged up. He moved closer, focusing on Larissa because she was the one doing all the talking.

Having picked up on the love vibe between Henry and Anne, Larissa was coping with this unexpected development by doing her best to execute a smooth U-turn. She'd walked into that party acting like Henry's date and was now trying to pass herself off as simply an old friend, because to do otherwise might jeopardize her position in his court. To that end she decided to gain Anne's trust by making several references to her own boyfriend and how he didn't mind when she hung out with Henry because they were just pals and Henry's girlfriends didn't mind because Larissa's rep was that she was one of those women who supported other women, "a girly girl." She complimented Anne on her outfit and Theresa on her house, galloping through her monologue as if she'd done a couple of lines of blow, though it was common knowledge in that circle that she'd given all that up a year ago.

Cliff wished he could pull her aside because he could see that with every word she was setting herself up for a bad exit. This was the problem with these "short-runners": they didn't understand the power that comes from being still. Cliff remembered the first time he met Larissa, a few years back at a dinner at Ago restaurant. A friend of Cliff's had brought her as his date and she was delightfully chatty, as these girls usually are on first meeting. She spoke enough Italian to joke around with the waiters and drank a couple of peach martinis, which she swore was the key to happiness. In the soft light of the restaurant's "garden patio" she looked like a green-eyed goddess right off the beaches of Rio. Later he found out that her sun-kissed skin was a spray-on tan, the eye color was contacts and Larissa wasn't even her real name. It was Allie, Allie from Hermosa Beach, a high school volleyball star who was now making a living doing commercials (her biggest credit: an ad for Twix). Cliff heard a rumor that she possessed a trio of driver's licenses—each with a different birth date—and the casting agents only knew her by her youngest age. Though he hadn't spent a lot of time around her over the years, whenever he did she seemed cranked up, always running as if in a race against time. He used to think she was one of those girls with a lot of vitality but the older she got the more her "vitality" looked manic, like the compulsive dancing of a person terrified of what'll happen when the music stops.

Henry could have derailed her with a word but he let her go on, and Larissa misinterpreted his silence for approval. She thought she was on a roll so she tapped into her memory bank for a tabloid item she'd been saving for just such an occasion.

"I read somewhere that Angelina Jolie said she would never sleep with a married man and I'm with Angie on that. Girls got to stick together, right, Anne?"

"Interesting point," Anne replied.

"Of course," Larissa continued, "if the man is separated and the relationship is dead except for the burying, then it's cool."

"Although . . . ," Anne replied and then stopped for dramatic effect the same way Cliff sometimes did when he was giving a speech about global warming and took a long pause before delivering the expiration date for the planet.

Cliff took a step closer, not wanting to miss a word. He noticed that Theresa, too, was waiting with bated breath and seemed to be vibrating with excitement but it was Henry who gave Anne the go-ahead. "Although what?" Even in the way he posed the question it was obvious Henry was smitten with his paramour.

"Well," Anne proceeded as if arguing her case in a debate, "what about those situations where a woman does everything in her power to attract a married man. She mentally fucks him. She emotionally fucks him. She might flaunt her naked body in front of him but she doesn't *actually* fuck him. Seems to me a woman like that can get a guy so worked up he'll not only divorce his wife, he'll desert his entire family just to get inside her pleasure palace." She turned to Larissa. "I've got nothing against Angelina and I agree with you about all that girly-girl stuff, but just because you don't allow penetration does not mean you're not fucking a married man."

Henry burst out laughing. "Well put."

Larissa looked like she'd just had a tiara ripped off her head and was demoted to a lady-in-waiting. Either that or she'd just caught her reflection in a mirror and saw her own expiration date on her forehead.

"Darling," Theresa said, once again gripping Anne's arm as if they were old chums, "you should write an essay about that for our website but of course you can't say 'fuck.'"

"Thanks but I think I have enough enemies already," Anne quipped.

Cliff could have sworn she was referring to him because she glanced in his direction. Whether she did or didn't, he'd seen enough to conclude that while Anne might be Mary's sister, they might as well be of different species. This one is clever, he thought. Maybe too clever.

Larissa struggled to find a response, finally settling on "You're a fun girl, Anne, love ya." She gave Anne a peck on the cheek before picking up someone else's abandoned mojito and walking away.

Cliff followed her down the hallway that led to the guest bathroom. A few people were already waiting their turn and Larissa took her place in the back of the line. Her eyes were teary as she finished off her drink, put the glass on a nearby table and snapped open her clutch purse. She pulled a tiny bottle out and unscrewed the cap as Cliff appeared.

"Can't talk now, Cliff," she said, as she put the bottle up to her nose and sharply inhaled.

"What is that? Smelling salts?"

"Aromatherapy. Lavender oil. Don't leave home without it." She inhaled again, savoring the calming scent of the oil before closing the bottle and putting it back in her purse. "What is it, Cliff?"

The directness of her question confounded him. Why was he doing this? He had no real stake in this game yet he knew that this was precisely the kind of moment when you could score the most points. People having a vulnerable episode remember acts of kindness and that can bring dividends to the do-gooder. Who knew how things would shake out? Maybe he'd need Larissa's help someday. As long as she was still in Henry's circle, she was potentially valuable.

Finally he found his voice. "You don't have to try so hard."

"What are you talking about?" she asked, not really wanting to know the answer.

"With Henry or with anyone. You're a terrific girl. You don't have to prove yourself."

"Oh Cliff, of course I do. We all have to prove ourselves. Every day. Over and over again. It's exhausting, but what's the alternative? Her?" She was referring to an overweight fortyish woman at the front of the line, whose graying hair, sensible shoes and pantsuit rendered her invisible to any men scouting hotness.

"She happens to be a well-known and respected pediatrician," Cliff pointed out.

"Yeah, well, I forgot to go to med school."

Larissa was doing her best to cover her hurt feelings with a little attitude and Cliff knew she was a pro at this kind of thing. Give her five more minutes and she'd be back into party mode. She could do a quick turnaround on her emotions, but it cost her. Every hit she took to her self-esteem added to her scar tissue and an underlying frustration that she would take out on her boyfriend—if in fact there was one. Cliff had never seen her with any guy who fit that bill but he did know a lot of these short-runners had "backup deals," so-called boyfriends who were kept around to build up the girl's ego and hand them aspirin when they woke up with a hangover, but who were rarely publicly acknowledged. What did these faux boyfriends get out of it? They got to fuck a girl who might otherwise be out of their league and they got "gifts." Tickets to concerts, good seats at Lakers games, invitations to parties, all courtesy of their girl who had access to the A-list people and places that these guys ached to be part of. It was a twisted deal but a fairly common one. Cliff wondered why these girls opted for such compromise, instability and confusion when they could easily find some nice, steady, professional guy to settle down with. Why put yourself at such emotional, financial and psychological risk? The answer was what it always is—because in Los Angeles, the prize doesn't seem that far out of reach. It's like an optical illusion, a mirror where objects appear closer than they in fact are. There's a feeling that if you keep at it just a little longer, reach just a little further you'll have it in hand. "It" being the big everything—fame, fortune and freedom. It was an illusion that was particularly dangerous to women, who more often than not had to look good to compete. The irony being that the maintenance required to stay looking good left little time to accomplish anything else, which, in girls like Larissa, created a weird combination of entitlement and panic. Thinking about it made Cliff hyperaware that he was glad he had a son, not a daughter.

"Larissa," he said, "take it as a compliment."

"Take what as a compliment?"

"Look, women are going to be threatened by your friendship with Henry. You're beautiful, you're fun and he obviously adores you."

Hearing himself pile on the sugar, Cliff thought, My God, you can choke on flattery in this town, not that Larissa was choking. His words were going down as smooth as the green tea honey elixirs he was hoping to market.

"Yeah, I know, I know. But she is a witty girl and Henry is a sucker for that." Larissa's omission of Anne's name was a clear sign it was war between these two.

The door to the bathroom opened and a famous man-about-town—an owner of a number of trendy hotels and a reputation for courting threesomes—stepped out, while a girl remained behind primping in the mirror above the sink. As the hotelier walked by Larissa, he checked her out, the way men who are always on the prowl check out new prospects.

That bit of attention worked better than the aromatherapy or Cliff's flattery. Larissa's mood lightened up considerably. "Hey, you got any pot on you, Cliff?"

"Me?"

"Yeah, I thought you were a pothead."

"Never."

He felt in his pocket for the rest of the Soma pill but wasn't about to offer it up. The night wasn't over yet and he might still need it. He checked his watch. He'd been there for an hour and a half but if he left now, Theresa wouldn't be happy. And what was the point of showing up at all if he was going to lose points for an early departure?

"You think anyone here has pot on them?" Larissa asked.

"I doubt it. This is more of a Xanax, Vicodin crowd."

"You got a cigarette?"

"I'm more likely to have pot."

She pulled out her compact and checked her face yet again. As usual it was the one thing she could rely on. She still looked better than anyone else at the party. "Damn, Cliff, what are you good for?" She snapped shut her compact and dropped it in her bag. "I'm just teasing," she said. "You know I love ya."

The bathroom door opened and the girl who had shared a moment behind those closed doors with the overlustful hotel honcho stepped out. She was one of those women of indeterminate age. Cosmetic surgery was blurring the age lines in L.A., especially with younger women having the same procedures as women twenty years their senior, which ironically left them looking so similar the young ones now appeared much older than their actual age.

"Thirty is the new fifty," Cliff said, which got a laugh out of Larissa.

"I'm much sexier than that woman. I should be hanging out with a cool guy who owns hotels." She leaned over and lightly kissed Cliff on the lips. "See you later, hotshot." She then stepped inside the bathroom to redo her makeup and erase any lingering signs of sadness.

Chapter 7

Anne

To be involved with a king is to live in the land of no information. Thank God I come up with this realization a few minutes after Henry shows up with that awful girl. For a moment there I feel like an explosion is ripping my heart out. I'm not good with confusion and chaos. It triggers a desire to act rash, which is a tough desire to suppress, but I do. I have to. Otherwise I'll end up damaging the very things I'm trying so hard to protect. But once I hang a label on something I can usually handle it. In search of that label I force myself to remember that being able to deal with moments like this separates the runners-up from the royals. I have to remind myself that handling situations like this well is how I earn an extraordinary life. I force myself to focus. Why am I so upset? If Henry walked in with his ex, Catherine, I might be mildly annoyed but that's all. Why do I feel so hurt? Is it because when I spoke to him earlier he said he'd see me at the party and left it at that? Henry has always been extremely vague when it comes to his intentions but there's vague and then there's a lie of omission. I do know he's like this with everyone. Even Catherine lived in the land of no information. Well, maybe not no information but minimum information. Why don't I just say, Fuck it, I don't need this? But the thing is I do. Henry may not have absolute power but he does hold the keys to many magic kingdoms and no one is more fun and fascinating than Henry when you're right there with him, alone, just the two of you. I can't walk away from that. If I could, I would.

The more I think about it the more I realize it's not so much Henry's habit of operating without regard to others' feelings, or his vagueness or even that he walked in the door with a young woman wearing over-the-knee black leather boots and a fuchsia mini. What bothers me is that he walked in the door with that *particular* woman in the leather boots and fuchsia mini.

I despise Larissa. I've seen her around town over the years. She's one of those girls who like to talk about being a girly girl and the girl code—whatever that is—and yet girls like her are always the ones you'll find ringing the bell outside their best friend's boyfriend's gate at 2 A.M. saying, "Hi, handsome, in the mood for some extra fun?" She's an "I love you, therefore you owe me" type of girl if I've ever seen one. She drops the L-word the way people place bets in Vegas, hoping she'll get lucky and land some guy who will set her up for life. I'm sure Larissa has some kind of troubled past, abandoned by daddy, a mommy who had too many boyfriends, plus her own early disappointments in romance. It's not that these stories don't deserve sympathy. There is a sisterhood of shared pain that can be tapped into. If she and I ever end up having a couple of drinks together someday I might even feel bad for her, want to help her, not that I'll ever really believe everything she says. Telling the truth is a luxury for girls like that. At an early age they learn to survive by lying, hoping that when they make it big someday they can drop the nasty habit but either they don't make it big or the habit is too ingrained to be exorcised. I get it, I do. Problem is, even when I finally figure Larissa out and slap a label on her, satisfied I've nailed her correctly, I still feel uneasy.

These thoughts occupy me as I let Theresa take my arm and lead me across the room. I'm not looking forward to what's coming but the second I make Henry laugh all my anxiety disappears. That beautiful hearty laugh of his captivates me and the way he looks at me, with such delight, makes it obvious that he and I have a special connection and Larissa is about as significant as a couple of melting ice cubes at the bottom of an empty cocktail glass.

I'm back in the game and I know exactly what move comes next. I leave Henry laughing and disappear, giving him time to wonder (and maybe worry a little) if everything with us is okay. I walk through the kitchen, looking around, hoping I might find an uncorked bottle of pinot noir but no luck. I grab a banana out of a bowl on the countertop. Perfect, just the way I like them, not too ripe. I slip out a side door that leads to a small area where the caterers have set up their equipment and supplies. There's a small table and a few chairs and I sit down assuming I'm alone but soon realize I'm not. In the shadows a man in his mid-twenties is helping himself to some bottled waters from the stash set up for the help. He turns to me, stares for a moment and then grins. "Smart girl," he says. I've never seen this young man before and I would have remembered. He's good-looking enough to be a heartthrob but lacks the vanity of one, which makes him even more attractive.

"Do I know you?" I ask. "Do you know me?"

"Nope," he says with a bit of a Southern accent. "But you're smart to be eating a banana. Potassium is what you need if you're going to drink at a party."

"Drink? If only. Seems Theresa skimped on the beverage selection."

He opens up his jacket and pulls out a silver flask that looks like an antique, maybe something that's been in his family for decades. I'm already imagining a Savannah, Georgia, background. He uncaps it and hands it to me. "You like vodka? This is the good stuff."

I don't usually drink vodka but considering I've just successfully survived an ambush I could use something to smooth out my emotions. I also don't usually drink from a flask, especially not a stranger's flask, but there's something about this guy that seems so normal and healthy that any germaphobe tendencies and fear of being drugged vanish.

He is right. It is the good stuff, probably Russian and very strong, stronger than America's idea of a Russian import. This tastes like something you might find in Putin's own liquor cabinet. A wave of warmth washes over me as a helicopter appears overhead, not so far overhead that the sound of its engine doesn't make me feel as if we're suddenly under attack.

"What do you think, robbery in the neighborhood?" he asks.

"A fire?" I ask as we go back and forth.

"Carjacking?"

"Celebrity sighting?"

"I got it," he says. "Another landslide. Did you hear that there've been a bunch of them recently and no one can figure out why?"

"Strange times," I say.

"Nostradamus?"

"This is what I want to know: Why is it that all those people who say Nostradamus predicted this and that only say so after the incident occurred? Where were they on 9/10 and where will they be when 2012 passes and the world doesn't end?"

"I hear you," he said. He smiled, a slightly crooked smile that made him appear both boyish and wise. "By the way, I'm Wyatt."

"I'm Anne."

We shook hands. He had good hands. Firm. Beautiful skin.

"Are you catering this?" I ask.

"Uh, no. Valet parking." He shrugs his shoulders as if to say I know, I know, you'd respect me more if I were part of the chef's crew.

Only then do I realize he's dressed in khaki pants and a white T-shirt like the other valets but somehow on him the clothes look cool. Must be that attitude of his or maybe it's that one gulp of the fast-acting vodka I consumed.

"I make more money as a valet," he adds. "This crowd tips big. I'm also a . . ."

Although the helicopter has moved on I don't hear the end of his sentence because Theresa has upped the volume on her outdoor speakers. I peek through the bushes to the backyard, where about thirty people are mingling, including Theresa, who has taken Henry by the arm and is introducing him to various guests. One of them says something to amuse "my king" and he breaks into a big smile. I've got to tell you about Henry's smile. His laugh is wonderful but it's his smile that is dangerous. He holds nothing back when he smiles. It is a smile so full of life and fun that very few can resist the urge not to be seduced into a sense of momentary optimism. I'm seduced from fifteen yards away. All is forgiven. At that moment if you ran down the list of all the things that are so, so difficult about Henry, including his lies of omission and his taste for awful girls who wear over-the-knee black leather boots with fuchsia miniskirts, I'd say yes, yes, I know but so what. You might roll your eyes and tell me I sound like a girl in love, which I wouldn't deny, but even scarier, I'm a woman in hope.

"What are you driving? I'll keep it up front."

The question brings my attention back to Wyatt, who is loaded down with a half-dozen water bottles.

"Oh, thanks. It's an old BMW, the cheap model. Black." I dig in my pocket for the ticket and give it to him.

He winces and I take it personally until he explains. "This music . . . someone needs to help Theresa out with her playlist. Her taste is just one step up from campaign theme songs."

He's right about that. As Wyatt goes back to work, some Fleetwood Mac song comes up on the CD loop. What was Theresa thinking? No alcohol selection and seventies rock? Not that I care because I decide that I'm ready to reenter the party now that the one taste of vodka got me thinking. I know just what the situation calls for, a little "private display of privates" or, as my sister Mary would put it, a little PDP. First step, ditch the underwear.

PDP should not be confused with flashing, though both are done in public. It's easy to flash. I once knew a girl who liked to flash her tits at restaurants. She only did it when she was at a table in the corner and in a chair that was not facing the middle of the room. One night she flashed a table nearby three times. The third time she did it no one cared except for a waitress who later told me that that was the moment she decided to become a lesbian. PDP is different. It's about revealing in such a way that the person you intend to see your privates is the only one who does see it. That's what makes it hot. The objective is to get your guy turned on while he's carrying on a serious conversation with someone who hasn't a clue there's a split focus going on. This requires skill on the part of the one doing the revealing and the one doing the watching.

It's one of the ways I keep Henry enthralled . . . by making less, *more*. It requires a number of sex tricks, which I learned through research and instinct, not practice. That's another thing I've got going for me. Henry loves that I've dated so few men in L.A. Apparently, women who are naughty by nature but have a good-girl résumé go into a special, honored category in his book.

I scout the location, walking around the backyard soiree. Theresa's property is typical of houses in her neighborhood. There's space for a small pool and a small lawn and not much more. Theresa definitely spent money on the exterior décor, bringing in couches and coffee tables to create an outdoor living room atmosphere, including a chandelier hanging from a tree. I see that Larissa is flitting about, making sure she's available if Henry wants her, but not hanging on to him the way she was when she made her entrance. I can tell she's teetering on that fine line between drinking to appear happy and accidentally falling into the pool. I note that she's steering clear of me and seems to be quite chummy with Cliff. I should probably worry about that but just then I see that Henry has taken a seat on one of the sofas and is in deep conversation with a couple of his golfing buddies. I know this is the best setup I'm going to find. I take a seat at the sofa catty-corner to his and chat up a guy in his forties who turns out to be a blogger whose area of expertise is state politics. As we discuss balancing the state budget, which I know nothing about, I make sure I catch Henry's eye. Once I have his attention, I shift my position slightly so even though I'm still talking sales tax my body is directly in Henry's sight line. Since I'm wearing a pencil skirt, it takes some finessing to nonchalantly push it up. For camouflage, I grab one of the cashmere throws that Theresa had tossed over the rented furniture to give the outdoor décor her personal touch. By the time we're on to fiscal responsibility my skirt is pulled up to my crotch and only a section of cashmere is covering my "golden triangle," actually red triangle, having just the night before used some Betty beauty dye for some visual spice "down there." By the time the blogger is explaining the cost of maintaining the city's infrastructure, I've unveiled and Henry is pulling off his split focus like the pro that he is. Not for a second do I risk having the blogger's eyes wander south of my face. Being incredibly curious about city versus state taxes is really working. Not for a second does Henry allow the two guys he's talking with to focus on anyone but him. Being the king, he has the easier assignment, seeing as he tends to get undivided attention even without trying. Plus, they're golf fanatics, which means stories of miracles on "the back nine" abound.

By the time the blogger is wrapping up his pitch for why the unified school district has mismanaged its yearly budget, my pencil skirt is now straightened out and ladylike, I've tossed the throw aside and my cell phone is beeping. An instant message coming in. I have no doubt it's from Henry, congratulating me on my little performance, but surprisingly, it's not. All anxiety returns as I check caller ID and see that it's my brother, George. "We've got to talk. Usual place? In an hour?" As always I am there for my brother as he is always there for me. We Boleyns have to stick together. Besides, George is my soul mate, though by no means a twin. He is far more reckless and gullible than I am, which is why I have good reason to worry and even better reason to show up. I text him back immediately. One word. "Yes."

As I make a quick exit from the party I run into Cliff.

"Having fun?" He has a weird grin on his face. I wonder if by any chance he may have seen any part of my "little performance." More likely he's just weird. In any case I can't dwell on it. George is in trouble.

Chapter 8

Theresa

Three people at the party told Theresa she looked great. Actually only one said great. Another said she looked invigorated and the third said she looked sexy. That's the word she wanted to hear. Too bad it didn't come from Henry. Although Henry had a well-documented appreciation for the sexuality of older women as well as his pretty young things, personal compliments had never been part of his dialogue with Theresa. He did, however, say the next-best thing. It happened when Theresa was escorting Henry and Larissa out to Henry's car, which, of course, was parked right out front. Can't keep the boss waiting.

At this point Larissa had had way too much to drink and was doing that thing that short-runners do when they want to make sure they'll be invited back . . . giving the hostess a verbal blow job.

"You look so bee . . . utiful in that dress, Theresa . . . so. So glamorous. Like Ava Garner or something."

"Gardner," Henry corrected, and then held the car door open

so she'd cut short the babbling and get inside. In a rare moment of defiance, Larissa wouldn't oblige until she had the last word.

"Theresa, you and I should do a hike one of these days. My favorite hiking trail is up the street."

"Darling, I'm sure I couldn't keep up with you." Theresa had a touch of genuine warmth in her voice, which was the key to her social success. She was genius when it came to making people feel so good they didn't notice they were being cut off.

Taking Theresa's comment as a compliment, Larissa concluded with her usual closer. "Love ya," she said and then with great care not to trip, she stumbled inside the Range Rover.

Finally the moment had arrived, the one Theresa had been planning all along. She now had her boss's full attention as he thanked her for a great party and she thanked him for the new job. Making sure she wasn't standing anywhere near the streetlamp, which cast too harsh a light, she gently touched his arm and said, "Let's do some great things together."

Theresa knew that competing with hot girls for Henry's attention required the excitement of a new project, or a new frontier. "I have so many ideas," she added, knowing this aggressive maneuver was risky. She was crossing a line. It was Henry's choice to expand the boundaries of an employee's working agenda, not hers.

"That's why you're here," he said. "You're my accomplice." With that he gave her a little squeeze, got in his car and drove off.

Theresa watched him leave, still reeling from the beauty of that word *accomplice* and what it could possibly mean. Accomplice, as in partner in crime? She didn't think Henry meant that literally but she loved the idea of doing something illicit with him, something secretive and risqué.

"Ms. Cromwell."

Theresa snapped out of her reverie. "What?"

Wyatt, the valet parking guy, was standing there with an envelope in his hand. "This is for you."

"Send the bill to my office."

"It's not a bill, it's a present. It's my CD."

Theresa was confused. Was she supposed to know about this? She took the envelope, gingerly, as if it might be contaminated.

"Self-produced. I'm shopping it around," Wyatt added.

Shopping it around? He was giving her a homemade CD? Theresa was tempted to give it back. Yeah, that's what she needed, another wannabe peddling his wares in the hope of using her connections. Not going to happen.

"I don't know anyone in the music biz who can help you," she replied.

"No, no, no. It's not that. It's for your personal use. Guaranteed to get the party started."

That made her pause, remembering that Nic Harcourt, the former host of KCRW's morning music show, once told her that there was a greater chance of discovering something new and interesting from a stranger handing him a CD in the bathroom of the Troubadour than from an official submission by an established record company.

She opened the envelope. "Two?"

"Actually I was hoping you could give one to one of your guests. Anne. Long dark hair. Black-as-coal eyes."

Black-as-coal eyes? Theresa hoped that wasn't an example of his song lyrics. "You mean Anne Boleyn?"

"Anne Boleyn," he repeated, as if he'd just found his mantra.

"I'll make sure that she gets it," Theresa said, thinking the beguiling Boleyn girl had struck again. As she was about to head back inside, a car drove past and she could have sworn Jake Winslow was at the wheel. What was L.A.'s notorious private detective doing on her street? This is not good, she thought. Not good at all.

Chapter 9

Cliff

It was midnight, three hours later than the time Cliff told his wife he'd be home and he was still at Theresa Cromwell's, upstairs in her bedroom, eating her pussy while thinking about anything and everything but sex. She didn't seem to notice or didn't seem to mind that he was on automatic pilot. Maybe it was because he'd always been good at this kind of sex, in part because he feared his dick wasn't as big as he'd like it to be and he was compensating. She seemed to be enjoying his attention though he wondered how much of it was due to his skill and how much was due to the Viagra cream, which she'd slathered on. It didn't taste all that great and Cliff couldn't help but worry that it might be toxic, though Theresa assured him it wasn't. That gave him an idea. Maybe he should look into the possibility of developing a line of organic sex lubricants.

Theresa's breathing got heavier, lost in her own fantasy, whatever that was. She was the queen of sexual compartmentalization.

Kissing or extraneous touching weren't even part of her playtime with Cliff and that suited him just fine. Guilt was part of his problem but less than one might think. Before they'd hit the bed, a deal had been struck though it was never put in those terms. Theresa offered him her old job (not for a lot of money, but still) editing *Daily*'s website now that she'd be doing more important work with Henry. It put Cliff back into play. Just thinking about the extras that would come, including a modest expense account, got his blood pumping and if he was expected to give his benefactress a little pleasure to seal the deal, so what. He also had a backup list of rationalizations that included the fact that he hadn't had sex with his wife (her choice) in two months and Theresa was attractive . . . in her own way. She had a nice body for a woman her age though a bikini wax wouldn't have been a bad idea. For a minute there he thought he was going to have to get a flashlight to find her clit. An exaggeration but still, in comparison to the standard Brazilian G-string wax job that was the standard fare in L.A., it was startling.

Theresa's short breaths grew more frequent and Cliff felt her body tense until finally, after a few false alarms, she had the orgasm she was looking for. She wasn't a screamer, which Cliff was grateful for but she did make a very unsettling sound when she came. It was some sort of a triumphant groan as if she'd been jamming a pickax into stone as she climbed Everest and had at long last reached the summit.

He rolled off her, assuming she was done with him.

"Nice," Theresa said, with genuine appreciation. And then reaching over the bed, she pulled a wad of tissues out of a Kleenex box on the floor and tossed them in his direction.

When straightened out and cleaned up, Cliff reached into his pocket for the remainder of his Soma pill. He'd performed better just knowing it was there, knowing if he needed to zone out a little, he had the means to get there. Now he popped it into his mouth, a treat to himself, his version of a nightcap for an evening that had its challenges but also its rewards.

"Cliff?" Theresa spoke in a voice that was relaxed but by no means vulnerable. "What did you think of my mojito cocktail?" This was her way of saying I saw you dump the drink. Of course she did, Cliff thought. She doesn't miss a thing.

"It was a hit," he replied, skirting the issue.

She just smiled, letting it go. Bringing it up had put him on notice. Sitting up in her queen-sized bed, she reached for her bottle of Pellegrino on the bedside table, while glancing over at her BlackBerry to see if the message light was on. It wasn't. "Give my best to your wife," she said.

He was being dismissed, as if Theresa, by virtue of her job promotion, was now infused with a bit of royal blood. She waved her hand, an indication his presence was no longer required. Cliff hesitated for a minute, not knowing the protocol here. For a second he considered, as a joke, bowing and backing out of the room, but he wasn't sure Theresa would find it amusing. Instead he blurted out a word he'd never used before and couldn't imagine where it came from.

"Cheerio," he said and saw himself out.

The neighborhood was quiet as it usually is after midnight. The valets had long gone and Cliff found the silence eerie. Even though it was a residential area, this far up in the canyon there was too much shrubbery, too many shadows. It wouldn't have surprised Cliff if someone jumped out at him from behind a bush or maybe worse, an animal appeared. There was a rumor that a baby mountain lion had been spotted not too far away. So when the quiet was disturbed by the sound of a helicopter approaching,

Cliff found it reassuring. Even when the chopper hovered right overhead, loud and threatening, its searchlights scanning the area, Cliff wasn't worried and no one else seemed to be, either. No door opened, no light was turned on in any of the houses. People just took it in stride. It was just business as usual up in the L.A. canyons.

Chapter 10

Anne

The first thing I notice about my brother George is that he's wearing a sweatshirt. It's from USC, his alma mater. Though George is a sufficiently proud member of the alumni, he never wears sweatshirts unless he is actually playing sports. Even when he's down at the Staples Center, watching his favorites, the Lakers, he puts on a jacket over a Helmut Lang T-shirt, or if slumming, a standard black or white one from the Gap. George takes great pride in his fashion sense. To show up at a restaurant in a sloppy sweatshirt tells me there's a problem.

When I arrive he's sitting in a corner booth drinking a beer. It's our favorite booth at Jinky's, which is our favorite off-the-radar hangout on Ventura Boulevard, not too far from the house we grew up in. There's something about this place that makes us feel safe and it isn't nostalgia, because neither of us is the nostalgic type. I think it has more to do with the fact that we rarely ever run into anyone we know, so we're safe from gossip. They also happen to have great pancakes, which comes as close as you can get to a short-term cure for depression.

"Sorry to call you out so late. You weren't in the middle of anything, were you?"

I know he means Henry. "It's okay, I was at a party. I'll give you a progress report later. What's up?"

"You want anything?" He slides a menu across the table.

"I'm good," I say, helping myself to a sip of his water.

He looks around the restaurant as if casing the joint. "I hate that you can't smoke in here anymore."

For a second he looks like he might light up anyway. He finishes off his beer, signals to a waitress for a refill and then gets down to it. "I ever tell you about my friend Ethan?"

I know exactly who he's talking about even though I haven't met Ethan and George has only dropped his name a few times but he dropped it in such a way, with a kind of irrepressible smile on his face, that told me there was a good reason he wasn't bringing him around.

"Ethan, the chef guy?"

"Yeah. Well, I've been trying to help him out, getting him some catering jobs and I guess someone who is competitive with him . . ."

George stops to let the waitress put a bottle of Heineken on the table. "Can I get you something, honey?" The waitress has a cheery yet world-weary tone.

"No thanks," I reply politely. She gives me a look that says, Oh great, I'm really earning the big bucks on this shift, and walks away.

As I wait for George to continue, the message light on his cell starts blinking and he checks to see what's incoming.

"Lacy," he explains.

Lacy Rochford is George's girlfriend, who works in fashion PR but only when she feels like it because her parents have always given her enough money so she doesn't have to do anything very seriously or for very long.

With noticeable nervousness, George instant-messages her right back, then puts the phone down on the table. Having his BlackBerry visible makes me feel as if Lacy is actually there with us, though if she were, she'd be sulking and complaining about being in a place like Jinky's on Ventura Boulevard.

"Where is she?"

"At my apartment, waiting for me." His eyes keep darting back to his phone as if he's worried about her possible response.

"So," I say to get him back on track.

"So," he says, "I guess because Ethan's career is starting to take off . . . he's even been approached about going on *Top Chef* . . ."

As troubled as George appears, he offers up this piece of information with noticeable pride.

"Anyway," he continues, "people get jealous and one of them started this rumor about Ethan being gay and accusing me . . ."

George pauses momentarily and then without diverting his eyes from mine delivers the punch: "of being his secret boyfriend."

"So," I repeat, and never has one tiny word packed so much in meaning. It's "So" as in . . . So why should we care about some stupid gossip? It's "So" as in even if it's true you can deny it. It's "So" as in even if it's true and you don't want to deny it, you don't have to let some jealous creep control your flow of information. It's "So" as in if it's not true and you're upset about it you shouldn't be. I'm about to launch into Henry's theory that every interesting person has at least one tabloidworthy rumor or story floating around about them when George interrupts me.

"So," he says nervously, tapping a piece of silverware against his bottle of beer. "So, Dad heard the rumor."

And that's when my "So" became an "Oh."

All families have complicated systems that determine what gets discussed and what gets ignored and my family is no different. There are certain things that are never mentioned (including George's possible bisexuality) and usually that's because it's the way my father wants it. At first glance my dad appears typical of the liberal, baby boomer generation that grew up in the upscale suburbs of the San Fernando Valley. Back then the Valley was paradise, clean air, mostly blue skies and a sense that things were only going to get better. My dad went to the same high school as Michael Milken, who later became infamous for being indicted for insider trading in the course of amassing enormous wealth, and Mike Ovitz, the onetime head of Creative Artists Agency, whose fall from power and grace was almost Shakespearean. My dad had the golden good looks of a classic Southern California beach boy (George and I are dark-haired like our mother), which brought him plenty of opportunities to live the good life. Surfing, rock and roll, and drugs (not that he's ever admitted to that) were all part of his high school life and the party continued at UCLA. Reality didn't grab his attention until his average grades landed him in a second-tier law school. A few years after graduating and toiling away at a small, not particularly illustrious firm in Century City, it became obvious to all that he was being outperformed by the very classmates he'd always felt superior to. It was right around this time that he married my mother, whose father was a senior partner at a Beverly Hills entertainment law firm. Marriage came with a job offer at his father-in-law's practice and a nice office with a view. Much to everyone's surprise, my dad proved to be good at negotiating contracts, specifically finding ways to screw whoever was on the opposing side. To his credit, he was fairly honest about his story up until this point, except he wouldn't refer to it as screwing an opponent but instead as protecting a client, and there is no question that when push comes to shove, my dad knows how to fight for his team.

The rest of his story I pieced together from bits and pieces of secondhand information and my own experiences growing up. Around the time I was ten, I thought of my dad as a star, maybe because that's how he saw himself as he took the leap and opened up his own law firm. He expected his new business would catapult him to the rank of major player in the biz but by the time I was twelve the dream was over and I've never been able to find out exactly what happened. This episode, like many others, falls in the no-speak zone in our family history. No one had to say a word for me to see that my father was devastated by this failure. It was the equivalent of having a shot at playing James Bond but ending up playing the backup detective on a TV drama, and not even one on a major network. The acting analogy comes to mind because it was around this time that my father met Suzy Samuels, an actress who had won a Golden Globe for her work in a drama about a woman who awakens from a coma and has no memory of being a supermodel and a killer. Apparently my father was quite taken with how Suzy looked in those skintight Azzedine Alaïa dresses that were so popular back then. Though they managed to keep their affair under the media radar my mother found out and the "D-word" was whispered around the house. It was always the "D-word," never divorce. My mother couldn't bring herself to say it, much less file for it. However, in her own passive-aggressive way she fought back, dropping hints about suicide and flirting inappropriately with the pool guy when she wasn't sipping chardonnay with her morning scrambled eggs. My dad on the other hand was ready to move on to Suzy and their red-carpet moment until Mary, George and I begged him not to leave us. It was a scene that, in retrospect, was almost comical. As the three of us stepped in front of the door to keep him from walking out with a suitcase in his hand and his prized possession, a Leo de Vince sketch in the other, Mary got so hysterical she broke out in hives and had to be rushed to the emergency room, which delayed my father's exit that night. He was all set to leave the next morning but something happened and he put it off another day and then a week and then a second week until finally one Sunday evening he gathered us children around and made a deal with us. He said he'd stay but from this point on we must all be one hundred percent committed to our family. It was going to be family first. He was very solemn and we all swore our allegiance and then we went into the dining room, where my mother had prepared lasagna, and life continued as if Suzy Samuels never existed.

Years later George and I joked that that vow we took that Sunday evening was like something out of a mafia movie. We also cynically concluded that Suzy was the one who dumped my dad because it was right around then that she started stepping out with a young, hot cinematographer who later directed her in a low-budget erotic thriller that couldn't find a distributor at Sundance or any other film festival. The one thing we didn't joke about, the one thing we never mentioned, was that the vow stuck. It glued us together in some kind of shared-guilt alliance. It was as if my father had changed our inner wiring that night and we all felt bound by the oath we took.

When I was younger that bond made me feel safe but as the years passed a strange thing happened. I started to view my father as weak and his control over me had more to do with my sense of loyalty and obligation to him than it did with his role as the chief of our little tribe. When he heard I was seeing Henry, he started acting like a manager, constantly advising me how to play the courtship game. Between the lines, what he was really doing was making me the designated savior of the family. It was now my job to take us up the next rung of the social and economic ladder. I could have rejected the assignment. I should have rejected the assignment . . . but I didn't.

I reach across the table and touch my brother's hand. "I'll deal with Dad. Just tell me what you want me to say."

"He wants me to marry Lacy. He thinks I should propose right away."

"You love her?"

"You're the only woman I love, Anne. You know that."

I smile remembering our childhood proclamations made to each other when we were too young to know what we were saying.

George glances around the room as if he's worried someone is stalking him. "I'm thinking maybe I should tell Dad to just mind his own fucking business."

We both laugh, knowing he won't and that if he did, my father wouldn't listen anyway.

"So what do you think I should do?" George asks. Although he really wants an answer he doesn't appear as panicked as he was when I first sat down. Could be because Lacy isn't calling him incessantly, which is her nature, or maybe it's because I haven't pushed for any details about Ethan. I respect his privacy in part because I need him to respect mine.

"Do you want me to answer as a Boleyn or as a sister who adores her brother and wants him to be happy?"

"Does it have to be either/or?"

"I don't think Lacy will make you happy," I say.

"Whatever happy is," he replies dismissively. At that moment I'm reminded of that famous video clip from an interview with Prince Charles on the day he announced his engagement to Diana. When asked if they were in love, he answered, "Whatever love is." That sentence was a red flag that warned of what was to come in the royal marriage and though George doesn't have the weight of a crown on his head, his equally cynical quip makes me uneasy, which he immediately picks up on.

"What do you want me to say?" he asks, looking at me with those soulful eyes of his that have always brought out my protective instincts. "I admit it. I don't have the kind of passion that would make me drive five hundred miles just to see her face."

The five-hundred-miles thing was another reference to our preteen years, when it was the ultimate declaration of adoration, as in, "I'd drive five hundred miles to meet Johnny Depp," a sentiment George and I were one hundred percent in sync on.

"Do you?" George asks. "Do you have that kind of passion for Henry?"

Before I can answer, the waitress puts down a bag of takeout food and George's credit card receipt.

"Lacy," he explains. "She's starving."

Just then a cell phone rings, mine not his. An instant message that reads, "Where are you darling?"

I quickly IM him back. "On my way."

"Henry?" George guesses.

"Henry." I smile and then squeeze George's hand. "Whatever you need me to do, I'll do."

We stay like that, without talking for a few moments. I have no idea what he's thinking but he probably knows that my mind is racing through a series of aggressive tactics. In that regard I am like my father, not my mother. I'm always going to opt for action and retribution. You'll never find me slurping white wine and crying into my scrambled eggs.

"What's the guy's name, the one spreading the gossip?" I ask.

"Doesn't matter who he is. He's insignificant."

"Still, what's his name? I'm just curious."

"Lionel."

"Lionel what?"

"Doesn't matter." George picks up the takeout food and his keys. "Fuck it," he says, as if he's surrendering to the inevitable.

He can tell by the look on my face that I'm not sure what he means.

"Don't worry, Anne. It's all going to work out fine."

At that moment I choose to believe him. Big mistake.

Chapter 11

Catherine

Catherine's insomnia had changed her life and she blamed it all on Henry. Ever since he ended their marriage, she didn't trust the darkness. She worried about what was going on in the world when she was asleep and her dreams were filled with such disturbing, haunting images she had to take anti-anxiety medication on awakening. The brilliant morning sunlight that comes with living in Southern California and the fact that she and her daughter Maren lived in a secure gated community—with a guard at the entrance to their road—did not reassure her. Even Carmen, her Mexican housekeeper, who though only five foot two was fearless and (somehow) intimidating to any and all trespassers, didn't diminish Catherine's anxiety. Not even Catherine's newly revived faith in Catholicism could quell her fears and that's what troubled her the most. If surrendering to God wasn't calming her soul, what would? Not that she would ever confess this to anyone, except possibly the pope.

The result of all this unrest was that Catherine had become a night person, a glaring contrast to the first years of her marriage, when she took great pride in waking early and accomplishing much while others (Henry) were still asleep. She had always boasted about coming from a long line of achievers. Throughout the house there were numerous photos (in Tiffany frames) of her family's accomplishments. Winning horse races, golf tournaments, elections. Catherine was often photographed at charity events, many of which she chaired. She loved it when people remarked that she got more done before ten in the morning than most people got done in a week. Not anymore. These days Catherine rarely got to bed before three and sometimes didn't rise until 11 A.M. She decided that being a nocturnal person was good for nothing except dealing with other nocturnal people, which is how it happened that she and Jake Winslow, the private detective she'd hired, were sitting in her downstairs den at midnight checking out the digital photographs he'd taken earlier that night.

"Henry's so predictable," Catherine said as she looked at a shot of her ex and Larissa getting out of his Range Rover in front of Theresa Cromwell's house.

Jake glanced over at the shot Catherine was referring to. "Larissa Lopez is her name."

"I know her name but I prefer to call her 'the seat-filler.'" This was Catherine's derogatory term for those indistinguishable girls Henry called on when he wanted to be surrounded by "scenery."

Jake nodded, to appear agreeable. His job wasn't to judge, though he could have easily built a case for why dallying with seat-fillers was often a better road than dealing with demanding women like Catherine. Fifteen years ago, back when Catherine first hooked up with Henry, it was a different story. Back then she was worth the drama. Now, at forty-six (six years older than her ex), she'd hardened on the inside and softened on the outside (he thought she could stand to lose a few pounds), making her appear asexual and matronly.

Jake watched her flip through the dozens of digital shots he'd taken, giving most of them no more than a glance until she came across one of Anne talking with the valet parking guy.

Catherine stared at the photo, fascinated by this creature that she despised even though they'd never met. She didn't need to be in a room with her to hate everything Anne stood for, which in Catherine's opinion came down to three words: *dark, Machiavellian, cunt.* Unconsciously she reached for the diamond cross necklace that she always wore, as if her holding on to a religious symbol while plotting Anne's demise meant God was on her side. "Who's the guy she's flirting with?"

"Just someone parking the cars. They were just talking."

"Flirting," Catherine admonished him.

Jake let her abrasive attitude slide because she was paying top dollar for a basic surveillance job and because her family was still a powerful force in politics and he might need a favor someday.

Catherine stared at the image of her nemesis and there was no hiding the pain this photographic evidence caused her. "Did Anne leave alone?"

"Arrived alone, left alone."

Catherine sighed, accepting defeat for a second before launching the next attack. "It's always the ones who arrive solo and leave solo that you have to worry about. They're the ones Henry is besotted with. He loves the ones who act like they don't need him."

Jake figured it was time to throw his client a bone. "I don't get it. I don't see what's so great about this Anne Boleyn."

"Apparently she's full of surprises." Catherine moved on to dozens more photos, all slight variations of what she'd already seen. It wasn't until she came to a completely different shot that she stopped.

"What is this?" She was looking at a picture of the small terrace off Theresa Cromwell's bedroom. Through the French doors was a clear view of Cliff, half dressed.

Jake explained. "I had some time to kill so I stuck around and bingo. You know this guy?"

"Cliff Craven. Nose firmly pressed to window at all times but relatively harmless. Poor guy. I don't know what's worse . . . that he's sleeping with that Theresa woman or that he's too stupid not to notice that the curtains aren't closed."

Wow, Jake thought. If Catherine doesn't slow down, she's going to OD on her own bitterness one of these days.

Ten minutes later, after being given further instructions, Jake was out of there. As he walked down the driveway, he had a moment of empathy, thinking about how hard it must be for Catherine to have any kind of normal life, given who she was and whom she was married to. The chance she'd be able to find a new husband who wasn't after her money or connections was remote. Worse was the kind of man who'd come around out of some perverse curiosity. He'd once heard a cocky real estate agent say he'd consider fucking Catherine, just once, for the historical significance of it. If that was the kind of offer she had in her future, maybe religious abstinence was the smarter move.

When he got to his car Jake noticed a van parked across the street and recognized the man sitting behind the wheel as one of the front-gate guards. Jake guessed he was pulling a second shift to provide extra protection for Catherine and wondered if this was standard operating procedure. Catherine was tricky, that's for sure. He wasn't one hundred percent clear on her whole story but that was okay; he was tricky, too. He hadn't told Catherine, nor did he plan to, that she wasn't the only one paying him to keep tabs on Henry.

As Jake drove by the parked van, he waved to the security guard—

even though they'd never met—and the guard waved back. They were two men acknowledging their membership in the same club, both of them part of the corps that serviced the troubled residents of these supermansions. Thank God for jealousy and paranoia, Jake thought. Talk about stimulating the economy. He then headed over the hill to North Hollywood to spend some of that money at one of his favorite Ventura Boulevard strip clubs.

Chapter 12

Anne

Someone in the parking lot at Jinky's says there's been an accident on the freeway. That explains why there's so much traffic on the boulevard. Usually at that hour, even on a weekend night, I can make it to Henry's in fifteen minutes. From the look of the gridlock in front of me, I know it's going to take, at the very least, a half an hour. Fuck. The second I say this I realize how far I've come from being so blissful and filled with generosity that I'd let every motorist cut in front of me. Now I hit the accelerator for the slightest advantage, narrowly averting a guy in one of those tiny "Smart" cars so I can get to Henry's a minute sooner. "Sorry," I blurt out, but with the windows up, of course he can't hear me. Too bad. Maybe if he could, he wouldn't go so psycho. Being the tiniest car on the road, the "Smartie" is able to navigate around traffic and catch up with me. In my rearview mirror I see that the driver is an angry-looking man and I don't know what surprises me more . . . that he's giving me a Charles Manson stare or that this is the first time I've seen a grown-up man driving one of those egg-shaped cars. He leans on his horn and I shrug as if to say, "Yeah, I know, I fucked up," but this doesn't appease him. I guess you have to expect this kind of road rage on a Saturday night in L.A., especially when you hit the midnight hour. I mean here's a guy, looks to be in his mid-thirties, going home alone, in the same kind of car that sixteen-year-old Beverly Hills kids get as their starter wheels. And if he's not drunk, there's a good chance he's not happy. Still, I'm not expecting an escalation in this little drama nor do I have time for any so I don't respond further to his horn blaring. My only thought is to take the next left and use Valley Vista Way as a shortcut to head up into the hills. I pull over into the turning lane and wait for the light to go green. The road-rager moves over into the same lane but instead of stopping, he intentionally slams into my back bumper. For a second I sit there shocked. I turn around and see that this lunatic is leaning out his car window. "How'd you like that?" he screams, pleased with himself. My options are to interact with someone who is clearly unhinged or to stay focused on my goal—Henry. I wait until the light is just about to go from yellow to red before I move through the intersection. Through-traffic prevents the Smart car from following. I get away clean, wondering what is going on in this city lately. Where is this rising tide of unrest and craziness coming from? Could Nostradamus be right? Are we headed for the big goodbye? L.A. has always been a place where hope and possibility spring eternal and a new better day is just around the corner. It's practically the city's birthright. Is that optimism in jeopardy? If Los Angeles loses its hope card . . . then what? These thoughts and questions make me appreciate, even more, the protection and safety Henry provides, and which at that moment attracts me like no other aphrodisiac ever has before. No wonder I'm flirting with disaster by going through three stop signs to reach him.

The downstairs door has been left open. Henry's security guy informs me of this as he opens the gate to the driveway. The other live-in staff members are ensconced in their rooms off the kitchen and over the six-car garage. Only two lights have been left on, one in the hallway illuminating a painting by Tamara de Lempicka and one at the top of the stairs illuminating a Leo de Vince portrait of a woman in a red dress. Henry is waiting for me, standing there naked. I walk up to him and curtsy, eye level with his beautiful cock.

I didn't plan for this to be the night I cross the line and abandon my strategy. God knows I have to ignore my father's advice to do so. He's cautioned me not to fuck Henry until I get an invitation to move in or some other form of public acknowledgment as "the number one girl." My father has made the point, on more than one occasion, that when you're dealing with a so-called king, you can't afford to ignore strategy. He has a point. Long-term desire and commitment don't happen by accident with Henry. They happen, like luck, because you create the right conditions for them to happen and sometimes that means knowing when to move the action up to the next level of play and when not to. My sister Mary didn't bother with strategy and look what it got her. A brief rush of attention and a Cartier watch as a parting gift. Worse, Mary discovered that once you've been with a king it's not easy to go back to civilians. She's had a number of relationships since Henry and though all start with declarations of love none has lasted more than a few months.

But tonight I can't rule with my brain anymore. Maybe the psycho with road rage rattled me. Maybe it's the thought of my brother being rattled by my father's demands or maybe I'm just tired of always forgoing gratification for a master plan. Probably it's all of that and something else, something bigger, some voice in my head that says . . . when a moment for true, emotional connection is within your reach, it's a gift from the gods; and they haven't been in a very giving mood lately. Take it.

I get more than I asked for. Of course the sex is amazing but there's also a bonus. There's something about surrendering to this authentically strong man that makes me feel empowered. So often women fall in love with a man's potential. I've done it and then felt silly later when he turned out to be a guy who drinks sea breezes and excels at cheesy pickup lines. That was back in my first year of college and I've been careful to avoid the poseurs since then. There's nothing fake about Henry. He's done what he set out to do and more. That's always been evident. The surprise is that fucking the real deal makes me feel like *I can rule the world*. I lie back with a big smile on my face.

"What are you thinking?" he asks.

"I'm thinking that I now know what the phrase 'sexually liberated' really means."

At 3 a.m. the phone rings. Henry is on top of me, both of us drenched in sweat. He looks over to see that the light on his third line is flashing, the line I call his recreation line because it's the number he freely gives out to any woman who attracts his attention. There's a good chance it could be Larissa calling or maybe it's another pretty young thing on her way home from a club or party, drunk enough to believe that a spontaneous call will be met with an invitation.

"Answer it," I say, not because Henry needs my permission but because I want him to know I can handle it. But he doesn't and after the fourth ring it goes to voice mail and everything gets quiet again. As he and I lie next to each other after our sex marathon he turns to me and says, "Libidos separated at birth." I laugh, delighted that he feels the same way I do. We are perfectly in sync and I know that a greater destiny is opening up in front of me and it's almost too much to handle. At that moment I believe we've found something in each other that makes who we are individually so much stronger. It's one thing to satisfy a king; it's another to embolden him. And yet another to do both. I know what we just experienced is unique so I'm not worried about Henry's history. Everyone knows his pattern is to conquer, enjoy and move on. I get that. Men who have options generally take them. It's a fact I'll have to deal with down the line but even more crucial, I'll have to find a way to make Henry's bad-boy behavior work in my favor. Alchemy. Lead into gold. I'll learn from Catherine's mistakes. She dealt with Henry's "needs" by looking the other way until there was no place left to look. I'm smarter than that. I'm a Boleyn. Flush with confidence in my abilities to have a future with Henry, I push my hair off my face and lovingly gaze at him.

"Just remember, Henry, you can get rid of me, but you can never, ever replace me."

He roars with laughter. "Why would I ever want to get rid of you?"

Trained by my father to never, ever, throw all caution to the wind, even when I'm falling in love and feeling like a winner, I whisper sweetly in his ear, "Because you can, darling, because you can."

Part Two

THE CONTENDER

Chapter 13

Anne

"Well, at least we don't have to be bridesmaids," Mary says as she pours herself more champagne.

"That's the upside of having the bride hate you," I reply.

"She doesn't hate me," Mary says laughing. "You're the one she can't stand."

We are in my old apartment, my one-bedroom on the "poor" side of Beverly Hills, getting in some sisterly bonding before heading over to our brother George's wedding. Mary took over the place after I moved in with Henry because she'd just ended another relationship (that didn't make it to the six-month mark) and needed somewhere to stay.

"Lacy pretends to adore me," I say.

"Duh," Mary says as she slips on a floral print dress that looks more appropriate for a wedding in Topanga Canyon than one in fancy Trousdale Estates. "She's got to pretend . . . *now*."

The operative word is *now*. It used to be that my about-to-be sister-in law, Lacy, was quite vocal about how "difficult" I am to get along with. By difficult she meant that she resented how close George and I are but now that I'm publicly with Henry she's all smiles and has channeled all her resentment into one curious habit. She seems to perversely enjoy calling me Annie.

Mary refills her champagne glass and looks over to mine, which is almost full. "My champagne isn't fancy enough for you? You just drink the hundred-dollar-a-bottle stuff now?" Mary is kidding but underneath the joke is a sensitive topic . . . our very different lifestyles.

"Just pacing myself," I say.

I look around the room. It's been a while since I've been here and I can't believe how shabby it is . . . and always was. The cracked plaster around the windows, watermarks on the walls from a leak in the roof and worst of all, the thinness of those walls. I can hear the downstairs neighbor's TV. A basketball game and judging by the loud cheering, his team is winning. None of this bothered me when I lived here but now, having been upgraded to Henry's very private and exquisitely designed and decorated architectural jewel of a house, I'm seeing my old home through different, more critical eyes. It's not that Mary hasn't warmed up the place in her newly acquired hippie style—lots of pillows covered in Indian fabrics, a vase filled with sunflowers, framed family photos—it's just that all of that only serves to semisuccessfully camouflage the fact that zip code aside, this place is not much better than an upscale tenement.

At Henry's there are no watermarks on the walls or stains on the carpets or flaws anywhere. Everywhere I look there's beauty, from the arrestingly beautiful Ellsworth Kelly on the wall in his dining room to the Picasso figurine sculptures on the coffee table to the custom-made floor-to-ceiling bookshelves filled with the greatest art books published in the last fifty years. That's another thing I notice about Mary's décor. No books. The shelves I left behind are now filled with her collection of small woven baskets, snow globes and candles. There is a stack of magazines by the bed. *Elle* and *Us Weekly*.

"So Henry is going to meet you there?" Something about the way Mary asks that makes me wonder if she thinks about Henry more than she admits.

"He's not coming to the ceremony, just the reception."

"Typical of him," Mary declares with the slightest edge to her voice. She always claims she's happy that Henry and I are together but I think she'd be even happier if Henry dumped me the way he dumped her. I don't blame her for that. Our parents have become obsessed with my life since I hooked up with him, and Mary—who had always been their dream child, their lottery ticket to the big time, their gorgeous blond-haired, blue-eyed girl—is now relegated to option B. Whenever any of their friends inquire about Mary, my mother always says, "She's fine, keeps herself busy." Five words sum up my sister now. It used to be that my mother could sing her praises for hours. Mary pretends she doesn't notice this shift in attention but she has started smoking pot. While we're talking, she pulls a joint out of her pocket and lights up.

"It's an appropriate thing to do," I say defensively. "It's not like Henry knows the bride or groom all that well. Two dinners does not mean he's obligated to spend his entire day celebrating a marriage that probably won't last."

"Whatever," Mary shrugs, as she slips on a pair of purple slingback stilettos that immediately give that floral nightmare she's wearing sex appeal. I have to admit she has a much better body than I have . . . longer legs and those perfect tits of hers, which are still a magnet for male attention. It's only her face that has lost its sparkle. No way to camouflage her disappointments.

"So who is part of Henry's entourage this time?" she asks.

And yes, Henry still has an entourage. This is what you're never going to see: Henry sitting alone at a party. "Theresa Cromwell and Cliff," I say. "Lacy was thrilled to put Henry and whoever he wanted to bring with him on the guest list. I didn't tell her he was only coming because I begged him to and because George begged me to get him there."

"Dad wants him there," Mary says and I nod. She's right but the Dad issue is a whole other conversation that neither of us has the stomach for at the moment. Better to stick with gossip.

"Are Theresa and Cliff an item?" Mary asks. "Tell me that isn't happening."

"Absolutely not. He's married and even if he wasn't, Theresa would never publicly date a guy she considers her inferior."

"Larissa's not part of the entourage anymore?" Mary laughs. Again a joke and again an edge.

"Absolutely not."

"Whatever happened to her?"

"She still calls Henry occasionally. She called the other day, in tears, saying someone had broken into her house and stolen money and jewelry. She was shaken up, wanted to come over."

"You're smiling, Anne."

"I've got a writer friend who works on a TV cop show. He's friends with a couple of LAPD detectives. He checked it out for me. No police report was ever filed."

"Did Henry let her come over?"

"I told him to. I answered the door when she arrived. That shocked her. She didn't know I had moved in."

"What is it with Henry always ambushing people like that . . . never giving them advance warning? Would it have killed him to say, 'Larissa, by the way, Anne is now living with me'? Anyway, not my problem anymore. So then what happened?" Mary leans forward to listen as if her concentration will keep a lid on any further outbursts.

"She told us her little story and we showed the requisite sympathy. I made her a drink. Henry gave her money for a couple of nights at a hotel because she didn't feel safe staying at her house. When she left, he was happy to see her go. Doesn't matter how much money Henry has, after a while it's annoying to be constantly doing favors for everyone. Constantly being everyone's ATM machine. He's starting to get that Larissa is a taker who comes disguised as a giver."

"And I'm sure you put that exact thought into his head."

"Of course I did. It would be stupid not to point that out."

Mary takes another hit of the joint and I see her growing pensive. "I can't believe George is getting married."

"I'm not sure George can believe it," I say.

Mary doesn't disagree but she prefers to see the glass half full. "It could work out. Lacy comes from a family with some money. She's social. George likes that. She seems to be crazy about him. Could be so much worse." Mary takes another hit and then studies the joint as if trying to determine exactly what she just ingested into her lungs. "I hope this is the happy-silly pot, not the painkiller-sleepy pot. I always forget which is which." She offers me some but I wave it off. "No thanks."

Mary drops the remainder of the joint into an ashtray, grabs her sunglasses, pops an Altoid in her mouth and spritzes herself with her favorite new perfume . . . grapefruit essence. She's ready.

Suddenly this wave of emotion hits me and I become acutely aware that with George's marriage our childhood is officially over, and in spite of being in love with Henry and living this big exciting life with him, there's a part of me that longs for those innocent days: Mary, George, me . . . little kids, playing in our backyard, jumping on the trampoline to the point of exhaustion while the summer afternoon turns into one of those gorgeous California sunsets and all seems right with the world.

At that moment, as if the cosmos is trying to remind me of the more dangerous world I now live in, Mary brings up the name of the woman who gives new meaning to the word *frenemy*. "So Theresa Cromwell is going to be at the wedding. Someone once told me she got thrown out of college for plagiarizing her senior thesis."

Mary looks at me as if she just shared a big scoop but I know what's going on here. She's doing that free-association thing that comes with a little intake of high-potency weed.

"Even if she did," I say, "no one cares about that anymore. No one cares what happened twenty years ago." I want to hold on to my childhood flashback a moment longer and in a perfect world not have to think about Theresa Cromwell ever again.

I stand up, pull the car keys out of my bag. "We got to get going. If we're late, Lacy will blame me."

I open the door to leave but Mary stops in the apartment hallway. "I hate that that's true. That things get forgotten." She's not looking at me when she says this but is staring at herself in the mirror near the door. For a second I wonder if she's doing some kind of quasi-spiritual thing, some leaving-the-house ritual. I notice she does have some sage on a tiny Buddha shrine on that tabletop. Maybe she's silently chanting *Nam-Myoho-Renge-Kyo*. It wouldn't surprise me but it turns out I'm wrong. Mary is looking at her curls. "Oh my God!" she shrieks in mock horror. "What's with my hair? I look like Roger Daltrey when he was in the Who. Where did all these curls come from? I told my hairstylist Botticelli, not Daltrey." And then she bursts out laughing.

No question about it. She's smoking the silly pot.

Theresa

The last couple of times Theresa saw Anne she was impressed and reassured. What impressed her was how Anne's wardrobe had greatly improved, as had her overall sense of style. What reassured Theresa was the knowledge that Henry was paying for those clothes, so that meant if he's buying her clothes, he's buying her. One plus one equals Anne is just another ho. It was a conclusion Theresa arrived at with great satisfaction. As she sat at a table at the wedding reception, which at 10 p.m. was still going strong, she watched Anne work the room like a star. Theresa did the calculations in her head. Louboutin shoes—$1,100; Lanvin dress—$3,000; Bulgari gold bracelet—$10,000.

Suddenly Theresa realized that Cliff was staring at her. "What?" she asked.

"You look so serious," Cliff replied.

"I'm watching 'her ladyship.' She's a fast learner, isn't she? You would think she was brought up to be the center of attention."

Theresa studied Anne, who was chatting with some guests and charming them all. She noted some of Anne's newly acquired mannerisms. The way she cocked her head to one side was reminiscent of Princess Diana.

"Where'd Henry go?" Cliff asked.

"He's over there, talking to Carl Wolsey." Theresa pointed to where Henry was sitting at a quiet table talking with an older man whose gray hair was slicked back. From a distance he bore a resemblance to ex–Lakers coach Pat Riley.

"What's Wolsey doing here?"

"He's Lacy's father's investment guy."

"You mean Carl has time to service clients other than Henry?"

"They're old college roommates," Theresa explained. She continued to scan the room, that calculator in her head still going, adding up the cost of the glamorous wedding reception: the tennis court tented and transformed into a midsummer night fantasy, crystal chandeliers; nontoxic, soy-based votive candles, specially made in Lacy's favorite color, lilac; the food, including a vegetarian option that was really yummy; the floral centerpieces on every table—black calla lilies surround by orchids; the band that played jazz standards and vintage pop classics. It was obvious the bride's father had shelled out plenty for his little girl on her special day but he got his money's worth. Lacy looked supremely happy and George Boleyn certainly looked the part of the dashing young man that young women dream of marrying. Theresa had to give him that. Though she had heard rumors about George's sexual inclination, that night he was playing his part to perfection . . . and it bored her. No juicy gossip there. She turned her attention back to Cliff, noticing he'd polished off his second piece of cake. She shot him a disapproving look.

"Now what's wrong?" he asked, knowing exactly what she was thinking.

"Nothing," she said.

He shrugged. "So I have a thing for sweets. But only when I'm depressed."

"What do you have to be depressed about? On second thought"—Theresa put her hand up like a traffic cop controlling an intersection—"I don't need to know. I have a different question for you. What's your definition of a hooker?"

"You mean there are multiple definitions?" His tone was dismissive, which irked Theresa. Didn't he get that part of his job description was engaging in whatever conversation she wanted to have.

"Yes, there are multiple definitions, Cliff."

"Why do you ask?"

Oh God, she thought, can't he fake a little enthusiasm? Why am I stuck here with a sullen man? "I'm asking because I wonder how many upscale hookers"—she was looking in Anne's direction when she said this—"justify their little deals by saying they're not charging for sex, they just have what it takes to inspire men to give them expensive presents."

Theresa fully expected Cliff to get with the program and come up with a few cutting lines about the paramour-turned-contender, something that would amuse Theresa and give her reason to laugh and appear vivacious. She'd like Henry to look over and see her laughing, her head thrown back, full of life and spirit. Maybe he'd wonder what was so funny. Maybe he'd come closer, wanting a piece of that fun. Instead Cliff said nothing.

"Well," she nudged him.

"I don't know, Theresa. I'm no authority on this subject." He picked up his fork and moved the few remaining crumbs around the plate.

"Well, if you want to get technical about it, you're not an authority on being an editor in chief of a national magazine website but I gave you the job anyway."

Theresa regretted saying it the second it popped out of her mouth but she wasn't good at apologies. The best she could do was smile and hope he'd roll with the punches. The band was playing a slowed-down version of the Beatles' "Something" . . . and Theresa thought about asking him to dance. That would be her way of saying "sorry" but before she could do that Cliff put down the fork and looked her straight in the eye. She noticed a vein in his neck was bulging and when his words came, they came in a rush of emotion.

"Theresa, what you don't understand is that men want to pay for it and they want to pay a lot. They want an expensive price tag hanging from a pussy. They want Tiffany pussy, not wholesale pussy."

Theresa felt like she'd been slapped. "What are you saying? That a woman's worth is measured by how much money a man spends on her?" His words had tapped into her inner feminist, the part of her that was once righteously enraged by misogynists before she realized she actually enjoyed fucking misogynists. She came back at him forcefully but not loudly—she wasn't about to advertise her insecurity, anger or any social disharmony—and made her case for why he had his head up his ass.

Challenged, Cliff backed down. He did know how to apologize. It was one of his specialties. His shoulders collapsed forward and he folded his hands together as if in prayer. He suppressed his anger and focused on the task that he did know was as much a part of his job as assigning writers stories: making his boss feel good about herself. "Of course as soon as they buy those girls they regret it and can't wait to dump them. What they really need is a smart woman, an equal. A smart, sexy woman," he hastily added. "Look at history: the men with smart women always accomplish more."

Theresa snorted, an actual, irrepressible snort. Did he expect her to believe that crock? But for the moment she let it go, as much as she could let anything go. She accepted that version of an apology but looked at him with a certain degree of pity. He reminded her of a schoolboy caught cheating. "No more sugar for you," she said as she got up and left him alone with his empty plate and his burgeoning guilt.

Chapter 15

Anne

My parents pose with me for a photo for the wedding album but my father isn't happy that Henry is not in the shot. "He hates having his picture taken," I explain. My mother giggles. "I got a shot of him with my cell phone."

We are in the backyard of Lacy's parents' house, high up in the hills, north of Sunset, inside the tented tennis court, which has been transformed into a plush palace that my mother finds gauche, though she is also impressed that Lacy's parents can afford all those antique Oriental rugs (except for the dance floor), silver candelabras and Baccarat goblets. "You do know cell phone photos are not allowed. Lacy's rule," I say.

"I'm the mother of the groom. I can do what I want."

My father rolls his eyes. I know what he's thinking. No point in arguing when she's had more than two glasses of champagne. My mother is one of those people who should never go for the third glass. And yet she usually does. I wouldn't call her an alcoholic but when my father is in a bad mood he sometimes can't resist.

"One more," the photographer says, "without the glass." He takes the champagne flute from my mother's hand and she lets him because he's attractive and sweet and though twenty years younger than she is, when she's on her third glass, she sees opportunities for courtly love everywhere. My father has his arm stiffly around my waist, and my mother is clutching my arm as if I'm her salvation and I'm thinking this is not a picture I'll be wanting a copy of.

"Lovely," the photographer says. "Now let's get Mary and do a few more."

"Where is Mary?" my mother asks.

"Who knows," I say. Mary lives on her own little cloud these days.

My father looks at my mother as if somehow this is her fault. "Go find her," he orders.

"I'll find her," the photographer says. His name is Alex and he's British and it occurs to me that Mary loves a British accent. "Good idea," I say.

My mother sits down at a table and my father joins her. For all their dysfunction, they are now a couple for the duration. There won't be any Tipper and Al Gore surprise split-ups after decades of marriage. Not now, when neither one has the energy to seriously start a new emotional relationship. They can't even change their TV-watching habits. They're not about to start changing partners. Besides, they are in this together. Always have been. Nothing illustrated this to me more than an incident that happened shortly after Mary and Henry broke up. While Mary quickly reclaimed her life away from the public glare, my father was devastated. You have to understand that my father has spent much of his career toiling in the business affairs department of the studio Henry owns. For too long he's been just one of many lawyers serving the kingdom. Sure, he makes a decent living (we grew up in a nice house in the hills of Encino), but after years poring over contracts and negotiating whether a star's perk package included meals cooked by their private chef and someone to walk their dog, he'd become intoxicated with the fantasy of being in the ultimate inner circle—his boss's family. Once I even heard him kid around about someday possibly being grandfather to Henry's scion and heir. Yes, that's far-fetched but stranger things have happened in this and other kingdoms.

It wasn't until about six months after Mary and Henry broke up that it hit me that there was no joking in my dad's jokes. It was a Saturday and he had contracts that Henry needed to look at immediately. Usually a messenger is sent to do this mundane task, unless the contracts are top secret, in which case a trusted agent can be called. So it was more than a little odd when my dad suggested I personally deliver the contracts to Henry *at his home.*

"Me?" I asked. "Why me?" I turned to my mother. "Is Daddy trying to pimp me out?" I expected her to laugh. Instead she said, "He means well."

"'He means well'? What kind of answer is that?"

She just shrugged and went back to her glass of pinot grigio and reading the latest issue of *Vanity Fair.*

I took a pass on delivering the contracts but I couldn't shake the feeling that my parents could easily rationalize pimping out their child as a good thing. It was their version of making a contribution to my retirement fund.

It's that point in the evening when the older crowd is thinking about leaving while the younger ones are table-hopping or on the dance floor or over at one of the bars or outside smoking or maybe having sex in a bathroom. My parents look as content as two people who have pulled off a quickie but their satisfaction comes from the fact that, at their urging, George has made a good match. *Ka-ching!*

I look over to see if Henry is still talking to Carl Wolsey. He is. They seem to be oblivious to everything around them. Since men only bond over work, sports or pussy, I'm guessing it's work that has them head-to-head. My father is eyeing them as well. He's like a live-action GPS system when it comes to Henry tonight, tracking his every move.

"Anne, sit down. I want to ask you something."

Lately when my father wants to ask me something it usually ends with me feeling annoyed, but I oblige him. It's amazing how clothes can inform behavior. Tonight I'm wearing a sapphire blue dress that Princess Grace might have admired and I find that I'm much less combative than I might otherwise be. I guess clothes can make the lady. When you're dressed like royalty, you feel compelled to act like royalty. Or at least not to act like a willful control freak who grew up in the Valley.

My father blurts it out. "How do I get a meeting with Wolsey?"

"A meeting about what?"

"I want to talk to him about handling my investments."

See what I mean about annoying? My father is always after something. He always has some angle, some agenda, some plan, which is fine except lately it always involves putting me in a difficult position. Carl Wolsey is a money manager/investment specialist known for consistently getting his select clients above-average returns. He only deals with people who have huge amounts of capital, making exceptions for old friends like Lacy's dad, who has a lot more than my father but a lot less than Henry. Carl is not going to be interested in the $250,000 my father is looking to play with.

I also have an issue with Carl, one that he'd rather forget. A few years back I was dating a client of Carl's, a thirty-five-year-old hotshot entertainment lawyer who was on the fast track to a big career in Hollywood. I was besotted with the guy and everything was going great until Carl, being a megalomaniac when it comes to his favorite clients, decided my boyfriend could do a lot better than me. He fixed him up with an actress who was then the star of a hit TV show. Now, I know you're thinking that if my guy had been sincerely into me he wouldn't have been so easily lured away. Wrong. If the girl looks like Bar Refaeli what guy can resist that? The only reason Henry can resist Hollywood's crop of gorgeous young actresses and models is that he's either already had them or had enough of them not to be tempted. My lawyer-boyfriend didn't know what hit him so no, I don't blame him. I blame myself for not figuring out how to keep him and I blame Carl, but do so silently. My moment will come. He'll be on the receiving end of my leverage and power one of these days. I don't dwell on past hurts but I never forget them.

"I'd like to meet with him in the next couple of weeks," my father says a little louder, aware that my focus is drifting.

"You don't have the kind of money it takes to get his attention," I gently point out.

"Maybe he can do it as a favor to Henry."

I look at my father, incredulous. His sense of entitlement is startling. He's not a naïve man and he's not lacking in intelligence, so what's left? Greed? This is probably the fifth favor he's asked for this week but the first time he's actually called it a "favor." The rest of the time it was, I need you to do this, that or the other. At times I've felt more like his employee than his daughter.

"I don't want to be one of those women constantly asking for favors. Henry's had plenty of those."

At this moment I make a decision. I've been holding on to some good news, waiting for the right moment to share. My plan was to tell my parents tonight but I have a change of heart. I now see that anything that feeds my father's entitlement will only increase the burdens he places on me. I don't need the headache.

"Let me think about it," I say.

My father takes my hand and pulls me closer. "Anne, my darling daughter." He speaks softly but his tone is stern. "This is about more than money. Don't you think it's a good idea to keep a closer eye on the man who has Henry's ear?"

At that moment my mother snaps a cell phone photo of my father and me in close conversation. "Good one," she says. At least she's smiling.

I wander around looking for my brother. I should explain that even though Henry and I sat side by side together during the reception dinner, we don't feel the need to stay attached the whole night. Now that the word is out that we're living together, my instinct tells me I've got to be extra careful not to crowd him. We're in love, no question about that, but as a director friend of my father's once said, passion only lasts a thousand nights. If there's any truth to that at all, I want to do everything I can to stretch out the shelf life of our passion; I know that with a king, the shelf life can be considerably shorter. I also know that now that it's public, people will be looking to pounce on any signs of trouble, ready to interpret anything other than conventional displays of coupleness as a sign of impending failure. My challenge is to not buy into anyone else's interpretation. To do so is to play by a rulebook that will spell doom for me. Of course the problem is, there is no rule book for women in my situation and how could there be? The rules change every day depending on the king's mood. I'm on my own when it comes to figuring all this out but my intuition tells me not to get too needy. I can't look like I want to catch the bouquet. Not yet anyway.

I spot my sister and Alex, the photographer, off in a corner laughing. She's put one of the lilies from the table centerpieces in her hair and has a glass of champagne in her hand. It doesn't look like they're talking about wedding photos. I'm thinking there's a good chance Mary will take him home with her tonight. She's got that fetching look that I've seen her have when she's zeroing in on her next crush. Her lips are in a pout and she's let her curls tumble down over her eyes. It's Mary's version of Lolita, which she's been doing since she was fourteen, and she's still good at it. Though the clock is ticking on that, too. I've seen L.A. girls morph from Sue Lyon into Shelley Winters by the time they're thirty-five.

I don't want to intrude on their fun so I keep moving, asking a couple of people if they've seen George. People are so different now that I've been anointed as Henry's girlfriend. They tend to linger and compliment. Before it would be "No, I haven't seen George" or "Yes, he was over there a second ago" and they'd be on their way. Now they want to chat and flatter, even if they don't mean a word of what they say. Pre-Henry I was attractive. Now, according to Henry's sycophants, I'm gorgeous. Pre-Henry I was a freelance writer who landed the occasional magazine assignment. Now I'm an author, though I have yet to write a book. Pre-Henry I was a girl like so many others. Now I've suddenly become dazzling. Pre-Henry no one would consider me a candidate for a "trophy wife." Now my critics accuse me of being just that.

I do my best to say a quick thank-you and keep circulating. I finally see George and Lacy walk in from outside. The newlyweds (were they off sneaking some fun?) are holding hands. Lacy has changed out of her wedding dress and is now wearing a little lilac cocktail dress . . . and for fun, a cropped black velvet jacket over it with the words *Mrs. Boleyn* written on the back in lilac embroidery. No matter how doomed I may think this marriage is, the two of them look blissful, as if they can't bear not to be touching each other or sharing a look of mutual adoration. They both convey unbridled optimism and I can't figure out if George has had a transformation or if he's just caught up in the excitement of the day. Then this thought occurs to me: George might make a really good actor. I should talk to him about that.

"Anne."

It's a man's voice and I turn to see a face I recognize but the name escapes me.

"Wyatt," he says. "We met at that party at Theresa Cromwell's. Shared a little vodka."

"Of course," I reply. I don't say "You're the valet guy," even though I know he's not a guest at the wedding. For starters he's dressed way too casual. A blazer over black jeans and a black T-shirt.

"I'm the deejay," he explains. Reading the confusion on my face, he adds, "Step up from parking cars, right?"

Only now do I realize that the six-piece band packed up their instruments and deejay turntables have been set up on the other side of the dance floor. The after-hours part of the party is about to kick into high gear.

"Did you ever get that CD I left for you?" he asks.

"You left me a CD? When? Where?"

"I left it with Theresa Cromwell. She said she'd get it to you."

Good to know, I think to myself. Theresa probably figured there was nothing in it for her to pass along; a valet's pet project.

"I gave her two copies. One for her, one for you."

"Casting your net wide, aren't you?" I tease.

He laughs. There's a quality about this guy that is really endearing. He's probably twenty-five years old and is filled with excitement and passion for his music. If he's talented, that's an intoxicating mix. If he's not, it could be excruciating.

"To tell you the truth," he explains, "I gave it to Theresa because I was thinking she knows a lot of people; maybe she knows someone in the music business."

"And you gave it to me because . . . ?"

"Because you never know."

"Never know what?"

"You feel a connection with someone and you never know."

He's flirting and I'm letting him, even encouraging him a little. I have no interest in anyone other than Henry but don't all kings want to know that other men desire their women? I never want to turn into one of those women who, once she has a man in her life, shuts down her sexuality around every other male on the planet. I'm not saying I want some lowlife staring at my tits, but a cute, smart flirt is all to the good. And excellent for the complexion. Keeps the glow going. "I'd love to hear your stuff," I say, and he knows I mean it.

He takes out his cell phone to program in my info. "I'll send you a CD of my new songs. What's your info?"

I give him Henry's address.

Wyatt programs it in and then looks at me. "Is that the big place up on Mulholland at Benedict Canyon?"

"That's the place."

I can see him figuring it out. Chances are if I'm living in *that* house I'm not living there alone. He glances at my hand to see if I'm wearing a wedding ring. I'm not but I am wearing a sapphire and diamond "friendship" ring, a gift from Henry. It's a ring that screams . . . *taken.*

"But," I add, "I don't really know anyone at any record company so I don't think I can be much help."

He takes a step back, as if he's a batter who needs another second before facing a fastball. He looks down for a second, regains his focus and looks back at me and I notice that he has beautiful brown, soulful eyes.

"Why do I feel like a hustler right now when all I did was meet a girl I want to sing a song to?"

His sweetness comes through and I can't help myself. "Sing to me right now."

"Right now?" He laughs, liking the game. He looks around to see if the bride's father or whoever hired him isn't wondering why he's not already spinning tunes. Reassured that he can steal another couple of minutes away from the job, he turns back to me and starts humming something melodic. Before he can get out a verse . . . *kabooom.*

I look over to see a commotion a few tables away. Already a small crowd has gathered, surrounding someone who appears to have fallen on the ground. All I can make out clearly are the person's shoes . . . purple slingback stilettos.

Chapter 16

Cliff

Cliff was on the phone having a fight with his wife when he saw Mary fall to the ground. Alex, the wedding photographer, tried helping her up, which wasn't easy because Mary was laughing and wincing. It was clear she was a little drunk and when she tried to stand and put weight on her right ankle, her face grimaced in pain.

"I got to call you back," Cliff said to his wife. He hung up and put the cell back in his pocket. He hated fighting and he hated phone calls that ended abruptly but when he saw Anne dashing over to help her sister, his curiosity got the better of him. This could be big. A drama at a wedding involving Anne jacked up his adrenaline and jolted him out of his free-floating depression.

Cliff waited respectfully a few feet away as Anne took control, helping her sister over to a chair. He couldn't hear much of what was being said but he got the feeling Anne wasn't too happy with Mary and that Mary was trying to make a joke, calling this a PDI, public display of indulgence.

Alex, the photographer, stood next to Cliff, trying to catch Mary's eye but having no luck. Cliff understood the guy's predicament. He was an employee, not a guest, but he was also somehow involved in this little scene and unsure of his obligation. Shouldn't he be helping the damsel in distress?

"What happened?" Cliff asked, picking up a whiff of weed in the air.

"She lost her balance," Alex said. "A little too much champagne."

Cliff loved putting together mental dossiers on everyone and it wasn't difficult to formulate a take on Alex. He judged him to be around thirty-five years old, one of those English blokes from a working-class background who had found his way to L.A. dreaming of being the next Ridley Scott but so far had only found a niche in wedding photography. Probably got more than his share of female attention but had difficulty hooking up with the more glamorous women he wanted to score.

"It's a wedding," Cliff said. "These kind of things happen." Cliff was always good at the generic supportive understanding comment that meant nothing.

At that moment the music from the deejay booth got started and the half-dozen people who had gathered to see what had happened started to disperse. Alex started to walk away too until . . .

"Alex." It was Anne calling out his name. She was standing up now and looking quite regal in that sapphire blue dress. Cliff noticed her posture had gotten a lot better. *Imperial* was the word that came to mind.

"You should have caught her," Anne said.

"I tried to," Alex replied, about to explain what actually happened.

But Anne's statement was a conclusion, not a conversation. She turned back to tend to Mary while Alex sheepishly slipped away.

The more Cliff observed Anne the more he was of two minds about her. On the one hand he had to give her credit for having the tenacity to come as far as she had. He thought of all the beautiful young women in L.A., in the world, who had more to offer Henry than Anne did and yet she was the one walking around with that sapphire and diamond ring on her finger. On the other hand he suspected she was a fraud, another one of those girls who bought the "fake it till you make it" philosophy that was popular back when Anne was still an adolescent. Although admittedly he had adopted the same philosophy from time to time, as did half of Hollywood. Whatever the case, Cliff saw an opening. "You know I might be of some help here."

Anne looked at him suspiciously

"I've done some training with emergency services and have seen a lot of ankle sprains," he explained. Truth is, fifteen years ago Cliff played an emergency room doctor on a TV show that lasted half a season. Still, in those thirteen episodes he'd picked up the lingo. "You want me to take a look at her ankle?"

Mary piped in. "I think it's going to be fine. I can move my foot around. See?" She stuck it out for Cliff's appraisal.

Anne nodded okay but hovered as Cliff went into M.D. mode. Kneeling in front of Mary he gently examined her injury while trying to recall exactly what he learned in episode three when his character, Dr. Lawrence, had to help heal a track-and-field star. He remembered something about there being three types of sprains and it came down to swelling, pain and motion.

"Does it hurt when you put weight on it?"

"Some pain, not horrible," Mary said.

He gently moved her ankle around, touching various points without causing any moans or cries. It was always easy to play a doctor, Cliff remembered. All you had to do to be convincing was deliver the information with the right touch of arrogance and add a little bedside manner.

"A mild sprain," he said. "If after two days there's still soreness, you might want to get an MRI but I think you'll be okay . . . though I wouldn't recommend hitting the dance floor for the next week or so."

Cliff turned his focus back to Anne, toning down his "professionalism" to prevent her from asking technical questions he couldn't answer. "That's my opinion, for whatever it's worth."

"Thank you so much." She smiled at him, a smile full of warmth and appreciation, and at that moment Cliff realized that whether she was a fighter or a fraud, he wanted her approval. This is what her upscale status has brought her, he thought. It makes people want to please her. Either please her or destroy her.

"Always there when you're needed, aren't you, Cliff?" This too was said graciously but it hit a nerve with Cliff. Was Anne suggesting that he was, ever so slightly, an opportunist? She was getting very good at equipoise while keeping those she was dealing with a bit off balance. He was surprised how much she had changed since the first time he met her up at Beverly Glen . . . Even her face looked different now, fuller, less hungry. Her eyes had become even more intense, and why wouldn't they? In her position everything has consequences. He'd seen enough women who had hooked up with powerful men to understand how it worked. These women gained so much from their involvement but the first thing they lost was their spontaneity.

After Anne went off to find Henry, Cliff lingered. The first thing Mary said when her sister was out of earshot was "Guess I'm OTP . . . again."

Cliff had no idea what she meant so she spelled it out: "Off The Pedestal." She laughed but it was the laugh of someone choosing humor to mask her insecurity. It aroused Cliff's sympathy.

"Give yourself a break," he said. "Although, if I were you, I'd go easy on the weed. Some of that stuff will knock you on your ass without warning." Cliff was so much looser and more relaxed around Mary. She wasn't as smart as Anne and she wasn't as tough. She was a pretty girl but not one with much ambition or complexity.

She was doing her best to play the role assigned her—as a Boleyn she was expected to make an illustrious marriage someday—but her heart wanted something easier. A bloke, not a baron. It didn't take a professional to figure that out. Mary wasn't cut out to strategize her way to a prize. She was the kind of girl who wants a nice but not flashy house on some leafy suburban street and a hunky guy with a normal job who comes homes after work, gives her a big kiss and is thrilled when she hands him a cold beer.

"Fuck," Mary blurted out. "I love this song."

The deejay was playing a Beyoncé tune. A few bridesmaids and their dates, who had been sitting nearby, got up to dance, giving Cliff a clear view of Anne sitting on Henry's lap. They were talking to each other in a way that seemed so intimate it felt like an invasion of privacy just to watch them. Henry had his hands around Anne's waist and when he whispered something in her ear, she burst out laughing. One of the things Cliff knew about alpha men, from all his years taking notes on L.A.'s social scene, is what they had in common. Without exception, one of their favorite things in life was making a beautiful woman laugh.

"My sister Anne is something, isn't she?" Mary said.

Odd choice of words, Cliff thought. Innocuous and yet they hinted at something a little more judgmental, something closer to "she's really a piece of work, isn't she?" Scratch the surface on the sisterly love and he was sure he'd find a growing resentment on both ends. But Mary wasn't ready to go there . . . not yet. Instead she changed the subject to something that made her feel better.

"You can do something for me, Cliff."

"Whatever you need."

"Tell Alex, the photographer guy, to call me."

"Will do," he said. "Is that all?"

"Yes."

He started to walk away.

"I mean no."

He stopped.

"No compliment?" she asked.

"What?"

"You always leave with a compliment. Did you know that? You do it a lot. You like to leave the girls smiling."

"I do?"

"Yes, that's your thing. Kind of your trademark."

He searched for something to say. "I like your curls."

Chapter 17

Anne

Henry takes care of things. When I tell him about Mary he calls one of the guys he has on staff and has him drive over so when she's ready to go home, she'll have a ride and someone to help her up her stairs. Problem solved, he's in exceptionally good spirits but for a much more important reason. Though he won't tell me the details, he informs me that he and Carl Wolsey had an interesting conversation and he's got to think about what they discussed and make a decision. It's something big. Has to be. Henry is not one to get excited about a stock tip.

He pulls me onto his lap and at that moment I'm as content as I've ever been in my life. Content and stimulated. We're still at that stage when a day without sex doesn't seem possible and it's not just because we're sexually compatible and passionate about each other. There's another factor here, one that surprised me. Over the last two weeks something has clicked and it now feels like a true partnership. We have plans, our ideas mesh and our opinions are always of interest to each other. We're excited about the future because adventures await and we believe we can accomplish a lot together. Being in love and lust always involves, to some extent, being enamored of the other person's potential but I never thought being in love with our potential together could be such a twenty-four-hour-a-day turn-on. Well, that and the fact that Henry has stamina. How long will our bliss last? I have no idea but I'm a happy girl sitting there on his lap.

"You know what I'm thinking?" he says. "You know what I'd love? To get out of here and go to In-N-Out Burger."

I get this goofy smile on my face. "Perfect." My evening just got a little more blissful as I imagine a burger from my favorite L.A. fast-food joint. Plus I'm starving because I can never eat very much at events. I was like that even before people began scrutinizing everything I do. Mary and I were raised to eat before parties so we wouldn't be "inelegant" (my mother's word) in social situations. Sometimes I think my mother thinks we're living in a different century. Her idea of eating at a function is a tiny bite of something, chased with a peppermint Altoid. Tonight, though, Mary was wolfing down the salmon and roasted potatoes. She's escaping my mother's training and my father's grip and I kind of envy her for that. "Let me just say goodbye to George and we can sneak out of here," I say to Henry.

"Okay," he says, but he holds me on his lap for another moment and kisses the back of my neck and it sends chills down my back. It's the first time in my life I feel cherished.

I find my brother on the front lawn. Lucky me . . . he's alone. Not completely alone but not with Lacy. George is saying goodbye to some guy who looks like he might have been one of his USC buddies. The guy is good-looking and they have such camaraderie you'd think he was George's best man but I've never seen him around before. At the time I don't think too much about it because I can't wait to pull George aside.

"What's going on?" he asks as I make him follow me, finding some privacy in the driveway next to a parked limo. "First," he says, "before you tell me . . . I can't fucking believe your wedding present. Do you know how long we've wanted a Leo de Vince painting?"

"I thought you'd like it."

"Like it? We love it. You've made my wife very happy."

There it is, the first time I've heard him call Lacy his wife, and it sounds so natural and he says it with pride and I'm wondering if somewhere between our conversation at Jinky's and this moment, he's fallen in love with this new chapter in his life, maybe even fallen in love with Lacy.

"I have something to tell you," I say. Seeing a few exiting guests heading in our direction, I take George's hand and lead him farther into the shadows. I'm leaning against the back of that limo because my four-inch-high Jimmy Choos are killing me.

"Don't tell me you're engaged." He's joking.

"No, but"—I can't stop smiling—"I *am* pregnant. Henry's ecstatic. We both are but we haven't told anyone yet. You're the first to know."

"Anne. Anne. Anne. Anne. This is fantastic."

We're giggling now, both of us giddy at the thought of everything that's happening. He's married. I'm pregnant. It's all happening so fast it feels like a whirlwind. It does occur to me that whirlwinds are dangerous but this is one of those times when danger feels so very, very good.

"You're going to be an uncle. There's going to be another Boleyn in the world." Interesting that I think of the child as a Boleyn, not a Tudor.

Caught up in the moment, George suddenly grabs me, twirls me around. No one has ever twirled me before and it's not my favorite thing but I go with it because I'm so grateful knowing that George and I will continue to be there for each other, as we've always been. When the twirling stops, George says, "I love you, Anne," and gives me a big hug and then a kiss right on the lips. It may not have been as intimate as the infamous kiss Angelina Jolie and her brother James Haven shared at the 2000 Oscars but some people might consider it inappropriate.

Lacy considers it an assault . . . on her. "Fuck you, Annie."

I look over to see her standing in the driveway, enraged.

George immediately takes a step away from me and tries to lighten things up.

"Anne was just telling me some good news." Unsure if he can share the baby info he glances over at me and I shake my head no. Not that Lacy appears interested in any information that could assuage her fury.

"Yeah, right. *'I love you, Anne'?* This is my wedding day, George. This is our wedding day. The only person you should be declaring love for and kissing on the mouth is me."

George tries to defend himself but she cuts him off and gets in one more shot.

"Fuck you, Annie. If being a courtesan doesn't fulfill your emotional needs don't come mooching around my house."

She walks away and George looks like he just woke up to a nightmare.

"It'll be okay," I say, worried about his feelings.

"You did nothing wrong," he says, worried about mine. "I got to go to her, Anne."

"Of course you do. Go."

He rushes off and I stand there alone, shell-shocked at how quickly one can go from content and stimulated to anxious and tired.

Right then the door to what I thought was an empty limo opens and a bridesmaid and her "date" stumble out, a bottle of champagne in her hand. The guy is trying to zip up his pants but can't quite get it to work. He looks down at his zipper like it's the most complicated math problem in the world. The bridesmaid looks at me, smiles.

"Don't worry, I didn't hear anything if you didn't see anything."

I nod. "Done deal."

In the distance I see that George has caught up with Lacy. He's talking to her, cajoling her and he's good at it and gets her to smile. It won't be long before she forgives him. Could be forever before she forgives me.

Chapter 18

Theresa

"What are the odds?" Theresa was sitting in Cliff's car on her way home from the wedding. She was tired and she was smoking. She'd made Cliff stop at 7-Eleven for some Marlboros even though she'd quit six months ago. She was desperate to get home and quietly think over the whole evening, evaluate the pluses and minuses like she always did. She did not want to be waiting for a cop to halt the traffic heading down the canyon so the cars headed up could pass through on what had become a single-lane road.

She put her window down and beckoned the cop who was in charge of directing the traffic.

"Officer, what's going on here?"

The cop took his time walking over to the car and took his time answering, checking out Theresa and Cliff and drawing his own conclusions.

"A sinkhole up the road."

"A sinkhole? How does that even happen in Brentwood? When did my street turn into something you'd find south of the 405?"

The cop aimed his flashlight at the interior of the car.

"Sorry to disappoint you. No drugs or stolen goods."

Cliff gave Theresa a look. Not a smart idea to be sarcastic with an L.A. cop. People have been arrested for less. She got the message and toned it down.

"I know none of this is your fault, Officer. We all appreciate the work you do."

She was laying it on a bit thick but it seemed to work. He put his flashlight away, told them to have a good night.

"That could have gone a lot worse," Cliff said.

Theresa shrugged. She had great confidence in her ability to talk her way out of trouble. It was one of her most valuable talents.

"What's going on in this city? Really," Theresa asked. "Every week something else seems to go wrong."

"Sinkholes happen everywhere," Cliff replied.

"Do they happen in communities that pay the kind of state and city taxes I'm paying?" Usually Theresa kept to the politically correct position when it came to taxes and all other political issues. She lived in one of the bluest neighborhoods in one of the bluest states in the country. Complaining about taxes was considered bad manners here, like burping at the dinner table. But if she was going to burp in front of anyone, it might as well be Cliff.

She took a long drag off her cigarette, blowing the smoke out slowly. That helped calm her down. "Since we're stuck here you're going to have to entertain me."

"What kind of entertainment did you have in mind?"

Theresa picked up on the sexual innuendo in Cliff's reply and it made her claustrophobic. If they didn't get the go-ahead to move soon she was going to get out and walk the rest of the way home.

"Did you say good night to your new best friend, Anne?"

"Come on, Theresa, I spoke to her for a minute and she thanked me for helping her sister. That's it. I'm not looking to be her friend. I'm sure it's a full-time job."

"Let me tell you something, Cliff. Everything is a full-time job. Staying healthy—full-time job. Having a career—full-time job. Having any kind of relationship—full-time job. We're all running around trying to do half a dozen full-time jobs."

"Good point," Cliff said.

Theresa relaxed a little. It was a good point, she thought, and she decided she'd share it with Henry at some future point. "What do you think makes Anne so difficult?"

Cliff inhaled the secondhand smoke from Theresa's cigarette. Even though an advocate for the eco-green lifestyle, he loved the stimulation that came from that first whiff of smoke. His dirty little secret was that he craved toxins and even a secondhand high put him in a talkative mood. "Oh, you know how it is, people who get a little power start to feel entitled. I watched her tonight and she told a guest to put out a cigar because it was making her sick. She picked at her food as if it wasn't good enough for her, ignoring the salmon for a couple of breadsticks. I saw her take the tiniest sip of champagne and no more . . ."

Theresa started to cough as if choking on something, but there was nothing in her throat.

"You want some water? I got water." Cliff reached back into the ice chest he always had in the backseat of his car, which was filled with glass-bottled water and organic juices.

She grabbed his arm and shook her head no as she continued to clear her throat.

The cop finally signaled they could start moving again. Cliff stepped on the accelerator, keeping one eye on the road, one eye on Theresa. "Are you okay?" he asked, not sure if she was being dramatic or was on the verge of a heart attack.

Finally she regained her voice. "I've seen Anne at parties. She loves champagne and this was the good stuff."

"It's not like I watched her all night," Cliff explained. "I'm just talking about what I saw."

Theresa looked stunned. She put her hand on the dashboard as if for support. "Oh my God, earlier you said she looked different, her face is fuller."

"Yeah, so?"

"I thought there was something different about her but I couldn't put my finger on it until now. Don't you see?"

"See what?"

"And when I saw Henry as they were leaving he said they were going to get a burger."

"Yeah, so?"

"She's pregnant."

Cliff wasn't sold on the theory. "I've left a party and gone for a burger. It's not that unusual. People do it all the time."

Theresa wasn't dissuaded. "She was probably having cravings. Didn't you tell me that when your wife was pregnant she craved Big Macs?"

"Even if she is, so what. Doesn't mean she'll actually have it."

"Of course she'll have it!" Theresa shouted. "Isn't that the whole point? Isn't that what she was after from the first kiss?"

"You're right, you're right." Though Cliff sounded cavalier his heart was pumping as he imagined all the various ways this story could play out. If only he had a genius talent for writing, he could be the Dominick Dunne of his generation.

He was ready to dissect this news from every angle but Theresa was done talking. She trusted her instincts on this and the thought of Anne pregnant was crushing. Of course she always knew it was a possibility, as it was with any woman Henry was with. Rumor was he hated condoms. But she wasn't prepared for how it gutted her. She had to dig deep to keep it together. She reminded herself of what her four-hundred-dollar-an-hour big-shot Hollywood therapist had said to her during her first session with him a year ago: "In every triumph there is the seed of future disappointments. In every disappointment there is the seed of future triumphs." That and a tall glass of vodka would get her through the night. It would have to.

*   *   *

Cliff pulled into Theresa's driveway, not sure what came next. "You want me to come in?"

"You know what?" She looked at him, thought about the kind of man he was, a depressed man who couldn't control his cravings for sweets but had no real craving for her. "I think we're done with all that."

She saw the panic in his eyes and knew he was worried about his job security. She could predict what was coming and the last thing she needed was to listen to Cliff try to sweet-talk his way back into her good graces. Maybe if she'd put some estrogen cream on tonight she would have been in the mood to . . . but on second thought, even that wouldn't do it. She couldn't be with beta men anymore. Better to masturbate than be in bed with a beta who was trying to pretend to be an alpha.

"Don't worry, Cliff. You still have your job."

"I wasn't even thinking about that."

"Of course you were."

"You're sure you want to end . . ." He stopped and Theresa thought, Poor guy, he doesn't even know what to call it. An affair? A romance? An arrangement?

". . . our thing," was the description he settled for.

"Yes, I'm sure I want to end 'our thing.' You can serve me in other ways."

Was that relief she saw on his face?

"Theresa . . . I don't know what to say here."

"I do. Go home to your wife."

He couldn't leave it at that. Before she could get out of the car, he grabbed her arm. "That's a beautiful bracelet."

She was wearing a simple but elegant silver cuff. "You like it? The designer is a young woman I recently met. Jane Seymour."

Chapter 19

Catherine

"The divorce is happening because this is California and even we can't keep it from happening." Catherine's father, Ferdinand, was sitting at the counter in the kitchen of her palatial Spanish-style mansion while she prepared two servings of sea bass for lunch. Still dapper and sharp as ever at seventy-five, he appeared fatigued while he tried to talk sense into his daughter.

"Well I'm not signing any papers," Catherine replied, adding a touch of spice to the marinade. Carmen, the housekeeper, was checking the rice cooking on the stove and making almost no sound, as if the quieter she stayed, the longer she'd be allowed to stick around and watch what was the best soap opera around . . . even better than her favorite Telemundo novellas.

"At this point signing papers doesn't matter." Ferdinand glanced over at the housekeeper and Catherine got his hint.

"Carmen, I'll take care of that."

"It's done," the housekeeper replied. "I'll just leave it on warm."

She adjusted the setting on the stove and then left the room. Theresa wasn't worried about Carmen overhearing her private business because she had every intention of filling her in later. How had it come to this? The person she trusted the most with her secrets was her housekeeper. Carmen's loyalty was never in doubt and she was fast becoming "family," a fact Catherine kept from her father, depriving him of another opportunity to lecture her about her judgment.

With Carmen off in a back room watching television, Ferdinand got down to business. "Henry has asked the court to bifurcate the issue of marital status from the remaining property issues. He'll get a judge to dissolve the marriage."

Catherine dropped the knife she had just picked up to slice the La Brea Bakery bread—Henry's favorite. "So the court just steamrolls over the wife? Is that what's going on here? I have no rights? We got married in a church. In the eyes of God we're still married but some corrupt judge can decide we're not? What about all our political connections? Can't we do something about this? Who is this judge anyway? Why can't we get one of our guys to rule on this?"

Ferdinand finished drinking his club soda. He looked like he'd prefer to be anywhere but sitting at this kitchen counter talking to his daughter about her desire for control and revenge.

"You've"—he stopped, corrected himself—"we've dragged this out to the point where a judge could decide . . . you know what? The husband in this case has tried everything to resolve this and there's been no cooperation, so I'm going to bifurcate."

"You sound like you're on his side."

"I'm on your side. You're my daughter. I'm always going to be on your side. I told you from the start that being married to Henry wasn't going to be easy. Look, we're still going to play hardball on the property settlement and there's a good chance we'll get the settlement we want. It's just a matter of how long it's going to take.

There's been talk about Henry's political ambitions. There's support for it but I can assure you that voters in California aren't going to rally behind someone going through an ugly property settlement. We can use that to our advantage. You're good at PR. You know how to get people to take your side. Women can relate to you. We can use that."

Catherine usually perked up when her father complimented her, even if it was simply on her PR skills, but she couldn't get over this new piece of information. Henry could get a court to terminate their marriage without her participation? "I want the name of the judge who will decide in Henry's favor. I'm going to expose him, write an op-ed piece about this for the *L.A. Times*."

"Stop. Catherine, you're making the McCourt divorce look like a walk in the park."

Catherine was about to say she admired Jamie McCourt, the wife of the owner of the Dodgers, and respected her refusal to be intimidated by her husband's big legal guns but she opted for a passive-aggressive approach instead. "I'm just trying to stick up for myself in a very difficult situation. This isn't about jurisprudence, what's acceptable under the law. This is about my life. My daughter's life. This is about a man who is being emotionally withholding and psychologically abusive. Aren't you outraged about that?"

Ferdinand had heard enough. He clenched his hands together as he often did when he was about to deliver his own final judgment on a matter. Catherine had seen him do this all her life. As a child it scared her; as an adult it frustrated her.

"Catherine, let me remind you that I was the first one to express reservations about Henry and now you're saying I'm not hating him enough, yet . . . *yet*," he emphasized, "you're standing there making him lunch. When was the last time you made lunch for anyone? For your daughter?"

Catherine poured herself a little wine. "I'm trying a new tactic. Maybe if Henry and I can have a nice lunch together . . . if I can make him his favorite meal . . . we can come to some understanding."

Ferdinand was done with the conversation but Catherine tried appeasing him. "I wish you'd stay for lunch, too." She was lying. She wanted Henry all to herself, and besides, she knew her father already had plans. Ferdinand just gave her a sweet, sad smile.

Was it Catherine's imagination or was he looking at her funny? The last few times she'd been around him she couldn't shake the idea that he was looking at her thinking she'd gotten fat. She was well aware that she was twenty pounds overweight and wasn't aging well. Every day, traces of the pretty little girl her father once adored, the young attractive woman he was once so proud of, disappeared a little more. A few weeks ago, after too much wine, she asked Carmen if she had completely lost the face she used to have. Had age wiped it out and replaced it with the face of a middle-aged stranger? Carmen reassured her. "You're only in your mid-forties and no it hasn't. You're still a beautiful woman." Then she went back to watching Telemundo.

"Have a sip of your wine; you're too wound up," Ferdinand said.

From upstairs came the sound of a young girl's voice. "Mom, Dad just pulled up to the front gate." The girl raced down the stairs. "He just texted me from the car."

Maren, Catherine and Henry's fourteen-year-old daughter, appeared in the kitchen, cell phone still in hand. The teenager didn't look at all like Henry except they had the same piercing blue eyes. She was wearing jeans, boots and a T-shirt that said "Free City."

"Here's my lunch date," Ferdinand said, pleased to see his granddaughter.

"Where you taking me, Gramps?"

"Wherever you want as long as I can get a decent martini."

Maren gave him a hug before noticing what Catherine was wearing. "You're showing cleavage? Oh God, Mom."

Catherine straightened out the V-neck sweater she was wearing to make it seem less revealing. "I wouldn't call this showing cleavage."

Maren turned away, embarrassed for her mom, but she had other things to think about. The sound of Henry's car pulling onto the circular gravel driveway had her dashing out the door. Before following her outside, Ferdinand blew Catherine a kiss and gave her some parting advice. "Have that sip of wine and be reasonable."

Catherine watched through the window as her father and Henry were cordial to each other. Men are so weird, she thought. They can compartmentalize their emotions so it's no problem to be civil. She watched Maren delight in the sight of her father. To Henry's credit he knew just what to say to make her feel special. Too bad it was only in small doses. Since Anne came into his life, he had less and less time for his daughter. Catherine knew it wasn't going to be an easy road for Maren. If Henry stayed with Anne it wasn't going to be easy because Anne would never unconditionally embrace Maren in their household. If Henry dumped Anne and went back to dating models, it wasn't going to be easy on Maren's self-esteem. She was a cute girl but would never be cover-girl beautiful. But mostly Catherine watched and thought about Henry. She hadn't seen him in a while and wasn't prepared for how his presence affected her. It was like a shooting pain that kept reshooting. She realized how much she missed him. Most people thought she missed being with a man who was so good-looking, powerful, smart and rich but that wasn't it at all. What she missed was the circle of warmth he could create around him. You would think someone like Henry would be exclusive, snobbish, an elitist, but quite the opposite. Unless he had a reason to turn cold, his personality was so appealing that even people like her father, with good reason to loathe him, found themselves enjoying his company. She was sure that's why Ferdinand walked away quickly and waited for Maren in his own car. To be around Henry was to want to be around him more.

The fish was cooked to perfection, as were the rice and vegetables. Everything was exactly the way Catherine planned except for one thing: the huge chasm separating the two of them. It was a chasm with a name . . . Anne. No one mentioned her, no one had to. Henry tried to explain why it was time he and Catherine resolved their issues and went their separate ways. Catherine tried to buy time, to keep things in limbo in the hope that God would soon come to her rescue. Every day and night, she got down on her knees and prayed for a divine intervention that would drive a permanent wedge between Henry and "that woman." Since none of Catherine's prayers or wishes seemed to be getting answered, she went for the one weapon she did have—Maren.

"This is her first year at boarding school and when she comes home to visit it's hard on her, thinking your house is off-limits. I think she needs more time to adjust to the new situation."

"Maren and I have no problems. We're fine." Henry was not going to be deterred from the topic he came to discuss.

Catherine crossed her arms across her chest. She knew her body language was defensive but it also served to increase her cleavage, not that Henry had so much as glanced in that direction. It was the only part of Catherine's body that she could semiconfidently flaunt and she wasn't getting a glance?

"Maren is going to act like everything's fine," Catherine said. "What do you expect? She wants to please you."

"Trust me. Maren and I are fine."

It was time for Catherine to try another approach. "What about us? What about you and me? What we built together?"

"I want you to be financially comfortable. You're a great mom and I appreciate how you've taken such great care of our daughter."

"Don't give me the 'you're a great mom but I'm moving on' speech."

"Not moving. I've moved. We split up years ago."

Catherine's eyes got teary and she let those tears slide down her face, a martyr bucking for sainthood.

Henry had seen this performance before. "I'm not doing this. We'll finish this conversation later. I'll call you." He got up to leave.

"No, let's finish it now." Catherine made a token attempt to wipe away the tears. "What do you want in the settlement? What's the most important thing for you?"

"That we end this marriage and settle things without drama."

"That's what matters to you? That will make you happy?" Her voice was calmer, almost conciliatory.

"Yes. That's what I want."

"Okay, well, that can be done . . . if you get rid of Anne."

Bingo, she got him. She saw his anger seething. She wanted him to unleash it. Bring it on. A big explosion. Drama equals significance. But damn it, he didn't lose it. He kept his anger focused and tight, more laser beam than kryptonite.

"Catherine, get help. Seriously. See somebody because this—whatever it is you're doing—is not healthy."

He got up from the table and headed out.

She called after him. "I can't believe you're walking out again." Her voice was back to being shrill and desperate. She couldn't help herself though she knew that approach never worked with him. She would have bet anything he wouldn't reply but he surprised her. Out of curiosity or exasperation, she didn't know.

He stopped, looked at her steadily and spoke assuredly. "What did you think would come out of this lunch?"

"Not this," she said.

"Well what do you know, we can finally agree on something."

When he left he slammed the door and the sound of it gave Catherine a jolt. It wasn't the goodbye she wanted but at least it made her feel alive. As long as she could still affect him, she'd keep on fighting and she knew just what weapon to pick up next. Her father was right. She did have a talent for self-promotion and getting an audience on her side. Maybe it was time to take a page out of Princess Diana's revenge playbook. Maybe Catherine should find a writer interested in doing an "unauthorized" biography of her life with most of the research provided by Catherine's close and of course very biased friends. This is America. People love victims and Catherine knew exactly how to position herself as the spurned first wife who deserved better treatment.

Cheered somewhat by this new plan of action, she walked down to the end of the driveway, where the security guard was sitting in his van. He put the window on the driver's side down as she approached.

"Did you search his car?" she asked.

"Yeah."

"Find anything interesting?"

"Nothing. Just a receipt from In-N-Out Burger."

She let that sink in for a minute. "He could have sea bass and broccolini and he settles for burgers and fries. What an idiot."

The security guard just shrugged. It wasn't his job to explain men to Catherine.

She went back inside the house. In the five minutes she'd been gone, Carmen had cleaned away the remnants from lunch and all signs that Henry had ever been there.

Chapter 20

Anne

We get married in the backyard of Henry's house. There is no better place. To begin with there's the light. Up there at the top of Bel Air, daylight is different, as if diffused of any harshness. It's also serene. The only ambient sound heard is the gentle wind rustling through the trees. It's the kind of light and serenity that comes with wealth, no other way to put it. We get married late in the afternoon. The sun is still golden but not too hot. Two days earlier I hit the three-month mark of my pregnancy and all morning sickness has disappeared. I'm wearing a long, white, sexy (stomach is still relatively flat) backless dress, no veil, and holding a small bouquet of white orchids. It's a small, private affair. My parents, my sister Mary, brother George and sister-in-law Lacy, who acts like we've never had a problem though I challenge anyone to find someone with a smile that's as fake as the one she directs my way when she tells me how happy she is for me. I don't let it bother me though because it's my wedding day. And I don't let it bother me that Carl Wolsey is there and so is Theresa Cromwell. There was some discussion about whether Maren should be there but since she's back at boarding school in Connecticut, Henry decided to go ahead without her in attendance. I was secretly relieved because unlike Lacy, Maren doesn't even try to fake it around me. I'm the enemy.

So there we are in the backyard of Henry's spectacular house and I'm too happy to worry about Maren or Lacy or Theresa or even my father, who has cornered Carl and is no doubt trying to talk his way into Carl's good graces. They beckon me over and I stand there and watch these two men trying to outmaneuver each other. My father hates Carl for that strict prenup he encouraged Henry to demand, one that guarantees me almost nothing. Yet he really wants to get in on Carl's investment pool. Carl has no respect for my father but knows there's no further advantage in alienating Henry's new in-law. So they make small talk and tell me I look lovely and I smile and take a sip of champagne, which I do not feel guilty about. I don't think there's anything wrong with my baby having a little bubbly on the day his (yes, I believe it is a boy) parents wed.

George comes over to take a picture of the three of us and as I pose I notice that in addition to the Cartier gold and steel Tank watch Carl always wears, he's also sporting a thin piece of braided leather. It's something you'd see on a teenage surfer, not a fifty-year-old finance guru, which gives credence to the gossip that's been circulating, rumors he and his wife of fifteen years are splitting up. I don't want to know the details even when George whispers about a younger woman involved and the word *burlesque* gets mentioned. I just shrug, say "whatever" and, for once, really mean it. I also choose not to be concerned that Mary is obsessively waiting for a call on her cell and that's all she seems to care about or that Theresa is getting very chummy with Lacy. If you can't suspend paranoia on your wedding day, when can you?

So the moment arrives. The vows. My "vow" is to Henry the man, not the king of Hollywood, because I wouldn't be there—no matter how much my father pushed me toward this—if I hadn't fallen in love with who Henry really is and that means his flaws and doubts. I don't know how you fall in love with any man without falling in love with the little boy in him, the part that wants a baseball cap on his head, not a crown. My vows are not inspired but I decide that I'm going to embrace romantic clichés because when a cliché proves to be true there's no reason to run from it. So I simply say, "This isn't a vow because *vow* implies that effort and vigilance are needed. I don't have to make a vow, a promise or a pledge because no effort is required to love and treasure this magnificent man in front of me." I'm sincere but let's face it, clichés don't get a lot of applause. People nod, yes, it's a wedding, nice, boring, next.

It's Henry's turn and he says, "When I was young it was easy to be optimistic but as I got older and became aware of how hard life can be, how risky, how dangerous, how—"

He stops when he sees the look on my face. "Don't look so worried, darling. This ends up in a good place."

Everyone laughs and he continues.

"—how disappointing life can be, I realized that when a wonderful woman comes into your life and without ignoring the lessons the years brought, makes you feel as optimistic as you felt in your youth, as excited as you felt in your youth, as passionate as you felt in your youth, there's only one thing to say. Stay with me. Stay with me forever."

I think the forever is overstating it because I'm not so naïve as to think that people and circumstances don't change, and neither is Henry. Still, the fact that he can say it and know that I understand that it's truthful in spirit, if not in fact, is one of the reasons we are standing there saying "I do." There are other reasons that are less clear. My father thinks men marry when they fear losing you. He's wrong in this case. Henry wouldn't give in to that kind of fear. If he feared losing me, he'd be more likely to walk away just to prove he could. Others, more romantically inclined, say a man like Henry marries when love transcends doubt. Maybe. Henry does believe in transcendence but I don't think marriage is his only opportunity for a bigger-than-life moment. The man has, literally, climbed mountains. There's also the possibility that Henry is marrying me because I fit into some agenda yet to be revealed. Whatever his reason is fine with me. I adore him. He's my guy and I now have a diamond and emerald ring on my hand and we have matching platinum wedding bands and we are united. "PDT," my sister says. "Public Declaration of Togetherness."

Everyone there wishes us the best and Theresa makes a lovely toast. She's good at that sort of thing and I know that Henry is impressed with her ability to handle herself in all kinds of situations. He always gives her the benefit of the doubt so I don't even bother telling him the remark she makes to me as she's leaving. She pulls me aside and says, "Well, Anne, I bet you're wondering what comes next. What comes after you've gotten everything you want?" Even with my paranoia on hold, I pick up on the dig in that comment. Theresa is reminding me that once you hit the mountaintop the only place left to go is down.

"Actually, Theresa," I reply, "I'm not wondering about that. Guess I'm too busy thinking about how much fun it'll be to fuck my husband once everyone leaves."

A little crass? Maybe. But she had it coming.

Chapter 21

Theresa

Theresa was one of the first members of L.A.'s Soho House. She was more than happy to pay the $1,500 membership fee in return for dining with people who had passed scrutiny and could afford a little exclusivity. Though the crowd skewed a little young on weekends, Theresa found the workday week diners to be more her scene. Plenty of businesspeople showed up, especially from the entertainment world. This was good for her now that she had taken on greater responsibility at Henry's company, including overseeing his philanthropic foundation. What a sweet reversal for someone who, as a child, had grown up on the receiving end of charity. Those church food baskets left on her family's front doorstep at Thanksgiving and Christmas always mortified her. Now she had the power to direct Henry's charity dollars, which afforded her some sweet payback when it came to those Hollywood "haves" who shunned her when she first came to town. That agent who ignored her when she called to ask his advice about getting a job with his agency . . . well, his favorite charity was the NRDC. Guess who was getting Henry's money? Oceana. Then there was the second wife of a current studio head. Everyone knew her story, knew that years before when she was an assistant to her boss, now husband, she would blow him in his office, though he was still married to wife number one. When Theresa first came to L.A. this woman, who considered herself the town's preeminent hostess, made a point of never remembering Theresa's name, no matter how many times they were introduced. The woman's favorite charity was PETA and she'd pitched it to Theresa numerous times in the hopes of getting a contribution. Guess who was getting Henry's money? The SPCA.

Carl Wolsey was there, sitting at the bar when Theresa arrived. She was always relieved to walk into that front room, which had flattering lighting, because getting there was always challenging for her self-esteem, starting with the harshly lit garage where the valet parking was located. Next came the elevator ride up to the penthouse floor . . . more bad lighting. Then, finally to make it to the top tier, there was a staircase that could give you vertigo and made Theresa feel older than her years. However, once she was there, in the club's main area, she felt rewarded by the spectacular view. To the east were the bright lights of Sunset Strip; to the west the twinkling lights of Beverly Hills suburbia.

After checking in with the hostess, Theresa joined Carl at the bar and the first thing she noticed was that he was wearing color . . . a burnt orange shirt, opened collar, under a black suit. This was a glaring departure from his usual monochromatic uniform: dark suit, white or pale blue shirt and classic Brooks Brothers tie.

"Are we the first?" Theresa asked, trying to be convivial.

"Seems so," he answered, barely looking at her. Lately, there was no love lost between these two, both at odds with each other, always vying for Henry's ear and his favors. Still, Carl usually had better manners.

"What are you drinking?" she asked.

"Some kind of vodka. With tonic or something. You want a drink?" Carl signaled to get the waiter's attention and continued to scan the room. Usually he was so focused and sure of himself, you got the feeling he knew what was going on in any room without even looking. The joke about Carl was that he could make anything he said (even if it was a drink order) sound as if it were backed up by canon law, but not tonight. Theresa wasn't sure what to make of it. Should she take it personally?

"I'll have a pinot noir."

He ordered it for her and then checked his watch. He seemed frazzled. Maybe it had something to do with his marriage falling apart or maybe it had to do with meeting for an eight-thirty dinner. Being a financial guy who had to be up early to track the markets when they opened, Carl's routine was a six o'clock dinner and home by seven-thirty. In all the time she'd worked for Henry, never before had the three of them had dinner together on a weekday night and Theresa worried about what it might mean. When Henry asked her to make a reservation somewhere, she opted for her turf to mitigate her anxiety. Unfortunately it wasn't working. Why was the waiter taking so long with her wine?

"Has Henry told you the news?" Carl asked.

"What news?"

"So he hasn't told you?" Carl kept looking around the room, not the entrance, as if searching for someone who might already be there.

"What? What is it?" It bugged her that Carl knew something she didn't. She wasn't enjoying this at all and she really didn't like what came next. She looked up to see that Henry had arrived but he wasn't alone. Anne was with him. The first thing Theresa thought when she saw her was damn . . . she's having a Gisele pregnancy. Like quarterback Tom Brady's supermodel wife, Anne's pregnant belly was showing but other than that cute bump and a slight fullness to the face she was still thin and sexy. So many horrible things happen in this world every day, Theresa thought. Why aren't any of them happening to Anne?

Henry waited until they were done with the appetizers before bringing up the reason for the dinner. He looked at Theresa when he made this announcement because she was the only one of the group who hadn't yet been told. "I'm considering running for governor of California."

Theresa was confused. She knew that Catherine's father and other honchos in the Democratic Party would never back Henry. Not with the fallout continuing from his ongoing settlement problems with Catherine. Just yesterday Catherine had written a blog on the *Huffington Post* about why morals matter, a thinly veiled attack on men like Henry.

"As an Independent," Henry explained.

In a second Theresa saw a wide road of opportunity opening up ahead of her. "Brilliant," she said. "You could pull this off. And why not be king of the state? Why not be the puppet master?"

"I don't think we want to use that phrase," Carl interjected.

It wasn't lost on Theresa that Carl's use of "we" sounded like he was more the campaign manager than Henry's finance guru.

Henry filled in more details. "Carl and I have been talking with some key people and the support seems to be there."

"Fund-raising won't be as easy running as an Independent," Anne said, "but that's not a deal breaker."

So when did Anne become strategy chairman? Theresa thought. Of course what went unsaid was that Henry could do a Mayor Bloomberg—finance his own campaign.

"There's a lot to be figured out yet," Henry said, "but I'm

confident we can handle whatever problems come up. What I'm not sure about is my sanity for wanting to step into politics at all."

He said it as a joke and Anne laughed. Theresa got the feeling Henry had said this line before and Anne always laughed on cue. No reason to dwell on that, though, when there were so many other things to consider. Theresa's mind was racing. She understood why Henry wanted to run. Control, power and to impact the decision-making process in a direct way. She got it. She liked it. She thought of all the trickle-down cachet that would come her way if he won. If people were sucking up to get a hundred-thousand-dollar contribution to their favorite charity now, they'd be kissing her ass to try to get closer to a man with the power to veto, the power to pardon and everything in between.

Life was good, soon to get better because an even more exciting thought occurred to her. Maybe this is why Henry married Anne . . . because he was already planning to get into politics and knew he'd need to have the domestic side of his life in order, especially with the pregnancy. Maybe their relationship isn't as much a grand passion as much as it is a grand strategy. It was a thought that reassured Theresa and thrilled her . . . and lately she'd been short on thrills.

"Are you okay?" Anne touched her arm. "Your face is flushed."

"It's the pinot noir," Theresa replied. "Every time I drink red wine, it happens. But I'm fine. I'm more than fine. I'm delighted."

Throughout dinner they talked strategy and logistics, with Anne contributing as much if not more than Carl and Theresa. It was looking like the paramour/contender had more Hillary Clinton in her than Theresa had first thought, which is why when Anne got up to go to the ladies' room, Theresa decided to do the girly thing and accompany her. It was the equivalent of letting the men step into the study for cigars and brandy while the women powdered their noses and did their own politicking. As they touched up their makeup, Theresa decided it was time for her to do a little sucking up. Since Anne was going to be actively involved in the campaign, Theresa needed to guide her into a niche that wouldn't infringe on her own power base.

"You ever meet Maria Shriver?" Theresa asked.

"Never," Anne replied.

"She was a great first lady of California. She started a women's conference that turned into a big deal. She even got Michelle Obama to show up."

"Were you there?"

"No." Leave it to Anne to ask the question that made Theresa feel like an outsider. "I bring it up because you should start thinking about all the things that you'll be able to do if Henry is elected."

"Oh, believe me, I have."

"And?"

"It's too early to talk about all that. I have to give birth first."

As they chatted away Theresa couldn't shake the feeling that she felt especially short. She looked down to check out Anne's footwear. She was wearing boots with three-inch heels but Anne often wore three- or even four-inch heels and Theresa didn't usually feel so small in comparison. She made a mental note to buy higher heels, as Anne finished touching up her lipstick.

While she was zipping up her cosmetic bag and dropping it back in her purse, Anne's demeanor changed as if she'd suddenly taken a sharp turn from a sun-filled boulevard onto a shaded private alleyway. She spoke softly to Theresa, in a conspiratorial tone. "You and I have to keep an eye on Carl. Henry can be loyal to a fault and doesn't want to hear it but I don't think Carl gives him the best advice. I think he gives Henry advice that works best for Carl."

"You don't have to convince me of that. I've thought the same thing for a long time. Besides, Carl is no fan of mine," Theresa added. "I heard he was spreading a rumor that I plagiarized my college thesis, as if anyone cares about anything anyone did in college. Not that I plagiarized."

"Sounds like something Carl might do," Anne said, sympathetically. "So you understand what I'm saying and agree?"

"Absolutely."

Anne's famous dark eyes sparkled and the effect on Theresa was a bit hypnotic. Even more so when Anne said, "Let's the two of us keep in touch about this and work together." She then leaned in closer to Theresa, whose first thought was, I love her perfume, a mix of citrus and a hint of exotic spice. Should she come right out and ask Anne what it was? Would it be too weird if Henry realized that she was now wearing the same perfume as his wife? All this internal debate stopped when Anne kissed her on each cheek and Theresa found her heart beating faster.

She wasn't a lesbian. She didn't have sex fantasies about women but Anne's talent for sexualizing a moment caught Theresa off guard and she was unprepared for how those kisses excited her. She felt as if she and Anne had actually stepped into a dark alley and had an illicit moment.

Emerging from the ladies' room Theresa struggled to regain her former disdain for "her ladyship." It was one thing to see Anne as a temporary ally; it was another to fall under her spell.

When they got back to the table Henry and Carl were not alone. This was not unusual. People were always coming up to Henry and wanting to meet him, or reminding him that they had met and hoping that he'd want to meet up again soon. This time the interlopers were two women wearing short, tight dresses. One was standing up and talking to Carl; the other one was Larissa, sitting in Anne's chair, flirting with Henry. You can spot that kind of flirting from across the room. Aggressively coquettish. The way she arched her back, crossed her legs, classic feline-in-pursuit body language. Larissa jumped up when she saw Anne and Theresa. "I just came over to say hi."

She looked at Anne, at her pregnant belly. "Congratulations on all of it." Larissa's hands made a circle in the air as if speaking in sign language.

"Thank you," Anne replied, taking her seat and putting her hand on Henry's leg, an obvious territorial gesture but one that Henry seemed to enjoy. Theresa noted that maybe the most impressive tool in Anne's skill set might be her ability to read Henry's moods accurately. Not an easy task.

The other girl standing next to Carl chimed in. "Yeah, congratulations."

No one introduced this girl so Theresa extended her hand. "I'm Theresa Cromwell, and you're . . ."

"I'm Kim." She had long wavy red hair that complemented her pale skin but Theresa suspected the color wasn't natural. Neither were the tits.

Larissa turned to Theresa. "We never did take our hike." She was referring to the suggestion she'd made at Theresa's party all those months ago.

Theresa laughed then and she laughed now. "God knows I could use the exercise but I've been so busy."

"Haven't we all," Larissa said, making light of the fact that if a woman like Theresa thinks you're someone she wants in her social web, she'll find the time to trek up a canyon or two.

"Well, nice seeing y'all," Larissa said, taking Kim's hand, as if they were on a date. Giggling, the twosome headed over to the bar.

Theresa was amused. "'Y'all'? When did Larissa go Southern?"

"She's nervous," Henry said.

Theresa did a quick pivot. If Henry wanted to make excuses for Larissa, Theresa would follow suit. "Understandable," she quickly added. She looked over to Anne to gauge her reaction but Anne's expression revealed no emotion at all. A perfect poker face. She had her head on Henry's shoulder and he began to rub the back of it like she was his favorite pet. He whispered something in her ear and she nodded yes.

Carl squirmed in his seat and signaled the waiter over. "Anyone want dessert, coffee?"

"We're going to get out of here," Henry replied, "but no need for the two of you to rush."

Carl handed his credit card to the waiter.

"Actually," Theresa spoke up, "I'd love some coffee. With the way they're handing out DUIs these days, you can't even have a second glass of wine without being over the limit."

Carl looked annoyed but what was he going to do . . . leave her there alone?

After Henry and Anne said their goodbyes and Theresa was waiting for her espresso, she caught Carl making eye contact with Kim, who was watching him from her perch at the bar. The two exchanged a look that told Theresa tonight wasn't the first time they'd met. Oh fuck, she thought . . . this is a two-headline dinner. Henry is going for the governorship and Carl is going for new pussy.

Chapter 22

Catherine

"Anxiety, dizziness, nausea, vomiting." Catherine was reading from a list off an Internet site. "Or in severe cases, possible swelling of the mouth and face, hallucinations, seizures, unusual or disturbing thoughts." When she got to the last side effect, she laughed. "I have that whether or not I take one of these pills." She clicked the Web page closed and tossed her prescription bottle, filled with Lunesta, across the kitchen countertop as if offering them to Jake Winslow. It was midnight and they were having another nocturnal meeting because Catherine's insomnia had only gotten worse since her divorce, with the ongoing war over the property settlement and Maren off at boarding school. Even with Carmen now living full-time in the guest quarters at the house, Catherine couldn't make peace with the night. Two thousand twelve had come and gone. Nostradamus was wrong. The world didn't end but the uneasiness in the air had only increased, worse now because it couldn't be explained as the buildup to Armageddon.

"I wouldn't worry about it," Jake replied, just to have something to say. He played the odds, and the chances of ending up in the ER because you took something to help you sleep were too slim to dwell on.

"Given my run of bad luck lately I can't be so sure."

Jake nodded to be agreeable and hide his boredom.

"I know what you're thinking, Jake. You're thinking that I'm out of touch with how ninety percent of the world lives, that my idea of bad luck is most people's idea of paradise."

"Bad luck is bad luck," he said. "And it's got nothing to do with how much money you have."

"You know, if Henry gets what he wants in our settlement I'll have to sell this house, downscale. And when Maren reaches eighteen and child support ends . . ." Catherine knew she was oversharing and exaggerating but she wasn't sure she was ready for whatever information Jake had in the manila envelope he'd brought with him.

"We'll keep on him," Jake said as he opened the envelope and pulled out his report, including the latest batch of photos. "It's only a matter of time before he fucks up and we catch him," he said with total confidence. "Running for office puts him on a short leash and that doesn't strike me as his style."

Catherine agreed. She knew Henry's foray into politics would curb his freedom and it was only a matter of time before he rebelled. Yet she worried, tossing and turning at night. She had visions of Henry becoming even more dynamic and in demand than he already was, which struck her as grossly unfair. Her way of striking back was by becoming a Republican. Her father, who had been an advisor to Democratic campaigns for the last thirty years and was still a behind-the-scenes confidant to candidates, was horrified at Catherine's swing to the right. Fact is, from Catherine's perspective, it wasn't even that big a swing. Once she embraced Catholicism, she started to embrace a value system that was more in line with red states than blue. She started talking to women's groups, stressing the importance of vows and the unfairness of divorce, always supporting those in favor of monogamy and the divine union of matrimony. Little by little she became more and more conservative about everything and was finding a niche as a defender of family values. She had contributed money to every Republican who might end up running against Henry, though she did this in secret. Her daughter, to the extent that she tuned in at all, was a liberal and was her dad's biggest fan. She wouldn't forgive her mother for trying to work against her father's campaign. Mother and daughter did share some common ground, though. They both believed in karmic justice. Maren came at it from a more California spiritual New Age style and Catherine's version was more New Testament. However, both believed that certain people were evil and would get their comeuppance someday. They both believed that a greater justice would eventually be restored and the evil one, aka Anne, would be punished.

Catherine shuffled through the photos Jake brought. "This is just Henry at a bunch of business lunches and fund-raisers. And why do all these women look like Nancy Pelosi? That can't be making him happy. He likes younger, hotter scenery. This is all you have?"

"He's been a good boy. If you want me to go deeper . . . ?" Jake held up his cell to make his point. Catherine had resisted asking him to tap Henry's phone, not only because it was illegal and she was terrified of getting caught but also because she was afraid of what might be said about her in Henry's private calls. What if he said something negative about her, about the way she looked? What if he said she was fat? She couldn't handle that.

"No, no, no," Catherine said, ready to shut down any further conversation about phone tapping. Suddenly a thought occurred to her, a mini epiphany. "I've got a better idea, Jake. Let's stop keeping tabs on Henry and start keeping an eye on Anne. Something tells me that following her might bring us interesting information."

Again he held up his cell. "An eye and an ear?"

Catherine was reluctant to cross that line, but then a second epiphany hit. If she ever got caught she would say that the Lunesta she was taking to fall asleep was responsible for unusual, disturbing thoughts and hallucinations. Not guilty because of diminished capacity would be her plea. "Do it," she said.

"I'm on it." Jake was ready to get out of there now that he had his marching orders.

"Wait," Catherine said. She opened up a kitchen drawer that held miscellaneous items and pulled out a medal on a chain.

"Saint Christopher. For protection. You'll need it being anywhere around that whore."

Chapter 23

Anne

I watch George act in a scene for a new TV series being shot on the back lot of Henry's studio. George is a natural, which isn't to say he's ever going to be a great actor, but he's not self-conscious and he knows how to listen to his fellow actors. He can, as they say in the biz, "commit to the moment." I think he feels more comfortable being himself inside a character than out of one. He's playing a police detective and he has a swagger that reminds me of the young cop in the movie *Under Suspicion*. He exudes energy and drive with just the right dose of mischief.

As I stand there and watch from the sidelines I'm well aware that I'm the boss's wife. The show's exec producers have offered me their assistants, their chairs and even their headphones so I can hear the audio as the scene is being shot. Not everyone is welcoming, though. Some of the crew go about their work, polite but not solicitous. I know there are people on the lot who resent my presence and resent that my brother got this break. Nepotism is a fact of life in

Hollywood and I don't fault anyone for taking advantage of it and I don't blame anyone for resenting the ones who do. It *is* cutting the line and you can't expect that the people forced to wait longer for their turn—or in some cases denied their turn altogether—are ever going to think that's okay.

"Do you need anything?" One of the show's network executives, a woman in her thirties, who has that crispness about her that females in corporate jobs often possess, is standing next to me watching them block the next scene.

"No, I'm fine but thanks."

I can tell she doesn't like me. It's in the crispness of her speech. There are so many negative stories about me in the media that I'm not surprised when someone dislikes me on sight. I've done my best to counter the bad press but I'm not very good at it. If someone asks me what I think, I tend to tell them. When am I going to learn that they don't really want to know what I think, they just want me to say something that'll make them feel good? With that in mind I try again.

"George says the best things about everyone he's working with here."

The executive smiles, without showing any teeth. "He has a lot of fans," she says. "All the girls have a crush on him."

"He's very sexy," I say. "Sweet and sexy."

"Yes, he is," she replies and I can see she's struggling to keep the conversation going. "When are you due?"

"Four weeks."

"Boy or girl?"

"I don't know. We want to be surprised."

But the problem is I do know, just found out, and it's the reason I've come to see George. "Is it okay if I wait in his trailer?"

"Of course. I'm sure there's water and snacks in there but if you need anything, anything at all, track me down and I'll get it done."

She walks away and for a second I envy her. She's a career

girl, honing a skill with value in the marketplace. For all the perks and favors and nepotism that come my way because of Henry, my résumé is looking thin and without a public record of accomplishment I could easily become one of those women fighting for credit. I've been to enough ladies' lunches and dinners over the years and have witnessed women married to powerful men trying to prove they're more than just a wife and mother. There was the older woman who claimed she advised her husband to green-light *Home Alone* and the younger woman who claimed she urged her now super-successful TV producer husband to get behind *American Idol*. I don't want to be a woman who, down the line, is searching for relevance by declaring that I was the one who suggested Henry run as an Independent. Fighting for credit may be standard operating procedure in Hollywood but it's never a sign of strength.

I locate George's trailer and make myself comfortable. It's not one of the fancier ones on the set because he's not the star of the show but it's a private oasis, which is all that matters. I lie down on the couch and put my hands gently on my stomach. So I've got an Elizabeth inside me, not an Edward. It's a terrible thing to admit but I'm disappointed. I feel like I've failed. And though I can't explain why, up until that moment the thought of childbirth didn't scare me—now for some reason, I'm terrified.

George is on an hour break and has ordered us salads and sandwiches. He still has his makeup on and with his ill-fitting cop suit, badge and prop gun, I'm reminded of our childhood again—the year he dressed up as a cop for Halloween. A year or so before that, I chose to dress up as a queen. I remember I refused to wear a cardboard crown and made my mother buy me one made out of plastic and then glued glass beads on it where the jewels would go. Thinking about that now, I wonder if we were precognitive, our subconscious knowing that down the line we'd be playing those parts for real . . . well, semi-real.

"I don't see why you're so upset," George says as he pours ketchup over his side order of fries. "Henry may prefer a boy but he'll get over it."

I try to explain my state of mind. "Today when I was at the doctor's, getting an ultrasound, I just had to ask. It was so crazy because I was so sure it was a boy that when the doctor said girl, I thought he said boy. I'm looking at the picture of my baby and I'm saying where's the penis and he looks at me like I'm a moron and he says . . . there is no penis, it's a *girl.*"

George sees that I've only taken a bite of my sandwich. "Eat something, Anne, and stop worrying. It's not like Henry is actual royalty and needs an heir to the throne."

"Yes he does. Men like Henry want and need a son. It's the 'I'm going to live forever' thing. The immortality gene works through a male child more than a female. I guess old traditions and thousands of years of DNA memory die hard."

George looks skeptical. He has no drive to have kids. He's not that kind of male. He doesn't think in terms of creating an empire or leaving a legacy. He thinks in terms of getting a new BMW and leaving personal updates on Facebook. "Once she's born, Henry will adore her. She'll be his little princess."

"He'll adore her eventually but it won't be when she's a baby. It won't be automatic."

"He's got a month to get used to the idea," George says, trying to be positive.

"I'm not telling him yet. I need these four weeks to figure out the best way to deal with his disappointment and because right now, as the mother of his 'son,' there's nothing he won't do to make me happy. How do you think you got this job?"

"Henry may have given me the job but I'm making it work."

George sounds hurt so I quickly boost his confidence. "Once

you make a big splash, which you will, nothing and nobody can take that away," I say. For a second I loathe myself for not being straight with him. I know, and he should know, too, how quickly hot can turn into not in this business.

My sensitivity inspires his sensitivity and he feeds me a french fry—the way I like them, with a touch of Dijon mustard. "I'm feeding my future niece," he says and then talking directly to my belly he says, "Elizabeth, I know you're going to rock the world. You're going to have a spectacular life."

"You're going to be a great uncle," I say and I have no doubts about that.

"Yes I am." He smiles and all is back to being right in his world. Well, almost all.

"You're a good guy," I say. "One of the few really good ones."

"Lacy doesn't think so." His reply is matter-of-fact.

Hmm. Now it's back to Lacy, not "my wife." I don't ask how things are going with them. I'm pretty sure I know.

Chapter 24

Cliff

Cliff sat in his backyard, one of his favorite places now that the chunk of dirt and foliage that had fallen from the canyon above had been cleaned up and the hillside reenforced. It was a Sunday afternoon and he was getting some sun and working at the same time, taking a meeting with George's wife, Lacy.

"Give her an assignment," Theresa had said. "We don't have to hire her or even pay her. Let her write a blog about something and eventually when there's an opening" . . . blah, blah, blah. He knew the routine. When Theresa was courting a friendship with someone she'd flatter them by saying, "Darling, you must write something for us." Usually the person was so flattered they didn't even think about the fact that they were providing Theresa content for free. Theresa was savvy, knew she could get away with it. There was no shortage of people in Hollywood who felt they had something to say and were rich enough not to need to be paid for saying it. What a business model, Cliff thought: capitalizing on ego.

Lacy fit that category perfectly. She had a husband who was getting paid decent money on his TV show and she had family money for backup. What she didn't have was her own identity and she was frantically searching for one. She was like a plane, circling, running out of fuel, desperately in need of a place to land. More and more these days people like Lacy were landing on the Internet.

"So what would you like to write about?" Cliff asked.

Lacy pulled a chic leather folder out of her tote bag, plucked out a page of notes and handed it to Cliff. "I'd love to write about fashion."

Cliff was clueless about the fashion world and everyone in it. Was Lacy fashionable? He had no idea. If pressed on the issue he'd say that she was always nicely put together and often wore scarves.

"I'm thinking I could write something about how every woman has her own uniform. For some it's jeans and a cashmere sweater, for others it's . . ."

Cliff pretended to be listening. None of it interested him but he had a gift for looking like he was paying attention, and beyond that, looking like he was moved by what he was hearing. He once played a shrink in a TV drama and the producer later said he was hired because he had the kind of face that made people want to open up. He made them feel safe. He looked like he gave a shit. Putting on his best Gabriel Byrne in *In Treatment* expression he sat there as Lacy went on and on.

"Or, in the case of other women it's boots, pants and a silk top. You know what I mean?"

Uh-oh, she was asking a question. Cliff scrambled to come up with a reply. "Now that you mention it, I've always had my version of a uniform: khaki pants and polo shirt."

"Are you two talking about clothes?" Cliff's wife had brought them out a tray of iced teas.

"Lacy may write some fashion pieces for the site," Cliff explained.

"Maybe branch out to other topics down the line," Lacy added.

"Other topics?" Cliff perked up.

"There's a topic, that, well, one of these days." Lacy trembled slightly, as if it weren't a story for a sunny California afternoon.

Now Cliff was intrigued. His wife wasn't.

"I'll leave you two to talk," she said.

"Actually," Lacy replied, "I'd love your opinion on this. It's a female issue."

"My opinion?" Cliff's wife took a seat, somewhat reluctantly. "Okay. Shoot."

Lacy took a deep breath and let it all out. "One of these days I want to write a piece on women who borrow other people's husbands."

Now Cliff was worried. His wife was amused. "I think I know something about that," she said.

Lacy took that as encouragement and continued her pitch. "I want to write about women who have attachments to other women's husbands. Under the guise of 'friendship' they meet these men for lunch. They confide in them. They send them emails. They ask for advice. They have secrets. And the guy is into it, servicing them—"

Cliff's wife interjected. "Hiring them?" And then added jokingly, "I didn't say that." She shot Cliff a look that said, Don't worry, I'm not going to trash Theresa . . . publicly.

Lacy continued. "And the husbands are always at their best with their special 'friend.' Meanwhile, at home, it's the wife who has to deal with her man being moody and insecure. It's the wife who gets yelled at if she doesn't have her husband's favorite muffin, toasted just the way he likes it, and ready for him when he sits down for breakfast."

She was getting worked up and Cliff knew what she really wanted to write and complain about . . . Anne and George. He could tell Lacy already had a fan in his wife, who rarely offered an opinion about anything having to do with the site. Now she did.

"Forget the fashion stuff: this is the story you should write first.

This is the story that'll bring the site thousands of hits. Trust me, women all over can relate to what you're saying."

This was news to Cliff but as he considered it he thought, They could be on to something here. Whether the "guilty party" was Anne or Theresa, maybe the habit (or the crime, depending upon your point of view) of borrowing another woman's husband was a widespread phenomenon. Aside from that, the opportunity to please his wife by saying yes to Lacy's idea might help thaw the chill that had been his domestic reality for the last few months.

"Why don't you write that up, Lacy, but don't name names. We don't want to get sued."

He looked over to his wife to see if that scored him a point or two.

"I'll leave you two to figure it out," she said. Though she clearly wanted to get back to whatever she was doing, there was no question she was in a more chipper mood. She even gave Cliff an affectionate pat on the head as she walked past him.

He was cautiously hopeful. She was unexpectedly hopeful. It was the first time they'd been anywhere near the same page in weeks.

He watched her cross the lawn and go back into the house. He noticed that she'd put on some weight and wasn't dressed in a very flattering way. This much he knew about fashion . . . yellow velour sweatpants were not a good look on women over forty who weighed more than they should, second only to overalls when it came to clothes that should be banned from all middle-aged women's closets. Yet he found himself desiring her and her imperfect body more than he'd ever desired Theresa or anyone else. When he and his wife were on the same page it was, for him, the biggest turn-on around.

Switching his focus back to Lacy he could see that her mood had changed, too, for the worse. Visibly upset, she'd pulled a cigarette out and was using an empty pill bottle for an ashtray. Cliff wanted to seize this opportunity as well. "So you want to write about Anne without actually saying so?"

"She's driving me fucking nuts . . . oh the things I could tell you."

He wanted to hear all of them. "What's going on?"

"I don't want to get into it now. Let me just say, she has my husband at her beck and call."

"Some siblings are close like that."

"It's not about close, it's about control. That's not even the right word. Control would be normal in comparison to what's going on."

Cliff felt her need to spill all the ugly details. All he had to do was gently nudge her in that direction and he guessed the very nudge that might do it. "That'll change when you and George start having kids."

Bull's-eye. The mention of kids made her eyes tear up. He had gotten too close to the exposed nerve and now she wanted to flee.

"Yeah, right, whenever that happens." She gathered her papers, putting them back in the chic leather folder. She reached for her tote bag, accidentally knocking over her glass of iced tea. *"Fuck."* She tried mopping up the spill with the ends of her long linen scarf until Cliff made her stop.

"Don't worry about that."

"I'm sorry, it's just that . . ."

Cliff knew what it was. She wanted kids. She didn't have any. Anne was having one. Anne had a husband. Anne also had Lacy's husband. Cliff was still thinking about Lacy's comment, ". . . oh the things I could tell you." He wanted those Anne stories. Theresa would want those Anne stories.

"Look, let's start with this piece but here's what I'm thinking: If you want, you could be a contributor to the site. Come into the office, be part of our meetings."

"Really?" Lacy regained some composure. "I'd like that."

"Great, you can start on Monday?" Cliff was pleased with himself. It would pay to have her around, plus the beauty of it all is they wouldn't have to actually pay her. A win-win.

Chapter 25

Anne

I knew that one of these days I would run into Carl Wolsey and we'd have some kind of a clash. I just never expected it to happen in the men's department at Barneys. I'm in my eighth month of pregnancy so I rarely go shopping at a store filled with fabulous clothes I can't fit into but this morning I decide to buy Henry a present. I'm trying to decide between a blue sweater and a plum one when I spot Carl checking out cashmere hoodies.

He waves, seems reluctant to come over so I go over to him.

"My father tells me he's invested with you."

Carl put the cashmere jacket back on the display table. "We're doing some business. How are you feeling? Any day now?" He's looking at my stomach.

"Actually I'm still three weeks away."

"Is that right?"

When someone says "Is that right?"—and I say it all the time— it's a sign that there really is nothing left to say. Unless Carl and I are going to talk about what's really going on, his disapproval of me and my distrust of him, saying "see you around" is probably the best option. We are moving in that direction when Smith shows up. He's one of the salesmen at Barneys. Second floor is his territory. High-end designer clothes for women.

"Anne!" he screams with delight. "Look at you. You're just going to pop out that baby and pop right into a size four. No problem."

Smith is my guy at Barneys, has been for years, even when I couldn't afford to buy anything that wasn't on the "40 percent off" sale. We bonded then and now he loves me because I spend a lot. A few weeks ago, in an attempt to make Maren feel better about having a sibling, I bought her lots of cool clothes and shipped them to her prep school. I never got a thank-you. I'll admit it: this stepmom business is harder than I ever thought it would be.

Smith hands Carl two large shopping bags and a credit card receipt, which Carl quickly signs.

I glance at an item sticking out of one of the bags. "Some girl is going to be very happy."

"A present for a client," Carl says.

Yeah, right. Who buys their client a Dolce & Gabbana polka-dot bustier?

"Lucky client," I say.

Smith chimes in. "A *very* lucky client." Fearing he said more than he was supposed to, Smith takes the signed receipt, shakes Carl's hand, kisses me on the cheek and heads over to the elevator.

"I got to get going, too."

Carl isn't going to let me drift away without evening the score. If I'm going to rattle him by speculating about the recipient of the bustier, he's going to rattle me in whatever way he can. He can't help himself any more than I can. We bring out the bad judgment in each other.

He smiles. "I hear it's a girl."

"What is?"

"Your child."

"My child? Is a girl?" I'm speechless. How does he know? Is he guessing? Fucking with me? Or does he actually know? Did he pay off someone who works in the doctor's office? All very possible. But why? Just to have the information?

"I have no idea," I say. "Henry and I want to be surprised."

"Then I must have been misinformed." He now sounds very proper. "Whatever it is, it's a blessing. All children are," he adds.

Now he's moved from proper to pious. Easy to imagine him in priestly garb doing the sign of the cross over my pregnant belly.

After we part, I seek out Smith. I know he'll tell me what the deal is with Carl's purchases because I'm the bigger spender and big spenders get perks . . . the number one being store gossip.

"What's the story with Carl?"

"No story."

"No story? He walked out of here looking like Santa Claus."

"Buying something for a client. I think."

If Smith is suddenly closedmouthed it can only mean Carl has become the bigger spender and Carl would only spend like that if he was really hooked.

"Maybe Carl's in love with 'bustier girl' . . . whoever she is." I'm hoping I can lure something out of Smith and he caves. He can't resist letting just one cat out of the bag.

"This girl is very good at seducing Santas. I know. When she wants a present, she sends them all to me . . . and that's all I'm going to say."

Chapter 26

Theresa

Theresa loved sitting outside at the Polo Lounge on a beautiful blue-sky day. She arrived before Anne and said hello to a number of people she knew as she made her way to her favorite table, a booth just to the right of the entrance of the patio—high-profile and yet private enough so your conversations couldn't be overheard. Anne had invited her to lunch and Theresa took that as a sign that their mutually self-serving friendship was intact. As Theresa sat there, waiting, drinking a mineral water, she looked around at the men lunching there that afternoon, and wondered if there were any interesting, single ones among them. Damn, why couldn't she find anyone appropriate to date or even fake date—someone to go out with every once in a while and they could act like they were together even if no intimate relationship existed. Every man she found attractive was married or seeing someone twenty years younger. She always knew L.A. would be a tough town for single women over forty; she just didn't think it would be this tough.

She checked her BlackBerry for messages. There was one from Jane Seymour returning her email, saying she would be coming to L.A. in a few weeks and yes would love to meet for a drink. Theresa had a good feeling about this new acquaintance, which she believed could be a potentially fruitful connection. When she put her phone back down on the table, Anne was there, looking very, very pregnant and quite beautiful.

"It's criminal how good you look," Theresa said.

"You haven't seen me naked: not so hot. I'm not one of those women who think the pregnant body is a thing of beauty." As Anne sat down and made herself comfortable a number of people checked her out. She might not be a celebrity by E! Entertainment standards, but this crowd knew money and to them she was a star. Any woman who was with Henry would be.

"I'm tempted to get a photo done just to see how people would respond to a candidate's wife doing a Demi Moore." Anne was referring to the often-copied shot of a nude and pregnant Demi on the cover of *Vanity Fair* two decades ago.

"Hey, a first lady of France, Carla Bruni, might have some naked photos floating out there on the Internet," Theresa teased.

"I'm no Carla Bruni. No one ever suggested modeling as a potential career for me."

Theresa appreciated the repartee. Anne was smart, self-deprecating and fun. They were picking up from the alliance they had forged at the Soho House. There they had found a small slice of common ground and were now discovering a way to enjoy each other's company.

"Are you hungry?" Anne asked. "I'm starving. You?"

"Famished."

When the food arrived, Theresa divided the single order of the hotel's signature entrée, the "McCarthy Salad," on two plates and she and Anne had some laughs over the silliness of two women who claimed to be starving, deciding to split a salad and forgo the bread. This was Hollywood-style hungry. But at least they went for the full salad combo. Splitting a McCarthy often took some negotiating. One person might want it without beets, another without cheese. Bacon? Always an issue. Tomatoes? Could be iffy. Salad dressing? Up for discussion. No problems today. Anne was fine with whatever Theresa wanted. She was the queen of acquiescence and though that would usually set off a warning bell for Theresa, this time she allowed herself to relax and enjoy.

Even Theresa needed to let down her guard every once in a while, if for no other reason than to keep her face from hardening into a frown that no amount of surgery could reverse. That's what so many women in Hollywood didn't get. Staying young had as much to do with letting go as it did with holding on. Sometimes it had as much to do with being bad as it did with being good, as much to do with being naughty as it did with being nice. It was said around Hollywood by the girls in Larissa's crowd that staying youthful-looking had as much to do with the muscle work you got from giving blow jobs as it did with $1,500 injections of Perlane filler for the lines and wrinkles around your mouth. Since letting go did not come easily to Theresa and she was no fan of blow jobs, the best she could do was, every so often, treat herself to some carefree girlfriend bonding.

But first things first. There was so much to discuss, starting with their mutual goal . . . seeing Henry become governor. Theresa wanted to talk about Henry's upcoming interview with Diane Sawyer and wanted to know what Anne thought of Henry doing an interview for *GQ*'s special issue about icons of style. Henry in a Brioni suit shot by Mario Testino would be fabulous. "Never underestimate the power of an image in a campaign," she said. Anne had no interest in these details. She was excited about something else. "I finally figured out what I should be doing for Henry."

"I think you're doing plenty for him already." Theresa meant it as a lighthearted compliment but Anne had no interest in flattery.

"I've decided I should run his philanthropy organization."

"What do you mean run it?"

"You're so busy working with Henry on so many things, all his various companies, the last thing you need is to be bothered with his charitable contributions."

"I've got it organized quite efficiently at this point. It's not a huge outlay of time or energy." Theresa snapped into business-speak because she didn't know what else to do. She suddenly realized she was standing over a trapdoor.

"It's very nice of you not to complain," Anne said, "but really, it's something I think I would be good at. I've been researching a middle school near the airport. Very poor neighborhood. The place looks like an army barracks, not a campus, but some of those kids are testing super-high on math and science. I want to fund a program at the school. Get them better computers, bring in lecturers, set up field trips, establish a support system of tutors so they even improve on their test scores and qualify for scholarships to the best private schools, and eventually, colleges."

Theresa had heard this pitch before and it had come to her from credible people who actually had already established programs set up to help disadvantaged students. Anne wasn't even pitching something original. Oh, I get it, Theresa thought. Anne now fancies herself a serious person with visions of nonfiction best sellers dancing in her head. Well, Theresa didn't see it that way. From her perspective Anne was no game changer, just another Bel Air housewife looking for a little gravitas.

But there was no debating the issue when Anne concluded with "Henry thinks it's a great idea." With that, Anne symbolically pulled the lever and the trapdoor opened. With a flip of a switch Theresa had been removed from the philanthropic arena and there was nothing she could do about it. While Theresa had been sitting there blithely dividing up the McCarthy Salad, Anne had been dividing up Henry's territory.

Theresa ached to tell Anne what she really thought of her but wasn't about to jeopardize her job to do so. Instead she kept her anger in check and assumed the position. Elbow on table, chin resting on her hand, she listened to Anne with mock fascination. When she finally replied, her words were supportive though she spoke in a monotone, an overcorrection of the surging emotion she was trying so hard to keep at bay. "I think you have a real talent for that kind of thing."

Theresa was furious with herself for letting her guard down with Anne and she was paying a big price for that slip. Running Henry's philanthropic interests had made Theresa feel important. She was the one who was good at it but now it was being taken away from her by a sperm trapper. Never again, she vowed. I will get rid of Anne, one way or another. She wasn't sure how or how long it would take but she was confident that she'd find a way to bring the bitch down.

"I've got to pee," Anne said. "Being this pregnant it seems all I ever say anymore is 'I'm starving' and 'I've go to pee.' Be right back."

Theresa watched Anne stop at a few tables and socialize on her way to the ladies' room. At one table where a small group of women were having a girls' lunch she let one of the more ebullient women actually touch her stomach. It was as if a queen were allowing a commoner a special favor. Who does she think she is, Theresa thought. The Virgin Mary about to give birth to Jesus? Get over yourself.

She recalled the first time she saw Anne up at Beverly Glen, when Cliff pointed her out as Henry's latest "girlfriend." She had a bad feeling about her then but never did she think Anne would get this far.

Across the patio, Theresa noticed someone waving to her. It was one of the board members of Oceana. Theresa waved back, thinking, He won't be so friendly when he finds out I'm no longer in control of Henry's charity dollars and won't be able to write the big check to protect sea turtles in the Galapagos.

A waiter approached to ask if she wanted to order anything else. "No, we're done," Theresa replied emphatically.

He placed the bill on the table. "Whenever you're ready," he said and walked away.

Theresa had her credit card in her jacket pocket, had put it there earlier so she could hand it to him before Anne beat her to it. She liked being the one who paid. Not this time. She put her credit card back in her wallet. Let the queen buy me lunch, she thought. She owes me.

Chapter 27

Anne

It's a warm, windy night and the baby is due in a few days. It's around midnight and Henry and I are in his bedroom, my favorite room in the whole world. Though the whole house is contemporary and some would say minimalist, this room is warm and inviting. It's not a huge area (the walk-in closet and his-and-her bath take up more square footage) but spacious enough not to feel crowded. The only furniture aside from the TV in its custom-designed console is a king-sized bed and a couple of bedside tables. That may not sound cozy but nothing warms up a room more than a Monet Impressionist landscape on the wall. In a house full of contemporary Expressionist art, this is the room of quiet masterpieces.

We are talking about all the things we want to do if (when) Henry gets elected. Recently we both became obsessed with an obscure book I found about the three ingredients necessary for happiness: integrity, passion and freedom. Henry jokingly suggests in my case there's a fourth—wardrobe. Jokes aside, we're having one of those conversations that make me feel like I'm high. When you're intoxicated by ideas and the person you're talking to is equally intoxicated, and there's not a drop of alcohol or weed or any chemical substance around, then you know you're clicking on a pretty magical level. We talk about how the happiness formula can apply to what he's trying to do politically and we get so carried away with all our ideas we start believing we can really make a difference and I make him open up his laptop and we start writing a speech. Even though it's not a speech for any particular occasion I feel like we're co-creating on a whole new level. I feel like this is the birth of a big idea and a winning campaign, a birth that might prove even more important to Henry than the arrival of our baby. I've made good use of these past four weeks and feel indispensable to him, at least for the short term, at least until I can get pregnant again . . . with a son. My security is intact.

And then the war starts. That's what it sounds like. Helicopters overhead are nothing unusual in L.A. but this is different. This helicopter is directly over the house, directly over the room we're in and it's not circling or moving on. It's loud and low and ominous and it feels as if we're under attack, reminding me of the first Vietnam scene in *The Deer Hunter*.

Henry grabs the remote, turns on the TV and switches to the channel hooked up to the high-tech security cameras around the property. We can't see the helicopters but we can see down the long driveway and outside the front gate, where a number of fire trucks are parked and firemen are dragging hoses over to flames shooting up on our side of the road.

Henry jumps up, puts on his shoes, grabs his cell and tells me not to worry. When I say tells me, I mean he really convinces me, takes a moment to talk to me calmly before he dashes out. As he leaves I'm thinking that if Henry can keep me calm when I'm nine months pregnant and there's a fire raging on the property, he's the man I've always hoped he would be.

For an hour I sit there on the edge of the bed and watch the security camera video and because I have the audio connected to the front gate buzzer speakerphone, I can even hear some of what's being said.

The firemen explain to Henry that a car went over the cliff and caught on fire, which ignited the brush. The two passengers managed to crawl out of the wreck and are waiting to be rescued from fifty feet below.

Brush fires are scary, especially when there are hot winds to feed them, so the fire department is out in force—six trucks. Southern California has a history of catastrophes that start with just one spark igniting a blaze that results in scorched earth and a declared disaster area. Within minutes Henry grasps the entire situation and knows how to make himself useful. He phones one of his always-on-call errand boys and has him bring up coffee and water and snacks for the firemen. He has the road blocked off before the cops even get there and becomes the go-to guy for the neighbors who trickle out, some in their bedclothes, all in a panic. Henry zeroes in on the real culprit in all this—the lack of guardrails on dangerous parts of the road—and already has the neighbors determined to do something about it.

I watch all this not expecting any levity but I burst out laughing when I overhear Henry talking to the driver of the car, once the guy and his date, a girl who looks like she's auditioning for the Pussycat Dolls, are finally hauled back up the canyon. The guy's story is that he was driving at normal speed and a coyote ran across the road and he swerved to avoid it. Through the hazy pictures from the security cams, I find the guy's story questionable because if any two people look like they were partying and probably driving too fast it's these two. Henry pulls the driver aside and says, "Say deer, not coyote."

That cracks me up. Great piece of advice. People on Mulholland won't be too forgiving of a guy driving too fast, who swerves to avoid a coyote and almost sets their very expensive real estate ablaze. But to avoid hitting a deer . . . well, that taps into everyone's Bambi nerve.

"There are deer up here?" the guy asks, incredulous.

Henry says, "It's the wild animal kingdom up in these hills."

As much as I love being on the top of this canyon, Henry wasn't exaggerating. There are all kinds of wild animals living up here. Though rarely seen, they can be heard, most often when the Santa Ana winds descend over the mountains. Sometimes I think L.A. is the most extreme of cities when it comes to day and night. When the sun is shining, this city feels like an open, safe, sparkling piece of heaven but at night all that wide-open space makes one feel more vulnerable to unseen threats. Add on to that L.A.'s own particular history, its tendency to attract unhinged people who arrive with unrealistic expectations and you've got, at best, a flawed paradise and at worst a compelling danger zone. Living here all my life I've never successfully been able to shake the feeling that we're all walking on shaky ground both geologically and psychologically. Being pregnant has only increased this feeling and my need to have a man around to protect me.

When the drama is over and the neighbors have returned to their homes and the firemen are packing up their equipment, I go outside to meet Henry as he walks back down the driveway. My hero. My man. My husband. The sky is clear but the smell of smoke hangs heavily in the air; still, all is well. We are safe. All is quiet. There is peace and calm throughout the canyon and in my heart. For a moment I'm not worried. For a moment I feel sure of what we have together and the strength we have as a couple. For a moment I forget to worry about the future and the unknown and what lurks in the shadows . . . and then my water breaks.

A week later the gardeners are already at work replanting the burnt-out area of the canyon on Henry's property. Plans for guardrails are under way even though there's no money in the city or state budget to pay for it. Henry has rallied the neighbors to chip in, with him contributing the bulk of the cost. Unquestionably he's picked up some votes along the way. The neighbors now look to him as their leader. His phone rings constantly. Everyone seems to want a piece of him but he does his fatherly duty by taking time out to take family photos of me with his daughter. Over the last week he's said all the right things . . . how beautiful I am . . . how beautiful Elizabeth is. He did, as is the custom these days, buy me a "push" present—a diamond necklace. He also said this: "You're still young and we'll have another." I don't know if he said that to reassure me or reassure himself. He never showed any outward disappointment at fathering a daughter, not a son, but I have a feeling that had I given him a boy he might have suggested a fireworks display in celebration.

I sit there with Elizabeth in my arms and I swear as tiny as she is, she appears poised and looks right at the camera. Henry doesn't say "smile" and I'm not because I can't stop thinking that something is slipping away and I can't stop thinking about the question Theresa asked me on my wedding day: "Are you wondering what comes after you've gotten to the top?" Now, I am wondering . . . and what I'm wondering is what if the answer is . . . trouble.

Part Three

THE PROBLEM

Chapter 28

Anne

It's my mother's birthday and the plan is for the whole family to get together at my parents' house for a celebratory lunch. It's one-fifteen and there's no sign of Mary. Granted, now that she's living out in Topanga Canyon with her photographer boyfriend, Alex, it's a drive to get to Encino, but so what. We all have our reasons and excuses. George (there without Lacy, who claims she's not feeling well) has an audition this week and would rather be working on his Boston accent. My mother suggests he stop obsessing and just throw some *r*'s in words that don't have them and take them out of words that do and he'll sound just like a Kennedy. I've got Elizabeth with me and didn't bring a nanny and my anxiety about my maternal skills has given me the worst headache. My father is grumpy because Henry didn't come with me. I think he thought that he and Henry would start hanging out together, golfing together at Bel-Air Country Club. He'll never broadcast his disappointment to the outside world. Quite the contrary: he can't stop advertising his connection to Henry. The last ten times I've seen my father, he's either had on a Tudor-for-governor T-shirt, hat or button, and election season hasn't even officially begun. On the other hand, my mother is becoming more cavalier about everything, except her granddaughter . . . though she does make an effort to effusively thank my father for organizing the lunch, which amounted to ordering in the takeout food and making sure the refrigerator is stocked with my mother's favorite pinot grigio. He's been in a generous mood lately because he got another profit check on the money he invested with Carl Wolsey, which he brags about until I can't take it anymore.

"How much can it be? You didn't have that much to invest."

"Nearly fifteen percent profit is a nice little dividend." He says this with some bravado.

"That sounds extraordinarily high."

"That's what Carl's good for. You should know that. I'm sure Henry is pulling in a nice profit."

"Wait a minute," I say, with growing concern. "I'm not following this miracle that Carl pulls off in a sluggish economy."

"Where's Mary?" my mother interjects. "Someone call her or text her or find out where she is. We want to sit down to lunch." My father gets the message. It's her birthday and she doesn't want to talk about Carl-fucking-Wolsey.

As George takes out his phone to track down my sister, my father pulls me aside for a private chat. My mother takes Elizabeth from me, and there are no tears from my child. It's as if my daughter already knows that being adaptable is a skill she better develop fast.

My father and I go outside to the patio, which my mother has recently redecorated with a proper table and wicker chairs with Liberty print–covered cushions. She's created a place to have high tea in the middle of the San Fernando Valley. It's like her design theme was scones and palm trees.

"Anne," he says, "I'm concerned about you, concerned about the family."

"Really," I say. "Why?"

"Because I think you're not being smart about your situation."

Oh God, I'm thinking, if he brings up (again) the prenup I happily signed, I'm leaving. "I think my situation is the best thing this family has going right now."

"Yes, yes, it's a very good thing but it could all go away tomorrow, unless you start thinking big."

"I have an infant and a brilliant but complicated husband who is running for political office. How much bigger am I supposed to be thinking?"

"You need things in your name. Real estate. Art. Valuables. A postnup. I'd be happy to have a conversation with Henry on your behalf."

"No." The word comes out of my mouth louder than I expected it to. "I'm not asking Henry for anything else. He's an incredibly generous man. We all know that." I say this in a tone that dares him to disagree so I can list all the gifts and perks my family has received since Henry and I got together.

"You're not asking for anything that women in your position don't get."

I feel the anger building and it's the worst kind of anger, mixed with hurt. I'm angry that he doesn't ever give me a break and I'm hurt that he thinks I'm not smart enough to run my life. "I don't care what other women get or don't get, ask for or don't ask for. I don't care!" I'm shouting now and my father is looking at me as if I'm crazy, unreasonable.

"I'm just saying you've got to think ahead so you don't find yourself in a situation where for a brief time, when you were still young, you lived like a queen."

He's speaking in a monotone as if trying to get through to a deranged child. If my mother were sitting here she'd say her usual, "He means well," and I do believe that. I have to believe that and I do feel guilty for losing my patience but I can't continue the conversation. "Sorry," I say. "It's my hormones. Since the baby, they're all screwed up. I've got to go find an aspirin." As I leave, my father takes a cigar out of his pocket and lights up. We both know this is only a pause in our tug-of-war.

My mother is holding Elizabeth while George takes photos of them with his iPhone.

"I spoke to Mary. They're stuck in traffic on the 405," he says as he snaps another shot. "You know she's bringing 'the boyfriend' with her and you know who else? Are you ready for this? Angela."

"Angela DeSoto?"

"She's temporarily moved back to L.A. Living out in Malibu."

Angela is an ex-model and an old friend of mine who spent a lot of time hanging out at our house when we were growing up. She lived in the neighborhood until she was sixteen, which was when she was discovered by a scout for Ford Models while shopping for Clinique cosmetics at the Galleria. Almost overnight she dropped out of school and moved to Paris. Her first cover, for *Elle* magazine, was on the newsstands four months later. She was an instant success but eventually got tired of the whole scene, had a few dramas and dropped out of the media spotlight. I haven't seen her in years.

"You know she's married to a big director now," George says. "That French guy who did that sci-fi thriller about vampires and angels." He hands me his cell phone so I can check out the shots he took of Elizabeth. "How cute is that one?"

"Very," I say, somewhat annoyed. Not by the photos, which are adorable, but because I thought this was just going to be a family lunch. Immediate family only. "I wish Mary had told me she was bringing guests."

"It's my birthday and she can bring anyone she likes," my mother says. "Anyway, I always liked Angela. She's lively. And I like Alex. He's a gentleman."

"You say that because you're a sucker for a British accent." George is teasing my mother but also getting his feelings across. He's no fan of Mary's new beau. George thinks Mary should be with someone who can, at the very least, help her pay her rent.

"He treats your sister with a lot of respect."

"Of course he does. He sucks up to the whole family. Sucking up is not actual respect. It just looks like it is."

My mother sighs and looks to me to resolve this.

"He seems like a nice guy," I say because I don't want to discuss the pluses and minuses of Alex and Mary. Do I think he's the right guy for her? No. They're living in a funky house up in Topanga with three dogs and a vegetable garden. If not for his posh British accent it would all be a little too rural for my taste. What am I saying? Even with the posh accent it's far too rural. Though that's not the main reason I don't think he's right for her. I think when you get right down to it, appearances aside, Mary is running away from a bigger life and Alex wants to run toward one. He may be going along with her bohemian lifestyle at the moment but I've seen him around Henry and I know he eyes that world and wants a piece of it.

I flip through more of the photos George took of Elizabeth. Cute, cute, cute and then . . . who is this? . . . followed quickly by . . . *what*? The fourth shot is one taken at another time and it's a smiling face I've seen before. It's the guy at George's wedding, the one I assumed was one of his old USC buddies. The fifth shot is the same guy but in this one, he's in some restaurant kitchen, cooking. That's when I put it together. This is Ethan, the gay guy that George was rumored to be involved with before he and Lacy got married.

George grabs the phone out of my hand, knowing what I'm thinking. "He's just an old friend."

"Who's an old friend?" my mother asks.

George and I exchange a look, a tacit agreement to go no further with this.

"Just some guy George went to college with," I say.

My mother lets that register and I know she's thinking the same thing I'm thinking and then she makes a move that reminds me of just how adept she is at getting life back on the track she needs it to be on.

"Well don't go trying to fix him up with Mary. Leave her be. She seems to be happy."

And with that the topic disappears as if it were nothing more than a piece of gossamer that my mother cleared away with a gentle sweep of her hand.

When George goes outside to keep my father company and share in the cigar-smoking ritual (though George hates cigars), my mother turns to me and says, "Now we can talk."

I'm thinking she's going to get into some neighborhood gossip but she shocks me when she says, "Postpartum depression." I look at her, wondering if she's getting a little too loopy. "What are you talking about? I'm not depressed."

"Howard women"—Howard is my mother's maiden name—"don't have the typical postpartum blues. We suffer in a different way."

"I'm not suffering."

My mother continues as if my denials are actually affirmations. "We marry men who are mesmerized by us as sex objects but men like that lose some of their ardor when their sex object has a baby. I've lived in this town a long time. I grew up in Beverly Hills. My father's firm had the biggest Hollywood clients. I know a little something about successful, powerful men and the appetites they have. Now I know you're not depressed because you had a baby. You love having Elizabeth. But you're concerned that having a baby has made you less alluring than you were before."

I'm hearing everything she's saying but I'm thinking did my mother just refer to her younger self as a sex object? And to me as one as well?

"I'm not a sex object."

"Hogwash. Mary got the body of a sex object and you got the brains of one. You're seductive as anyone . . . when you want to be."

My mother is definitely on her third glass and so the brakes are off.

"Well, if I'm as seductive as anyone then I've nothing to worry about."

"You will always have something to worry about with Henry."

"I've got it under control."

"Okay, good. I was just checking."

My mother is the queen of suggest and retreat. Her point made, she has no need to go further. She's leaving it to me to talk or walk. I look at Elizabeth, who is falling asleep on the couch right next to me. A little angel. I don't want her to grow up avoiding the truth, so I can't avoid it, either. I take the plunge.

"What does one do when they're suffering from Howard postpartum?"

"You find new ways to keep Henry engaged."

"Could you be more specific?"

"Absolutely not. I'm your mother. I'm not comfortable talking to you about the details of your sex life. Besides, you have to figure that part out for yourself. But I will tell you this: don't be lazy and do be naughty."

"What?"

"That's all I'm saying."

My mother's nonadvice advice makes me wonder what she was like in her younger years and how much my father has done to oppress her spirit since then. It also makes me think that when my parents almost got divorced when I was a kid, maybe there was more to my father's decision to end it with his new girlfriend and move back home than guilt and three children begging him to stay. Maybe my mother stopped crying long enough and got naughty enough to keep him nice.

Now that she got out what she wanted to say my mother is

anxious to leave that topic behind. She picks up a *People* magazine off the table. "Did you see this?" She opens it up to a picture of a fifty-year-old woman, Jayne Keller, who also once lived in the neighborhood and is now the star of a reality show along with her two daughters.

"You know how much she made last year? Thirty-five million dollars." My mother is apoplectic. "They'll pimp anything. Gum, lipstick, Tampax. They sign their name to any product. And that show . . . have you seen it? Guess privacy is a taboo for that family."

She keeps talking but all I'm hearing is that someone she once used to have mid-morning coffee with and talk to over the backyard fence is now making millions with her daughters. My mother claims to find it shameful but is she also suggesting that as this family's designated savior I'm slacking off?

A Jeep pulls into the driveway. Finally Mary has arrived. I open the front door to greet her . . . and her entourage. She steps out of the car carefully because she's carrying a cake box (I'm guessing carrot cake) and a bottle of champagne. Alex offers her his arm to lean on. Angela runs past them with big hugs for everyone. She's still gorgeous and still has that impulsive wild streak that made her a star and ultimately cost her that stardom.

My mother puts one arm around Mary and one arm around Angela as we go back inside. "Let's be a family," my mother says, as if one can decide to be one or not be one and it's a choice you renew every day. Maybe she's right about that or maybe it's the pinot grigio talking.

Chapter 29

Catherine

Catherine agreed to a 7 P.M. meeting with Carl Wolsey. Since Catherine didn't get up until noon, it felt like the middle of the day to her. Turns out it was the middle of the day for Carl as well. He said he'd been having trouble sleeping, too, but Catherine wasn't so sure that was his problem. Usually people with insomnia have some interest in possible remedies, but not Carl. When she tried to tell him about a new homeopathic cure he listened without interest, thanked her for the information and asked for a little more coffee. It's true that Carmen made the best coffee, made Starbucks seem like dishwater in comparison, but this was Carl's third cup and he'd only been there a half hour.

"I feel we should toast to the future," Catherine said, "but why waste champagne when you're washing it down with all that coffee."

Carl did his best to reply civilly, though he found Catherine's manner grating. "You got a point there. We can save that toast for when you get your first dividend check."

"I look forward to that." Catherine hoped that didn't sound too flirtatious. She was well aware that Carl had separated from his wife and she didn't want him to think she was one of those L.A. women who turn into a barracuda at the news of an available man on the market. She was devout when it came to her ongoing obsession with her ex-husband. She had channeled all her Catholic fervor into a state of near rapture when it came to Henry. Love or hate but always with fervor. That's why she was getting into business with Carl, giving him a chunk of her money to invest, with a promise of more to come when her divorce settlement was finalized. Though it was indisputable that Carl was "the" financial manager in town and having him was a status symbol, akin to walking around with an alligator Kelly bag, it was his proximity to Henry that sealed the deal and the fact that he was no friend of Anne. The enemy of Catherine's enemy was her ally. She was hoping she could eventually get information out of Carl, anything she could use against Anne or something that would, at the very least, make her feel better about herself. At this point she'd delight in hearing that Anne and Henry got into a disagreement over whether to dine on Chinese food or Italian.

"I've got some poppy seed cake Carmen made this afternoon. Would you like a piece?" Carl looked haggard and Catherine thought he could use a little attention. Maybe champagne wasn't the way to go but cake and tea would keep him hanging around. Or was he a steak guy? Carmen had one marinating for dinner.

"No, thanks. I've got to get going." He gathered up all the paperwork, now signed, her money now wired into his company's account.

But she wasn't letting him go so quickly. "Are you okay? I know you're going through a divorce and I know how hard that can be."

Carl understood that he had to humor her, at least for a few minutes. She had just given him a significant amount of her money to invest. "It's tough but I'm getting through it."

"And your wife?"

"We're both sad about it but . . ."

"But you left her, right?"

If only he could say this is none of your fucking business, but again, he thought of the money she had just given him and the promise of more. "I'll probably regret it. What if one of these days I wake up, come to my senses and realize I want her back but she's moved on?" He was no idiot. He knew this was exactly what she wanted to hear, exactly what all "first wives club" members want to hear.

"Speaking of coming to one's senses, how is my ex-husband doing?"

Carl was not about to betray Henry by talking behind his back. No amount of money could get him to do that. "You know Henry. He seems good but none of us will ever really know what he's thinking"

"Not even his new wife?"

Carl finished his coffee. He could feel the acid from three cups of caffeine burning his stomach. Maybe a piece of cake wasn't such a bad idea but he couldn't stay there and have a conversation that had no upside. "Anne," he said dismissively. As if to say anything more than the new wife's name was unnecessary between two people who saw eye to eye on the topic.

He checked his watch though he knew what time it was. The kitchen clock on the counter was digital and easy to read. "I've got another appointment I've got to get to and then hopefully get home early and get some sleep tonight."

"Sure you don't want some of this?" She held up a small bottle of pills. "My homeopathic insomnia cure?"

"Not right now, but I may be calling you about it in a few days if this goes on."

"I'll be calling you regardless." Catherine wanted to let him know that she wasn't one of those women who just handed over their money without being catered to. He might be a big-shot money manager, but she was still a woman from a prominent family and the father of her child was a king among men. She would always outrank Carl Wolsey.

She watched him drive off in his brand-new Ferrari. At least it was black. Male menopause, she thought. Divorces the wife, gets a sports car. For a second she wondered if this behavior wasn't unbecoming for the head of an investment fund and if signing on with a moneyman when he was having a second adolescence wasn't foolhardy. Yet just last week she was at a ladies' lunch and two of the women there, married to very successful men in the entertainment business, were bragging about how great Carl is, how his judgment is uncanny, always knowing which stocks and bonds to buy and when to sell. One rumor was that his marriage failed because the only thing he was really devoted to was making money. That was the only god he worshipped, the only loyalty he could sustain.

Once he was out of sight, Catherine, as was her custom, went outside and walked over to her security guard's van. He was waiting there, window down, a bit of a smirk on his face. He got a lot of self-esteem out of being able to break into locked cars and snoop around people's belongings.

"Find anything in the Ferrari?"

"The guy's a smoker and he also had a pack of condoms in the glove compartment."

Catherine frowned. Men devoted to their careers don't keep a supply of condoms in their car. "Is that all?"

"Yep."

She pulled something out of her pocket, handed it to him. It was a piece of poppy seed cake wrapped in a napkin. "Homemade."

"Thanks," he said.

As she walked away, he felt a little bad that he didn't mention one other thing he found in the glove compartment. Matches from a strip club on Ventura Boulevard. But hey, the man had tipped him twenty bucks for watching his car, making sure no one came near it. Besides, the poor guy looked exhausted and probably needed some R&R at a place where he wouldn't run into demanding clients like Catherine. At a certain point, the guard figured, no matter who you're working for, men got to stick together.

Chapter 30

Anne

Later I would explain that I knew long before I admitted to knowing but had talked myself out of the truth. Women do know when their guy is cheating on them, or contemplating cheating. I know that there's another woman in Henry's life, maybe more than one, though I don't know names or places. I know, but not because there are any obvious signs or clues . . . and I've looked. There are no phone numbers on scraps of paper or suspicious names added to his cell phone or anything unusual coming in to his email account. On the other hand, I don't have access to his office phones and for all I know he might have another secret BlackBerry. It's also possible that any one of his aides could be a go-between messenger. There's no way I can police Henry's life, nor do I really want to. I hate myself every time I check his Yahoo Mail in-box. If I wanted to stick to logic, the fact is that there's nothing major for me to worry about . . . yet. Henry and I still have a great sex life (now that I've taken my mother's advice and gotten even more adventurous), we don't argue and we still have a lot of laughs. But logic isn't as powerful as what I feel this evening when we're in the living room talking about what events and appointments we have scheduled for the next week. A message comes in on his phone and he checks it out with great interest.

"Everything okay?" I ask.

"Yeah, I'm just making sure I have all the information I need for tomorrow night."

He's referring to a political fund-raiser he's going to at the Sunset Tower Hotel. "Just a small group of businessmen" is how he'd explained it to me a week ago, which was his way of saying it isn't the kind of thing I need to attend. But he's reading that message and as the seconds turn into minutes, I'm thinking to myself, How much info does he need? The time of the event is pretty much the only fact required. It's not a big hotel and it's not a place that's hard to find or that we haven't been to dozens of times before. I can tell that he's pleased with whatever he's reading and now I'm really sure this isn't just a reminder about an appointment.

I get up and walk over to the glass doors and look out onto the garden and pool. It's a picture of perfection, a picture of order. Not a weed anywhere, not a fallen leaf to be found. There are also no toys or swing sets outside. We have all that for Elizabeth but it's on a piece of property that can't be seen from the house. Nothing in this room or anything that can be seen from this room would indicate that there's a child in this house. Thinking about that makes me realize that there's also nothing of me in this room. At this moment I feel very much like a guest. If I disappeared tomorrow nothing here would look any different. Nothing in this house would look any different except there'd be one big empty closet upstairs.

"That's a long message," I say. My slightly snarky tone doesn't keep Henry from staring at that cell screen and scrolling down as he continues reading an email that can't possibly be from his assistants.

They're all quite young and their version of a message is nothing more than twenty-five letters. Brevity is their lifestyle.

"Just a sec," he says . . . as he continues reading and I continue to wait, telling myself the real test will come when he gets to the end. Does he save or delete? If he deletes then I know he's guilty of something. I'm standing behind him now and with the light from the lamp next to his chair I have a clear view of his phone keyboard. Finally he's done and I watch his fingers very carefully. One click means he's saving the message; two means he's deleting. He clicks twice.

We go upstairs and fuck and have a good time. I don't mention a thing about my suspicions but he senses something is bothering me. He doesn't ask me what it is right away. That's not his style. Instead he changes my mood by surprising me. That's one of the things he's smart about. Like a parent who always keeps a few new toys hidden away in case they should someday need a treat to soothe an especially upset child, Henry always has a few surprises he can pull out to make sure I keep my suspicions to myself.

"I forgot to tell you what I did today," he said. "I made a deal with Leo de Vince to do a painting of you."

"Of me?" I'm speechless. Leo de Vince is not only the painter that everyone considers a genius; he almost never does portraits by commission.

"It wasn't easy," Henry adds just in case I'm not aware of how monumental this is.

I jump into his arms because this is proof of his love. I do a mental accounting. Let's see, on one side Henry wants Leo de Vince to immortalize me in a painting. On the other side is my worry that some girl might be sending him a flirty message. I choose to focus on the painting though I'm not delusional. I do know that this doesn't mean I'm safe or spared an ambush in my future but

Henry wouldn't hire Leo de Vince to do a painting of me if he wasn't committed to this relationship. What man would want a very expensive painting of an ex-wife around? The thought of the cost of this surprise brings another issue to mind. There's no question that a Leo de Vince painting is a major asset and one that I don't think I'm entitled to if we should split up. That prenup I signed was a motherfucker.

Right before I'm about to fall asleep, Henry says, "Everything okay, baby? You seemed so pensive earlier."

"Pensive. Yes, I guess I was."

"About what?"

God, he's good, I think. He knows that he can ask this question now because there's no way I'm going to bring up anything that will ruin the serenity of the moment. "I was just thinking about Carl Wolsey. Something seems very off about him lately."

"That's what you were thinking about?"

"Yes."

"Carl? You were thinking about Carl?"

"Yes," I lie.

Henry laughs. "There are a lot of things to contemplate in this life. Carl is not one of them."

"Anyway, now I have more important things to worry about," I say.

"Like what?"

"Like what do I wear for my portrait?"

Chapter 31

Theresa

Theresa associated Beverly Glen with Anne. She sometimes referred to the Glen as the crime scene because the second Cliff pointed Anne out as Henry's new girl was also the second Theresa came under attack. This according to her therapist, who told her that Anne's negative energy was like an airborne virus that could only be resisted by a strong psychological immune system. And just what did that mean? It meant no guilt about destroying this virus.

Theresa thought about all this as she searched for a parking spot. It was noon and the lot at the Glen was often full by then. Today it was jammed; even the valets had stopped taking any more cars. She drove around and around, hoping to get lucky since she was in no mood to park on the street. She spotted Anne's car in a spot right next to the sushi restaurant where they were meeting. Of course, she got the best spot, Theresa thought. The astrological forces are still on her side. Theresa had recently checked in with her astrologer and was told that she needed to hold on a while longer and that Anne's

Saturn would soon be in a harsh angle to Pluto in her tenth house of career and prestige. It was an opposition that spelled trouble. Finally, Theresa thought, I'll get a break.

She slowed down when she thought there was an empty spot up ahead but damn, it wasn't empty. A motorcycle was parked there. The guy getting off it was in his twenties, wearing jeans and a leather jacket, eyes hidden behind sunglasses. He was carrying his helmet as if it were a trophy. Seeing him in all his young, cocky glory made her feel old. She kept driving.

Up ahead a Volvo was pulling out of a space. Theresa hit the accelerator but an aggressive driver in a Prius snagged it. Theresa was about to lean on her horn and scream at the hybrid-loving, space-robbing bitch but "held on" and calmed herself down with this thought: Okay, I'll park on the fucking street but with every step I take I'll remind myself that the clock is ticking and the universe has better days in store for me . . . and worse ones in store for Anne. It was a good plan but, in fact, that's not what she thought about with every step because she was wearing very high heels so as not to feel small around Anne, and she could already feel the blisters forming as she trudged up the hill to the restaurant.

They ordered sushi. Anne went for vegetarian rolls . . . cucumber and avocado, which irked Theresa. Who orders vegetarian sushi when there are all those yummy items on the menu: crab rolls, spicy tuna rolls, yellowtail. It struck Theresa as overly competitive. Was Anne flaunting her steely resolve?

The two women kept things friendly and got down to business. Anne had suggested they meet to discuss Carl Wolsey. Theresa had been doing her homework and she and Anne traded information in a subtle game of one-upmanship.

Anne led, sharing her concern about the unusually high percentage her father was getting from his investments with Carl.

Anne had done a little investigating, comparing these earnings to other financial firms'. Though Carl's numbers weren't as off the charts as Madoff's had been, it appeared that Wolsey was either a fraud or a genius.

Theresa listened with great interest, not yet ready to reveal the ace in her pocket. Instead she shared the gossip she'd heard about Carl dating Kim.

"Kim?" Anne was confused.

"Kim, Larissa's friend. Fake red hair. Fake tits. We met her at Soho House."

"She's Carl's girlfriend?"

"It happens," Theresa said. "I've seen it happen before. There's a certain kind of man who is all about work and money and power. For years he gets up at five A.M., works hard, is focused because all he really wants is the respect of his male peers. Then he gets in his forties and he's bored with his wife of fifteen years and some young woman comes into his life and gives him the kind of blow job he never knew existed and suddenly all he can think about is sex with his new hottie. He loses his ability to compartmentalize. Everything becomes about her and getting more of her—whatever that takes, and usually it takes a lot of money. I know one guy who spent hundreds of thousands of dollars trying to launch his girlfriend's singing career. Another who invested in his girlfriend's bathing suit line . . . because that's what the world needs, more bathing suits that look just like all the other ones that are already on the market."

Anne was impressed. Theresa had nailed it. One good piece of analysis deserved another so she confided about the screwups Carl had recently been guilty of on her end. Screwups with money that was supposed to be wired into her account from Henry's dividend checks but mysteriously went missing. She'd call Carl and he'd apologize, blame it on one of his underlings, fix it immediately and then it would happen again a week later.

"You know," Anne said, "I have a theory about these screwups.

Now that I know about Kim, I'm thinking maybe it's impossible to have a conventional job and an unconventional relationship. Or an unconventional job and a conventional relationship. For years Carl was in sync. He had a conventional job that required him to go to the office every day and he had a conventional marriage to a stay-at-home wife who made sure his suits were pressed and his dinner was always on the table when he got home. That's not Kim's world. She's out partying late and when she shows up at his door at one A.M. wanting to have some fun, she doesn't care that he has to get up at five and function in a conventional world. And he's going to let her in and pay the price for it later."

The two women were practically head-to-head as they gossiped and shared notes and enjoyed, for the moment, being on the same side. That fleeting alliance was interrupted by Anne's cell phone beep—email message. When Anne saw who it was from she opened it and read it with great interest. As Theresa waited patiently for Anne to type in a rather long reply, she noticed that Anne's skin looked amazing. That's always the thing that happens with Henry's girls, Theresa realized. They get more beautiful because suddenly they have the money for the best skin care treatments and best beauty products. Their pores disappear. That's what money buys . . . pore-free skin.

"Sorry about that," Anne said, putting her phone back down on the table. "I had to get back to that person right away."

That "person," whoever it was, changed Anne's mood. Suddenly she had a cat-ate-the-canary smile on her face and instead of enjoying the deconstruction of Carl Wolsey, she was now anxious to wrap things up. "Look, I had this thought last night. I think you should talk to Henry about Carl. Tell him everything we've been talking about lately. I think it's better if it comes from you."

Theresa was getting very good at reading the dance moves in the Henry and Anne relationship and she knew what this two-step was all about. Anne wanted Theresa to talk to Henry about this because for Anne to do so might make it seem as if Henry wasn't on top of the situation. Even said sweetly it wouldn't land right. What Henry would hear is his wife saying, "I know you're the king and all but you're slipping a little 'cause you're putting your trust in a guy who is slipping." It could come across as ball-busting. It wasn't that Anne was shy about expressing her opinion. She was known for speaking out, but never when it called into question Henry's ability to rule his own kingdom.

"Of course, darling, whatever you want." Theresa was still fingering that ace in her pocket. "But let me ask you something. What are you worried about?"

Anne already had her car keys in hand. "Well a lot of things, including that the last thing Henry needs before his campaign kicks into gear is someone screwing up his investments, and now that you've told me about Carl and Kim who knows where this will lead. Does Henry need his financial wizard to be involved in some scandal? Carl and his L.A. party girl getting busted for a DUI? Will Kim sell her story to some tabloid? Will TMZ start shooting video of them stumbling out of clubs? All possible."

Just then Theresa noticed that the guy with the motorcycle, the one she'd seen in the parking lot, was paying his check. Up close and with his sunglasses off, she realized she recognized him. As he passed the table where Anne and Theresa sat, he gave them a big, beautiful smile. "Hello, ladies."

As he continued on his way, Anne laughed, a laugh full of delight.

"I know that guy," Theresa said. "He parks cars."

"And writes songs."

"Do you know him?"

"I've run into him."

"What's his name?"

"Wyatt."

"Good name for a musician."

"Good name for anything."

Anne seemed quite pleased with herself, as if somehow the joke was on Theresa. Problem was, Theresa was in no mood for jokes. The "queen's" giggly innuendo hit a raw nerve that touched on memories that took Theresa all the way back to her childhood in Boston's tenement slums. She didn't work hard all these years, make the sacrifices she made so she could still feel like the outsider who just doesn't get it. It was time for her to put her ace on the table and wipe that look of self-satisfaction off Anne's face.

"Getting back to the Carl problem, don't worry about a thing. Henry is well aware of the situation and he's got it under control. In fact it's taken care of." It was a statement that was sort of true. Henry had been keeping closer tabs on Carl and did say he was going to make some changes but Theresa didn't know how, what or when. The point was she knew more than Anne did and that had never happened before.

"Taken care of? How?"

"Henry will explain. I'm sure he just hasn't gotten around to it yet."

"Oh, okay." Anne was taken aback. There was no hiding it. She didn't like it when Theresa had information that she should have had first. Though Anne had a dozen questions she wanted to ask, her pride prevented her from probing further. "Well then good," she said, regaining her composure. "Problem solved."

The two women smiled at each other but had they been liberated from all pretense and free to speak the truth, Theresa would gloat over the fact that Anne's husband confides in her and Anne would remind Theresa that beating someone across the finish line in a practice session doesn't make one a winner.

"Got to get going. Let's talk soon," Anne said, keeping her curiosity in check.

Discipline and pride, Theresa thought. All "royals" needed both but if they had too much of the latter . . . bad things could happen. Being a "civilian," Theresa didn't have to get the balance perfect every time and right now she didn't mind throwing pride out the window. "Quick question for you, Anne. What kind of moisturizer are you using? You must tell me. I'm desperate for some help in this area."

By the time Theresa got back to her car, she had a bloody callus on her foot. The second she got inside her Lexus she took off her high heels and reached around to the floor of the backseat for the pair of flats she always kept there. As she did, a car drove by and she got a good look at the driver. It was Jake Winslow, Hollywood's notorious private detective. She recalled that that car, or one very similar, had been behind her when she arrived. She flashed back to Jake lurking around her house the night of her party. Coincidence? Maybe. Maybe not. She picked up her cell phone and speed-dialed Cliff. Without saying hello, she got to the point.

"I need you to do something for me. I need you to call Jake Winslow."

Chapter 32

Anne

I pull up behind the motorcycle and walk the steep steps up to the front door to his tiny house. I didn't plan on showing up at Wyatt's but I'm not ready to go home and I don't want to be alone with my thoughts. When Wyatt sent me that message while I was sitting there with Theresa it was like I'd been offered a cool drink in between rounds of a psychological boxing match. It was a simple message and an invitation to take a break. "Now that you're in my neighborhood, come on over and visit. I'll be waiting."

And he is . . . waiting at the front door.

"It's not a palace, but it's a home," Wyatt says as he shows me around.

He lives in one of those tiny canyon houses off a narrow lane (it can hardly be called a road) that's very picturesque unless it rains and that lane turns into a river of mud. The inside is comfortable and clean but messy.

"It's sweet," I say.

"Too sweet? I was actually thinking of getting rid of all the junk and going minimalist. But if you're going to do that, whatever minimal you're left with better look good. I realized this place needs clutter so you don't notice how everything's falling apart."

He hands me a cold beer, which suits the moment. Champagne, wine or sake just wouldn't fit the mood. I check out his stuff: guitar collection, vinyl collection, books everywhere. "There's no way you're a minimalist guy."

"I'm very adaptable," he says.

"I can tell. Excellent Russian vodka out of a flask one day, good old cold American beer on another. You got range."

I keep looking around, fascinated by how he lives. So different from Henry's world. My *second* closet is as big as his living room . . . and dining area.

He also has an interesting collection of framed photographs of rock-and-roll legends: Bob Marley at the Roxy in the seventies, Sting backstage in New York in the nineties.

Twang. Wyatt has picked up one of his guitars and is tuning it. "Now I can finally sing that song for you. Just one thing you should know: I wrote it for you."

I spend two hours there listening to music. The song he wrote for me is no "Layla" but it's a good song, one that any girl would be pleased to have written about her. Every tune he sings shows talent and I find myself appreciating his voice and mind a lot more than I expected to.

"Hey, I thought you were going to send this CD to me. I never got it."

"Every day I kept saying I got to send this to Anne, but something always stopped me. I think it was the thought that if I sent it and never heard from you I'd get so depressed I wouldn't be able to function."

"I thought songwriters did their best work when they're suffering."

"Some do. I'm not one of them." He puts his guitar down, takes my hand, pulls me next to him on the couch.

"I'm not going to fuck you," I say.

"I didn't invite you over for that. We're just hanging out getting to know each other."

"What I mean is I'm not going to do it today, tomorrow, next week, next month or ever."

"I get it," he says. "Whatever you want."

"Whatever I want?"

"Just say it."

"I want to relax and not worry about anything."

"Nothing to worry about when you're here with me."

It sounds like a corny line in some country song and that's just fine with me.

It has been a gray, overcast day but over the next couple of hours the sun breaks through and though the wind has picked up, there's something about this cabin tucked high up in the canyon that makes me feel like I'm in a magical tree house. I feel above all the craziness that's happening down on the streets and boulevards. We lie on opposite sides of the couch, our legs entangled but not in any kind of sexual way, listening to an eclectic mix of music: Raphael Saadiq, some jazz and some Beatles classics. It feels almost too right. I could easily drift off to sleep right here in this cluttered room next to my poet/songwriter/music man . . . which is exactly why I know I have to leave.

I jump up. "As nice as this is . . . I can't stay any longer."

"Now you know how to find me," he says as he walks me to the door. "Anytime you want, you're always welcome."

"Thanks," I say. We kiss goodbye . . . on the lips. Though it's a quick kiss, it's not an innocent one. I could do a whole hour on the various kinds of kisses and what each one means. Wyatt and I could write a whole song about it but now that I've stepped out of the cocoon of my music man's world, I have to step back into Tudor-land and there's no place in that world for cute lyrics about kissing a poor singer-songwriter.

When I get to the bottom of Wyatt's road and head up the hill toward Mulholland, I'm back in cell phone range and my phone starts beeping like crazy. Lots of messages have come in over the last two hours. I pull over to the side of the road when I see that three are from Henry. He never calls me three times right in a row. Ever. Is it possible that he knows where I am, what I'm doing and whom I'm with?

I'm shaking as I check voice mail and I'm still shaking after I find out that the first two messages were dropped calls. His cell phone glitch, not mine. The third message is to tell me that Leo de Vince called and wants to know if I can come to his studio sometime in the next two weeks so he can do some sketches. I call Henry back immediately and say, "Yes, of course, whatever works for Leo's schedule, I'll be there."

I'm so relieved I forget to ask if he knows Carl Wolsey is seeing a friend of Larissa's. A loaded question because it puts Larissa three degrees away from Henry even if they're no longer in touch . . . which is a big if. Fear. Relief. Panic. Excitement. My mood is all over the place these days. What's going on with me? Either I'm not as good as I thought I'd be at a royal life . . . or . . . could it be . . . I'm pregnant again.

Chapter 33

Cliff

As if Cliff didn't have enough to do, trying to keep the *Daily* website lucrative, pulling in those advertising dollars and at the same time trying to get something going on the side. Right now he was obsessing over a new business idea, selling compost pails, a device that turns household garbage into fertilizer for your garden. "You never know when something like this could take off, especially in California." That was his pitch to his wife, when, earlier that week, she'd quizzed him about why he spent so much time on "garbage" and she meant it in more ways than one.

As Cliff sat at the bar at the Kat Klub, a strip joint on Ventura Boulevard, he thought about all the things he should have said to his wife. Why couldn't he have put it to her firmly and decisively? He wished he'd pointed out that in a slow economy you always have to be on the lookout for new opportunities. You have to have skin in some game somewhere. His Web job wasn't ever going to be their ticket out of debt and he wasn't going to sit around and hope someone offered him an acting job after all these years. He didn't say any of that because he and his wife were getting along better precisely because they were both getting better at letting things slide—though that garbage comment was a step back. Saying less had translated into getting more . . . more peace, more quiet and more (though not a lot) sex.

Besides, standing up to her would have been exhausting. Although he had to admit that not standing up to her was also exhausting. Lately everything was exhausting. Was this a sign of the times or something that happens after forty? It used to be he could have a regular job, a side job, a relationship, a hobby and still fit in regular workouts at the gym with energy to spare. Now it was only eight o'clock and all he wanted was to be home, crashed out on the couch, watching a basketball game with his son. But how could Cliff say no to Theresa even though she was taking advantage of his good nature? He really needed to hold on to this job. Last week he panicked when Theresa had complained about all the articles he was running on the environment. "*Bor*ing," she said. Cliff's contract was a short-term one and the option to renew was all her call. He promised her he was backing off on the green news and Lacy would be doing more blogs about relationships and marriage and hopefully he'd convinced her to do a gossip column using a pseudonym, which should get a lot of buzz. "Don't use that word *buzz*," Theresa said. "Buzz is *bor*ing. Find another word."

Since it was easier to find another word than another job, he agreed. Every so often he would think, Fuck it, let her fire me. I can find something else. But then he'd be at Starbucks and look around at all the out-of-work journalists and editors, some of them brilliant with illustrious credits. There they'd be, shoulders hunched over their laptops, on their second refill of coffee, desperately waiting for some important email that never came. Every so often he'd get into a conversation with one of them and inevitably they'd talk about some freelance assignment they were pitching or actually doing and they'd have a hungry look in their eye, hoping one of their articles or ideas would get optioned for a TV series but as weeks and months went by, he'd find them at Starbucks, still waiting, hope ebbing out of them with every caffe latte. Cliff knew he could end up being one of those guys . . . but with even fewer options. Those guys were actual journalists, professional writers. He was just an ex-actor turned environmentalist who was good at following orders. This is why he had to have something else cooking . . . even if it was as far-fetched as a compost pail. Why didn't his wife understand that? People made millions on offbeat ideas. This was California. Offbeat was the rule here, not the exception.

Cliff looked around the Klub and had to admit this place wasn't what he expected. The interior was more upscale and the customers weren't weirdos. The bartender explained it was Burlesque Night. Once a month a group of professional dancers, who called themselves "The B-Dolls," put on a show and drew in a high-end crowd from the other side of the hill. Cliff could never understand the appeal of entertainment establishments along Ventura Boulevard. Every so often a restaurant or club would open up in the Valley and people would talk about it as if it was something worth checking out but at the end of the day, at best, it was a place offering good food or maybe a good show, but couldn't shake off the second-rate vibe of the Valley. Glamour didn't stick here. No matter the effort, money and taste put into anything on this side of the hill, it always ended up feeling overdone or underdone. As did this place. The dark leather booths, the well-appointed bar, the pricey lighting fixtures, the framed Vargas prints . . . on the other side of the hill it could be a VIP hangout where a glass of house wine cost twenty-five bucks. Here it just felt garish and overpriced.

Cliff ordered a Coke with ice and then ordered another. He needed the caffeine and the sugar and it was working. He was starting to feel as if he could actually focus on something for more than a minute. He noticed someone had left a magazine on the bar stool next to his . . . and Anne was on the cover with a caption that read, "Meet California's New Royalty." The photo was done in a tongue-in-cheek style with Anne standing on Mulholland Drive, a panoramic view of L.A. in the background. She was wearing jeans and an "I Love California" T-shirt. She had a tiara on her head and diamonds on her fingers.

"That's someone's magazine," the bartender said.

Cliff quickly put it down. "Sorry." It was only then that he realized the bartender was wearing a vest and nothing underneath.

"I'm kidding," she said. "I put that there to save the seat."

"This seat is saved? Then I'm going to need to get a table because I'm meeting someone." He looked around the room but there wasn't a vacant one in sight.

"You're fine. You're meeting Jake Winslow. I know."

"How did you know?"

"He called earlier, reserved two seats at the bar. Left your name. I recognized you from that sitcom you did back in the early nineties. Loved that show."

"You're one of the few. It didn't even last one season."

"So you had your one season there and then went on to another interesting experience. That's not so bad."

"That's one way of looking at it," Cliff said, thinking this girl is still young enough to optimistically think life is just a series of interesting experiences.

As the bartender helped other customers, Cliff checked out the crowd, surprised to see a couple of up-and-coming agents and studio executives in the mix. He noticed they were all wearing business suits and drinking bottled water. This was the new breed of professional, not his generation. This crop approached their careers like they were in training to be marines. It was all about who could work the hardest, be the strongest. The one with the fewest vices wins. Cliff concluded that they must be there for business. Maybe the B-Dolls had just signed with a big agency or were trying to. A bidding war? It's not like these Hollywood "marines" were here looking for dates. These guys, if they were straight and looking to climb Hollywood's power ladder, only dated three types of girls. Established celebrities, who gave them job security. Rich girls, who gave them financial stability. Or A-list models, who boosted their image and gave them good genes for their future progeny.

Looking up at the large mirror above the bar, Cliff noticed a man at a corner table who was a doppelganger for Carl Wolsey. He was surrounded by a few women, who were showering him with attention and listening to his every word as if he had the inside information on the fountain of youth. One in particular, a redhead, looked like she'd do him right there if he was up for it. It wasn't until Cliff took a closer look that he realized it was actually Carl. What a shock. He'd transformed himself from a risk manager into a risk taker. Or so it seemed. Maybe this was just Carl blowing off some steam in his after-hours life but still it was startling, like seeing a cardinal cavorting at the Playboy Mansion.

"Cliff?"

Jake took his seat on the bar stool that had been reserved for him.

"How'd you know it was me?" Cliff was joking.

"Not hard to figure it out. You're the only one here wearing seersucker."

The bartender put a drink in front of Jake. His usual. Chopin vodka martini, two olives.

"Guess you're a regular," Cliff said.

"We all have our territory, don't we?" Jake took a sip of his drink. Chilled to perfection. "So what can I do for you? Domestic issue? My company handles a lot of that but I'm not personally doing much of that anymore."

"No, nothing like that."

"So what's your problem?"

Jake wasn't going to go for any small talk and that was okay with Cliff. If he got this over with fast, he could get back in time to see the fourth quarter of the Lakers game. "I'm here on behalf of Theresa Cromwell. You know who that is, right?"

"I know who she is. What's her problem?"

"She'd like to know if you're following her."

"Who said I'm following her?"

"Maybe you're not. That's what I'm here to find out."

"Now if I were following her, why would I tell you that?" Jake's voice dropped in volume and he spoke calmly, which actually made him seem more menacing.

"Because Theresa's not a bad person to have on your side. She always returns favors."

"You mean Henry's not a bad person to have on my side."

"Well, yes, she does work very closely with him."

Two of the B-Dolls, working the room before the show, squeezed through the crowd at the bar, one of them brushing against Cliff's arm and almost dislodging his glass from his hand. His quick reflexes saved the day and she smiled at him but it wasn't her smile that captivated Cliff. In true burlesque style the corset she was wearing pushed her firm tits up so high he could have balanced that glass right on them. When he finally turned back to Jake the detective had an amused look on his face.

Cliff felt himself blushing. "It's just that . . ."

"I get it," Jake replied, not needing an explanation, but Cliff felt compelled to give one anyway.

"I forget what a twenty-two-year-old body looks like up close."

"Want me to introduce you to some of the girls?"

"Uh, no . . . thanks."

Jake waved to another sexy B-Doll across the room. "Look, Cliff, I'm not following Theresa."

"Good. I'm glad to hear it because she's a very private person."

"Is that right?" A smile on Jake's face made Cliff uneasy, as if the detective knew more than he should. "Privacy doesn't exist anymore, Cliff. You know how easy it would be to find out stuff about you."

"What kind of stuff?"

"Anything and everything."

"How much have you already looked up about me?"

"I know you were a cheerleader in high school."

"I was just the megaphone guy," Cliff replied defensively.

"Hey, I don't care if you walked around with a pom-pom sticking out of your ass. I'm just telling you, privacy . . . gone. Secrets, impossible to keep for long."

The B-Doll Jake had waved to now sidled up to him and provocatively grabbed his leg. "You better be here after the show."

"I'm planning on it."

As Jake and his hottie firmed up their late-night plans, Cliff couldn't stop staring at all that nubile flesh around him. Their stomachs so flat, their tits so perky, their delicate tattoos so sexy. Tiny stars. Buttercups. Hearts. Truth is, he would be even more aroused if women like this didn't scare him. It had been his experience that unless you're rich or famous, you're not going to get these girls. And even if he splurged and paid for some version of this, even if he hired a hooker who looked and acted like one of these girls, he wasn't sure he could deliver what they were used to. Jake may not have millions but he had the bad-boy thing going for him, a bad boy who would protect them if they ever got in trouble. Cliff couldn't compete with that and at this point didn't want to. For him it was no longer about finding women who were hot; he wanted a woman to find him hot, which his wife still did when she wasn't annoyed with him for talking garbage.

When Jake's B-Doll sashayed away, the detective turned back to Cliff. "We done here?"

"So it was a coincidence that you and Theresa crossed paths?"

"Call it whatever you want."

Cliff was not about to call it anything that might piss off Jake, as it appeared the detective was one of those guys who had mastered the art of being threatening with minimum movement and barely speaking over a whisper.

"Okay, we're all good then." Cliff put money down for his drinks.

Jake pushed it back at him. "They're already on my tab."

"Thanks."

"Sure you don't want to stick around? These girls are smarter than they look."

"I appreciate the offer," Cliff said, "but after a while you lose your appetite for what you're never going to have." He wanted to sound self-deprecating. That was his survival trick. Flatter women, be self-deprecating around powerful men, which included men who could take you in a fight.

Jake shook his head. "If that were true the high-end porno business wouldn't be making millions."

Outside the club, Cliff headed down the block to where he'd parked his car to avoid the seven-dollar valet parking charge. Halfway there he saw a girl, on her cell phone, singing, doing her best Marilyn Monroe.

> *Happy birthday to you.*
> *Happy birthday to you.*
> *Happy birthday, Mr. Governor.*

She giggled before finishing up with

> *Happy birthday to you.*

Then she giggled some more and started talking excitedly. "I know, I know, but someday you will be. I'll get all my friends to vote for you."

It was Larissa. She was surprised but not upset that Cliff might have overheard her. She said goodbye to the birthday boy and came running over to Cliff and gave him a kiss like they were long-lost friends. "What are you doing around here?"

"I had a meeting with someone at the Kat Klub."

"And you're leaving? You've got to stay and see the show. The B-Dolls are fab. Want to join our table? I'm meeting my friend Kim and her new boyfriend. You might know him? Carl Wolsey."

"I know who he is but I've got to get home. Nice to see you. You look great."

"I'm very happy." Very happy. She was inviting him to probe further.

"Got a part in some new movie? TV pilot?"

"No, but I'm happy, happy, happy. And though I can't talk about why, it's all good."

It was like she was begging Cliff to guess and he had a pretty good idea why.

"Good for you," he said. What else could he say?

She gave him another kiss on the cheek. "Sorry you can't stay but go home to your lucky wife."

Now Cliff was sure. No question about it. When a party girl like Larissa refers to his wife as lucky that can only mean one thing. It means her generosity of spirit is in overdrive and there's only one thing that got Larissa in overdrive: Henry.

When Cliff got in his car, he took out his cell and went online to the Wikipedia website. Was it Henry's birthday today? It sure was.

Chapter 34

Anne

I now know how to do my face. I'm practically a pro with the mascara brush and the lip pencil. I know how to create a mask of artificial beauty with just a few subtle tricks. It's something I forced myself to learn because I want Henry to be proud to be seen with me and more importantly because every famous person, or person involved with a famous person, needs a mask. People will always be looking to see the cracks in your emotional armor and I'm not about to give them that satisfaction.

When I show up at Leo de Vince's studio, I'm confident he won't detect the agony I'm in as long as he doesn't look too closely into my eyes. If he does and detects sadness, I have an excuse. It's raining and has been for six days. That's biblical by L.A. standards. The whole city is sad when we are subjected to almost a week of gray skies. We're a city of addicts, jonesing for our sun fix. Where is it? It's part of the contract. We put up with earthquakes because we get the sun. Six days of rain is five too many.

It's a decent excuse and one that I prepared in the car because the true story is the last thing I'll reveal to a stranger, even if that stranger is a genius and probably would have great advice. I'm not about to divulge that a week ago I had a miscarriage. I was barely pregnant and so Henry didn't rush to my side. He did wonder if it was a boy. He didn't ask why it happened. He didn't consult with my doctor. He did have his assistant reschedule my appointment with Leo for the following week and he did offer to send me to a spa to help me recuperate.

"Henry," I said, "you don't go to a spa to get better when you're ailing. You go to a spa when you're feeling good so you can feel even better. It's like the difference between drinking when you're sad versus drinking when you're happy."

"Are you sad?'

"Disappointed but I'll be fine."

"I know you will be. You're strong."

When, I wondered, did strong go from being a compliment to being a justification for him to walk out the door?

The first time I lay eyes on Leo it's through the dark lenses of my oversized Gucci glasses. He greets me at the door to his oceanfront studio looking every bit the grand artist. He's wearing loose olive-green cotton pants and a black T-shirt. Clothes comfortable to paint in. He has piercing green eyes and a lot of hair for a man his age. It's thick and gray, not white. He has an aura about him and a confidence that probably comes with knowing he sees clearer than most people and can translate what he sees into something that puts people in a state of awe.

He leads me into his work area, a loft space filled with works in progress. Everywhere I look there are paintings and sketches on large and small pieces of paper: sketches of the human body, male and female, hundreds of drawings of hands, more of torsos. There are also a handful of paintings of familiar faces. One of Dennis Hopper, another of a teenage Leonardo DiCaprio. At the other end of the large room is a sitting area, a couple of chairs around a coffee table upon which is a pitcher of water, two glasses and a bowl of guavas.

Leo comments on the color of the dress I'm wearing. It's sapphire blue, the same blue as the stone in the first ring Henry ever gave me. Reluctantly I take off my Gucci shades because there's only so long you can wear sunglasses indoors. The only person who has ever gotten away with that is Jack Nicholson and I'm no Jack Nicholson. Leo points to a chair near the window and I'm happy to see it's a comfortable one. I don't have the strength or posture to pull off an armless or straight-backed wooden chair.

"I've never had my portrait done before. How do we go about this?"

"I'm going to make some sketches, maybe take some photos. Mostly I just want to get a sense of you." He is already sketching something on his drawing pad.

"Oh God, anything but that," I say. "A sense of me? Can you use someone else's sense and attach it to my portrait?" I'm joking. Sort of.

Leo gets the joke and gets that it's not a joke. "Missing anonymity? Craving privacy?"

"I did spend an hour trying to get off LinkedIn this morning. Got off Facebook last week. Well I tried to. They don't let you off those sites so easily."

Leo picks up a camera and takes some shots. "They own you forever now. Own all of us. My new definition of bliss is wiping all traces of myself off the Internet."

"How do you do that?"

"One delete at a time."

We spend the next half hour saying very little. I expected that. He works with a high degree of concentration and isn't the type to fill up the pauses with small talk and I'm fine with the silence. My entertainment is looking out the window at the ocean. Whenever I'm down at the beach I wonder why I don't get down here more often. There's something so soothing about just looking at the magnificent Pacific. It puts me in a very contemplative mood and I let my thoughts flow, which is like a vacation for me. No matter what comes to mind eventually all thoughts and images lead back to Henry. The more I think about him the more it becomes obvious that something is seriously not right with us. The other day when I walked into his office at home, he didn't acknowledge me. He was reading a financial report and for twenty minutes didn't look up once. There was a time when nothing would have kept Henry from looking up the second I arrived. Nothing would have stopped him from giving me his undivided attention. When he finally tore himself away from his reading I made a comment about his impressive level of concentration and he tossed off a token apology. I let it go because my father has always impressed upon me the importance of not making the same mistakes the women who preceded me made. Even now I can hear his voice reminding me "there's a fine line between getting the respect you deserve and being a nag."

As I sit there, posing, I can feel my body temperature rising and that pitcher of water on the table is looking awfully appealing but I decide to sit still just awhile longer because I don't want to interrupt Leo's focus and because a thought is beginning to take form and it's such a potentially explosive one that I want to examine it carefully. I recall various times over the last week when Henry brought up my appointment with Leo, making sure he knew the exact time and day. He also, now that I think of it, has been much more interested than usual in my schedule in general. I think about another small but unsettling incident. He was late for the birthday dinner I planned for him, and he explained his tardiness by saying he had to have a drink with a campaign donor. But now that I think of it he never did mention the donor's name.

And the other evening when I went out to his car to see if I'd left my phone in there, it was locked. Henry never locks his cars. Why would he? His very private property is behind secure gates and we have around-the-clock security. Even more telling is how the staff has acted toward me recently. "Are you okay, Anne?" It's a question I've heard more often than seems necessary. I thought it had to do with my miscarriage but now when I replay it in my brain there's more pity in their questioning than concern for my health. As the list of incidents grows, I reach a point where there is only one conclusion: Henry is seeing another woman . . . and seeing her this very moment when he knows that I'm detained at Leo de Vince's studio *all afternoon*. There is every reason to believe that at this very moment he's in bed with this woman . . . possibly even . . . *in our bed*.

My impulse is to make my excuses, get out of there and drive as fast as possible back home. I remember Mary once told me about coming home to Henry and finding a half-naked girl hiding in the pool house. Yet as much as I'd love to confront Henry and his afternoon delight, I don't move a muscle. I talk myself into inaction by reminding myself that I gain nothing by acting impulsively. I remind myself that extraordinary things don't happen to those who react in an ordinary fashion. I reach down, deep and deeper still, even though I feel imprisoned by my circumstances. At least at this point I'm a voluntary prisoner.

I'm not perfect, though. I can't completely shut down my emotional responses. My temperature rises even more and I feel the heat building and building on the back of my neck. To keep myself from dwelling on the image of Henry getting blown by some love-struck intern who works at his office or by Larissa or by another girl just like Larissa, I start babbling about Henry's family crest and my family's motto, not that Leo is at all interested. That doesn't stop me. I try to engage his attention by explaining that the Boleyns' motto is "to always do what will make you happy, not what will make you happy this minute." I explain how my father has interpreted that to mean that our salvation lies in delayed gratification.

Leo puts down his sketchpad. "Are you okay, Anne?"

"Yes, fine."

He walks over to me, takes my hand, pulls me up and over to a mirror.

I gasp. There are red blotches all over my neck and arms. Hives. I stand there, in shock at proof that my body can't handle the truth.

"To me, you're still the fairest of them all," Leo says. "But you won't be for long unless you let go."

"Let go of what?"

"Only you know the answer to that."

Chapter 35

Theresa

The view from Henry's Century City corporate offices was breathtaking. Very easy to feel like a master of the universe when you looked out on the entire expanse of L.A.'s west side, all the way to the ocean. Easy to feel like a master of the universe when your offices were the entire penthouse floor. Yet Henry's personal office was surprisingly small in size, his theory being that any meeting consisting of more than three people was what a conference room was for. He preferred a more intimate space and Theresa did feel safe and comfortable in there . . . as long as she didn't walk over to the window and look out at that billion-dollar view. She had a fear of heights and elevators so the fact that she came to the twenty-sixth floor in this building every workday was part of the price she paid to be at the hub of a "master's" world.

As she waited for Henry to finish a call, she noticed a new piece of art . . . a small, framed painting of a bowl of guavas by Leo de Vince. Not your typical office art but anything by Leo de Vince was a sign of being on the right side of the art world's latest trend.

She opened up her leather iPad case, powered up to the Internet, clicked on to Google News and typed in Henry's name. She did this five or six times a day to monitor all stories and information circulating on the Web. Since the last time she checked, a few hours ago, there were a number of items but the only one that caught her attention was a *Newsweek* blog about the three-way race for governor of California. This one was no different from so many others. Can an Independent candidate win in blue state California? The essay was an analysis of the pros and cons of Henry and his two opponents: a Democratic congresswoman from San Francisco and a Republican congressman from San Diego. Hadn't she read this exact article a week ago? A month ago? She had the same urge now that she did then, a desire to post a screaming comment done all in CAPS saying, "You don't need to go on and on trying to explain this. It's simple. Democrats will tell you the answer is to tax and spend. Republicans will tell you the road to ruin is taxing and spending. Henry will tell you he'll tax more than the Republicans want but not as much as the Democrats insist upon and he'll spend less than the Democrats want but not as little as the Republicans insist upon and he'll be able to pull this off because he's smarter, sexier, funnier, and more charismatic than anything the state has ever seen." How many times had she written that comment (using a fake name, of course) but at the last minute didn't hit send. In this world of traceable emails, free speech came with too many consequences.

Henry got off the phone and seemed to be in a good mood because he indulged in some uncharacteristic small talk.

"You look different, Theresa. What is it?"

"I do?" What she was thinking is, I better look different. In the last year she had spent thousands of dollars on maintenance. Numerous "boot camp" exercise classes . . . and she was the oldest person there . . . pushing herself hard on the treadmill and then almost collapsing afterward, needing to chug a 5-Hour Energy drink just to make it back to her car. There were also weekly facials, the occasional Botox and the best skin care products on the market, which she'd discovered, thanks to Anne's beauty tips. She'd also spent a fortune on clothes. Her new style being the two J's: J as in Jil Sander and J as in Jimmy Choo. Her style concept was simple: classy clothes and shoes that said, Don't think I don't know how to have fun.

"Better nutrition," Theresa said. "No wheat, no dairy, no sugar."

"No alcohol?"

"Hell no, I'm not giving that up."

Though enjoying this banter, Theresa wanted to share some good news. "Have you seen the new poll numbers? They're good."

"Forget about the polls right now. Give me any updates on Carl Wolsey."

It was a topic that always made Theresa uneasy. She was thrilled that Carl was in Henry's crosshairs and after her lunch with Anne she did her part in keeping him there by passing along all damaging information. Since then Henry quizzed her on Carl on a regular basis. As much as she liked being Henry's go-to source she couldn't help but wonder if this could somehow backfire on her.

"Anything new on him this week?"

"Aside from the fact that he looks completely different? The transformation is now complete. He's gone from Brooks Brothers to Roberto Cavalli. From Wall Street to Saint-Tropez. From ties to gold chains."

Actually there were no gold chains and he wasn't wearing Cavalli but her exaggeration amused Henry.

"What else?"

"I heard that that new house he bought for himself and his new girlfriend Kim is a very expensive property up in Mandeville Canyon with stables for her horses. Apparently Kim likes to ride horses, which probably means when she was living in whatever small town in Texas she's from, she rode a few and now she's walking around in equestrian gear talking about breeding. I'm sure she's got breeding on her mind . . . and not just horses. I'll be shocked if she doesn't get pregnant soon. That would guarantee her at least eighteen years of free rent and child support. Men are so stupid when it comes to girls like Kim. They all spend a fortune trying to turn a 'ho' into a socialite."

She had to slow down and be careful. She was treading awfully close to accusing Henry of being stupid for marrying Anne.

"Keep going," Henry said.

Theresa loved showing off her verbal skills and talking trash but it did occur to her that maybe she should put a little more distance between herself and Carl's destiny. She might have stopped there had Henry not said, "I love hearing your observations."

She had to keep going now.

"I've noticed he has a smug look on his face these days, as if he's getting the best sex in the world and we should all be jealous. Doesn't he know how many men were there before him? And how many of them dumped her? I'm not saying he's not having a fun time and good for him but the smugness has got to go. It makes him look silly, which is all right if you're some Hollywood producer dude but not okay if you're a money manager who is supposed to have no time or interest in anything that doesn't make your clients boatloads of money."

"But he *is* making his clients plenty of money. Have you heard anything different?"

She'd heard a few rumors but they were all unsubstantiated and she didn't want to dilute Henry's esteem of her by giving him second-rate innuendo. It also was beginning to occur to her that she was turning into a character assassin just to get Henry's approval and ultimately he wouldn't respect her for it. "No, but I don't know anyone who invests with him except you. My friends don't play in that league."

But the questions didn't cease. Henry, like a lot of men who have had spectacular success, was good at asking questions. He understood that it was an art, a seduction. You had to be persistent but do it in a way that made the person being questioned feel flattered and Theresa was flattered. She loved having his attention and he did look at her in a way that made her feel they were in this together and she was his one true accomplice.

"Is Carl out at the clubs? Having parties, going to parties?" Henry especially wanted to know about Carl's girlfriend, Kim. Did she do drugs? Did they do drugs together?

Alarm bells went off in Theresa's mind. Kim was Larissa's best friend and if Cliff's speculation was accurate, Henry and Larissa were seeing each other again. So . . . wouldn't Henry already have all this information? It's not as if Larissa would ever hold any information back from Henry. She'd probably sell her family's deepest dark secrets just to get him to fuck her one more time. Oh my God, Theresa thought. Is Henry just getting me to say stuff he already knows so he can name me as the source if it ever comes up with Anne? Or worse, was this some kind of Plan B setup in case he should end up needing a fall guy? This was fast becoming her new phobia . . . fear of being the fall guy. Without warning, she was hit by a new sensation, one that made her more fearful than the view from the twenty-sixth floor. She felt paranoid and feeling paranoid about a man she worshipped was not something she knew how to handle. It wasn't just a case of wires crossing: it was wires shorting out and causing a shutdown of the whole electrical grid.

Luckily his assistant buzzed to inform him of a call waiting. He hesitated before saying, "Put her through."

Theresa pantomimed "do you want me to go?" Henry shook his head no and then settled back in his chair as if to say, Okay, bring on the madness.

"What is it, Catherine?"

Theresa didn't have to hear Catherine's end of the conversation to know what was going on. They were fighting about money but really they were each fighting to win. Henry was happy to give her a generous settlement but he wanted assurances that she wouldn't trash him all over town. She was happy not to trash him all over town if he assured her that the only heir who would ever be allowed to work in an executive capacity at his company was Maren, not "Elizabeth. Never Elizabeth."

Theresa knew all this because Henry had been arguing this point for months and had shared his concerns with Theresa. After a few more minutes of back-and-forth accusations, he abruptly hung up.

"Was there a fuck-you on the other end? Did she go to her crazy place again?" Theresa felt comfortable kidding about Catherine's craziness. Henry didn't seem to mind. In fact it could be said that part of Theresa's job was saying the things about Catherine that he didn't feel comfortable saying himself but wanted vocalized.

"If not handled right, she could hurt us in the press. And she's not the only one." Henry didn't sound worried but he was taking the threat seriously.

Theresa said a silent thank-you to Catherine for getting Henry off the Carl topic. "Who else can hurt you?"

"Sometimes I worry about Anne. She can be . . . difficult."

Now Henry was pulling Theresa into the heart of his inner circle, that inner sanctum where what is said dare not be repeated. She tiptoed in. "How?"

"She's high-spirited."

Theresa knew that was a euphemism for something.

He followed that up with something even more enigmatic. "Do you think being divorced is a liability in an election in California?"

She had the feeling what he was really asking was, did she think it was a liability to be divorced *twice*? Was Anne in jeopardy? The question required a careful answer.

"You know, Henry, sometimes two messes cancel each other out . . . and a third, new element wipes the slate clean."

"A third element?"

"I have to give it a little more thought but I think I have an interesting idea."

"Work on it and get back to me."

That was her cue that today's meeting was over. She gathered her bag and iPad and headed for the door.

"Nice shoes, Theresa."

"Why thank you, Mr. Tudor."

She tossed her head back and laughed in that carefree way she always wanted to laugh in his presence.

As she waited for the elevator she wondered if her new cell phone would work this high up. When the doors finally opened, Carl Wolsey stepped out. He was dressed casually, in a sport jacket that was acceptable dress for a meeting with Henry, except for one thing. He had a diamond stud in one ear.

"Hello, Theresa."

"Carl."

"I'm late for a meeting with the man," he said, rushing right by her.

"Don't worry, he's running late. My meeting with him ran fifteen minutes over."

"Good to know."

He was almost at the receptionist's desk when Theresa stuck her hand on the elevator door to keep it open. "Carl, could you give me a second?"

Reluctantly he walked over, the same look on his face he'd had when she delayed his fun time by ordering coffee at the Soho House. He hated to be slowed down by anyone who wasn't paying him good money or showing him a good time.

"What?"

"You might want to take that diamond stud out before you walk in there."

His hand checked his earlobe. "I forgot it was in there. Thanks."

That made Theresa feel better about having trashed him without mercy ten minutes earlier. I'm a good person, she thought. I do what I have to do to get ahead but I'm a good person. And feeling like one, she was not surprised when the universe rewarded her. As the elevator door closed she saw that the Verizon network was keeping her connected. Thinking about her promise to Henry to offer him a third element, she put in a call to Jane Seymour. When she heard Jane's voice on the other end, she forgot all about the fact that elevators scared her or that she'd had a moment of panic twenty-six floors up.

Chapter 36

Anne

When things get desperate, Boleyns grow bold. My father always says that but it's my mother's encouragement to get a little naughty that continues to rule the day. Rather than confront Henry with my suspicions about Larissa, I keep him focused on me by keeping our sex life interesting. Having had a few days of feeling out of sync—when I'm feeling hopeful, he's dismissive; when he's feeling playful, I'm tired—I make a bold move and call Angela.

When she showed up at my mother's birthday, we picked right up where we left off. She's still a lot of fun and at thirty is even more stunning than I remembered. She reminded me of all the good times we had that summer in Paris and we sure did. A year before Mary met Henry I'd gone to France with my sister because she had some modeling work over there and I was going to tag along and take a course at the Sorbonne, which I never got around to doing. I also thought traveling would be good research for the novel I was planning on writing one of these days, which I also never got around to doing, though I did get assignments to do some magazine articles for travel publications. Angela was already a big deal on the European modeling circuit and knew how to survive all the sharks in the water. She had excellent advice for spurning the lecherous men who lurked around that world without making them feel so rejected they would sabotage your career. It came down to two options: either claim to be engaged or claim to be a lesbian. And in certain situations claim both. We called that doubling up on condoms, like when a man wears two just to make sure none of his little guys slip through. Angela was brilliantly convincing at saying she was really only into women. Of course the second she met a guy she was attracted to she was off to Ibiza or London with him, claiming he turned her straight.

Mary paid no attention to this advice or to Angela or me. About five minutes after we arrived she got swooped up by some guy and moved into his place in St. Germain and became obsessed with him to the exclusion of anything else except her modeling gigs. Angela and I ended up spending a lot of time together and often did our faux lesbian act when we went out to clubs. We got very good at our roles. In fact by the end of the summer I realized Angela was bisexual to the extent that she's attracted to beauty and excitement and doesn't care all that much if it comes in a male or female package. She prefers men because she likes all the male things that go along with the Y chromosome. She likes that they can be her bodyguard/ daddy/mentor . . . and her ticket to a world and lifestyle that even her good looks and high modeling fees couldn't access. I learned a lot about men from Angela that summer. I also learned how to talk dirty in French, how to dress like a lady and all about the power of the pussy.

The reason I call Angela is that she is perfect for what I need. She's married, interested in staying married, but also looking for a little excitement. There is no question she loves her husband but in that European way, which means that having a little fun on the side isn't a deal breaker so long as it's very discreet. She has security and is looking for excitement and I'm looking for excitement in order to hang on to my security. We're a match made in fast-lane heaven.

Ever since I mentioned a threesome with Angela to Henry he has been much more attentive. Ever since I suggested it to Angela she's been more attentive, too . . . to her own husband. She confesses this to me in one of our many phone calls. We've become best pals again, chatting a few times a day, and have concocted a simple plan.

Since her husband is scheduled to go on an overnight location-scout to Palm Springs, Angela tells him she's spending the night with me because she doesn't want to be all alone in their isolated Malibu house. I make arrangements for Elizabeth to spend the night with Mary and Alex because Mary adores Elizabeth and all she talks about lately is having kids. Of course, I intend to a send a nanny along because Mary and Alex love their pot almost as much as they love my child.

The days leading up to the big night are fun. I order Angela's favorite rosé champagne. I go shopping for sexy underwear and pick up some beautiful scents and erotic oils from the "Strange Invisible Perfumes" store in Venice. Henry also seems to be enjoying the days leading up to our date. He buys me presents and is more thoughtful and sweet than he's been in weeks. One day I come down to breakfast to a wrapped present: a beautiful leather bag designed by Kendall Conrad, my favorite handbag designer. What makes this so special is not only the thoughtfulness of getting me a great present but the fact that he heard me mention Kendall's name weeks ago and actually filed it away so he would know where to go to get me something special. It was the kind of gesture an adoring husband might make on Valentine's Day. And even more impressive is that the very next day he comes home with the cutest little fluffy white puppy for Elizabeth. The irony doesn't escape me. We are having wonderful conventional family moments precisely because I've introduced a nonconventional element into our relationship.

What we don't mention is the wisdom of someone running for public office indulging in the kind of behavior that has sunk the careers of plenty of elected officials. I'm sure Henry is quite aware of the risk factor but reasonable risks are how he got to be kingly in the first place. It's his nature to flirt with danger. It's part of what gives him the requisite ego to think big. Besides, this isn't much of a risk. Henry knows he can trust me, and Angela is less a wild card than she appears. She's played around with a lot of high-profile people and knows lots of secrets and never once has she gossiped about who and what she's seen and done. That said, there will be no video or audio record of any of this. Risk is one thing, recklessness quite another.

When the night finally arrives, we start things off with dinner at a favorite restaurant because nights like this one require a stage and sometimes an audience—it's part of what gives the evening liftoff. Henry takes us to Il Covo, a new place that has a garden patio that is the closest thing to Italy you can find in West Hollywood. That night there's an eclectic mix of diners there: an actor and his wife, a journalist who just got back from six months in Greece, a guy in from New York who owns three hotels, a professional poker player who is just back from a big tournament in Vegas, and Henry's cousin, who just divorced a minor European prince and is starting her life over working for *Vogue* magazine in L.A. I'd call that a pretty nice liftoff.

After dinner we go to Tower Bar for another round of drinks. Having a car and driver makes it so much easier to say yes to another drink. We are silly happy at that point and Angela runs into some people she knows from the movie business as well as a fashion designer dining with a few of his arty L.A. pals. Looking at us no one would draw any conclusion other than that a married couple is taking a good friend, also married, to dinner while her husband is out of town. The only tiny possibility that maybe there's something more going on is that every so often Angela and Henry smile at each other in a way that two very attractive people should not smile at each other when the wife of the attractive man is sitting right there. The fact that I smile at them smiling would be enough evidence to get someone thinking this is no innocent trio. But no one notices or if they do I don't notice them noticing and our good time continues to build.

When we get back to Henry's house, we're all a little drunk and it's a very good high.

"You know, Angela," Henry says as we walk inside, "I can't get Anne to call this place home. She still thinks of this as my house."

"Because it *is* your house," I say. Since I am a little drunk, that fact doesn't bother me as much as it usually does. If I have one more drink I might decide I wouldn't have it any other way.

"You live here. You're married. It's your house, too," Angela insists as we all make our way into the kitchen. "Don't be so accommodating or shy or insecure or whatever it is you are underneath that regal ice princess thing that you've learned to do."

"What I am is a good hostess," I say as I bring out one of the bottles of rosé champagne and pop it open like an expert.

Angela takes a sip and then she does the funniest thing. She curtsies and says, "My lord, my lady, whatever you command, I am your trusted servant."

There comes a point in the partying when I look at the clock and it's 1:45 and Angela is dancing around in her underwear and we're kissing and then next thing I know we're all in bed together and everything keeps shifting so at times Henry and I feel connected and she's our toy or she and I are connected and he's our toy or the best point of all when we're all so connected to each other we feel immortal. Then suddenly it's 5:30 and we're standing in the driveway hugging and saying goodbye and we're all proclaiming love for one another and Angela goes home to her own bed to await her husband's return and Henry and I go back into the kitchen and raid the refrigerator for some apple pie.

Later, back in bed, I say something about Larissa, and Henry assures me she's not a factor. Never has been and never will be. I'm confused, not knowing if he's saying she doesn't mean anything to him or that whatever she means to him isn't a factor in our relationship. I do know this: Larissa couldn't deliver what I just did. I'm sure she could arrange a threesome but not with a quality woman like Angela and not done the way we did it. We were classy naughty. Larissa is slutty naughty. Two very different worlds. No contest.

When I wake up late the next morning, I'm alone in our bed. I buzz the intercom in the kitchen expecting the cook to answer but Henry does. He's making coffee and fixing me a bowl of fruit. I'm a happy girl. I take a quick shower and when I walk back into the room I notice Henry's computer is on and out of curiosity I look to see what site he's been on. I hit the space bar and the home page of the *Wall Street Journal* pops up. Their headline is a story on Carl Wolsey being arrested by the feds for running a Ponzi scheme that involved numerous people, including several Hollywood celebrities. I scan the list of well-known people. Henry's name is not there but Catherine's is and so is Angela's husband's.

Henry walks in with a tray of food and sees the shocked look on my face as I stare at the computer screen.

"Pretty wild, isn't it?" His voice is calm, as if he is commenting on someone he barely knows.

I'm not so calm. "What does this mean?"

"It means Carl's going to be spending some time in prison. Don't worry, I got all my money out a few weeks ago."

"A few weeks ago? And you didn't mention it?"

"I mentioned it to the SEC."

"When did you know Carl was stealing?"

"When he found his mojo but lost his judgment."

"Did you call my father about this?"

"Calling anyone other than the SEC would not be appropriate."

"My father has money invested with Carl. Not a lot but all the extra cash he has. He can't lose that money. We have to pay him back."

"'We'? Are you saying I should pay him back? I had nothing to do with your father's investments."

My mind is racing. My father thought he was so clever, keeping an eye on Carl as a way of neutralizing any threat he might pose for our family and getting a nice return on his investments at the same time. This reversal is a disaster. Worse than when he tried opening his own law firm and failed all those many years ago. I pick up my cell, turn the ringer back on and see that I've gotten half a dozen calls from him.

"I can't believe that you didn't look out for him, Henry. He's family. He's your daughter's grandfather."

I'm getting more and more upset. This isn't just about my father. I'm also having another attack of Larissa-inspired paranoia. Was she the source of the insider information on Carl? Was she the one who reported back to Henry about just how much mojo was gained and judgment lost? Was she the one who warned Henry in the first place? Did she provide more and better information than anything he got from me through Theresa? And if so, does this mean Henry is now in Larissa's debt?

Henry continues to speak in a measured tone. "I don't think you understand how these things work, Anne."

My tone is far from measured. It's borderline hysterical. "I don't understand how you can be so detached about all of this. Untouched by it all. Carl was someone you worked with for years. He considered you his best friend." What's really worrying me is how easily Henry can move on from Carl, which makes me wonder if he can just as easily move on from me.

"Anne, you hated the guy. You've been after me forever to get rid of him."

"And Angela's husband. Did you know he was an investor?"

"Now how would I know that? And even if I did, it was too late. There was nothing I could do about it."

"But you're the guy who is supposed to know how to fix things. That's what we all expect of you. That's what a king does."

"Sorry if I disappointed you. Heavy is the head that wears the crown and all of that."

I have my phone in my hand and can't delay any longer. I've got to call my father back. I feel like I'm holding a grenade and I'm in the middle of a war I didn't sign up for. "What about my father?"

"We'll talk about this later."

"No, we have to talk about this now."

"I'm going to the office now. I've got a campaign to plan."

"Yes, let's not do anything to fuck with your campaign."

"Careful, Anne." A touch of menace creeps into his voice.

"What does that mean?"

"Just that . . . careful."

Chapter 37

Catherine

It was midnight and Catherine was sitting up in bed watching TV, a rerun of the early edition of CNN's report on Carl Wolsey's arrest. She'd seen this same piece a half-dozen times but couldn't stop watching, as if somehow on the seventh time she watched or the eighth or whatever, she would hear something new, some word or clue that would help her understand how she was duped . . . and Henry wasn't.

She'd invested a big chunk of her own money with Carl for a lot of reasons and it was now apparent none of them were good. Apart from wanting a better-than-average return on her investments, other fantasies had been a factor. She actually imagined becoming friends with Carl, maybe even having dinner with him occasionally. She imagined Carl mentioning the friendship to Henry, making her ex, if not jealous, at least a little possessive. She imagined that maybe after a drink or two Carl might become loose-lipped enough to gossip about Anne. She had all kinds of ideas about how he might be helpful but never once did she entertain the idea that he would make everything so much worse. Now Catherine would really need that settlement money from Henry. She was losing her leverage and she wasn't a good loser. Ferdinand was outraged by her stupidity. Yes, he used that word and then quickly apologized and blamed himself for not being a better father and overseeing all her financial moves, which really infuriated Catherine. Instead of erupting or defending herself, she took a pill. Everything about this situation made her heart hurt. Really physically hurt. It was beating so erratically that she popped a Xanax, just to get back to normal. She felt her world was falling apart and so was her body. She had a headache, her allergies were acting up, her nerves had given her an upset stomach and she was so tired she didn't have the energy to get out of bed and yet her mind wouldn't shut off. There was no peace to be had anywhere. In the end she did drag herself over to the medicine cabinet and took a pill for each ailment.

The second after she swallowed two aspirin she realized they had a lot of caffeine in them and now she worried about her insomnia. She couldn't stand being awake all night with so many problems haunting her. Where was her homeopathic sleeping cure? She stumbled over to her bedside table, tripping over a notebook, which she then kicked across the room. That felt good. Maybe she should start throwing things. Maybe she'd throw a lamp against the wall like they do in movies. But first she needed her magic herbs. Found them. Sitting right there, next to the alarm clock. There's something she wouldn't need anymore since there was no longer any reason to get up early. She popped off the top of the pill bottle. How many should she take? She decided that since she took two aspirin, she needed to take an equal amount of these downers. She popped two tablets in her mouth and washed them down with some wine.

She called out for Carmen, thinking she'd like some company, and then remembered her housekeeper was asleep by ten o'clock and her room was on the other end of the house. She envied Carmen's ability to hit the pillow and fall asleep immediately, no matter what problems she had in her life . . . and Carmen had her fair share of them. She had a son who got into some trouble with the law, a mother with health problems, whom Carmen supported, and assorted family members in El Salvador who were always in some kind of crisis. Even so, somehow Carmen's life seemed so much less complicated than Catherine's, or was it just as complicated but Carmen was uncomplicated? Catherine mulled that over until it led her into thinking about her own complicated family.

Maren was slipping away. She was already talking about spending the next Thanksgiving break with her boarding school roommate's family back in New York. She's gone, Catherine thought. Oh sure, she'll come back to visit but she's got her own world now, her own friends. Just when I need her she's finding her own independence. It wasn't fair. Catherine wasn't ready to be alone. She couldn't be alone. Maybe, she thought, Carmen's family could move in here. A second later she realized that would never work. Maybe she could adopt a baby? That thought cheered her for about five minutes, until she considered she didn't have the stamina for mommy-and-me classes.

The report on CNN showed a photo of Henry and the reporter was talking about how he had alerted the SEC. The message was clear: Henry was the good guy, the smart guy. "Are you really the good guy, Henry?" Catherine was talking to the TV screen. "Because you're not being very good to me." Seeing his face made her want to see more of it. She went over to the closet and pulled a leather-bound album off a top shelf. She opened it up and flipped through pages of photos of her and Henry in their early days. They loved each other once. She wished she knew what happened. Did she get too old? Did he get bored?

She tossed the album aside. Oh God, she thought, if only religion had given her the strength to handle this moment. When I die, she thought, I want to confront God and say, Why are you so mean? Why do you allow so much suffering? Are you a sadist? Even thinking those thoughts felt like a sin so Catherine continued her talk with God in a more respectful tone. "But I do love your churches, the candles, the music, the altar, the stained glass windows, the religious art." Religious art. That gave her an idea. Maybe that's what she should invest in next, with whatever money she had left. Or even better, she could build a small church. Mel Gibson built one. And didn't she read that some basketball player in Florida built one for his mom?

All these thoughts swirled in her head, keeping her awake. Why weren't those homeopathic pills working? Maybe she needed something more hard-core. She searched around the drawers in her bathroom and found some downer pain pills. Real ones, the kind they give you after surgery. She took another swig of wine and then stopped. Wait. Did she take a pill or was she about to take one? She couldn't remember. Her memory was getting fuzzy but she was still wide awake.

The TV was now starting a new hour of headlines. She spotted one of the pain pills in the folds of the blanket on the bed. Figuring it was the one she didn't take, she popped it into her mouth. As she swallowed it, she remembered that she had taken one of these already. *Oh my God* . . . should I worry about this? Should I worry about anything at all? That was her last thought before the pills sucked her into the big sleep that she never awoke from.

Carmen found Catherine dead the next morning, the photo album nearby, CNN still on and still reporting the Carl Wolsey story. Carmen burst into tears and then called 911. As she waited for them to arrive, she thought about how much she loved her boss. What a good woman she was, a little loco, but good. She thought about how deeply Catherine cared about things and how much fun she could be when she had a couple of drinks. While she was sitting there with her memories and waiting for the sound of an ambulance siren, she noticed the notebook on the floor where Catherine had kicked it. Carmen had never seen this book before and out of curiosity picked it up and flipped through the pages. Holy Jesus, she thought. The notebook was filled with Catherine's anger and bitterness as well as intimate details of her marriage to Henry. Carmen made a quick decision. She put the notebook in her handbag. She told herself she was doing what Catherine would have wanted. She was protecting her boss in death as she had in life. As the sound of a siren grew louder she couldn't help but wonder—and she made the sign of the cross and asked God's forgiveness for this—if she was mentioned in Catherine's will.

Chapter 38

Anne

When Maren returns for her mother's funeral she stays with us for the whole week. I tell her that she will always be welcome in our house. What I don't say, but which is understood, is that the welcome comes with a condition. I expect her to respect me and to understand this is my home now. She informs me that she'd rather live in a motel in the Valley than have to deal with me as the mistress of the house. She stresses the word *mistress* to let me know that in her mind I'm no wife. I'm just a slut who scammed her dad into marriage.

It's an emotional time. Catherine's death created tremendous upheaval and I know she would have been thrilled about that. She got her wish. Her unexpected exit affects Henry greatly. He wasn't prepared for her to be gone so suddenly. Now Maren is motherless and Henry is being blamed for Catherine's death. No one blames him to his face but the word going around is that had he treated her better she wouldn't have accidentally overdosed. My instinct is to protect my man but my defense only adds to his problems. I'm not good at tempering my thoughts when I'm upset and that leads to statements that can easily be taken out of context because the media couldn't care less about context. The quote that gets me in trouble is "Catherine was a victim of her own anger." I was making a point about how often women turn their anger inward, unlike men, who direct it toward the world, but my observation was ignored for the more salacious quote.

Henry and I do have some moments that bring us closer. We both are amused when we read a blog posting by Carl Wolsey. Suddenly he's a big fan of Catherine, bemoaning her early passing. This is the new Carl, the accused felon, trying to reinvent himself as a compassionate soul. Had he been more compassionate, he wouldn't have stolen Catherine's money, hiding who knows how much of it in overseas accounts and spending the rest of it on expensive presents for his girlfriend, including an interest in a Thoroughbred horse ranch.

Henry and I spend more time talking. It's been a while since he confided in me and he's never been comfortable talking about anything having to do with his ex. He admits Catherine's family never liked him to begin with and now they really hate him. He never expected them to back his candidacy but now he hears they're planning on doing whatever it takes to get his major opponent elected. And when Catherine's father, Ferdinand, says he's going to back someone he's talking Chicago-style support . . . money and muscle.

Catherine's death has also made Henry and me appreciate our own family. We spend more time with Elizabeth, who is turning into a precocious child. The day before Maren is due to return to boarding school is a Saturday and Henry and I are talking to our landscape architect about whether we should put in an English garden or do something more tropical, arid, something more befitting a city on the edge of a desert. There are photographs of the various options on the table, next to where Elizabeth is sitting, playing with one of her dolls. As the discussion continues our landscape guy suggests we consider a more classical option . . . hedges, which are making a comeback. Elizabeth puts down her doll and checks out the photographs, pretty shots of flowers and trees.

"Mommy," she says in a voice that has a lot of authority for a toddler. "That," she says, pointing to a photo of an exotic bright orange leopard lily. "Not that," she says, pointing to a traditional box hedge.

Henry bursts out laughing. Elizabeth has inherited his decisiveness and confidence. She might as well have a tiara on her head. She's ready to rule.

Maren walks in as we're enjoying this moment. She doesn't even look in my direction. "Daddy, can I talk to you?" It goes without saying she means in private.

They take a walk outside. I watch them through the window. Henry is listening attentively to whatever Maren is saying. He puts an arm around her and she smiles. He's doing his best to make her happy and feel safe. It's what he wants for all of us. But this is a house divided and Maren is a teenager with a grudge. This could get a lot worse before it gets a little better.

Chapter 39

Cliff

Cliff enjoyed driving his son to school because now that Cliff Junior, whom everyone called C.J., was twelve, the boy had become more interesting than any adult Cliff knew. Teachers told Cliff his son was not only exceptionally smart but had a moral code rarely seen in someone his age. One teacher summed it up by saying the child had integrity, which wasn't a word that was often used to describe a preteen. Cliff wondered where C.J. got his integrity. Cliff didn't think of himself as an advertisement for the high moral ground and though his wife was, at her core, a good person, she didn't have the other thing one needed to keep integrity alive . . . guts. His wife was strong and resourceful but she wasn't a fighter. She would cut people off if she didn't like what they were doing but rarely took a stand.

During the drive to school Cliff always picked up interesting information from his son about music, movies and pop culture. The student had become the teacher. Today the conversation took a more serious turn to politics. C.J. talked about Henry's campaign for governor. He was writing a paper on the role of charisma in American politics and wanted to know what his dad thought about Henry's chances of winning.

"I think charisma can help you and hurt you."

"How can it hurt you?"

"Things can come so easily you start counting on that to always be the case."

"Small price to pay though, right?"

"Depends. Could be a big price to pay."

"So do you think people vote for the person who's best for the job or the person they like the most?"

"I think they vote for the person who will protect their own job."

"Whether they like them or not?"

The topic was getting a little too close to the gray area of Cliff's own murky moral ground and for a moment he wished his son was more like one of those surly teens who listen to Kanye West on their iPods and have little interest in anything a parent has to say. Or was Kanye what C.J. listened to two years ago? Cliff couldn't keep up.

"They find a way to like the person who's protecting their job."

"Can you do that, Dad?"

"Me, personally?" Cliff was stalling.

"Yeah, you personally."

Cliff thought about his feelings toward Theresa. He had found a way to like things about her and his acting training had come in handy. He knew how to pretend and knew that if he committed to the pretense it felt real. He was proud of himself for that survival trick and intended to pass it along to his son but not until C.J. was a grown-up. Twelve years old was a little young to find out that your dad was a pretty good fake.

"You know me," Cliff said. "I'm a people person. I pretty much like everyone."

C.J. didn't question that conclusion but he did reach into his backpack for his iPod.

A wave of relief washed over Cliff after he dropped off his son. Lately he worried that at any moment his kid might bust him on something, catch him in a lie or challenge him on one of his choices. At the same time he was fiercely proud of C.J. This combination of feelings had an odd effect. Rather than inspire a reexamination of his own moral shortcomings, it made Cliff more determined than ever to do whatever he had to do to make the money needed to give his extraordinary child all the advantages life could offer. Justifiable duplicity seemed reasonable to him and it was with that in mind that he headed to the meeting he'd been dreading.

Lacy wasn't happy that Cliff was ten minutes late. Ever since her gossip blog became a hit her diva tendencies had flourished. When she first started working for the website she wouldn't have considered asking for an out-of-the-office meeting at a location that was only convenient for her . . . and Clint wouldn't have acquiesced. Now she had leverage and not just because she got more hits on her blog than almost anything else on the *Daily* site. After the death of Catherine, she had reached out to Maren and the two had struck up a friendship, with Lacy playing the part of the older sister Maren never had. That alliance had emboldened Lacy. Not only was she now less solicitous of her boss, she was also more publicly critical of her husband. These days when George's name came up she might make some snide remark about his acting career and even ridicule the accents he used for his roles.

Cliff apologized for being late but it took him a moment to get out the apology because he was distracted by two women at the next table. They were young and typical of the type you see around this upscale shopping area. Both were dressed in the latest trendy outfits and had so many hair extensions they looked like a different species: half girl, half she-lion.

Lacy finished her cappuccino and got right to the point. "I'm leaving."

"Why?" Cliff wasn't really surprised. He suspected another site was wooing her away, offering decent money, and money had become more of an issue for Lacy. Her father, too, had lost some money in Carl Wolsey's scam but having diversified his investments, the financial hit wasn't life-changing, though it did mean Lacy had to cut back on her shopping trips to Barneys. "Did you get a better job offer?"

"Yes, but that's not the only reason."

"We can renegotiate your deal."

"But you can't renegotiate more freedom. There are things I want to say that can't be said on a website controlled by Henry."

"Henry has nothing to do with the site anymore. He stepped away. Had to while campaigning."

"Oh please. Let's not even go there. You're not going to allow anything negative to be written about Henry . . . on that site. You're not stupid."

Cliff wasn't about to debate the pluses and minuses of his own corrupt ethics.

"What kind of things do you want to write?"

"My first piece will be about Maren Tudor and the fact that she blames Anne for her mother's death. Anne is the one who drove her mother to the brink. You know in some parts of this country there's this thing called alienation of affection."

Cliff laughed. "I think Henry did the wooing."

"Not according to Maren."

"She was still a kid when they hooked up. She knows nothing."

"She has stories."

The promise of juicy, gossipy stories was always hard for Cliff to resist but Lacy was being naïve. "Maren's not going to expose the family's personal business. If she did she'd alienate the affections of her father."

"There'll be no direct quotes from her. I'm a journalist and I don't have to reveal my sources."

"Good luck with that. There was a court ruling that came down recently. Bloggers aren't protected by the shield law."

Nothing like watching a diva deflate, Cliff thought. But this diva had backup.

"We'll see," she said. "Meanwhile, there's something else I want to talk to you about. I'm thinking of doing a book on Anne. I've got two publishers interested."

"I assume not a flattering book. How will your husband feel about you writing trash about his sister?"

Lacy sat up straight as if testifying. "I've done a lot to keep my marriage together. And yet none of it seems to matter. When Anne needs something, the least little thing, George is out the door . . . no matter what time she calls. *No matter what* George is doing." She stressed this part, leaving Cliff to fill in the blank, his mind going to a coitus interruptus scenario with Lacy left to fend for herself.

"A nonfiction book?"

"No, fiction. Truth disguised as fiction."

"Whose truth?"

"A lot of people's."

She pulled some notes out of her purse and handed them to him. "My idea is that we can partner up on this, share information. I know you know stuff and we can get a ghostwriter to get it done quickly. We can publish under a pseudonym."

Cliff scanned the notes and then handed them back to her. "There's explosive stuff there."

"It's 'fiction,'" she said. "We're covered legally. Don't need any fucking shield law for that."

The idea of Lacy mounting a hate campaign against Anne made

Cliff a little sick. It was so twisted, but being an ardent opportunist he couldn't turn his back on a potentially lucrative offer.

As he considered her proposition, Lacy pressed her case. "There are a lot of stories out there about Anne." She stated this as if all the people shopping and having lunch around them at that very minute were all whispering and plotting. "It's going to come to a point where sides are drawn. You know how many copies a book like this could sell?"

Cliff didn't have to be sold on the profit possibilities. He had a different issue. Could he trust Lacy? How under the radar could his involvement be?

"What side are you on, Cliff?" She laughed as if his dilemma was highly entertaining, which made her look a little cross-species herself: half woman, half hyena.

"I'll get back to you on that," he said. He wasn't hesitating out of any moral quandary; he just had to make sure he picked the right side, which was whichever side exposed him the least and still earned him the money he needed to buy his integrity-blessed son an Ivy League education.

"Sooner rather than later," Lacy said. "Timing is everything."

Chapter 40

Anne

It's a wonderful day. It's a wonderful life. Henry and I are the guests of honor at an afternoon party given by William Gardiner, a self-made Hollywood billionaire who went from creating entertainment empires to creating political dynasties. The candidates he backs usually win and win big, their legacy and influence continuing long after they leave office. Such is the power of William Gardiner. He would be considered a political contender himself except he wasn't born in this country (he's Canadian) and his looks work against him. He's over sixty years old, tall but hunched over, sunken chest, with thick-framed glasses that sit on a large, bulbous nose. He's been married to the same unglamorous woman for thirty years, has no kids . . . and never wanted any. None of this fits the narrative for a popular political leader. However, he is a formidable power behind a throne. No one works the phones better than he does and no one wants to get on his bad side. Having him on our team is a big coup but that's not why I'm so happy.

It's also a wonderful day because of the guest list, an elite gathering of celebrities, artists, entrepreneurs, sports stars, Henry's inner circle and all my family and for once no one has any issues or complaints. Mary and Alex don't appear stoned and Alex isn't sniffing around Henry trying to get a job, which could be because he thinks if he keeps getting invited to these kinds of parties it's only a matter of time before he makes a career connection. My sister seems to be having a good time without tripping over herself and landing on her ass. My mother put the brakes on drinking after her second glass of wine and my father, though never at ease around Henry and always looking to increase his advantage, pulls me aside for a chat and instead of another request it's a thank-you.

"Nice of Henry to make that two-hundred-and-fifty-thousand-dollar 'loan' to my account," he says. "He really should have given me the heads-up about Carl."

"Now that you have the money you can't ever bring this up again," I say. "Especially not to Henry." I'm adamant about this but not too worried. My father is embarrassed by his own bad judgment and doesn't want to be reminded that he doesn't know as much about everything as he pretends to.

"I won't," he says and before I can move on to chat with other guests, he adds, "Anne, you look beautiful in that yellow dress."

My father never compliments me and it does make me feel good but that's not why I'm so happy.

It's also a wonderful day because I see my brother George and he's in good spirits because he just got a major part in a feature film being done at Henry's studio. Lacy is with him even though their marriage is on the rocks. She's on her best behavior because she desperately wanted to come to a party at William Gardiner's estate. Today she's all smiles, even refers to me as Anne, not Annie, though she claims the "Annie" was always only said out of affection. Yeah, right.

"You'll have to come visit me on the set," George says. "This time I get a deluxe trailer."

"How great is that!" Lacy says. She's suddenly very chatty and for once isn't complaining about me but that's not why I'm so happy.

It's also a wonderful day because Leo de Vince is there. He tells me he's moving to Santa Barbara. "Time for me to get away from Los Angeles, at least for a while. Get away from all this," he says looking around the room. He doesn't say this with a drop of bitterness. Why would he? Los Angeles and the people at this party have been very good to him and his career but he requires a quieter environment for the next stage of his work . . . whatever that work might be.

"Quieter than your place at the beach?"

"The sound of the waves can either lull you to sleep or drive you crazy."

I laugh and he tells me I'm one of the few people who don't think he's being grim when he says things like that.

He's carrying a canvas shoulder bag, which would be considered bad taste on anyone else but geniuses get a free pass. Out of it he pulls a small, framed sketch—one of the drawings he did that first afternoon I went to his studio. Though it wasn't my finest hour he managed to capture my vulnerability in a way that doesn't repulse me. "Your portrait isn't finished yet but I thought you might like to have this." I'm thrilled to own my very own Leo de Vince sketch but that's not why I'm so happy.

It's also a wonderful day because Larissa is finally crushed. Proof of that is she's now openly chasing after Henry's single friends (and some of the married ones, too) which she would never do if she thought she still had a chance with the king. Even more telling, the word around town is she's dropping Henry's name more and more. This is called cashing in. Girls like Larissa only get loose-lipped once they realize they're permanently out of the running for the big prize. Larissa isn't trashing Henry. She would never do that. On the contrary, she tells stories about her "good, close friendship" with him in order to try to salvage some cachet points. I don't fault her for that. The girl put in at least half a dozen years (she was around when Catherine was still in the picture) trying to close the deal with Henry and never even got to the position of girlfriend number one. I think she thinks these stories will give her a higher profile in town and maybe get her an acting job. Someone should tell her that what gets a higher profile in this town is new, fresh talent. Or, lacking that, Kim Kardashian's butt. I guess it's possible some small advantage could come out of Larissa's tall tales. Maybe she will get a job or a date but chances are I won't hear about it. She's off my radar except for one last stab. I made sure she knew that I was the one who put her name on the guest list, not Henry. I did it so she could see that Henry is no longer interested in her. All afternoon he and I are stealing loving glances and kissing, acting like new lovers. Larissa has been relegated to a witness to our renewed passion. But that's not why I'm so happy.

It's also a wonderful day because I get to checkmate Theresa. I see her across the room with her guest. Instead of Cliff, her plus one is a jewelry designer from San Francisco named Jane Seymour. Theresa has a habit of befriending socialites and I can see her flattering this girl who must be well connected because there's nothing else compelling about her. She's one of those washed-out blondes who has a regal air about her that comes from birthright, not accomplishment. Knowing Theresa I'm sure she's calling her new friend "darling" and telling her how fabulous she is but she also leaves her behind to come over and talk to me.

"Isn't this marvelous?" she says.

I've never heard Theresa use the word *marvelous* before and I wonder if this is something she picked up from Jane.

"It's a glorious day," I say.

I watch Elizabeth running around with her nanny and Wyatt, who is, as I might have guessed, very good with kids. Elizabeth is laughing and full of joy. Maybe the sight of that is too sunny for Theresa because she has to get in a slight dig.

"I see your daughter has her father's golden coloring and her mother's alluring charm."

Wyatt is now twirling Elizabeth around and she's insisting he do it again and again and he complies with pleasure.

"Wyatt has practically become part of our family," I say. "Henry and I are even thinking of asking him to write a lullaby . . . for the new baby."

Theresa is speechless

I place a hand on my stomach. "Yes, our family is growing and I feel so blessed."

"Congratulations." It's all she can manage to say because she's still reeling from the unexpected turn of events. I know what she's thinking so I answer without her having to pose the question.

"Yes, it's a boy."

"I'm thrilled for you . . . and Henry," she says, and does the equivalent of a verbal curtsy as she finds her balance and blabs on about her respect for me. Though it's nice to have her back in a nonthreatening position, that's not why I'm so happy.

It's a wonderful day because this child inside of me, my little prince, has restored my sense of security and brought new excitement to my marriage. God does work in mysterious ways, I think, because I'm sure this child was conceived the night of the threesome. How many kings and princes in the world have been conceived in less than sacred circumstances? You don't have to have an immaculate conception to create a savior and that's what my son is. My savior. The connection I have to this child is like nothing I've ever experienced. That's why I'm so happy. This is a new beginning. I know there are a lot of people saying all kinds of bad things about me but it doesn't matter. I'm back on safe ground, more powerful than before because I'm now very clear about who wishes me well and who wishes me gone.

Part Four

ANNE, THE QUEEN?

Chapter 41

Anne

Mary and Alex elope but that isn't the big headline. Though my father is furious and my mother is resigned, the bigger and worse headline is that to celebrate their wedding bliss the impetuous couple proclaim themselves cannabis activists, taking to the Internet to post their statement calling for the legalization of pot. Since Mary still has some kind of celebrity status from her own days with Henry and continues to have the trickle-down cachet that comes with being his sister-in-law, the item is picked up and goes viral.

"What were you thinking?" I shout, though I'm not supposed to get upset. My doctor said I must avoid stress and now that I'm pregnant with my precious prince I'm not about to put any drugs in my system. So what exactly am I supposed to do to stay calm in a situation like this? Mary doesn't say anything but gives me that hurt-child look that has so effectively gotten her off the hook for her entire life.

We're in the kitchen of her cluttered Topanga Canyon bungalow, which feels like a shack. She's making tacos and the smell is enough to bring back the morning sickness I thought I was over. Wyatt senses I'm feeling a little queasy and pours me a glass of mint tea from a pitcher on the counter.

Wyatt is with me because Henry was concerned about me driving all the way out here alone and he wasn't about to come with me. I don't even want to dwell on the fact that what I first thought was a good thing—Henry appreciating Wyatt's talent and even giving him some money to make a few demos of his best songs—has become another thing stressing me out. Why is Henry so comfortable giving Wyatt the assignment to take care of me? Doesn't he see that Wyatt is in love with me? Or maybe Wyatt is no longer in love with me and I'm the one who isn't seeing clearly? Is Henry going to use Wyatt's presence in my life to justify his own liaisons? Except I don't think there have been any other women and as we await the birth of our son, Henry seems completely devoted. What is happening here? Why is it getting harder and harder for me to figure out where the line is between paranoia and intuition?

The one thing I do see clearly is that Alex stands by their decision to out themselves as potheads.

"It's something we believe strongly in," he says.

"Really? You believe strongly in this?" I pick up one of the small containers of pot they have lined up on the kitchen counter along with their array of vitamins and read the label. "You believe strongly in 'Purple Haze'?"

He immediately gets defensive. "I know people who were hooked on prescription drugs, heavy painkillers, antidepressants and now they just have a couple of hits of this and they're fine. Blood pressure normal, no sleeping problems, happier."

"Fine, great, but you do know that my husband is running for public office and having this out there is not helping him? Which means it's not helping me . . . which means it's not helping you."

That's as close as I'm getting to saying, Who do you think pays the rent on this house every month? Who do you think bought Mary that Prius she loves so much?

"This isn't going to hurt Henry's campaign," Mary pipes in.

Alex nods. "Nothing else has hurt him. Come on, how many guys could have dated sisters, dumping one and marrying the other . . . survived an ugly divorce and his ex-wife's accidental overdose, has dated more wild girls in the past than a rock star and still be leading in the polls for a major political office?"

"Why do you think that is?" Wyatt's question is addressed to me. Like so many others he's become obsessed with figuring out the enigma that is Henry. People are fascinated with Henry and the fact that he continues to thrive. They are waiting for something to take him down a few pegs but so far nothing has slowed him down for long. Not even Catherine's death. Not even the aging process. He has a few stray gray hairs and the lines around the eyes are deepening but he's not accumulating the same nicks and dents that most people accumulate as they move through life. It's as if the bad stuff bounces off him. It doesn't stick, doesn't come close to stopping him.

"Because he's Henry," is the only answer I have.

We all think about that for a moment and no one says a word until Mary speaks up. "He didn't dump me. We drifted apart."

"That's right," I say, backing her up, though the truth is that Henry drifted first. Mary and I then get to the point we always get to lately. She says she's sorry but I'm the one who ends up feeling guilty.

"I have a wedding present for you in the car," I say.

"You didn't have to do that."

I turn to Wyatt. "Sweetie, will you do me a favor and bring it in?"

"Sure," he says, happy to be helpful.

As the door shuts behind him Mary looks at me. "'Sweetie'? You call him sweetie?"

"We're friends."

"You call your friends sweetie? What do you call Henry?"

"Your Majesty," I say jokingly.

She laughs. "I once called him that, one night when we were—" She stops, realizing this isn't the kind of story she should tell in front of her new husband. "Doesn't matter," she adds. "It's just a silly story." To get off the topic she holds out her hand to show off two interlocking circles of gold on her finger. "Isn't my ring pretty? Alex designed it."

"Beautiful," I say. Suddenly I'm extremely self-conscious about all the dazzling bling I'm sporting. I'm wearing my friendship ring, engagement ring and wedding ring. What's with me lately? Am I wearing all the rings because I need proof of Henry's love? Am I reminding myself or everyone else? I remove the friendship ring and put it in my pocket.

"Marrying Mary was the happiest day in my life," Alex said.

"Don't say that." My words come out a little harsher than I intended.

"Why not?"

"The happiest is yet to come. Don't doom yourself to having already hit your peak."

"Okay, one of the happiest days of my life. Is that better?"

"Much."

Mary unwraps the present slowly, carefully, undoing the ribbon knot . . . and I recall how much she always took such great care with her presents as a child, even on Christmas morning. Unlike George and me, who would tear through ours, ripping the packaging apart like little savages.

I look around the room and notice a number of Alex's photographs framed and hung. One is a beautiful shot of Mary on the beach. Another is a shot of the L.A. skyline from up on Mulholland.

"Nice work, Alex."

"Thanks," he says with a bit of a chip on his shoulder, the kind that creative people in Hollywood often have when they feel their talents haven't been acknowledged while lesser talents are signing the big deals.

"I really love them," Mary says.

For a second Alex thinks she means his photographs and his face softens until he realizes that's not what she means at all. Mary is holding up the crystal red goblets I bought her, the ones she practically salivated over the last time we shopped together at Barneys. Apparently fancy stemware doesn't conflict with her bohemian lifestyle.

"There's a card in there," I say. She knows that means there's a check in there, too.

She comes over to me and gives me a hug. Over her shoulder I give Wyatt a look and he gets my cue.

"Uh . . . Anne, if we want to get back before the traffic gets crazy, we should hit the road soon."

"Sure you don't want to stay for dinner?" Mary is holding my hand and though I miss spending time with her alone, the smell of those tacos and the grumpiness of her husband would keep me away even if rush-hour traffic on the Pacific Coast Highway wasn't a factor.

"Can't," I say, "but walk with me for a second, will you?"

We head down to the car, which is parked on the street, Alex and Wyatt keeping their distance behind to give us some privacy.

"Put it on hold," I say.

Mary pulls a jasmine blossom off a bush and puts it in her hair. "Put what on hold?"

"Your crusade about pot."

"Are you asking me to go against what I believe?"

"It's not in the family's best interest."

"But it's in my best interest."

"The family's interest is in your best interest."

"No, Anne, that's not how it goes." She looks over her shoulder as if she might call Alex to help her but gets another idea. "You know what, take your presents back. Thanks, but no thanks."

I can feel myself getting exasperated with her self-righteousness. "Don't be melodramatic, Mary."

"Take them back, I don't want them. They're not presents anyway; they're bribes."

That's when I snap. Sometimes I get so tired of being the grown-up to my irresponsible sister. I get so tired of being the bad guy to her innocent child. I get so tired of her arrogance, always thinking she's on the high road and never acknowledging who pays for that road.

"You're going to rip up my check and then what? Go to George for money? Someone is always coming to your rescue and you're always the pure one? Well maybe you're pure because we pay for your life in fantasyland. There's a price for everything, Mary, even free speech."

Tears well up in her eyes. Once again she takes the role of the victim and I'm cast as the shrew.

"I can't do this," I say. "I can't get upset. I can't watch you get upset. Do whatever you want with the gift and the money. I don't give a fuck."

We're on the road for at least ten minutes before I say another word. Wyatt is very sensitive to my moods and doesn't try to talk to me about how I feel. He waits until I'm ready to share but I'm not ready and never will be. The only reason I finally speak is that when I put my hands in my pockets I realize the "friendship" ring Henry gave me isn't there. It must have fallen out at Mary's. Now I am in a panic.

"You want to go back and get it?" Wyatt is ready to do a U-turn but I stop him. The thought of revisiting that drama is more than I can handle.

"No, let me call Mary, see if she's found it." Yet even that is more than I want to deal with. "On second thought, will you call her for me?"

He pulls into a gas station and I step out of the car. I need a little ocean air to fight back the nausea that's building. What's so upsetting about all this is how alone I feel though there's no reason for me to feel so isolated. I have a husband who has been very attentive. I have a good friend in Wyatt. I have a beautiful daughter. I have my precious son growing inside of me. There are so many riches in my life but like some kind of afternoon nightmare I feel uneasy, as if I'm in some precognitive state and know that something very scary is approaching fast.

Wyatt walks toward me, smiling. "Mary found it on the couch. Do you want to go back for it now?"

"No, I'll get it another time."

I give him a hug and find myself holding on to him because being in his embrace makes my fears recede. There's no question we're more than friends though no line has been crossed . . . and won't be. I'm married. I'm pregnant. I'm happy. I keep silently repeating this to myself though I hold on to him until . . .

"Oh my God." I violently break away.

Wyatt can't figure out what just happened until he spots a man getting into a car parked in front of the gas station's mini-mart. Though he is seemingly just another customer stocking up on cigs and sodas, I know what this man is capable of. One click of his cell phone camera could spell trouble for me.

"Do you know who that is?" I say. "It's Jake Winslow. A private detective."

"So." Wyatt has no fears, perhaps because he's unaware of how much he has to lose.

"Do you think Henry is having us followed?" I say.

Now Wyatt seems a little more agitated. "God, I hope not. That wouldn't be good for anybody."

"Could mean bye-bye to those demos of yours Henry is paying for." It's a mean thing to say but it might have a lot of truth in it.

"Do you trust anyone anymore, Anne?"

I don't answer. What I'm thinking is I trust my son. I rest my hands over my stomach . . . a protective gesture, but already this unborn child is protecting me even more than I am protecting him.

Chapter 42

Cliff

Cliff loved his new thousand-dollar ergonomic desk chair. Theresa had signed off on the purchase because the site had been doing so well. Ads were selling; people were making it part of their morning habit. Though Theresa took credit for it, it was Cliff who had shaped it to its more successful formula. Fifty percent of the site was headline stories (economy, environment and politics, though nothing too partisan now that Henry was involved in a gubernatorial race), one-quarter was lifestyle (sports, interior design, food) and one-quarter was entertainment and celebrity pieces, which included gossip.

Lacy's blog had been a big success and Cliff knew he had to bring in someone not to merely maintain that level of popularity but in fact to top it. He had tried one last time to lean on her to stay, approaching the topic delicately, not wanting to jeopardize their future business deals. Their under-the-radar collaboration on a book about Anne was still a possibility even though Cliff was dragging out their financial negotiations because he wasn't sure he could trust her. Still, his job at the site required him to do what he could to keep her around so he reminded Lacy that they gave her a forum when no one else would. He also offered her a sizable salary and even made an attempt at playing shrink, giving her advice about the challenges of marriage and how to survive them.

She looked at him with hurt eyes but steely resolve and said, "Cliff, I don't think you're in any position to give anybody relationship advice."

He shut up fast because she was right. His marriage had been foundering for some time. They'd have a good day followed by a bad week or a good week followed by a bad month. Today, however, was different. He was willing to believe that the marriage not only could be saved but *was* saved. He and his wife had sex that morning and he couldn't remember the last time that happened. Their pattern was to fight, followed by an icy detente. Occasionally the ice would thaw and they'd have a few laughs and a few drinks. On those nights maybe they'd fuck, quickly, and then the second it was over, as if suffering from amnesia, they'd act like it never happened. That morning the pattern was broken.

Their son had spent the night at a friend's house. When his wife awoke at 7 A.M. it was drizzling and the shades were drawn though the window was cracked open just enough so the rain was a calming sound track. Cliff had already been up for a half hour but got back into bed. His wife's feet were cold and he rubbed his feet next to hers to warm them. She nuzzled her back up against him and that's when he heard the sound. A moan. He looked around the room as if there might be someone else there. It had been so long since he heard a moan like that from his wife, it took him a moment to realize that it was her voice. But it was and he made another move, followed by another moan and so it went and when it was over, she didn't leap out of bed as if she couldn't wait to eliminate all evidence of her momentary weakness. This morning she stayed in bed, looked over at him and said, "That was something, wasn't it?"

"It sure was," Cliff said, and after living for so long with nothing, "something" was a nice change.

By the time he got to the office he was late for his first appointment. It was with a young man interviewing for Lacy's old job. In the end Lacy had turned down Cliff's offer and went off to her new job, saying, "Thanks for giving me my first shot at blogging and now get your fucking lawyer to finish our partnership agreement so we can get started on the Anne book."

The young man's name was Lionel Chase and he was there waiting, sitting outside Cliff's small office. He had already made friends with a few other staffers and he'd only been there for fifteen minutes. That tells you a lot about Lionel. He was like the guys in *Wedding Crashers* . . . both of them. He had Owen Wilson's quirky charm and Vince Vaughn's fast mouth.

He sat across from Cliff in a non-ergonomic chair and before Cliff could fire off one question, Lionel got the meeting started. He talked about his experience as a gossip columnist, which started because it was easy money to sell a few items here and there when you worked as a waiter at the fourth-floor restaurant at Neiman Marcus.

"You would not believe the scene up there. You see the same women at the Ivy and they'll be drinking mineral water but for some reason when they stop off at the fourth floor, after one of their shopping sprees, they pound back the wine or martinis. And there are no tables up there; it's just a round counter and they don't keep their voices down. After their first drink I'm hearing all this stuff about what famous person has money problems and what other famous person is a bad fuck and why some actress who says she went to rehab for prescription drugs is really there because she was caught selling stolen goods and they plea-bargained it out before it ever hit the courts."

Cliff was mesmerized. Lionel had the cocky confidence of someone who believes they can go through life without any blowback for their actions because they're bullshit busters. He acted as if that got him some special dispensation from the gods. But this is Hollywood and busting people on their lies can get you fired . . . unless you're Ricky Gervais and can give the Golden Globes show a big spike in the ratings. Lionel didn't seem at all worried about repercussions. He was still reveling in the power that came from having information.

"When I first started blogging about all this stuff, I loved going after the stupid girls who think they're smart. The ones who think that because they're on a reality show for a couple of seasons and making some money, they're business savvy. No, moron, you're decoration. You're a girl in a bikini having an immature moment on camera with a guy who is cheating on you with a girl who actually is hot in bed. You're decoration the network is using to sell light beer."

Every so often Cliff got a question in, like one about whether Lionel did blind items.

"Blind items? I love blind items. I got in trouble for one of my better ones."

Cliff was enjoying this far more than he thought he would. "Details?"

"Okay, the guy I wrote about is an actor now but at the time he wasn't. So my item read, 'What hunky brother of two sisters who both dated the same king of the scene isn't as much of a ladies' man as he would have everyone believe, especially his family? He'll deny, deny, deny but what's with his very close friendship with an up-and-coming chef who was one of his fraternity brothers at USC . . . or so they claim. As if fraternity brothers are as "close" as these two are.'"

Two sisters dating the same king of the scene? Technically this could have been a reference to a chapter in Hef's life or a couple of Hollywood playboys but Cliff knew Lionel was talking about the Boleyns and the guy in question was George.

"What kind of trouble did you get into?"

"I was fired and the item was pulled after some big-dog attorney sent my boss a cease-and-desist letter."

"We would never run anything like that here," Cliff said.

Lionel got the message. "I would never write anything about the Boleyns, if that's what you're worried about, though I know a lot about them."

"How do you know so much?"

"Because I dated chef guy, too."

Cliff had to hand it to Lionel. He was playing it just right. Instead of assuming that his involvement in previous Boleyn gossip would take him out of the running for a position at a website owned by Anne's husband, he played it right down the middle, letting Cliff know that what he knew about the Boleyns was not something he'd write about but something he might talk about exclusively . . . to Cliff.

When the interview wrapped, Cliff shook Lionel's hand and told him that the decision would be made in the next two days. He didn't want to hire him on the spot, lest Lionel think the Boleyn information was what sealed the deal.

Before leaving, Lionel said some flattering things about Cliff's efforts to protect the environment and the good work he'd done for Conservation International. He had done his research and even knew about the compost pails Cliff was trying to sell to Whole Foods. It was the only part of the interview that felt ass-kissy but Cliff didn't mind getting his ass kissed for a change.

He picked up the phone and called Theresa. "You're not going to believe who just walked into my office. You're going to love this."

Chapter 43

Anne

Seeing your guy in charge is the most powerful aphrodisiac in the world. I'm reminded of that when I accompany Henry on a visit to his campaign headquarters. No storefront space for Henry. He has taken over an industrial building in Santa Monica and converted it to a highly functional but creative environment. The main room downstairs is large with high ceilings and filled with desks (no cubicles) like something you might find in a newsroom. Most of the volunteers working on that floor are attractive, energetic and in their early twenties. The private, executive offices on the second level overlook this central space so there is a feeling of cooperation and integration. Everyone is invited to the party.

It amazes me to see how Henry's presence electrifies the room. They believe in him. He represents something to them. They are ready to go into battle for him. As I watch him stop to talk to various people I am in awe of his ability to inspire. People want to talk to him about everything. Not just the campaign but sports, art, movies and what teams he thinks might make it into the Final Four.

Maren is there, on a break from school, and she's in the middle of all the activity and loving being the daughter of the man everyone wants to get close to.

"Hello, Anne," she says, giving me a perfunctory kiss on the cheek, which she only did to please her dad. If he weren't standing right there, there'd be no kiss and only the briefest acknowledgment. Maren does realize that she can't push her father too far. As it is she's already made a stand by staying with her grandfather while back in California, under the pretext that he's getting old and she rarely gets to see him. No one doesn't see through that excuse, but there's no point in making the rift between us any wider.

Her look has changed since going to boarding school. Her hair is messier, her clothes more East Coast. She's wearing riding boots over skinny jeans and a plaid shirt over a Columbia University tee, even though, last I heard, she doesn't have the grades to get in there—even with a generous "mandatory contribution" from Henry. If anything her attitude toward me has become even more defiant. She exudes an air that says, I'm so much smarter than you, so much more clued in. Poor Maren, she hasn't even begun to get clued in. She will always hate any women her dad chooses, unless they're pretty enough to try to steal him away from me. Then she'll love them until they succeed and become the new threat.

"How's everything going?" I ask.

"Great," she says. A text message comes in on her phone and she reads it and shrieks the way young girls do when they think that whatever little thing going on in their lives is so important. "My roommate," she says. "Got to call her." She runs off and I'm left standing there feeling old and cynical even with my powerful aphrodisiac standing right next to me, covertly pinching my ass.

Theresa is there and when I first spot her she's leaning over the desk of the same woman she brought to the party at William Gardiner's—Jane Seymour, the jewelry designer and San Francisco socialite. As

Henry and I stop to talk to some of the volunteers, Theresa and Jane come over to say hello. I notice that Jane is wearing five or six gold bracelets with tiny jewels embedded in the gold. If this is her claim to fame, her signature design, I'm underwhelmed. You can find some version of the same bracelet in the jewelry department of any upscale store from Fred Segal to Saks. Theresa is her usual self. Very darling this, darling that.

"Darling Anne, have you met Jane Seymour?"

"Hello, Jane."

"Such a pleasure to meet you," she replies. I have to give her credit. She does have a sweetness about her. I'm almost ready to like her until she turns to Henry and says, "Hello, Mr. Tudor." It's said with almost the exact inflection that I used back in the early days of my relationship with Henry. It's the excessive formality that a playful young woman at court might use to camouflage the fact that she had her hand down the king's pants a half hour before.

"Hello, Jane," he replies, but his hello doesn't seem excessively anything. Not even excessively flat. Am I overreacting or has Henry gotten better at deceit?

In any case, Jane scurries away and Theresa takes my arm. "I want to give you a tour." I look at Henry and he's smiling. "Yes, give my lovely wife the tour."

After Theresa fills me in on the architectural and design choices that were made throughout the building, we end up in the kitchen. There are plenty of healthy snacks on the big communal dining table. Green tea. Vitamin water. Fruit. Salads. Bags of almonds. Whole-wheat bagels. The only nod to indulgence is a glass jar of red licorice sticks.

"Want something to eat?" Theresa opens the refrigerator, brings out a bowl of sliced apples and sets it on the table. As she helps herself to one I notice she's wearing a bracelet, just like the ones Jane had on.

"No thanks, Henry and I are going to lunch when we leave here." I'm looking right at her, a look that screams, *Don't think I don't see what's happening.* She sits down and so do I because the truth is, I'm much more tired than I was when pregnant with Elizabeth. Theresa continues to avoid my gaze and keeps talking about the campaign and how much Henry is enjoying it. "It's all good," she says.

"Well, mostly all good."

"Mostly?" She reacts like I insulted her.

"It's easy to get hooked on all the attention, makes him vulnerable. Wanting this too much, wanting anything too much jeopardizes your power."

"But what's life without great passion? You know that, Anne."

"Passion isn't the same thing as need."

"But it often is."

"Theresa, you have great passion for your job but you don't *need* it. There are other jobs out there in the world for you. You've made a name for yourself here. You could easily find another situation . . . if you had to."

Her mood changes immediately. Earlier in our "friendship" we might have danced around this conversation a little more, but now we're two women who have earned the right to say what we mean.

"Just the other day, Henry told me how much he counts on me, how much he needs me to run things for him. This isn't about my needs, Anne. It's about his."

"And mine," I say. "So don't fuck with me."

I pick up her arm. "Nice bracelet. Did Jane Seymour give you a discount? Or was this a thank-you present for getting her a job on the campaign?"

"I don't have as much sway over Henry as you give me credit for."

"I don't think you have much sway at all. But I do think you do or say what you think he wants to hear."

"I'm just an employee trying to do a good job."

"You're going for more than a gold star on your report card."

At that moment Henry walks in, oblivious to the big chill in the room. He opens the glass jar and helps himself to some red licorice.

Chapter 44

Theresa

Traffic lights were out and a cop was at an intersection up ahead directing traffic, which had slowed to a crawl. Theresa was in no mood to slow down. She didn't care that winds had unexpectedly kicked up and knocked the power out in a ten-block area north of Sunset. She wanted to be home. She wanted a break from Henry's world, even if it was only for an evening. Usually she loved nothing more than working for him and plotting ways to become his invaluable ally. She loved finding a book he might be interested in or getting him excited about some new challenge. Lately political gossip was becoming her specialty and she loved entertaining Henry with gossip items fed to her by Lionel Chase. Every so often, though, she needed to decompress and when that need hit, it hit fast and being delayed by Mother Nature was not okay with her.

As her car crept along in bumper-to-bumper traffic, she called Cliff, who thankfully picked up.

"What's going on?"

"Power outage. I hate the DWP. I hate weather."

"Where are you?"

"I should be ten minutes from home but it could be an hour. Keep me company."

There was the slightest pause on the other end, the kind someone might take to adjust to doing an onerous task.

"Anything particular you want to talk about?"

"Anything but Henry, my job, your job, anyone else's job . . . and especially let's not discuss Anne."

Maybe it was because it was after work hours and Cliff also needed a break. Or because he thought he had been doing a great job with the site and Theresa got all the credit. Maybe it was because he wasn't getting paid all that much. Or because he'd gone off his healthy diet and ate a Snickers bar. Whatever the reason, he was short on patience.

"What do you want, Theresa? What would make you happy?"

She wasn't in the habit of confiding in Cliff about her inner needs and desires but she was stuck in that car and was feeling vulnerable. Her last run-in with Anne a week ago had scared her.

"That's a big question."

Cliff sighed. "I don't get it. You've got the job you want. You got a boss who respects you. You make good money. You don't seem interested in getting married or having kids or any of that."

Theresa cut him off. "You have no idea what interests me. And it's not always about getting what you want. Sometimes it's about keeping what you've got."

"That's what contracts are for." Cliff was making a not so thinly veiled reference to his own contract renegotiation. He was trying to be cute. Theresa wasn't in the mood for cute.

She actually sounded a little panicked. "What if I'm the fall guy? What if Henry loses the election and I'm the fall guy?"

Cliff didn't bother to point out that in spite of her wishes they were back to talking about Henry. "He's not going to lose."

"If he does, someone is going to have to pay."

"It won't be you," Cliff insisted. "No one is going to make you the fall guy."

"You can't be sure about that. You know these people never think they're to blame."

"If heads are going to roll, your head will not be one of them."

Now Cliff was annoying her. His reassurances were based on nothing but his desire to get off the phone quickly. "Forget it," she said. "I'm having a bad day, that's all."

"That's what I'm here for . . . download on me, baby."

His use of "baby" made her cringe. A reminder of the intimate connection they once had, which now seemed like another life-time ago.

Her silence felt like a rebuke to Cliff, so he tried a less chummy approach. "You got a generator, flashlight, candles?"

"I've got it all, Cliff. I've got the whole fucking hardware store."

After she hung up, she thought about Cliff's comment about her lack of interest in marriage and kids. She rarely thought about those things, but now, going home to an empty house on a stormy evening, she had to wonder . . . Did she sacrifice too much for this job? For Henry?

A gust came down the canyon.

"Two riders were approaching and the wind began to howl."

She thought about that line from Jimi Hendrix's version of "Watchtower." It was a song that played often on the jukebox in a club in Boston she hung out at back in her law school days. Though not her usual kind of music, that song always got to her. Hendrix's guitar sounded like it was in pain and it made her aware of her own pain . . . the kind you get when you realize it's not going to be an easy road but there's no turning back. She put down the driver's-side window and let the wind howl.

By the time she got to her intersection and turned right up her street, she was more anxious than ever to get home and didn't bother to obey the stop sign. Unfortunately a cop on a motorcycle, hiding in the shadows, pulled her over.

"I admit it. I'm guilty. Just give me the ticket." She wasn't even going to try to talk him out of it, so when she started to cry it was a great shock to her. "I'm sorry, I'm sorry," she said. "I guess it's all too much."

"What's too much?" The cop seemed to genuinely want to help.

"The thought of going home to a dark house, no electricity, no security system."

"Where do you live?"

"A few minutes up this street."

"I'll come check out your house, make sure it's safe."

"That's so very nice of you, Officer . . . ?"

"O'Neal. Kevin O'Neal"

Turns out the electricity was only out at the bottom half of the canyon, so Theresa did have lights and power, but the cop came inside anyway since he'd come this far. He walked through the downstairs with her and when they got to the kitchen she made herself a drink. She noticed he wasn't a bad-looking guy.

"Want one?" She got another glass out for a shot of vodka.

"I'm not off duty yet."

"When do you get off duty?"

"Ten minutes."

He picked up a framed picture on a shelf in the breakfast nook. "You know Henry Tudor?"

"I work for him"

"What do you do?"

"Oversee various divisions of his company."

"So you're a big shot." He was flirting.

"You're funny."

"I'm a cop. I have to be. Without humor, you don't survive twenty years on the force."

Theresa got him to stick around by asking questions about crime in the neighborhood and whether she should get a guard dog. He said yes and she said she'd look into it but that was never going to happen. She didn't want any animals in her house. Too messy, too needy.

"Do you have a card or something? In case I ever need someone to protect and serve me." Now she was flirting and she wasn't being subtle.

He wrote his number on a piece of paper he pulled from his pocket. "You don't remember me, do you?"

Theresa had no recollection of ever having seen Officer O'Neal before.

"A while back. The night there was a sinkhole on this street. Only one lane for traffic. Me and my partner were making sure all you rich people didn't break out in any fights over right of way."

He was teasing her and she liked it.

"I'm not rich."

"You're not poor."

As they bantered Theresa felt a surge of energy like the kind she always got when she realized she could probably fuck the stranger she was talking to. She noticed he wore no wedding ring, not that she cared if this one was taken. Even more exciting, a plan was beginning to form, an idea about how she could use Officer O'Neal to discredit Anne. Once again Theresa remembered what her shrink had said about the seed of something good that could be found in a bad situation. She had started the evening off depressed, had gone through a stop sign, been caught . . . but now was on the verge of sex and a new plan.

When he handed her that piece of paper with his number on it she started fantasizing about his uniform and how if they were going to have sex, he had to keep on at least part of it. Definitely the boots.

"What's with that look?"

She smiled. "I have a look?"

"That look that women sometimes get."

"I was just looking at your gun."

"That's what they all say."

She looked at the clock. It was a minute after six. Officer O'Neal was now officially off duty.

Chapter 45

Anne

Leo de Vince and I keep in touch and continue the friendship that started with my first visit to his studio. After my hives episode, I sent him a note of apology, telling him I was sorry to have been so distracted I couldn't sit still and so worried about so many things I couldn't get rid of the scowl on my face. He responded with a note saying . . . no scowl and nothing to worry about and invites me to stop by the studio again when in the neighborhood. I rarely get to his side of town but since becoming pregnant with my son I have an urge to go for drives, always heading west, toward the ocean in Santa Monica and Venice, never up to Malibu or any of the fancy part of the coast. I like the public areas and I'm fascinated by the busy street life down on Abbot Kinney. People are out shopping, eating. There are dogs, bikes and kids everywhere. It's a snapshot of what normal looks like and I need to visit it occasionally now that I'm no longer living it. And when down there, I often check in with the master.

My plan is to swing by and surprise Leo later but first I'm headed southeast to Lennox Middle School. I'm due there for a one o'clock lunch meeting about the educational programs I've set up using the financing provided by Henry's philanthropic trust. As I head down on La Cienega, passing more and more houses with security bars on all windows and doors, an email pops up from Leo. He tells me the portrait is finished and has been sent over to the house. For weeks I've put the painting out of my mind, a part of me hoping it would never be done because I'm not comfortable seeing my image anymore. Is it the pregnancy? Lately I feel like I've lost my photo face. Cameras scare me. Who is the woman in those photos? Maybe seeing myself through Leo's eyes will show me who I've become.

I call the school and say I'm not feeling well and would it be okay if I came by tomorrow instead. When you're pregnant and have given them lots of money, everybody is accommodating. Meanwhile my foot is on the gas and I'm driving much faster than I should but my curiosity can't be downshifted. This is my chance to meet myself. Anne, this is Anne, or at least Anne as seen through a master's eyes.

At first I don't think anything of the new silver BMW parked next to Henry's cars in the driveway. There are always lots of people around when Henry is home, though he usually isn't home in the middle of the day. But then I think maybe he's curious about seeing me immortalized by Leo de Vince or, equally possible, curious to see what all those thousands of dollars bought him.

As I walk through the hallway, I hear the housekeeper talking in Spanish to someone on her cell. Instinctually I head upstairs to look for Henry even though he could be in his downstairs office or out by the pool, conducting business on the phone from his favorite lounge chair. Provoked by nothing, I remember years ago when my father wanted me to drop off contracts at Henry's house, his ploy for getting us together. It seems like an odd thing to pop into my head at that moment but when I open the door to the master bedroom, I gasp and it all makes sense. There was nothing random about that memory. My intuition provided that flashback. Henry is sitting on the edge of the bed with Jane Seymour on his lap, her arms around his neck. She jumps up when she sees me and one of her bracelets falls to the floor along with some campaign paperwork, her excuse for being there.

"Get out!" I scream.

"Anne, Anne." Henry tries to calm me down.

"Get out of my house."

Jane can't figure out if she should pick her bracelet up or get out of there fast. She looks to Henry to give her some guidance but he's focused on my hysteria.

"Anne, let me explain." He's talking in that silky voice of his and Jane finally locates her bracelet on the floor, picks it up and runs out of there as if fleeing a fire.

"How could you . . . in my home when I'm pregnant with your son." I have my hand over my stomach, protecting my child.

"You're being dramatic for no reason." Henry tries to put his arms around me but I push him away.

"No, no . . . you're killing me," I say. "How could you? How could you?" We go on like that for several minutes and I don't know if I want to hit him or just fall on the floor and sob. From outside I hear the sound of Jane starting up her BMW and putting it in gear. As devastated as I am I'm aware that she goes back and forth a number of times. No genius. She can't even manage a three-point turn. "Can someone teach that moron how to drive?"

Henry is trying to get me to sit down and calm down but I don't want him near me. I run out of the room but don't get far. As I head down the hallway I feel a pain in my stomach that feels like a dagger and I know even before I feel the trickle of blood between my legs . . . I know I'm losing my son. He's leaving me alone, unprotected.

"My baby, my baby, my baby."

"Call 911!" Henry shouts to the housekeeper.

As I wait for the ambulance I notice that the Leo de Vince portrait of me is leaning up against the wall. There I am. No scowl. No royal haughtiness. No sense of entitlement. A woman like any other except he captured a sparkle in my eyes. He captured the spirit that I've always counted on. Looking at my eyes in that photo, I try to tap into that spirit once again. I pray that I still have it in me somewhere and it will give me the strength to hang tough while the sound of the ambulance siren gets closer.

Theresa

Theresa wrote this down in the private journal she kept: "Heard that Anne lost the baby and I have compassion for her pain." She wanted that on record, not that she intended to show her diaries to anyone but it was part of her ritual. A show of kindness and compassion mitigated the guilt she might feel for any damage she might cause in the pursuit of her mission. The miscarriage had given Anne a bump in public opinion polls. Women cut her some slack because of her loss and there was even a rumor that *Vogue* was going to put her on their cover. Theresa knew this was a critical time. The window of opportunity to get rid of Anne and replace her with the more congenial and malleable Jane could narrow, even close, and then where would Theresa be?

She knew she had to be careful but decisive about how she operated. And she had to do all this and still feel good about herself. It was the curse of her gender. Men just plowed ahead toward their goals, not as worried about methods and sins until they got old and suddenly awareness of their mortality made them more self-reflective. But being a woman, there was always a part of her that wanted to be nice. Theresa always came out of this struggle with enough rationalization to keep her being aggressive. Her rationalization this time was that Anne was no slouch when it came to replacing people and would have no problem getting Theresa fired.

The universe seemed to support this conclusion because it gave her another gift. A phone call from the Lennox School. The head of the program didn't want to trouble Anne as she recovered both mentally and physically from the loss of her child so they contacted who they thought was still in charge of all Henry's philanthropic endeavors. Seems that a $250,000 payment that was supposed to be in their account hadn't yet been made. They were sure it was just a bank error and Theresa agreed and promised she would look into it and correct it. Theresa immediately understood that Anne had "borrowed" that money because a few days earlier Theresa's new best source of information, gossip star Lionel Chase, told her he heard Thomas Boleyn had lost $250,000 in Carl Wolsey's Ponzi scheme. Theresa was no slouch at connecting the dots. The dollar number was no coincidence. This was classic Anne, typical Boleyn behavior. Protect the family no matter what has to be done, except usually Anne was sharper. This was an amateur's mistake, which meant it was done without Henry's knowledge. You can't take tax-deductible money and give it to your father . . . even on a temporary basis. Theresa guessed that Anne was thrown off her game by the miscarriage and paranoia about Henry. The question was, What should Theresa do with this information? She could go directly to Henry. Or she could call Anne and put step one of her plan to get rid of "the queen" into action. She picked up the phone and suggested they meet for a truce lunch. Anne didn't seem all that interested so Theresa sweetened the pot by saying, "I have some interesting information you should hear." That clinched it.

The location for the lunch was a restaurant in Theresa's neighborhood. The place was on the small side, dark wood paneling, soft lighting. It was a place known for its steaks, not its salads.

Anne got there ten minutes late. Stress had taken its toll. Her face looked thin, and if she didn't watch out, could become gaunt . . . old. For once Theresa was glad she had a more round figure and face. Less wrinkles. More volume. It was the upside to not being a size two. Theresa had ordered a bottle of wine before Anne arrived. Though a bottle was not customary for a ladies' lunch, Anne seemed to welcome the sight of it because the first thing she said was, "And you didn't even wimp out and go for a bottle of white."

"Some days only a pinot noir will do."

"What's the occasion or maybe I should say what's the problem?"

"First things first," Theresa said as she filled Anne's glass. "How are you feeling?"

They did fifteen minutes of small talk but none of it was pointless. Theresa was laying the groundwork with every word she spoke. Her approach was to disarm Anne by talking about her own miscarriage at the age of twenty-four (it was actually an abortion but who was going to check) and she followed that up with her usual well-researched helpful hints. A yoga class that would balance Anne's hormones. An acupuncturist whose treatments make women hyperfertile and a brain spa ("Darling, you know they already have a chain of them in San Francisco") that does marvelous things for your brain chemistry when you are going through any kind of trauma.

Theresa waited until they were on their second glass before she brought up the big topic. She started by complimenting Anne on all the good work she was doing down at the Lennox School, mentioning the new computers, terrific tutors, stellar test scores.

"Are you monitoring me?" Anne smiled, the first smile Theresa had seen from her in a while.

"I'm praising all your good work but . . . there is some monitoring going on."

"Oh really?" The smile on Anne's face retreated slowly, gracefully, as if making a voluntary exit.

And then Theresa brought up the pesky problem of the $250,000. She brought it up with the perfect touch of seriousness and reassurance, saying she understood how these errors happen from time to time. Anne showed no sign of being alarmed except she did drink a bit more wine, which was exactly what Theresa hoped she would do.

"Don't worry about it," Anne said. "I'll look into it and take care of it."

"I'm sure you will but it might not be so easy. If I've heard about it, others may know and be drawing the wrong conclusions."

"I'll take care of it," Anne said, and this time her tone made it clear the topic was closed.

Theresa refilled both their glasses. "Might as well finish off the bottle," she said.

"Might as well," Anne agreed.

While the two women waited at the valet stand at the back of the restaurant, Theresa couldn't be more thrilled with how part one of her plan was going. Anne had consumed plenty of wine, not so much that getting behind the wheel of a car was a danger but enough so it could be a problem. Theresa made sure Anne's car was brought around first. She held her breath to see if the back right-side taillight had been tampered with as she'd instructed Lionel Chase to do. *Yes!* It was the type of equipment malfunction that might inspire a very diligent, highly motivated cop to legitimately pull Anne over.

The women said their goodbyes with more warmth than they would have felt had they not had some pinot noir in them. Theresa waited until Anne drove away and was down the block before she walked over to the taxi she had called earlier. Not a big drinker (Theresa had consumed more than usual to ensure that Anne did, too), she didn't trust herself to drive safely. Besides, she wanted to watch all the action without being seen.

She instructed the cabbie to take a right at the end of the street and then pull over. Just as she'd planned, Officer O'Neal had stopped Anne for that broken taillight and from there it was just one small step to "Step out of the car, ma'am." Theresa got a thrill watching her new secret lover in action. He made Anne stand on the street, in full view of anyone passing by, and go through the series of balance tests to determine her degree of intoxication.

A van pulled up behind the cop car. Out of it jumped Lionel and a tabloid photographer who started snapping pictures. There was nothing Anne could do to stop them and Officer O'Neal didn't even try.

"Okay we can go now."

The cabdriver looked at his passenger in the rearview mirror. "Go where? You didn't give me an address, lady."

"Go up to Wilshire and make a left."

As the cab sped down the street, it hit a pothole and a wave of nausea came over Theresa. Whoa, she thought. Maybe she should have eaten some bread to soak up some of the wine. They hit another pothole and Theresa felt an even bigger wave of nausea.

"Stop, stop!" She was screaming now.

"Go. Stop. Make up your mind, lady."

He pulled over, not a second too soon. Theresa opened the door and puked into the gutter. People walking by looked at her like she was some pathetic wino lush. As she heaved up the last of the red grape she thought, Well at least I'm not famous and no one cares enough to take my picture.

The cabdriver tossed her a box of Kleenex, checking to make sure no vomit got on his cab. He didn't ask if she was okay.

Theresa wiped her mouth and tossed the soiled Kleenex into the street. She sat up and closed the door. "Don't worry. You're getting a big tip."

The cabbie took out a canister of air freshener he kept in his glove compartment. The stench of the sweet gardenia perfume made Theresa want to puke some more but she managed to stifle the urge. She pulled a Hermès scarf out of her purse and wrapped it around her mouth and nose like she was a bandit. Resting her head back on the seat, she tried to concentrate on why this would all be worth it.

Chapter 47

Anne

I'm not drunk. I don't get drunk. When I was a teenager, my father explained to me that drinking too much is not an option for a Boleyn. Judgment gets abandoned, secrets are revealed. It never ends well. When my mother, on occasion, drinks more than she should, my father doesn't approve but doesn't say too much . . . part of the tacit trade-off that comes with more than thirty years of marriage. Besides, my mother isn't a lottery ticket for my dad the way his three children are. We carry the burden of building up the Boleyn fortunes. Even without my father's expectations, I wouldn't be a big drinker because I'm too vain. I don't like how sloppy and silly people get when they drink beyond their capacity. And as Henry's wife, it's too dangerous. If I lose my balance for a second or use the wrong grammatical syntax, rumors could spread (and have spread) that I'm drinking or doing drugs. Such is the public minefield of anyone in the news, and any wife of Henry's is always going to be a target for those who make their living writing gossip . . . or creating gossip when none exists.

So for all those reasons I have trained myself, over the years, to be able to enjoy a drink, or even two, but never lose sight of my cutoff point, even when I'm upset about something and Theresa gets to me good when she mentions the $250,000. I don't let her see my concern though it's all I can think about. How did she find out about this so quickly? I know I acted rashly when I wrote my father that big check but I had every intention of putting that money back by the end of the week. My plan was to talk to Henry about loaning me that money and if need be, I'd sell some of the jewelry he's given me, including a couple of outrageously expensive watches that I don't wear and wouldn't miss. Doesn't everyone use their cell phone to tell time these days? This isn't about theft, it's about accounting. Yet Theresa won't see it that way. Now that she has something on me I need to regroup. In the meantime I sit there and sip my wine.

Before I'm finished with my first glass, Theresa is already on her second. Okay, I think, she's in the mood to get a little wasted and I attribute that to the stress of the campaign or maybe some personal unhappiness. I've always thought of her as one of those women who is only interested in having relationships with the kind of rich powerful men who only want to have relationships with young attractive women. She sets herself up to fail and in the meantime hooks up with "civilians" who think of her as a rung up on their ladder. It's the worst of both worlds. No wonder she sometimes has to go for a bottle of wine at lunch.

We order light salads but neither of us eats very much. At one point I look for our waiter to ask for some bread (can't find him) and when I turn back I notice Theresa has refilled my glass. I realize she's trying to get me drunk and I assume it's because she thinks I'll start babbling about personal stuff. So begins another chess game. I pretend not to notice what she's trying to do and Theresa makes moves based on the belief that I don't notice. When she goes to the ladies' room I empty my glass into hers. When I go to the ladies' room, she refills my glass again. So it goes, a cat-and-mouse game. I sneak an Excedrin, which is full of caffeine and keeps me from getting tipsy. At the same time, Theresa gets more and more intoxicated and *her* secrets begin to pour out. I think some of what she says is true but she's laying it on thick, probably because she's running that tried-and-true girl-bonding trick . . . pretending to share secrets to get another to genuinely share theirs.

It's a chess game that I win because I walk out of there having given nothing up and though I've got a tiny buzz going, I'm fine. Meanwhile, the alcohol has made Theresa maternal. "Call me when you get home, Anne, so I won't worry." When the valet brings my car around and I see the back taillight is smashed, Theresa berates the valet for his carelessness and when he defends himself, claiming it wasn't his fault, she changes the topic and reassures me that she has a great mechanic who will fix it immediately.

By the time I get in my car, I'm happy to be away from her and looking forward to being alone with my thoughts. I'm still thinking about Theresa and the $250,000 problem so I open the glove compartment and reach for Wyatt's CD. I need to hear his soothing voice. That's when it happens.

The siren, the flashing lights in my rearview mirror. A cop on a motorcycle, telling me to pull over. At first I think I made an illegal turn but I check the street signs and I did nothing wrong. He does the standard move, asking for license, registration and proof of insurance. He shows no surprise or interest at seeing my name is Tudor, which is unusual. Almost no one in L.A. doesn't know the name Tudor.

"You've got a broken taillight," he says.

"I know. It just happened. I was having lunch around the corner—"

He cuts me off. "Did you have any alcohol at lunch?"

This is the critical question. To tell the truth is to open the door to a nightmare. To lie is to open the door to getting caught.

I lie. "No."

"Step out of the car," he says.

"What?"

"Step out of the car." His tone is forceful, belligerent.

I get out of the car, wondering if it's legal to make me get out of the car and how long it will be before some passerby recognizes me. Not long. A guy with a camera gets out of a van and starts clicking away, so many photos one right after another that it makes me hate the digital age.

The cop is in his mid-forties and his motorcycle helmet is not a good look for him, makes his head look gigantic in proportion to the rest of his body. I get the feeling that he hates wearing it and for a second I feel bad for him.

He orders me around. "Stand there. Don't move. Drop your hands by your side. Close your eyes and count backward from thirty." We run through the whole series of balance tests and I pass them all. Am I perfect? No, but I wouldn't be perfect if I'd been drinking green tea all day. I'm hoping the worst is over when he says, "I want you to take a Breathalyzer test."

That's when I realize something is very wrong here. The cop is strange. It's weird how quickly he decides to test me for alcohol even though I show no signs of intoxication and gobbled three Altoids. There was never any credible reason for him to think I was drinking.

He sees me wavering so he adopts a different attitude. "Look just breathe into this." He shows me the Breathalyzer contraption. "Assuming you pass, you'll be on your way in thirty seconds."

I weigh my options.

"These portable machines are more giving than the equipment down at the station." He's really trying to sell me on doing it now, which only makes me more suspicious. He's selling me hard on his "good" advice. He's like one of those salespeople working on commission who tell you that a certain color lipstick brings out the blush in your cheeks. Well, my cheeks don't blush for no reason and I'm not buying that this cop is trying to give me a break.

"You know, officer, I've read a number of reports saying the police have gotten a lot of false positives with this portable equipment."

The second I say that his friendly sales pitch is over and he turns into big bad cop.

"You don't want to take this test? Okay, here's what we can do. I can call backup and have you handcuffed, thrown in the back of a police car and hauled down to the station. If you don't want to do a blow test there, we can stick a needle in your arm and do a blood test and make you sit it out in a jail cell for a few hours while we wait for the results . . . and you know sometimes those labs take a really long time. Sometimes a whole day."

I consider saying, Do you know who I'm married to? I'm pretty sure he does know so I don't bother making that point. I'm trying to reason this out. I do have alcohol in my system and the legal limit in L.A. is lower than it used to be and who knows, maybe one glass of wine is over the limit. I know with each tick of the clock that alcohol is leaving my system and the equipment back at the station is probably a higher quality and has better accuracy. I'm not trusting this cop and his portable machine and I'm pretty sure this is not one of those moments when my paranoia is overboard. My choices are take this test here, which might come out positive and also might be rigged, or have him call backup and be hauled off to the station (and publicly humiliated) but have a better shot of not getting charged. Calm comes over me and I'm grateful for that. I've been so emotional for the last few weeks that I welcome a problem that, as nightmarish as it is, forces me to think analytically.

"Call backup," I say.

The cop looks at me with contempt and goes for his phone.

I'm tired and sit down on the curb until he yells at me to stand up and not to move or I'll be arrested for . . .

He gives me another list of charges and punishments that await me if I don't do exactly what he says but I'm not listening. I only have one question and I know I'm entitled to an answer.

"Excuse me, sir, what's your name?"

"Officer O'Neal."

Backup comes fast. The two rookies in the black-and-white are sweet and do their very best not to hurt me when they put on the cuffs and gently help me into the backseat of the car. Those backseats are so tiny. My God, how do they arrest fat people? It takes fifteen minutes to get to the station. Tick tock. Less alcohol in my system.

Sergeant Kent, who is in charge, is younger than Officer O'Neal and asks the three questions he's required to ask. "You know why you're here? Any medical problems? Any questions?"

"Yes, one question. Is it legal to make someone get out of their car and submit to all kinds of testing without probable cause?"

He checks his notes. "You told Officer O'Neal you had wine at lunch."

"No, I didn't."

"That's what it says right here."

"I never said that." I look over to Officer O'Neal, who is standing right there, his arms crossed over his chest. He won't look at me.

It's becoming surreal. When the thought hits you that someone is trying to frame you and you don't know who or why but you have your suspicions—but even those suspicions seem extreme—reality as you know it disappears.

"I'd like to call my husband, Henry Tudor."

The sergeant is not immune to the Tudor name but he has to abide by the rules . . . at least outwardly. He politely explains that as soon as I take the Breathalyzer test, I can make whatever calls I want. Then as if the divine protection that Henry seems to have been born with has trickled down to me—at least for the moment—they can't get the Breathalyzer computer to work. Tick tock. Tick tock. Officer O'Neal fidgets with the settings, getting more frustrated as his superior gets more apologetic and therefore more chatty.

"You go to a lot of basketball games?" His way of saying I know your husband owns a team.

"Next time Henry's team plays L.A. you can have my floor seats if . . ."

I'm kidding and he takes it that way. Last thing I need is a bribery charge. While we continue to talk basketball, Officer O'Neal morphs into a Keystone Kop as he brings another cop over and the two of them can't get the machinery to work, forcing them to unplug the computer and reboot. Tick tock. Tick tock.

"No crime today?" I say to the sergeant. It's three o'clock in the afternoon and I'm their only action.

"Comes in waves," he says. "You don't want to be here around midnight tonight."

"I don't want to be here now."

He laughs and then, probably worried that he's being too unprofessional, he clams up and goes back to his paperwork. Tick tock. Tick tock.

I'm left alone and tell myself that I should write about this someday. Funny how all through my early and mid-twenties "someday" seemed like a reasonable plan. As I hit the end of my twenties, "someday" is beginning to feel like an excuse. What happened to my career, to my hopes of being a writer? People think when you marry a wealthy man you have more time to pursue whatever interests you have and I guess I do but somehow along the way I lost the drive to sit down and write or maybe what I lost was my belief that I had anything worthwhile to say. When the world perceives you as lucky, your audience shrinks unless you want to expose your privileged life as a sham. Unless you do, your problems are considered minor, your anguish considered an indulgence.

A woman is brought in under arrest for shoplifting. She's in her late thirties and I'm wondering what she stole and if her "someday" plan fell by the wayside and eventually led to her desperate measures. She looks like she's had a hard life but I notice her nails are perfect.

That's her source of pride. Her life might be a mess but she has beautiful manicured nails. My life might look Bel Air perfect but my nails are bitten practically to the point of bleeding.

She eyes me with disdain. "What are you looking at, bitch?"

Tick tock. Tick tock.

Finally they get the computer running and I'm led over to it by Officer O'Neal, who tells me to blow hard into a small funnel-shaped tube. I do.

"Blow harder."

I do

"Look, either you blow harder or . . ." He rattles off another litany of threats but in a softer voice, not wanting anyone to hear.

So I blow with all the power I have in my lungs and the machine beeps, the signal that the results are now being analyzed. The sergeant comes over and waits with us for the computer's verdict. It's a freeze-frame moment. No talking. No sounds at all except for the computer. I notice Officer O'Neal has no wedding ring on but I can't imagine he's never been married. He's a decent-looking guy, now that he's got his helmet off. Probably twenty years ago was an attractive police academy graduate with a solid future ahead of him. I guess that he's divorced, his ex-wife gets half the pension, he has to pay child support and he never made detective. Not an easy life but no reason to take it out on me.

Finally the computer spits out a piece of paper with the numbers of my blood alcohol content. The sergeant grabs it, reads it. He looks at me with an apologetic grimace. "Mrs. Tudor, you're going home."

I walk out of the station feeling like I escaped a term in the gulag. Now that the ordeal is over and I'm free, I'm shaking. Why? Why? Why? What is going on here? Why is someone trying to frame me? I add it up. Theresa, trying to get me drunk. The broken taillight. Officer O'Neal's lie. It's scary and I'm not used to this kind of fear. I feel like I'm the target of some kind of vigilante justice but what am

I guilty of? Being with a king? "Be careful what you inspire," Leo de Vince once counseled me. As usual he's proven to be right.

The two rookie cops are parked outside in a black-and-white, ready to give me a ride back to my car, but before I can get into the backseat I spot the same two guys across the street who were hounding me earlier. This time the photographer has a video camera.

"Uh . . . no thanks," I say to the rookies. "I'll call a cab."

I take out my phone. "By the way . . ."

One of the rookies looks up.

"I know traffic isn't your beat but those vultures in the van are parked in a red zone."

The rookie smiles. He has no love for these parasites, either. "We'll take care of it."

Chapter 48

Cliff

So this is what a sociopath looks like, Cliff thought. He was in his office, sitting across from Lionel, who was discussing his latest blog idea, a piece he's calling, "My Pledge to Celebrities." It was his promise to honor the line between what's public and what's private, though he had no intention of doing so.

"I think something like this can get a lot of play," Lionel said. "It'll be picked up by the mainstream press. Who knows, maybe I'll get invited on the *Today* show."

Though Cliff had hired the guy, with every passing day he found him more repulsive. Lionel thought he was smarter than everyone else, so much more plugged into the whole scene. He always dressed as if he had cash to burn. Hundred-dollar T-shirts. Tom Ford sunglasses. Prada jackets. On Cliff's desk was a copy of the weekly tabloids and the reason Lionel could afford the finery. Splashed across the covers were pictures and stories about Anne's "incarceration." The fact that she wasn't charged with driving under the influence didn't seem to affect the speculation that she was unhinged, a mess and a danger to herself. How much money Lionel and his pal got for those pix and items was pure speculation but no one speculated a lowball amount. Lionel, of course, swore he had no involvement in those trash stories (though Cliff knew otherwise) and his "Pledge" was a reaction to rumors that claimed otherwise.

"I think it's the perfect time for something like this," Lionel said.

Cliff quickly read the "Pledge" and thought, Are you fucking kidding me? It was nothing but empty promises wrapped in emptier proclamations. "Are you going to be able to honor this? The part about not harassing celebrities?"

"Harassing isn't my style. I hear things. I have a lot of contacts. I report."

"But you never instigate, provoke?"

"Half these celebrities are calling me up, wanting me to plant items about them, wanting me to get photographers to show up and snap them. It's not like I'm hiding in the shoe department at Barneys waiting to snap some C-list reality star trying on a pair of pumps. I don't chase them; they chase me."

He looked at Cliff as if he actually believed his own lies. That's where the sociopath thing came in. Lionel could look anyone straight in the eye. He could pass a lie detector. He had the good-guy thing nailed down perfectly. He could have played Matt Damon's role in *The Talented Mr. Ripley.* A chill went through Cliff as he listened to Lionel talk about his "Pledge." Here's a guy who can both stalk a celebrity and write a blog expressing outrage at celebrity stalkers.

"Hey," Lionel said, "I heard something you and Theresa are going to love . . . obviously not to leave this room but a friend of mine was at a party that Maren Tudor was at and she was a little wasted and she was bragging about how when her dad first started dating Anne, she sent Anne a tarot card of the Queen of Pentacles with the head sliced off."

Oh great, Cliff thought. Now Maren's becoming a wasted teen.

And in what world does someone brag about sending that tarot card? In what world does that become a funny story for a gossip columnist and his cohorts? In what world does a guy like Lionel, with allegiance to none and exploitation of all, get rewarded? The truth was these things happened in Cliff's world, the world he chose to make his home and career.

"Here's the thing about your pledge piece, Lionel. It's all take and no give. It's a way of drawing attention to yourself but you and I know there's not a chance you're going to live up to it so the celebrities get nothing out of it."

Lionel laughed good-naturedly. "It'll get the site some attention, more hits, more traffic. I bet you we run this and get hundreds of comments in the first five minutes. If we don't I'll buy you a new T-shirt."

Under his new suit jacket Cliff was wearing an old NRDC tee that had been washed almost to the point of transparency.

"Not just any T-shirt . . . a Prada T-shirt," Lionel said.

Cliff backed off a little, not because he cared about a new shirt and not because it wasn't his job to police sociopaths. He also didn't care that the pledge would get the site some attention. He backed off because he had to choose his battles and this one wasn't worth fighting.

"Cliff, did I tell you what I heard the other day?" Lionel was like a stand-up not ready to leave the stage. "About the actress who had surgery to make her pussy smaller? You and Theresa are going to love this story. So this actress, wait till you find out who it is . . . tells her boyfriend—"

"Stop," Cliff said. "Theresa and I love very different things." Though that wasn't always true, it was starting to be true more often. Cliff had a growing distaste for Theresa's take-no-prisoners approach to survival. In the past his own survival depended on not being judgmental but he was beginning to feel a change in his moral compass and it terrified him.

"Oh lighten up," Lionel said. "It's just a fun story. You're not anti-fun, are you?"

Cliff shot him a look.

"Sometimes I'm not so sure." Lionel smiled and he did have one of those dazzling smiles that can make you feel anti-life if you don't join in on the fun.

Lionel continued his pussy story but Cliff wasn't really listening. This guy is dangerous, he thought. In time that smile of his will turn him into a caricature. When he's older and all his manipulative skills won't be able to keep his eyes from growing cold, he'll have the face he deserves . . . an exaggerated tragicomic mask that will be impossible to love. But in the meantime, he's a well-dressed, skilled storyteller with no conscience. In Hollywood, New York, Washington and in the royal courts of the past and future, the Lionels of the world thrive.

Cliff did sit up and pay attention when the sociopath said, "I've left the best for last. Guess who's in the running to be your brain double?"

"My what?"

"That's what I call myself when I'm hired to write someone else's story. Lacy called me about doing your Anne book though I know your actual name won't be on the cover. What name will you use?"

Cliff couldn't have felt more ambushed had Lacy appeared with a SWAT team. Deny, deny, deny, he told himself.

"I know nothing about any book." There was no way Cliff could be associated with an anti-Anne book. What was Lacy doing mentioning the project and his name to a gossip columnist?

Lionel ignored the denial and just kept talking. "Usually I don't brain-double for a novel but I make exceptions for something like this. Last month I got a job offer to do a novel for a C-list actress. I said, 'Honey, you're not a writer so why are you pretending you're going to write a book? Why even put your name on the cover? We all know you can't write anything beyond a one-hundred-and-sixty-character text message.'"

"Stop," Cliff said and this time he had a real point to make. "You can't be associated with a roman à clef about Anne Boleyn and still work for this website."

"Let's cross that bridge when we come to it," Lionel said, unfazed. He then continued his one-man show with stories about an actor doing rehab at the Peninsula hotel, a twenty-year-old son of a politician who was fucking a forty-year-old heiress and a rumor about a chemist in Silver Lake who was making high-quality quaaludes for a select group who have the money to pay for the pleasure.

Cliff couldn't care less about any of it because all he could think about was that because of Lacy, he was now forced to stay on a sociopath's good side.

"Okay, we'll run the 'Pledge' on Monday."

Chapter 49

Theresa

With the exception of Henry and maybe a dozen other major players in Los Angeles, Theresa rarely went to anyone else's office for a meeting. She made them come to her, which is why her assistant was shocked when Theresa scheduled a meeting outside the office with a "nobody." Angela DeSoto wasn't a total nobody. She had been a big model years ago but years ago was ancient history in Hollywood, a place that proudly embraced "what have you done for me lately" as a legitimate philosophy.

Angela and her director husband had been two of the high-profile people who had invested a considerable amount of money with Carl Wolsey and lost most of their wealth. They'd become the face of the scandal, in part because Angela wasn't shy about talking to the press, as long as the photo shoot or on-camera interview production team picked up the cost of her favorite makeup artist and hair stylist.

It was while watching Angela in a TV segment that featured

photos of Angela back in her early days, including one photo of her with the Boleyn girls, that Theresa decided she needed to meet the once famous, now broke, former model. So she tracked down Angela's number, called and introduced herself as someone who was about to change Angela's life.

Even with that promise and Theresa's fancy job title, Angela acted like she was doing Theresa a favor by even taking the call. Once a diva, always a diva.

Theresa humored her and agreed to come to Angela's house the next day . . . though she was on the verge of dropping the whole idea after Angela rescheduled three times. Does this broad not get that her celebrity days are numbered? When she got annoyed Theresa often fell back on the way her father in Boston talked. Yet she ended up driving all the way out to the beach to meet with Angela, who kept her waiting for fifteen minutes. That took Theresa to the breaking point but as she was about to leave, Angela swept into the room, a towering six-foot-tall blonde, her hair tucked inside a newsboy cap. She was wearing skinny jeans and a slouchy black top that drew attention to her swanlike neck.

"Don't ever split up with your husband, get a bad haircut and get your period all on the same day." She tossed this off as if broken marriages were not more serious than a split end.

Not giving Theresa room to respond, Angela continued her rant. "You won't believe what it's been like around here since being reduced to poverty. So much is going wrong, it's getting biblical."

Theresa didn't bother pointing out that there were no signs here of a downgrade to a poverty lifestyle. Gardeners and the pool guy were on the premises and when she arrived, Gelson's was making a delivery that included a case of wine. "Something is about to go very right," Theresa said, which momentarily shut Angela up.

Then, as if she'd left the room and come back in again, Angela cordially extended her hand. "*Hi,* Theresa, welcome to my nervous breakdown. Would you like something to drink . . . water, tea, tequila?"

"Water would be nice."

"Carly!" Angela screamed. "Carly's my assistant," she explained. "I swear she's got a hearing problem. *Carly!*"

While they waited, Angela sprawled on the couch. "Tell me something good."

"How would you like to write a book for Tudor Publishing?"

"Tudor as in Henry?"

"Yes. He's starting up a new company, an imprint for art books." The fact that no such company yet existed did not seem to worry Theresa.

"A book about what?"

"When you modeled and were hanging out with Bono and Sting and Mick and every other big name who only needs one name, you were always taking pictures. Before everyone was running around digitizing every breath they take, you were getting the shots. This was before people learned to hate having a camera in their face. Your pix are fun. No one is posing. They document an era. I think a book with those photos and your recollection of the stories behind those photos would be fascinating."

"I got them all," Angela said. "Lorne Michaels. Kate Moss. Johnny Depp."

A woman in her late twenties rushed into the room. She was wearing motorcycle boots, jeans and a velour zip-up jacket. She looked exhausted and was carrying a bunch of clothes in her arms.

Angela looked up languidly. "Carly, can you bring us some Fiji water and a shot of Cuervo."

"Yes, right away but I need to know, do you want to check these dresses before I ship them off?"

"Throw them on the chair over there and I'll get to it."

Carly did as she was told and Theresa got the feeling that those dresses could still be sitting there a month from now. Angela operated by her own clock. Theresa looked a little closer at the dress on the top of the heap. "Is that a Dior?"

"Dior, YSL, Chanel. They're all couture. The red one is Alaïa;

I was wearing it the night I met my husband. Now I'm selling everything. Shipping them off to Decades, that store on Melrose that sells vintage for a ton of money. This is what I'm reduced to because of Carl-fucking-Wolsey."

"I have no love for the man," Theresa replied.

"Did you get screwed, too?"

"No, thank God. He never would have taken me on as a client . . . or a lover. I'm not rich enough for the former or glamorous enough for the latter."

Angela sat up and reached for a cigarette from a leather box on the coffee table. "There's a lesson in all this," she said, though she seemed uninterested in discovering what that lesson might be.

Realizing it was time to get to the point, Theresa took charge of the conversation. "I imagine you have pictures of Anne and Mary Tudor from your modeling days."

"Some. We spent some time together one summer."

"Are you still friends?"

"Sure. Why not?"

This was the tricky part, the part that separated people who waited for things to go their way and people who made their way the way things will go. Theresa moved in for the kill. "You know what's so great about you is you're not one to apologize for anything you've ever done. You own it."

"Better me than someone else," Angela said. "You know I have had people steal pieces of my story."

"This book will be your chance to own your wild days. Take us inside that era and put a frame around it. This could put you back in the spotlight. Who knows where this could lead. You know how much money Tyra Banks makes?" Theresa knew she was getting close to sounding like one of those pitchmen hawking men's suits for ninety-nine dollars and throwing a shirt and tie in to close the deal.

Angela put out her cigarette and got down to business. "Just how truthful do you want me to be and how much will you pay me?"

"I guess that depends on what you have to say."

"You'll want me to leave my Anne stories out of it, right?"

"Why don't you tell me all your stories and we'll worry about the editing later."

Carly came back carrying a tray with two bottles of Fiji water, a bottle of tequila and two glasses.

"Only need one glass," Angela said. "I'm the only lush here right now but hey if you can't drink when you're getting divorced and your husband is on location seeking solace with the script girl—how pathetic is that?—when can you?"

Carly went to remove the second shot glass from the tray but Theresa stopped her. "I'll take that." She poured herself a drink, raised her glass to Angela. "To the next new chapter in your life."

Angela raised her glass as well. "I'll drink to getting a big check from Tudor Publishing."

This was going to be easy, Theresa thought. Angela might act like a diva but Theresa knew the type. She suspected that Angela would end up giving away half her stories and selling the other half for less than they were worth to pay for a pair of Louboutin boots or a Lanvin trench she just had to have.

"That must have been wild . . . you and Anne in Paris that summer. What was she like back then?"

Angela chugged the tequila and bit into a piece of lime. "We used to have a saying that summer . . . 'try me.'"

Theresa wasn't sure what that meant.

"It means don't assume anything about me and definitely don't assume I won't surprise you. It wasn't 'try me' like in 'I'm available.' It was more like a dare. Like 'I might be available if it's an interesting proposition.'"

"Anne was quite young that summer, wasn't she?"

"Young and curious," Angela replied.

Ah, Theresa thought. Now it's all making sense. No wonder Anne has such an erotic hold on Henry. No wonder she knows the right tricks to trap him. She's far more experienced then she's ever let on.

Theresa took a gulp of tequila and bit into her slice of lime. It was bitter and made her wince . . . and yet life was getting sweeter all the time.

Chapter 50

Cliff

"Well what do you know? Theresa Cromwell is in the building." This was what Cliff said when he looked up from his computer screen to see Theresa standing in the doorway.

"Got to pop in every now and then to make sure the patients haven't taken over the asylum." She waved a few pieces of paper in front of him . . . his new contract.

"Finally." He reached for it but she yanked it away.

"There are a couple of things we need to discuss first." She closed the door and took a seat.

There's no question that power changes how people look, Cliff thought, because as Theresa's power had grown, she had developed an aura that made her seem less drab, more Technicolor.

"Remember that night of my party, when I announced my promotion?"

"Of course." Cliff was thinking that if he had to pick a color that best described Theresa at that moment it would be red.

"Remember afterward when we were talking and you made a joke about Anne flashing Henry?"

"I said for a second there I thought she might be."

"Well, let's say she flashed you and that you were shocked because she wasn't wearing any underwear."

"Me? Why would she ever flash me? She would be more likely to flash one of the cute bartenders."

"Okay, let's say you saw her do that."

"But I didn't."

"No one is asking you to swear on a Bible."

"Why would anyone ask me about this at all?"

"But if anyone does . . . now you know what to say."

Cliff couldn't believe what Theresa was saying. Her red aura was not the red associated with love; it was the red associated with battle. What Cliff really couldn't believe was that he'd ever fucked her. Thank God that was done with a long time ago. Now she was fucking some cop and she loved telling Cliff about it. He didn't understand why she would think he'd be interested in those details. She was always saying, "We were Dionysian for two hours last night" or "We were fucking for an hour and a half." Did she have a timer next to the bed?

He looked out his window and saw that his wife was dropping off his son. He and C.J. had tickets to the Lakers game and he had been looking forward to it before Theresa ruined his mood. He had to tackle this head-on. "What's this all about? What's going on, Theresa?"

"What's going on? Look at the polls. Henry is slipping and Anne is the problem. That run-in she had with a cop—"

Cliff interrupted. "There was no DUI."

"People think there was but Henry had it fixed."

"And why would they think that?" Was this more of Theresa's California Scheming? It was starting to get to him. He was getting perilously close to accusing her of being the source of the misinformation but Theresa either didn't notice his annoyance or was too intent on making her point.

"Anne is not liked. People think she's a gold-digging whore with a substance abuse problem who killed Catherine."

"That's all crap and you know it."

"I'm talking about polls. I'm talking about people's emotional response to a candidate. And then there's Jane Seymour. The more people find out about her, the more they love her. Her family is one of the most powerful in California politics, second only to Catherine's. They practically own Sacramento and control San Francisco. Do you know what an asset that can be for Henry in this election?"

"Are you suggesting Henry should get rid of Anne?"

"I'm not suggesting anything. I'm just seeing which way the wind is blowing and I suggest you do, too."

Cliff heard his son's voice outside the door to his office. C.J. was talking to Cliff's assistant, who told him his dad was in a meeting. The two were chatting about basketball and C.J. had all the excitement you might expect from someone his age going to his first Lakers game.

Theresa picked up on it, too. "Lakers game tonight. Got good seats?"

"Very good. It's my son's birthday this weekend. Turning thirteen."

"Those seats are expensive, aren't they?"

"Very expensive."

"Life is expensive," Theresa said, to drive home what was at stake here.

She dropped his new contract on his desk. "Did I mention you'll also get a nice signing bonus if we both agree that we can continue to work together . . . amicably?"

Cliff heard the ultimatum and found it astonishing. Was Theresa really going to circulate more lies about Anne and get him to do it, too? Was she really saying go along with the program or be out of a job?

As if reading his thoughts Theresa put a kinder spin on her proposition. "I like you. I always have. I hope you agree to the terms so we can do some exciting projects together."

He nodded as if he were considering it but he was thinking he hoped that somewhere in her there was still some humanity. He was hoping that maybe it came out when she was with her cop. He hoped that despite her rabid ambition, maybe when she was in bed with her latest "maintenance program" and they were lying next to each other she occasionally reached out and touched him, not out of lust or need but to give him affection. He hoped she was capable of a gesture that said to another person, You're important . . . not because of what I can get from you but simply because you're you. He wanted to believe that she had that in there somewhere, and not for her sake but for his. He would hate to think he'd once fucked a monster.

When Cliff's answer wasn't forthcoming, Theresa was forced to be a little less kind.

"Not a great job market out there these days, is it?"

Cliff had to laugh. "This is like a scene in a bad TV show."

"Life is like that sometimes, isn't it?" Theresa chuckled. "Maybe that's why sometimes bad TV does so well. People feel right at home watching it."

She let herself out and he heard her turn on the charm with his son.

"Lakers going to win tonight, C.J.?"

"They're going to kill." His voice was full of optimism and anticipation.

"I hear you've got good seats."

"Fourth row."

"Wow, fourth row. You're lucky to have such a generous dad."

She said it loud enough to make sure Cliff heard, as if he needed a reminder. Her parting shot hit its target.

C.J. walked in with a FedEx package in his hand. "Hey Dad, this just arrived for you."

Cliff looked at the return address. Lacy. He opened it to find a book proposal and the first two chapters of the Anne book. After Lionel had brought up Cliff's name in connection with the secret project, Cliff had called Lacy, upset at her lack of discretion. She told him he was getting riled up for nothing. She admitted she had mentioned Cliff's name to Lionel but claimed she never said Cliff was actually involved. His anonymity was, she assured him, intact. She also told him the publishers were willing to spend big money if Lionel ghostwrote the book—that meant Cliff might eventually get a six-figure check. He had let her calming words and his desire for six figures keep him on board but now reading these pages it was worse than he'd imagined. He thought the book might be a light, fun, trashy read but this was dark, blistering . . . and wrong.

"Guess what, Dad? I'm covering tonight's game for the school website and if I do a good job they might let me do a regular sports column. How cool would that be? I'd really like to write an analysis of how the Lakers match up with the top eight teams in the Western Conference." His son seemed to have gone from boy to young man overnight. He was getting to that age when he would be looking at his father through more critical eyes, seeing how his old dad matched up with other players. Did Cliff really want to go through these next years fearing his son would uncover another ugly truth about how he made a buck? How did Cliff want to be seen by his child? As a hardworking dad who didn't always take the high road but did the best he could . . . or as a scumbag? He made a decision right there—and he knew he had to act on it fast or he'd lose the guts to follow through.

He gathered up the book proposal and handed it to his assistant. "Shred it."

He then emailed Lacy a brief message. "Thanks but no thanks, I'm out." As for the contract Theresa had left behind, he put it in his desk and locked the drawer. He'd sign it tomorrow but . . . he'd finesse the Anne stuff. If anyone ever asked him about her he would say she has a naughty side—which was to her credit. If asked about that night at the party, he'd keep it vague. He'd say . . . she might have flashed. He'd add that he was a little confused because he'd had a dream about it and now with so much time having passed, he wasn't sure how much was real and how much was his dream embellishment. He'd find a way to hold on to his job by lying as little as possible. He'd figure it out tomorrow. Right now he was celebrating his son's milestone into manhood and his own decision to be poorer but happier. Fourth row (tonight) at a Lakers game was great. Twentieth row (next year) wasn't horrible.

Chapter 51

Anne

A false-bottom moment. That's what George and I call it. That moment when you think, Okay, this is the bottom and now things will start turning around, but then you realize that there are levels below that bottom and all you can do is hang on and hope you're tougher than you feel.

When I drive over to the Valley to meet George at Jinky's, I keep thinking about the events of the last few weeks and how they've brought me to my knees. The almost DUI, the problems in my relationship, losing my baby, the sight of Jane making herself comfortable on my husband's lap, the problem with the $250,000 that Henry has begrudgingly reimbursed the philanthropic trust for but is still an unresolved issue with us, my failed attempts to get pregnant again, Theresa's growing influence over Henry, and Maren's continued disdain for me . . . now she doesn't even try to hide it from her dad. All of that and more have reduced me to an insecure mess with only occasional moments of spark and courage.

On the way over to Jinky's something happens that I take as a sign that things might be turning around. In one of those ground shifts (possibly a tremor from a small earthquake) that happen all the time in L.A., a boulder from the top of Laurel Canyon falls onto the street below where I'm driving. It scrapes the left side of the back bumper before landing so hard it tears a big hole in the pavement. I screech to a halt, pulling my car over to the side of the road, as does another motorist who was driving right behind me.

"My God," the motorist says. "You missed that by a millisecond. You must have a guardian angel looking out for you."

I'm too shaken to speak. Why are these bizarre things happening? Two thousand twelve has long since come and gone and yet the threat of the end seems still to be hanging in the air. This new era of *Post*radamus seems no different from what the sixteenth-century seer predicted. Did he just get his dates wrong? Is Armageddon still on the calendar?

"Are you okay, Anne?"

He recognizes me, which isn't unusual. There are so many photos of me all over the Internet, for good and bad reasons.

"Yes, I'm fine." I search my purse for some money, feeling I should tip him because when you're famous and you don't tip people they trash you. Locating a twenty, I force the cash into his hand even though I realize that's stupid. What am I tipping him for? For being relieved that I escaped death? Is that what it's come to? Thank you for not hating me?

He mumbles thanks and something about wishing me well but I barely hear him. I get back in my car, thinking what if he's right? What if I do have a guardian angel out there protecting me? It was a silly thought and I don't usually go in for that kind of thing but this is L.A. Hope springs eternal here as long as the sun shines. Besides, these days I'll take whatever lucky omen I can find.

George is already at Jinky's when I arrive. Middle of the afternoon, it's like nap time in there, which is why we chose it. One of the waitresses in the back booth even looks like she's nodding off until a busboy nudges her and she gets up and slowly comes over to our table to get our order. We only ask for Diet Cokes and she's bummed that she had to get up for so little.

"So glad you called today," I say. I notice that George looks tired and hasn't shaved. "I've been thinking about you, missing you. How's everything going?"

"It's not going. Everything is stuck."

I know that the one feature he'd starred in was shot but hasn't been put on a release schedule yet and that just about everyone knows his marriage is falling apart but is there more?

"Anything I can do to help?"

He shrugs, defeated. "Two weeks ago my agent tells me I'm a front-runner for the second lead in the next James Cameron movie. That falls through but my agent says, 'Don't worry you're going to get an offer for a cool action movie that Henry's studio is doing.' The director is the one who really wants me. I don't even think Henry knows I'm up for the part. So I don't bother playing that card. I figure I'll save it just in case it comes down to me and another actor. Then this morning they tell me I didn't get the part and now the director isn't interested in me even for a small supporting role. This, after the *Hollywood Reporter* ran a story three days ago saying the part was mine."

George isn't complaining so much as he's trying to figure out what happened. It's not like these things don't sometimes occur in Hollywood; it's just that when they do there's almost always some political, not artistic reason for the change.

More often than not, people get jobs in this town because whoever is hiring them is doing what's best for their own personal agenda, not what's best for the project. If those two things happen to coincide, great. If they don't, you can find yourself hanging out at Jinky's at three in the afternoon, wondering how you fell through the cracks.

"Do you think, by any chance, this was Henry's decision?" George asks, knowing that if the answer to that is yes it does not bode well for either of us.

"Let me see what I can find out."

"That's not why I called you, though." He sucks down that Diet Coke fast and is looking for a refill but the waitress is on her cell phone and doesn't respond. The busboy does, however, and George waits for him to be out of hearing range before continuing. "You've got to be careful."

I'm about to tell him I just survived near decapitation by a flying boulder when he says, "You've got to watch out for Theresa Cromwell."

"What do you mean?"

"I mean she's plotting against you. Look, as you know things are bad with Lacy, basically we're done. Neither one of us has filed for divorce but it'll happen. We got into this big fight last night because I forgot to leave the light on in the garage when she came home late and she said it was hostile. That's how nuts she is. She thinks I left the light off so she would have to stumble in the dark before she could reach the light switch, maybe trip and fall. At this point I don't even bother to argue anymore. I tell her I'll install a light that goes on automatically when the garage door opens. But she won't let it go. Finally I say enough, I've had a bad day, didn't get the part in the movie and she says of course you didn't. People have had enough of all you Boleyns."

"What people?" I can feel the defensiveness in me building at the thought of that twit Lacy attacking my family.

"I'm not sure except I know she's pals with Theresa. I'm not saying they get manicures together but they're an unholy alliance. She rarely talks about it but that light thing set her off and she starts saying that she's tired of hearing me put you on a pedestal and that 'Annie's days are numbered.' That's what she said. 'Annie's days are numbered because when someone becomes a liability, they're gone.'"

"Gone? Gone where?"

"I don't know. The point is Theresa is serious trouble for you."

"I know that. I've always known that."

"But now she might be winning. You've got to do something about it."

While I'm trying to figure out what exactly I might do about this, George's attention veers away from me and over to the entrance, where a young man has just walked in. He looks vaguely familiar but I can't place him immediately. When he spots George, he waves.

George nods, smiles and then explains. "He's early. I'll tell him to wait at the counter."

He gets up and has a short conversation with his friend. Now that I get a closer look I see that the guy is George's age, good-looking with a face that's easy to like. It has nice guy written all over it. If I had to guess I'd say he loves dogs, recycles and never forgets a birthday. I also remember where I've seen him before. He was at George's wedding and in George's iPhone pix. All the pieces fall into place. He's the chef guy George was linked to before he married Lacy.

When George returns to our table I say, "Aren't you going to introduce me?"

"Okay, if you want. We're just friends," he reminds me.

I don't know if he's telling the truth or not but I know that we all have our secrets. I never told him all the things I ended up doing that summer I spent in Paris.

"Friends are important," I say. "I don't think I have any left."

"Anne, that's the saddest thing I've ever heard." I can see he's trying to come up with names and finally finds one. "Wyatt is your friend."

"Yes, Wyatt is my friend."

"And I'm your best friend."

"Yes, you are, George."

"And Ethan will be your friend."

He beckons Ethan over and makes the introductions and I realize that whatever their relationship, Ethan makes George feel less alone and that's no small thing. I feel comfortable leaving George in his hands.

"I should head back home. You two stay and hang out." I look around. "Where's the waitress?" Not finding her I throw ten bucks on the table.

"She's over there," Ethan says. "Talking to the enemy."

He points across the room. She's peering out the front glass window and signaling something to a photographer outside. The paparazzo takes a step closer, holds his camera up, points it in our direction and starts shooting.

"Fuck," George says. "That's all Lacy needs to see. A photo of the three of us together."

"Don't worry," I say. "I'll take care of the gossip terrorist."

I go out there and I know I shouldn't do this and my intention is to be rational but reason isn't an option with guys like this. I'm sure they think they're just trying to make a living and though there are lots of bad and annoying jobs that can be justified by that explanation, this isn't one of them. I know some celebrities seek out attention from the paparazzi and that's a different case. If you're going to call for the cameras then you forfeit your right to privacy. I've never sought them out except maybe once . . . that first time Henry and I went out in public as a couple.

I march right up to the photographer. "Leave us alone."

He keeps clicking away.

The sound of a camera getting off multiple shots can drive you crazy. It's like a bully in the schoolyard spitting out insults and daring you to spit back. Or push back. And I do. I put my hand in front of the camera but still he keeps clicking and I know he's not going to stop so I manage to grab the camera out of his hand and throw it against the wall of Jinky's, where it smashes into bits.

He'll sue me. He'll do whatever it is he has to do but he didn't get a shot of George and Ethan. Protecting my brother makes me feel like I've saved him from a tumbling boulder . . . at least for the minute.

Back in my car, the weight of George's warning about Theresa hits me hard. I know he's right and I don't know exactly what to do so I fall back on a tried-and-true strategy. I decide to shop for some trashy lingerie. Satin push-up bra, ankle-strap stilettos, a long strand of (fake) pearls, body cream with a slight tint to it that makes your skin look amazing . . . and doesn't rub off on the sheets.

My purchases made, I call up my guy. "Hey, Henry, I'm on my way home with surprises for you."

"I'm in a meeting right now," he says, "and I have another one after this."

I picture him in his office at home, in one wing of the house and me in my trashy sexy outfit alone in the other wing.

"Okay, I'll just see you when you're a free man again."

He sort of laughs and says, "See you later."

He hangs up abruptly. I drive to the bins behind Rite Aid and toss my new purchases into the trash.

Chapter 52

Theresa

Theresa would not have even approached Henry with all the information she had gathered had she not seen that he was clearly falling for Jane Seymour and that things with Anne had reached a tipping point . . . too much against, not enough in favor. Theresa did make the distinction between falling and falling in love. Henry might act like he's in love with Jane but it had more to do with the right timing than the right girl. Or the right girl for the right time. However you wanted to look at it, it wasn't the eternal connection that might be immortalized in history books but it was a very, very good thing for everyone involved except the Boleyns.

Theresa prided herself on looking at the cold, hard facts and had they added up to a plus sign next to Anne's name she would have suppressed her feelings and pretended to be a cheerleader for Team Anne but that's not the way things were going. It had reached a point where she could rationalize that it was her job to hasten Anne's defeat. Henry was way down in the polls . . . and much of it was because of his wife and all the bad press she'd been getting. What if he went down in a big ugly, public, embarrassing defeat? Then there was the matter of all the money he'd spent on the campaign, a small fortune. Theresa understood the very rich. Didn't matter how many billions they had, they still hated to be overcharged for a cable bill. Losing money hurt and losing a small fortune was a hurt with no quick fix. Theresa felt she had no choice but to lay it all on the line for Henry. Since the problem was Anne, removal of Anne would be the solution.

"How?" Henry asked. It was the only question he put to her through the first part of her presentation. He then sat back and attentively listened as Theresa, like a litigator, pled her case to this one-man jury.

She pointed to the unsavory rumors about Anne and her brother being intimate, the gossip about Anne and her secret visits to Wyatt's and the stories about Anne and her private sessions with Leo de Vince. She brought up all the nasty talk about Anne's $250,000 "mistake," which hadn't been squashed even though the money had been paid and the incident resolved. She didn't say that the columnist Lionel Chase, who had become her good friend, had helped keep that story alive through blind items he sold to the tabloids, and had stoked the story to make it appear that Anne was guilty of fraud. Theresa talked about Anne's racy past in Paris, the details of which Angela DeSoto would, out of her affection for Henry, leave out of the book. Of course, further protection was the fact that Angela's book was being published by the newly formed Tudor Publishing . . . an idea that was surprisingly easy to sell Henry on. Theresa had assembled clippings from newspapers and had printed up disparaging articles about Anne off the Internet. She never once voiced an insulting personal opinion about Anne but instead let the so-called evidence speak for itself. She talked about Anne's reputation as a pothead who loved getting high with her sister and the gossip about how she'd occasionally flash her pussy at parties. She drank too much. She was violent—the lawsuit with the paparazzo was still in the news—and, whether fair or not, was widely considered a wicked stepmother.

Theresa had worked with Henry long enough at this point to know that you never ever present him with a problem if you don't have at least one solution at hand.

"I'm only telling you all this, Henry, because I know you like to have all the information that's out there. I don't presume to know what's going on in your personal life but if it isn't working out with Anne and you want out I can help make that exit happen smoothly and quickly."

"Go on," he said. His expression revealed not even a hint as to what he was thinking.

For a second Theresa feared she'd gone too far but there was no turning back.

"Okay, first thing we do is get the word out there that Anne recognizes she has problems and has to go away to deal with them. Maybe rehab, maybe Betty Ford, probably someplace out of state would be even better. We say she's there for depression and addiction to prescription drugs or something like that. We make it clear that it's her choice to end the marriage because she needs to be alone. You make a statement about how brave her decision is and how you will always support her efforts to be healthy. Then we make sure there are plenty of photos out there with you and Maren and Elizabeth. Very slowly we start to leak photos of you and Jane at some school event for Maren. Maybe the two of you at the Pediatric AIDS fund-raiser with Elizabeth.

"Now, to really turn these poll numbers around we'll need the support of some conservatives and moderates. Jane's family is uniquely suited to help you with their ties to political groups in the middle and northern part of the state. They can pull in the undecided voters, which is the bloc that will determine the outcome of the race."

Theresa got so swept up in her "closing remarks" that if she had ended with "God bless America" it wouldn't have seemed inappropriate.

Henry stood up and poured himself a drink. He didn't offer her one.

"Thank you for all your hard work. Obviously I've got a lot to think about."

She knew he wanted her to leave. She ached to give him a hug but she kept her professional distance.

"Call me if you need me," she said.

"Theresa?"

"Yes."

"Did you get taller?"

She was about to say it's the shoes but she was beginning to accept that even without the extra inches she was no longer so small. "Yes," she said. "As a matter of fact I have."

When she walked out of Henry's house, the late afternoon sun made everything appear golden. California, the land of plenty. Of thee I sing. She had never before felt such a mix of patriotism and eroticism as she felt at that moment.

A car came up the driveway. She hoped it wasn't Anne. She was feeling too good about everything to want to deal with Ms. Buzzkill. Good news. It wasn't the so-called queen. The car was an old but mint-condition Mercedes and the man behind the wheel was someone she had heard about but never met. Ferdinand Aragon, Catherine's father and Maren's grandfather.

He got out of the car, holding a manila envelope.

What she wouldn't give to be in on his meeting with Henry. Can Ferdinand help or hurt my agenda? she wondered. She concluded he could only help. The Aragons were no fans of the Boleyns.

As she drove down the canyon, this thought occurred to her. What if she toppled Anne and Jane turned out to be a problem? That won't happen, she reasoned. Jane is not the type that turns into a problem. But what if Jane disappoints Henry or, God forbid, she should die and then Theresa has to figure out her replacement? What if that replacement displeases Henry? What if the seed of Theresa's undoing is being planted right now in her triumph? No, no, no, she told herself. Not going to go there. Instead of thinking about everything that could go wrong, Theresa decided to follow another tip from her shrink and once a day think about everything that's going right. And with that in mind, she called Officer O'Neal to see if he was off duty tonight.

Chapter 53

Anne

It was 11 P.M. when Henry finally came upstairs to our bedroom. I had been waiting for hours and changed my outfit three times. At eight-thirty I was wearing a Versace dress, thinking that possibly I could lure Henry out to one of our favorite restaurants for a late dinner. At ten o'clock I changed into a silk negligee that he bought me for Valentine's Day. No point in not trying to look somewhat appealing. At 10:45 I looked at myself in the mirror and thought, Why am I trying to look good for a man who hasn't even bothered to say hello to me since I got home? How much effort does it take for him to hit the intercom button? So now I'm wearing drawstring velvet pants and a sexy T-shirt. Can't abandon all hope. Not that any of it matters.

He doesn't say those four words that all married women who want to stay married dread hearing—"we have to talk"—but he might as well say them because that is the conversation we're having.

He tells me it hasn't been working out for some time and for a while he thought he was to blame but now people—he didn't say Theresa and Ferdinand, but I found that out later—had brought facts to his attention. He has papers, clippings, audiotapes of my phone conversations and a manila envelope that he empties on the bed. There are photos of me and Wyatt embracing, photos of me walking arm in arm with Leo de Vince down at the beach, photos of me kissing (on the mouth) my brother hello and goodbye. There are numerous shots of me being put in the police car in handcuffs and compromising shots of me taken that summer in Paris. There's a whole series of shots of me looking wrecked at some club; my dress has slipped down and one of my tits is exposed. I was only nineteen years old at the time. Doesn't a nineteen-year-old get to make a few mistakes? Not that it mattered.

I sweep the photos aside. "Have you had a private detective following me?"

"No."

"Then where did all this come from? Did Theresa hire someone to dig up all this dirt?"

"No. Catherine did."

"Why am I not surprised?"

"And Ferdinand. Jake Winslow was working for both of them without the other one knowing."

"Catherine and her father doubling up on their efforts to spy on me? You've got to be kidding. Are they that dysfunctional or just completely insane?"

He cracks a bit of a smile. It's the kind of comment that, in the past, we would have laughed about, both of us appreciating the absurdity of the private detective taking advantage of the Aragon family's disunity and appetite for information. Jake Winslow outsmarts the royals. How modern.

Henry talks about how all my bad behavior has made it impossible to stay together. He doesn't talk about the election but I know my man. I know my king. He wants what he wants and what he wants right now is never to lose.

He does seem unusually upset about Wyatt.

"I know you cheated on me with him," he says.

"Not true." I do admit to flirting with Wyatt and crossing a few little lines but it's not like Henry isn't a guilty man. "You cheated on me with Larissa and Jane."

"I never promised you I wouldn't see other women."

"You encouraged me to believe you wouldn't."

"Did you really think I was never ever going to be with another woman? What I promised, and I kept to it, was that I would be sensitive to and protective of your feelings. You don't see stories about me and other women in the tabloids or all over the Internet."

The conversation was veering off into a place of confusion and frustration. How had it come to this point, where I was faithful to Henry and he wasn't faithful to me but I'm the bad guy?

"What are you saying, Henry? If something isn't in the tabloids or on the Internet it doesn't count?"

"There's a way to behave, Anne." He says this as if I'm too common to grasp the rules. "And the way you and George carry on, it's sick."

"You never seemed to think it was sick before."

"I didn't know everything before."

"There was nothing to know!" I scream.

Lacy, I'm thinking. And Theresa. God only knows what they said . . . what they made up. I'm beginning to see what's going on here. In this era of rapid communication and selective viewing, people can string together whatever stories, lies and innuendos they choose about someone and if they get that "portrait" out there big enough and scream about it loud enough it becomes a reality that diminishes and drowns out all logic and truth.

I could explain that to Henry but he's a very smart man, a man who so far as I know has never lost a game of chess, so he's got to be aware that I'm being unfairly accused and maligned. Not that it matters.

There was a time when I was Henry's future and he wanted a son with me and now he wants a future and a son with someone else. That's what matters and everything else is just a way to package his change of direction. I knew from the start it was my job to inspire and excite him and if I failed to do that, he would drift. What I now see is that all the love, passion and excitement a woman can give may not be enough to fulfill the needs of a king in his prime.

I'm not going to passively cave, that's not in my Boleyn blood, so I fight back.

"Let me tell you about your 'devoted servant' Theresa. She's one of those women who know you're never going to fuck them, which is all they really want, so they'll settle for the next-best thing . . . to exert control over who you do fuck. The truth is she hates women and has no use for them and she especially hates any woman you desire."

"False," Henry interjects. "She's quite close to—"

He stops, doesn't want to get into it, but I do.

"Jane. Close to, maybe. Friends with? Never. Theresa just prefers Jane because she doesn't threaten her, isn't as smart."

"Jane is quite accomplished." He says this with pride.

"You mean that 'jewelry line' she has? A half-dozen pieces on consignment at Neiman's is not a career. It's a hobby. A hobby for rich girls. That's all it is and all it'll ever be."

I can see he's getting angry but I can't stop. "I know right now you think she's the answer, you may even believe you're in love with her, but she's not going to be enough for you sexually. I know you, Henry. I know what you like, I know your passions, and after the first six months when the newness wears off you'll be bored and we know what happens when you get bored."

"Anne, you should stop before you make an even bigger fool out of yourself. Jane and I have a very special connection."

"Oh, I'm sure she connects really well when she's playing geisha. How good is she? You're the one who always said that only five percent of women really know how to give a good blow job. Is she in the five percent club? Somehow I doubt it."

"That's enough." His voice is thunderous.

I shut up, relieved to stop, because my own bitterness is making me sick. Moments pass before I speak again, quietly. "What are you asking of me?"

"I think you should go away. I think you should go to my ranch in Santa Ynez, until we figure out what to do next."

"Am I being banished?"

"We need to be apart. It will be good for us."

Ah . . . the power of a pronoun: *us*. Hearing it rallies hope.

"Okay," I say, "I'll go up to Santa Ynez, give you time to think."

I'm surprised by my own acquiescence. I never thought I'd be the kind of woman who would go away this quietly but now I understand the hope that doomed women of the past have mustered when defeat was inevitable. I can imagine queens of other centuries being sent to the tower but thinking I'm getting the fancy rooms in the tower . . . the rooms that just got the new rugs . . . so it's just a test. The king just needs to assert his authority and then when that's out of his system, I'll be back in the castle. The brain is fascinating, isn't it? One can put both paranoia and intuition on hold and have faith even when it's not in one's own best interest. Or is it? I know I can say, "fuck you Henry," and walk out of there with my daughter . . . but what would that bring? Henry has considerable power and my whole family is, in one way or another, dependent on him. Being defiant isn't going to get me what I need. Doing what feels good at the moment . . . telling him to go fuck himself is one way to go. Letting things roll, letting this new situation find its own form and trusting that tomorrow will be a better day to settle things or save things is the smarter way to go.

"When should I leave?"

"Now? Tomorrow? Soon."

"Now," I say. I wouldn't mind being in my car, on the freeway, moving fast. I suddenly wish I had a convertible.

"You don't have to pack a lot of things," Henry says. "I can have one of my assistants drive up in a few days with more of your stuff."

"And Elizabeth?"

"I'll tell her Mommy had to go away, just for a little while."

"A little while?" That's just a little too vague even for a woman with few options. "I want to see her this weekend."

"No problem. We'll make arrangements."

Is he just saying that now, to get me to go? My heart is broken but I can't give in to that emotion. I remind myself that I won't arrive at an extraordinary outcome if I don't make extraordinary choices.

"I'll call you," Henry says.

I'm tempted to ask when but I'm sure Catherine asked that very same thing on more than one occasion and there's no way that question doesn't sound cloying and desperate at a time like this. Besides, I don't doubt that Henry will call. What I can't predict is whether that call will be a new start or the final end. And then this thought: just what exactly is an extraordinary choice in this situation?

Chapter 54

Henry

My father once said kings can't afford sentimentality. He didn't say it to me. He said it to my older brother, Arthur, who was being groomed to take over the family's media holdings. Being the younger son I escaped much of my father's tutorials. As it is in so many families my role was decided at an early age. My brother was the brilliant one and I was the athlete, the gregarious one, the one who wasn't expected to graduate at the very top of the class and didn't. My brother excelled enough to take the heat off of me. He did everything that was expected of him, becoming a gifted scholar at Exeter, Yale and Wharton Business School. I was left alone to get a decent education at USC but not one that interrupted my love for sports and having a good time. There was a moment when my father was pushing me to make the U.S. Olympic ski team but I wasn't disciplined enough for that routine and had taken up golf and was on a mission to play at the best courses before I hit twenty-five. My brother died in a car accident shortly after he got engaged to

Catherine Aragon and I knew I was expected to step into his shoes. Ironically I found that the contacts I made on those golf courses, ski holidays and tennis courts proved more useful than a Ph.D. My personal life was a different story. I never intended to marry my brother's girlfriend though my father was obsessed with the alliance of our families. I wasn't about to be forced into a marriage. What happened is that Catherine and I started spending time together and before we thought of ourselves as a couple, the world did. Our picture was constantly being taken and showed up in magazines all over the world. We were a media sensation and we both got caught up in it. The world saw us as a golden couple and we let them inform our own sense of identity.

I don't usually think about my past, because I don't see the value in nostalgia and my present has always been an improvement on what came before and until that's not the case I'm not going to be looking in my rearview mirror. Yet, that night, after Anne left to drive up to Santa Ynez, I took a walk on my property . . . to my favorite spot on the other side of the pool where the dark brush of the canyon was to my right and to my left in the distance was the glittering city. There it was the darkness and the light all in the same vista, and a constant reminder of the line I walked. That's the thing about living where I do. It's ten minutes away from the busy clubs and restaurants on Sunset Boulevard and yet I'm sharing the same canyon with wild animals that, on full moon nights especially, make their presence known with the isolated, unnerving howl.

My father always believed the line between civilization and chaos was thinner than people want to accept. And as thin as that line is, the line between being the ruler of your destiny and one who is ruled is even thinner. My father also taught me that the best the world has to offer is there for the taking if—and it was a very important if—you know that the game is constantly changing and an ability to adapt one step ahead of others keeps you on the right side of that line. People who can't do that are what my father called "the new illiterates." My life with Anne and the promise that it once had were gone. All the information, gossip, facts, pictures presented to me by Theresa and Ferdinand would mean nothing if Anne and I had not already lost all forward motion. The reasons for that can be debated but the fact of it cannot. Theresa made her case dramatically; Ferdinand made his coldly. He told me he would help me get elected, promising to bring his formidable political clout in California politics over to my side if I would agree to Catherine's last request: To make Maren (on her twenty-fifth birthday) a voting member on the board of my corporation. He wanted assurances that she would be in primary position over any other children I might have and Elizabeth would be completely shut out of the family business. Though not accustomed to making such deals, I do see the advantage in doing so. Elizabeth will always be taken care of financially but her future role on my board is not an issue that I have much stake in . . . at the moment. More complicated is the question of my feelings about her mother. Anne is a combination of so many forces. Compelling and challenging. I loved this woman deeply. Love her still? Not a question I'll ponder. She was right for me then. I can't refashion her to make her right for me now. Jane is my future and I do love her but not in the way . . . the passionate way . . . that Anne and I came together. But future trumps passion. It also trumps love. And you think it's easy being a king?

In order for me to do the kingly thing I must keep one step ahead of changing circumstances. I have to end this relationship quickly and with the least amount of room for speculation. I know that deep down Anne understands this. We are very alike, both brought up with an addiction to achieving more and climbing higher. Energy comes from health. Sentimentality makes you weak. If you don't watch out, my father would say, you'll be like an old man asking "do I dare to eat a peach?" My father liked to toss out a line of poetry in his tutorials but I didn't need T. S. Eliot to be taught that lesson. I'm now in my forties. When I'm sixty I know I will feel differently but you don't stay on top of the mountain by acting decades older than you are. You don't give up the throne before your time. Power is not something anyone gives up easily or voluntarily. You don't stay on the top of the mountain by doing what others want you to do or expect you to do, or what is politically correct to do. You stay there by doing what you must do.

One of my household staff comes out looking for me, worried that something has happened. It's not like me to take a walk at night and be gone for what he informs me has been more than an hour. And then, as if cued, the sound of a coyote closing in for a kill echoes across the canyon.

"I'll be in, in a minute."

"Anne called," he said. "Gave me a list of things she'll need. I packed them up, put them in the hall closet and will drive up there first thing in the morning."

"Okay. Thanks."

"You need anything else before I go, boss?" I wonder if he's thinking, Look at this guy, king of the mountain but at the end of the day . . . all alone.

"No, I'm fine. Have a good night."

As I hear him drive off and silence descends again, I turn my back on the dark canyon side of the property and look out toward the lights of the city.

Before going to sleep, I open the hall closet and take out the two suitcases packed with Anne's stuff and a canvas bag with one item inside. It's the small sketch of Anne by Leo de Vince. It's Anne without artifice, raw and spirited. Looking at it, I remember a piece of advice my father gave me around the time I turned eighteen, when it became clear that I intended to have plenty of women and relationships in my life. He took me aside one day for a talk. I expected him to give me the standard talk—"be careful, don't get them pregnant, they'll want to sperm-trap you and take your money." I was ready to say, "You don't have to give me the lecture. I'm aware of all that."

But instead he said, "As you go through life, you're going to find yourself in relationships that are no longer right for you but you might still feel an attachment to the woman. Maybe the sex is great, maybe she's someone you like talking to but you know it's not right. I'm going to give you my best piece of advice and it will always be the correct thing to do in these situations: leave before you're ready."

He was right. It was the best advice he ever gave me.

Chapter 55

Anne

Henry is flying up from L.A. today, due in Santa Ynez at 6 P.M. He called last night to inform me. He didn't say much more than that on the phone but the tone of his voice was telling . . . not very warm. The sorrow I felt when I hung up seemed bottomless, the grief overwhelming.

When I wake up this morning, all that is gone. I feel like I'm in an altered state. Is this what acceptance brings? I feel so detached it's as if I'm already gone from this life. It's surreal. I feel like everyone else is still tethered to the ground but I'm released from gravitational forces. Is this the way you feel right before you die? If I'm departing this world as I've known it, there is one person I want to see before that happens. Leo de Vince. Now that he's living in Santa Barbara, he's only an hour and a half south of Henry's ranch. I email him for directions, grab the keys to my car and tell the housekeeper I'll be back by five o'clock. She seems nervous, not sure what she's supposed to do. I'm not a prisoner but I am expected to stick around.

"Don't worry," I say. "I'm not escaping, just getting out for air."
What can she do but hope I'm not lying.

Leo de Vince has relocated to a small house and studio up in the
hills. He takes a break from his work and we sit outside and catch
up. He explains that he decided to leave Los Angeles and the Hollywood scene because he woke up one day hating what he was working on. A blockbuster producer had offered him three times his
normal fee to do a portrait of the producer's third wife, who was an
exact but younger version of the two wives who preceded her.

"When you get to be my age," he says, "you have to consider
that this could be the last painting you ever do. And I knew that
I couldn't spend another minute painting Hollywood's version of
royalty. So I gave back the money, gave up those assignments. I'll
live a smaller life with more freedom."

His simple life looks good to me. His backyard has lemon trees
and rosemary bushes. He has a woman who cooks for him. She brings
us out a bowl of fruit and iced lemonade. It's a safe environment to
share my nightmare.

"My life fell apart," I say.

He holds up the bowl. "Have a slice of guava."

Over the next hour I tell him all and with each word the nightmare
fades a little more, even though what I say isn't pretty. I talk about
what happens to girls like me in a fast-lane world . . . if they're not
lucky or brave. I tell him what he already knows, that those who have
more power can take everything away from you. They can paint me
how they want the world to see me, not how I am. They can say I'm
a lying addict, an incestuous slut, a drunken embezzler, a flasher, a
party girl . . . and therefore a terrible mom. They can get custody of
my child. They can cancel my credit cards. They can take back what

they've given and blackball me so getting a job and career will be a struggle. They can kill my brother's career, fire my father and put my sister's house in foreclosure. Never do I mention Henry's name or say anything bad about him. When I'm done speaking I look to Leo for his reaction.

"Have some more guava," he says.

It's not what I expected from Leo but it turns out to be just what I need. We talk about other things and have some laughs. He asks about my family. I tell him that Elizabeth and her nanny were flown up to see me for the afternoon and my adorable daughter's new favorite response to any question is "perhaps." Already weighing her options. I talk about George and my mother driving up for a brief visit and my mother's epiphany. She's decided if you can't beat them, join them, so she's reached out to Jayne Keller, our old neighbor who is now queen of reality TV, for advice about how I can reinvent myself. Jayne's big idea is that I should follow Sarah Ferguson's example and get a "spill your guts" show on Oprah's new network. Never. The last thing I want is a camera in my face and the job of being faux sincere. I talk about my father, who has a different idea, offering to negotiate with Henry on my behalf, which I want even less than I want a camera in my face.

Leo listens to everything attentively and passes judgment on none of it. It's not until I'm ready to go that he takes my hand and says, "And your question is?"

"My question?"

"There must be a question that you came to me with."

"I've made a lot of mistakes so there are lots of questions but if I'm limited to one it would be, What would you do if you were me?"

He doesn't hesitate. "When you came to my studio the first day you told me about some family motto."

"Yes. The Boleyns believe that in making any decision, do what makes you happy tomorrow, not what'll make you happy right now."

"Whatever. It doesn't matter what the motto is. What matters is that having a motto is a good thing. Living according to your motto is usually a very good thing. But an even better thing is to every so often consider not following your motto."

While I was thinking that over, he handed me another slice of guava.

Had I not driven to Leo's and back I would have more time to dress and put myself together for Henry. I can't deny that there is a small part of my heart that yearns for him to walk in the door and say, Let's start again. We can do this. We can fix this. Instead he walks in with a let's-get-down-to-business look. He's coming to cut me off. He starts talking about what money he'll allocate for my relocation and what my visitation rights with Elizabeth will be. While he's talking his phone keeps ringing. I know it's Jane but I don't make a big deal about it. What's the point? He steps out of the room to take the call and then comes back in and continues listing what I'll get and won't get, what I'll no longer have access to and how much longer he'll pay my car lease.

I cut him off. "You know what, Henry, how about you give me nothing? How about you keep all your money and things? How about all the jewelry you bought me; you keep that, too?" I take off my wedding ring and engagement diamond and put it on the table. "How about even the small amount of money I'm entitled to from the prenup; that's yours, too. I'll take the car and pay the lease myself and we'll call it even. When I figure out where I'm going to be, I'll come for Elizabeth. I know your lawyers will fight me and you'll win but I'll do what I can to be a good mother."

I grab my wallet, keys and the small Leo de Vince sketch and then stop. I don't want my exit from this marriage to be some exaggerated heroine's declaration of independence. I don't want this scene to play out like a formulaic Hollywood movie, with myself in the role of the plucky feminist. The truth is more complicated than that.

"Henry," I say, "I hope you'll be happy. I do. I know what a good person you truly are and I know how hard it is for anything good to stay that way when so many people are rooting for it to fail. I don't know why that is but that's how it goes, isn't it? Is it because in our world people are always so fucking terrified there won't be enough to go around they only feel better when someone else has less? I don't wish you less. Whatever you think will make you happy, I hope you get it. Oh, and one more thing, Henry, just in case you forgot, you can reject me, but you can never ever replace me."

We both laugh, fondly remembering the first time I whispered that in his ear.

"My Anne," he says.

And that's how we leave it. I love that he still thinks of me as his Anne but what's really happened here is that his Anne is gone. Anne Tudor was killed but Anne Boleyn is still hanging around.

As I get back on the freeway I'm not sure where I'm going until I see the exit for Topanga Canyon and realize that my new life begins with a stop at Mary's. It has to because the only thing I have of any monetary value is there—my "friendship" ring, which fell out of my pocket on my last visit. Though not the most expensive piece of jewelry from Henry it does have sentimental value. For that reason and because whatever I can get for it will go toward renting an apartment, I knock on Mary's door at 9 P.M. She's alone; Alex is out working, photographing leather bags for a friend's website. She's excited about that because "it's decent money and the bags are soooo beautiful and I get a forty percent discount." That's my sister, living like a bohemian with a thousand-dollar bag slung over her shoulder.

She gives me my ring and I tell her my story and we stay up for hours talking about everything and it occurs to me that my sister no longer uses letters for shorthand. In the past she might have referred to my impending divorce as a PDD, Public Display of Disaster. I point this out to her and she says, "Alex doesn't like the letter-shorthand thing."

We look at each other and laugh, both of us thinking . . . the adjustments women make for the men they love.

I'm on the road the next morning at eight. I get to Beverly Hills as the stores are opening. I go to a little jewelry shop off Rodeo Drive and sell my ring. I get ten thousand dollars for it, which will allow me to rent a place to live. I drive around the streets south of Wilshire, the poor side of Beverly Hills, my old neighborhood, and see that there's a place for rent in my old building. I look up to the top floor—my floor—and I can see the windows are open as if the place is being aired out after a new paint job. I go to the intercom at the front door and buzz the manager.

"Boris, it's Anne Boleyn. Is 501 available?"

"Yeah, why, you know somebody looking?"

"Yeah, me."

"You?"

"Me."

What's great about Boris is he has no hesitation or curiosity about my reversal of fortune. He doesn't ask what happened to my king and my castle. He doesn't care. He manages six buildings. All he cares about is making sure everybody pays their rent on time and that there's no problem with the hot water. "You can move in today, if you want."

"Great."

Epilogue

Anne

A month has passed since I moved back into my old apartment. I don't think of my return to the old neighborhood as a step back, though I know everyone else does. I think of it as a new start. When in crisis, start over by counting your blessings. That's my new motto. Topping my gratitude list: I'm not living in another century or another culture where, at the whim of a king, women can be permanently sent to "the Tower" (either literally or symbolically) or worse. I'm an L.A. girl and attitude is my birthright. I'm strong, I'm healthy and as long as my brain is intact, I'll figure something out. I already have. I'm back to life as a freelance writer, only now I feel like I've found my voice. Funny thing is, the "you can reject me but you can never replace me" concept that was the foundation of my confidence with Henry now pertains to my career. So I lost my man but found my voice and so life goes on and who can say on some crazy level it isn't getting better? I'm certainly more motivated than I've been in a long time. Rejection either kills you or it gives you enough "I'll show them" energy to fuel another climb to the top. In Hollywood reinventing oneself is a way of life, even if few pull it off successfully. The other thing I've learned is . . . never try to know or predict everything. Always leave room for surprises. I got a call at home the other night (late) from Henry. He didn't leave a message but his private cell number showed up on caller ID. I knew it wasn't about Elizabeth because he would have tried reaching me on my cell. I didn't call back. More importantly I didn't fantasize the call meant anything other than that there is still a connection between us. We think about each other. Jane Seymour or any future wife Henry might have will never be able to take that away. That's not a fantasy. That's an emotional truth. This is not coming from the left side of my neocortex. It's truth that doesn't need logic or facts to support it.

Meanwhile I'm busy building a new life. I still find it annoying that my neighbor plays loud music and the walls are too thin but I also know that in an emergency, I can knock on his door and he will respond. I'm not alone. "People either have a will to participate in life or they don't." That's something Leo de Vince said to me last week when I called to thank him for the basket of guavas he sent over as a housewarming present.

No one can say I'm out of the game for good. I know the odds are against me but so what. Maybe I won't end up ruling the world like I once thought I would. Even if I don't, who knows, maybe my daughter will.

Acknowledgments

Many thanks to Jamie Brenner for her brilliant guidance and advice and to all my girlfriends who so generously shared their stories with me.